BLARNEY

12 TALES OF LIES, CRIME & MYSTERY

by Steve Hockensmith

CONTENTS

INTRODUCTION

I'd like to think I'm not a bloviator, backslapper or braggart. But I do know a thing or two about blarney. Every writer does. Because blarney is what we do.

Blarney is the art of telling people what they want to hear so that you can get what you want. For most writers, that works out really well, because all they want is to tell stories. So long as someone's paying attention—and not throwing rotten fruit—they're happy. Ish. (There could always be *more* people paying attention.)

I first got serious about the variety of blarney known as the short story about 15 years ago. Before anyone paid much attention to me, I had to dodge a lot of rotten fruit. (It came at me in self-addressed stamped envelopes and always began the same way: "Dear Contributor.") Eventually, though, I got it right. I told someone a story she wanted to hear. And she sent me a contract.

The story was "Erie's Last Day," and in the spring of 2000 it appeared in *Alfred Hitchcock's Mystery Magazine*. Over the next few years, I wrote a lot more stories for *AHMM* (and its sister magazine, *Ellery Queen*, and various anthologies, too). Then another kind of blarney started taking up all my time: novels. Reluctantly, sadly and with great gratitude for everything they'd taught me, I set short stories aside.

So what you have here is a pretty good portrait of my blarneying skills circa the first half of the first decade of the 21st century. I've made some minor revisions to the stories, but I decided to keep most of the passé pop culture and technology references as is. (That's why the criminal enterprise revealed in "Strays" is soooooooooo Old

School, for instance. That particular scheme would have only made sense for about two years out of all human history. In fact, "Strays" was probably already outdated by the time it first appeared, but let's not dwell on that.)

I'm guessing it won't bother you that these stories feature no iPhones or Facebook but do include the occasional shout-out to Britney Spears. Fads come and go. But a good story, hopefully, is forever.

Steve Hockensmith
Alameda, Calif.
April 2012

P.S.: If that "a good story is forever" stuff didn't set off your blarney detector, please contact me at steve@stevehockensmith.com. I'm gearing up for my next project—an overhaul of the Brooklyn Bridge funded by an elite group of visionary investors—and I think you're just the kind of person we're looking for....

ERIE'S LAST DAY

7:00 a.m.: The radio alarm by Larry Erie's queen-sized bed turned itself on. A deep-voiced announcer began telling Erie about the morning's top stories. Erie didn't really care what the morning's top stories might be, but he lay there for a while and let the announcer ramble.

There was nobody there to give him a playful kick and tell him to shut that noise off. There was nobody there to make breakfast for. There was nobody there to fetch pills for. It was just him and the announcer.

7:19 a.m.: Erie pulled himself out of bed and went out onto the porch in his pajamas and robe to pick up the morning paper. It was cool outside, just like the cheerful people on the radio said it would be. A storm passing through in the night had left puddles on the pavement.

Erie scanned the yard for the little black shape that sometimes came bounding up to him from behind shrubs or garbage cans, meowing greetings at him as if he were a long-lost relative. But the cat wasn't there. Erie went back inside.

He ate breakfast sitting on the edge of the bed. It was a habit he couldn't drop even though there was no longer anyone there to keep company.

7:42 a.m.: Erie showered, shaved, flossed, brushed, gargled, rinsed and repeated. Then he carefully picked out his clothes. He pulled on his best white shirt, his best suit, his favorite tie. He shined his

3

shoes before putting them on. He looked at himself in the mirror, straightened his tie, smoothed a few errant hairs into place. Then he pulled his gun off the bureau and clipped it onto his belt.

Some cops started to get a little sloppy years before they retired. Others waited just a few months or weeks before their last day to start letting themselves go. Erie remembered one cop, a fellow detective, who came in for his last day in a Hawaiian shirt and Bermuda shorts. It gave everybody a good laugh.

But that wasn't Erie's way. He was determined to make every day of his time on the force count. Even his last.

8:07 a.m.: Erie was reaching out to open his car door when he heard the cat. She was hurrying up the driveway toward him, meowing loudly. He kneeled and stretched out his right arm. Like always, the cat came up and rubbed her face on his hand a few times before flopping over on her back and stretching out her legs. He rubbed her stomach. Her hair was long and matted.

"How do you like that, buddy? How do you like that?" Erie asked the cat.

The cat purred.

Erie had never owned a cat, never really known a cat, never been interested in them. He had no idea how old the little black cat was. She'd been hanging around the neighborhood about a month. She had grown noticeably bigger since he'd first seen her. She had also become friendlier. She wore no collar or tags.

Occasionally, Erie had found himself worrying about the cat. Where was she sleeping? What was she eating? He'd seen her once over by Green River Road, and the thought of her trying to cross busy streets had haunted him for hours.

But Erie always reminded himself that he wasn't a cat person. And he had bigger things to worry about than dumb animals.

"That's enough for today," he told the cat as he stood up. The cat rolled over on her stomach and looked up at him expectantly. "Nope. No more. So long."

Erie climbed into his car and started the engine. He backed out of the driveway slowly, keeping an eye on the cat lest she jump up and dart under the tires. But she stayed where she was, watching him, seemingly puzzled by his desire to leave this perfectly wonderful driveway and this perfectly wonderful cat.

8:33 a.m.: On his way into police headquarters from the parking lot, Erie was stopped by three cops. They were all men he hadn't seen or spoken to in the last week. Each one stopped him separately and said the same thing.

"I'm sorry about your wife."

Erie said the only thing he could: "Thanks."

On his way past the Human Resources office, a female coworker called out, "Look who's early! Hey, Larry, don't you know you're not supposed to come in before noon on your last day!"

"The early bird catches the worm," Erie said.

A uniformed officer stopped as she passed by. "You don't have to worry about catching worms anymore, Detective Erie. You just head down to Arizona and catch some sun. Leave the worms to us."

8:45 a.m.: Erie had already cleaned out his office, for the most part. The walls were bare, his desktop was free of clutter, the drawers were practically empty aside from a few stray pens and paperclips and leftover forms. So it was impossible to miss the yellow Post-It Note stuck to the exact center of his desktop. It was from Hal Allen, director of Detective Services/Homicide—his boss. The note read, "See me in my office ASAP." Erie hoped it was a special assignment, a favor he could do for Allen or the department, something that would draw on his decades of experience, something that would make his last eight hours as a police officer count.

8:48 a.m.: Erie knew he was in trouble the second he stepped into the office of May Davis, Allen's administrative assistant and official gatekeeper. He had walked into a trap, and there was no way out.

Twenty people were crammed behind Davis's desk. Behind them was a banner reading, "WE'LL MISS YOU, BIG GUY!" On it were dozens of signatures surrounded by drawings of handcuffs and police badges and men in striped prison uniforms. The people waiting for him, the entire Homicide Division reinforced by a couple evidence technicians and some of his old buddies from other departments, began singing "For He's a Jolly Good Fellow."

Erie stood there, smiling dutifully, and took it like a man.

9:09 a.m.: Erie endured the song and the hugs and the slaps on the back and the vanilla cake with the outline of Arizona in orange frosting. He endured Allen's speech about 33 years of service and 112 murderers behind bars. He endured it all without ever saying, "What about those 29 *unsolved* murders?" or "Why would I move to Arizona without Nancy?"

And after the ordeal was over and the revelers had drifted away one by one, it became clear that he was supposed to drift away, too. There were forms to fill out and drawers to empty, right? Instead, he asked Hal Allen if they could step into his office.

"What's on your mind, Larry?"

Allen was a different breed of cop. He was younger than Erie. He worked out every day. His walls weren't covered with pictures of his kids or newspaper articles about his big busts. He had his degrees—a B.A. in Criminal Justice, a Masters in Psychology—and inspirational posters about Leadership and Goals. For him, being a cop wasn't a calling. It was a career choice. But Erie liked him and hoped he would understand.

"I was wondering if I could take back one of my cases."

"Come on, Larry," Allen said. "You're going to have to let go."

"Just for today, Hal. I just want to make some inquiries, see if I can get the ball rolling again. At the end of the day I'll turn it back over to Sophie Rogers with a full briefing."

Allen shook his head, grinning. "I've heard of this condition. It's called dedication to duty. We're going to have to cure you of it. I prescribe a day playing computer solitaire followed by a much-deserved retirement in beautiful, sunny Arizona."

"Nancy liked Arizona, Hal. We were moving there for her."

"Oh." The smile melted off Allen's face. "So you're not—?"

"I don't know. We hadn't signed anything yet when Nancy took that last turn for the worse. I'm not sure I want to leave Indiana. I've lived here all my life." Erie shifted nervously in his seat. "But that's neither here nor there. I'm just asking for one more day to protect and serve."

Allen leaned forward and gave Erie a long, thoughtful look, as if really seeing him for the first time. "You're not going to solve your 113th homicide today, Larry. You're just going to end up chasing around stone-cold leads and getting nowhere."

"I love days like that."

Allen nodded. "O.K., Larry. Do what you have to do. But drop by my office before you go home tonight. I want to talk to you again."

Erie practically jumped up from his chair. For the first time that day, he actually felt awake.

"Yes, sir," he said. "Anything you say."

9:31 a.m.: Detective Sophie Rogers was on the phone when Erie appeared in the doorway to her office. Rogers waved Erie in, said "No problem" and hung up. "The boss says you want to catch a bad guy today," she said to Erie.

"I just want to borrow back one of my cases. Is that O.K. with you?"

Rogers smiled and pointed at a stack of bound folders on one corner of her desk. "Pick your poison. If you insist on working your last day, I'm not going to stop you."

"Thanks, Sophie."

Erie shuffled through the case files. Did he want the 16-year-old meth dealer, four months dead? The unidentified, twentysomething woman found in the woods of Lloyd Park, six months dead? Or the middle-aged insurance salesman, ten months dead?

Lifeless eyes stared up at him from Polaroids paperclipped to Xeroxed autopsy reports. They looked inside him, told him, "Do something. Avenge me. Avenge *me*."

But justice isn't for the dead. That was one of the things Erie had learned in his years working homicide. It's no use fighting a crusade for a corpse. It will still be a corpse even if somebody turns its killer into a corpse, too. But the family, the loved ones, *the living*—they can be helped.

He picked a file and left.

10:07 a.m.: Unlike most of the older, lower-middle class neighborhoods around town, Pine Hills actually lived up to its name. It had both pines and hills, though not too many of either. It also had a reputation among Erie's fellow cops for producing wild kids. On Halloween night, patrol cars cruised through the neighborhood as if it were Compton or Watts, and EMT crews waited on stand-by for the inevitable wounds from bottle rockets, M-80s, broken glass and exploding mailboxes.

O'Hara Drive was a short, crooked, sloping street in the heart of the neighborhood. It was all of one block long, bracketed on each side by longer streets that curved up to the neighborhood's highest hills. From the top of one you could see the airport a mile away. From the other you could see the county dump.

The house at 1701 O'Hara Drive wasn't just where Joel Korfmann, insurance salesman, had lived. It was where he had died, too. There were two vehicles in the driveway when Erie arrived—a silver, early '90s model Ford Taurus and a newer Ford pickup, red. The Taurus he remembered.

Erie parked on the street and walked toward the house. All the curtains had been drawn. A big plastic trash can lay on its side near the foot of the driveway.

He rang the doorbell. And waited. He knocked on the rickety metal of the screen door. The curtains in the front window fluttered, and a woman's face hovered in the shadows beyond. Erie tried to smile reassuringly. He pulled out his badge.

"It's Detective Erie, Mrs. Korfmann."

The face disappeared. Erie waited again. Finally, the front door opened. The screen door in front of it remained closed.

All the lights of the house were off. Candace Korfmann stood back from the door, away from the sunlight.

"Hello."

"Hello, Mrs. Korfmann. I'm just dropping by this morning to ask a few follow-up questions. Is now a good time to talk?"

"Sure," Korfmann replied lifelessly. She was dressed in a bathrobe. Erie recalled that she was what people used to call a "housewife" or "homemaker." She didn't have a job to give her life focus again after her husband died. And she didn't have any children to distract her, keep her mind from dwelling on the past, what had happened in her own kitchen. He pictured her brooding in the darkness of the little white house all day, every day, alone.

"Good," Erie said. "First off, I'm afraid I have to tell you that we haven't uncovered any new leads. But we're putting a new investigator on the case next week. Detective Rogers. She's good at her job. So don't lose hope, Mrs. Korfmann."

After a moment's pause, Korfmann nodded. "O.K. I won't."

"Good. Now, secondly, I was wondering if there was anything new you could tell me—any new memories or thoughts you've had that might help our investigation."

Korfmann stared at him blankly. Standing in the shadows, perfectly still, she looked flat, one-dimensional, like the mere outline of a woman. Her shape—the slumped shoulders and tousled hair and slightly titled head—reminded him of Nancy toward the end, when she was so weak she could barely stand.

"It could be anything, even just a rumor going around the neighborhood," Erie prompted. "Every little bit helps."

Korfmann shook her head slowly. "I don't know what to tell you. I haven't heard a thing."

"That's alright. No reason you should do our job for us. I have just one more thing to talk to you about." Erie pulled a card from his jacket pocket. "I'd like to give you this. It's the number of a woman I know. She runs a group for...those who've been left behind. A survivor support group. You might want to give her a call."

Korfmann didn't move for a long moment. Then she opened the screen door and reached out to take the card. As she leaned into the light, Erie could see that her skin was pale, her eyes hollow. He noticed a slight swelling of her lower lip and a dark, bluish smudge of bruised flesh under her left eye.

"Thanks," she said.

"Sure. You take care now, Mrs. Korfmann."

She nodded, then closed the door.

10:24 a.m.: Erie started his car. The clock on the dashboard came to life. Not even an hour back on the Korfmann case, and already he was done. He'd driven across town just to stir up painful memories for a sad and lonely woman. There was nothing to do now but head back to the office and shoot the breeze with whoever he could find goofing off. Reminisce about the good old days, trot out old stories and legends, fart around, do nothing. Then go home.

Erie shut off the ignition and got out of the car. He walked to the house across from 1701 O'Hara Drive and rang the doorbell. An old man opened the door. He was wearing glasses so thick Erie couldn't see his eyes, just big, shimmering ovals of pale blue.

"Yes?"

Erie took out his badge. "Good morning, Mr. Wallender. I'm Detective Erie. You and I spoke about ten months ago."

"Of course. I remember, Detective. Come on in." The old man ushered Erie into the living room. "You have a seat, and I'll get some coffee." He disappeared around a corner. "I've got some just sitting in here. Every day I make a whole pot and then drink two cups. I don't know why I keep doing that. I pour more coffee down the drain in a morning than most people drink in a week."

Erie could hear cabinet doors and drawers opening and closing, porcelain sliding over countertops, the hum of an open refrigerator.

"I'll take mine black, Mr. Wallender," Erie said.

"Have you arrested Joel Korfmann's killer yet?"

"Not yet. That's why I'm here today. I'm making a few follow-up inquiries."

Wallender shuffled into the living room with a mug in each hand. He gave one to Erie. The liquid in it had the dingy brown color of coffee with skim milk. Erie didn't take a sip.

"I was wondering if you'd heard or seen anything else that might have a bearing on the case," he said.

Wallender lowered himself slowly into a recliner. "I've been keeping my eye on the neighborhood kids. They're always planning some kind of prank. I called the police a couple months ago. Thought I saw a boy with some dynamite. A policeman came out. Do you know an Officer Pyke?"

"Sure."

The old man's hearing and eyesight might not have been so great anymore, but his memory didn't have any problems.

"Have you spoken to Mrs. Korfmann at all?" Erie asked. "Do you know how she's doing?"

Wallender brought his mug to his lips with both hands. They were trembling.

"She kind of dropped out of sight for a while there. I figured she went to be with her family or some such," the old man said. "She was gone maybe two months. When she came back, she seemed to be doing fine. I took it upon myself to drop in and chat with her from time to time."

"And her state of mind seemed good?"

Wallender shrugged. "Far as I could tell. They were always stand-offish people, her and her husband both. She seemed a little more friendly for a while there, but then her young man began hanging around and she was the same old Candace again."

"Her young man? You mean she has a boyfriend?"

"I guess you could call him that, seeing as his truck's there most nights."

"And how long has this been going on?"

"Maybe two months, maybe a little longer." Wallender's thin lips curled into a sly smile. "Now don't go thinking evil thoughts, Detective Erie. She needed a man around so she found one. It's understandable. People get lonely. I know a little something about that. It's not easy living alone."

Erie tried to smile back, but found he couldn't. His mouth, his whole face, felt stiff, dead.

"I'm not thinking evil thoughts, Mr. Wallender. I'm just curious. That's my job."

"Sure, sure. I understand. I guess I'm curious, too. Except when it's a neighbor being curious, people call it 'nosy.'"

"Have you ever spoken to Mrs. Korfmann's young man?"

"Well, I've tried. He's not a very talkative fella. I've been over to chat once or twice when I noticed him out working on his truck. He didn't have a lot to say. Actually, he reminds me a lot of Joel— Mr. Korfmann."

"Did you happen to catch his name?"

"Ray. He didn't mention his last name. He works over at DeRogatis Ford as a mechanic." The old man grinned again. "That's all I got out of him, chief. If you want me to try again, maybe I could get his social security number for you."

Erie finally found himself able to smile back. "You're a real character, Mr. Wallender."

"I certainly am," the old man said with obvious pride. "I just wish more people knew it."

10:43 a.m.: Erie was back in his car, faced again with the drive back to the station, the afternoon killing time, the evening killing time, the weekend killing time, the years killing time until time finally killed him.

He thought about Candace Korfmann. Her hollow stare, the way she'd stayed away from the light, the black eye. He tried not to think evil thoughts about "Ray." But he couldn't stop himself. Maybe he couldn't catch a killer in one day, but he sure as hell could catch a woman-beater. What he would do about it, he wasn't sure.

Erie started up his car and put it in gear. As he pulled away from the curb, he noticed movement in one of the windows of the Korfmann house—a dark shape quickly replaced by the swaying of a blind. Someone had been watching him.

Erie drove to the intersection of Oak Hill Road and Highway 41, home of DeRogatis Ford.

11:10 p.m.: A salesman swooped down on Erie before he could even get out of his car.

"Good afternoon. What can I help you with today?"

Erie flipped out his badge. "I'd like a word with whoever runs your service department."

"Oh."

The salesman went pale.

"Don't worry," Erie told him. "It has nothing to do with the dealership. I'm just trying to locate someone who might be an employee. He's not in any trouble."

The salesman nodded and gave Erie an unconvincing smile. "Sure, officer. We're always happy to help River City's finest. Right this way."

The salesman lead him through the showroom to a bustling garage. Eight cars were being worked on, some with their hoods up, some hovering on hydraulic lifts. Off to the side, customers lounged in a waiting room watching *The Jerry Springer Show*. The salesman pointed out a short, middle-aged Asian man leaning over an Escort's engine.

"That's Frank Takarada. He runs things back here," the salesman said. He slipped a business card out of his shirt pocket and handed it to Erie. "If you ever want to talk cars, I'm your man. I'm here Tuesday through Saturday."

He shook Erie's hand and hustled away.

Erie pocketed the card and headed toward Takarada. The mechanic noticed his approach and eyed him warily.

"Mr. Takarada, could I have a word with you, please?"

"I'm very busy. Maybe later."

Sometimes the badge-flash routine got quick results. Sometimes—especially in public places—it just irritated or embarrassed people. Takarada looked like the irritable type.

13

Erie leaned close and lowered his voice. "I'm a police detective, Mr. Takarada. I promise I only need five minutes of your time. Do you have an office where we can speak?"

Takarada pulled a greasy rag from his pocket and began wiping off his hands.

"Come on."

He led Erie to the far corner of the garage. Auto parts in plastic bags hung from pegs on a large partition. Takarada stepped around it. When Erie followed, he found himself in a cramped, cluttered office complete with desk, computer, fan and filing cabinets covered with crinkled paperwork. A large board studded with pegs hung on the wall. Car keys dangled from the pegs.

"So what do you want?" Takarada said.

"I'd like to know if you have a mechanic here by the name of Ray or Raymond."

"Nope."

Erie felt like a fool. He'd followed up a blind hunch, something that had nothing to do with his job, based on the memory of a doddering old recluse. He was about to apologize and leave when Takarada spoke again.

"Not anymore, anyway. Had one a few months ago, though. Raymond Long."

"What happened?"

"We were obliged to let him go," Takarada said with mock gentility. He didn't volunteer anything further.

"This is off the record, Mr. Takarada. Just between you and me. You can be plainspoken."

Takarada thought it over, then nodded. He seemed like the kind of man who usually didn't wait for permission to be blunt.

"Raymond Long is a horse's ass," he said. "Always was, always will be. I put up with him for two years and then—"

Takarada mimed dropping a ball and punting it.

"When was this?"

"Six weeks, maybe two months ago, something like that."

"What happened?"

"Instead of being late once or twice a week, he was late every day. Instead of being hung over some of the time, he was hung over all of the time."

"How did he react when you fired him?"

Takarada barked out a bitter laugh. "Typical macho B.S." His voice took on a Southern Indiana twang. "'Oh yeah, little man? Well, I don't need this stupid job, anyhow! I'm set up! So screw you!'"

Erie's fingers and toes began to tingle. He took a deep breath and forced himself to relax before speaking again.

"He said, 'I'm set up.'"

"Something like that, yeah."

The tingling wouldn't go away.

"Can you tell me if a Candace Korfmann had her car serviced in this shop in the last few months?" Erie said. "She drives a silver Taurus, looks like a '93 or '94."

The mechanic scowled. "I'd have to look that up."

"I would appreciate that, Mr. Takarada. It's very important."

Takarada sighed heavily. "How do you spell that?" He walked to his computer and took a seat.

"K-o-r-f-m-a-n-n."

Erie's mind raced ahead of Takarada as he typed.

The dealership's records would show that Candace Korfmann had brought her car in two or three months ago. Raymond Long had worked on the car. He'd noticed her waiting—she wasn't an unattractive woman. He brought her over to show her something, began flirting. He could sense that she was vulnerable. He got her to agree to a date. He found out she was a widow. Her husband had been an insurance agent. She'd received a large amount of money upon his death. Raymond Long saw an opportunity. He wormed his way into her heart, then her home. Now he figured he ran the show.

Erie would think of a way to prove him wrong.

"Yeah, we've got a Candace Korfmann in here. Drives a 1994 Taurus, like you said."

"Does it show who worked on her car last?"

"Sure. Got the initials right here. 'R.L.'"

Erie nodded with satisfaction. The pieces were falling into place.

"Raymond Long. And this was around June or July?"

"Not even close. Try May—of last year."

"What?"

Erie gaped at the mechanic. His theory was blown.

Within seconds, another one took its place.

He gestured at the key rack on the wall. "These are for the cars you're working on?"

"And the ones waiting out back, yeah."

"You ever work on vans here?"

Takarada shrugged. "Sure, every now and then."

Erie mulled that over.

"Anything else?" asked Takarada, obviously anxious to get back to work.

"If you could print that out for me, I'd appreciate it." Before Takarada could groan or sigh or roll his eyes, Erie added, "Then I'll be leaving. You've been a big help. Thanks."

Takarada started to swivel back to the keyboard, then stopped himself. "So is Long in some kind of trouble?"

Erie gave the safe cop answer: "This is just a routine inquiry." But he knew trouble was headed Raymond Long's way. Erie hoped to deliver it himself before the day was over.

11:44 a.m.: Erie ate lunch at a Denny's across from the Ford dealership. A few too many people were probably expecting him to drop by Peppy's, the diner around the corner from police headquarters. But he wanted a chance to think.

His turkey club and fries went down untasted. The file on Joel Korfmann's murder was spread across the table before him.

Erie was pleased to see that the report was neat, thorough, precise. He'd put it together himself months before.

On New Year's Eve, at approximately 9:15 p.m., Joel Korfmann had been bludgeoned to death in his home. The victim, age 41, was a Lutheran Family Insurance representative who'd spent the day making calls on potential customers. In the evening, he'd been at the office filing paperwork. (In parentheses after this were the words "Indicative of victim's character?" Those were code words. What they meant was, "What kind of jerk makes cold calls selling insurance on New Year's Eve? Then spends the evening doing paperwork when he could be with family and friends?") Security surveillance tapes showed that he left work at 8:43 p.m. It would have taken him about half an hour to drive home.

The victim's wife, Candace Lane Korfmann, age 38, spent the evening with her sister, Carol Lane Biggs, and brother-in-law, Rudy Biggs. Witnesses placed them at the Dew Drop Inn on Division Street from 8:30 p.m. until approximately 12:30 a.m.

Carol and Rudy Biggs drove Candace Korfmann home, arriving at 12:55 a.m. All three entered the house. Mrs. Korfmann immediately noticed that several items—a GoldStar television, a Sony VCR, a Sony stereo—were missing. In the kitchen, Rudy Biggs discovered the body of Joel Korfmann. He'd been hit from behind by a large, heavy object. Forensic examinations would later conclude that he had been struck five times with the butt of his own shotgun, which was also reported missing.

Most of the Korfmanns' neighbors had been away for the evening celebrating the holiday. But a James Wallender, an elderly man who lived by himself across the street, reported seeing a dark van parked near the house at approximately 8:30 p.m. Later, Wallender said, he saw it in the Korfmanns' driveway. (In parentheses here: "Witness seems anxious to help investigation." That was Erie's way of hinting that the old man might not be the most reliable witness. Sometimes lonely people were so eager to please they would "remember" things they'd never seen.)

The report concluded that the victim had surprised someone in the house—an individual or individuals who were in the process of burglarizing the Korfmann home. Seeing the house dark on a holiday, the perpetrators must have assumed the residents were out of town or would be out all night partying. It was a common scenario.

There had been no evidence when Erie had written his report. There were no fingerprints, no hairs, no tire tracks that could be linked to the crime, and the stolen items had never surfaced. And that hadn't changed. Erie still had no evidence. But he did have something new: a hunch.

As he drove back to headquarters after lunch, he thought about Raymond Long. He pictured him as a young, long-haired redneck with tattooed arms and fiery eyes. He pictured him killing Joel Korfmann. He pictured him beating Candace Korfmann, finally killing her in a rage—or just because it suited him.

He saw it all, crystal clear in his mind. Long the manipulator, Long the killer. Joel and Candace Korfmann, the victims.

The only thing that interrupted these thoughts was a stray that crept in from another part of his brain as he maneuvered through afternoon traffic. It was the image of cars and trucks whipping up and down Green River Road, leaving roadkill behind them on the asphalt, on the side of the road, tumbling into ditches. He hoped the little black cat was safe.

1:10 p.m.: Back at headquarters, Erie checked to see if "Long, Raymond" had a criminal record. He wasn't disappointed. There were three charges of disturbing the peace, two charges of battery, two disorderly conducts, one assault and the inevitable DWI and resisting arrest. Over the years, he'd served a grand total of 15 months in the Vanderburgh County lock-up.

The pictures came as a surprise, though. Long was 37, and he looked every day of it. He was balding, pug-nosed and jowly. He didn't look like the kind of handsome young devil who could charm a vulnerable widow—or widow-to-be. Erie assumed he was one hell of a talker.

Erie went back to his office (accepting a number of handshakes and pats on the back on the way) and began calling all the U-Stor-Its and Storage Lands in town. The people he spoke to knew him, knew what he was looking for, knew the drill, but they couldn't help. No, they hadn't rented out space to a Raymond Long in the last year. Yes, they'd give him a call if a Raymond Long came in.

After saying "Thanks, have a good one" for the eighth time, Erie hung up the phone and left his office. It was time to have a talk with Raymond Long.

2:17 p.m.: There was something different at 1701 O'Hara Drive when Erie pulled up. He walked toward the house slowly, trying to pin down what it was.

The curtains were still drawn shut. The Taurus and the pickup were still parked out front. The trash can still lay on its side in the yard.

Erie was walking up the driveway past the pickup when he realized what it was. The truck was splattered with mud—mud that hadn't been there that morning. Erie turned and walked across the street and rang James Wallender's doorbell.

"Hello there, chief," the old man said as he opened the door. "I was wondering if you'd come back again. Why don't you come in?"

"I'm sorry, Mr. Wallender. I don't have time to visit right now. I just wanted to ask if you'd seen any activity at the Korfmann house today."

"Well, I might have peeked out the window a time or two since you were here." Wallender winked. "Hold on a minute." He shuffled away, then returned a moment later with a small notepad clutched in one shaky hand. "You left here at approximately 10:45 a.m. Around 11, that fella Ray pulled his truck into the garage and brought the garage door down. At 11:20, he drove back out again and left for a while."

"Was there anything in the pickup when he left?"

"Oh, yeah. Something big and green."

"Green?"

Wallender checked his notepad. "Yes, green. At least that's what it looked like to me." He tapped his eyeglasses. "I have to look at everything through these Coke bottles."

"Could it have been a tarp thrown over something in the back of the truck?"

Wallender nodded. "Could have been."

"And how long was Ray gone?"

Wallender looked at his notepad again. "Forty-five minutes."

Erie extended a hand. Wallender took it, and the two men shook.

"Mr. Wallender, by the power vested in me by the state of Indiana, I hereby declare you a junior G-man."

Wallender smiled. "I always said I wanted to be a detective when I grew up."

3:10 p.m.: The shoes Erie had shined so carefully that morning were now covered with mud and coffee grounds and mysterious flecks of filth. His trousers were similarly splattered, and there was a new rip where a piece of jagged metal had snagged his pants leg. Even his tie was beginning to smell bad.

Early on, there had been two other scavengers, a heavy-set couple with prodigious guts spilling out from under their dirty T-shirts. They'd seen him—a well-dressed, middle-aged man picking through piles of garbage at the county dump—and stared as if he were some exotic, dangerous animal pacing back and forth in a cage at the zoo. They kept their distance, eventually driving off in a beaten-up station wagon loaded with discarded toys and clothes and broken appliances.

Erie told himself he'd only look for another half hour. If he couldn't find anything, he'd head back down to Pine Hills and have that talk with Raymond Long. Not that he was going to make much of an impression in his current condition. Maybe after another 30 minutes wading through garbage, he'd smell so putrid Long would confess just to get away from the stench.

The ridiculousness of it made him long for Nancy. He wanted to go home and tell her everything that had happened. He didn't even know if his last day had been sad, funny, triumphant or disastrous without her face to gauge it by.

From off in the distance came the popping and clicking of tires rolling over gravel. More scavengers were headed up the winding dirt road to the dump. Erie was going to be on exhibit again. He thought about abandoning his crazy theory and just going home for a nice, long bath.

And then he found it. It was underneath a big, flattened-out cardboard box, the kind washing machines are delivered in. A GoldStar TV. The screen had been broken in and the plastic cracked on top, but it was relatively free of mud and grime. Erie checked the back. Even though someone had made a half-hearted effort to bust up the television and make it look old, they hadn't bothered scratching off the serial number.

Erie tore into the nearest heap of garbage, tossing aside trash bags and rotting boxes. At the bottom of the pile, he found a Sony VCR, the top crushed, as if someone had jumped on top of it. He picked it up and looked at the back. Again, the serial number was still there.

It only took him another minute of digging to find the stereo. It was underneath a pile of newspapers. It had hardly been damaged at all. There was still a serial number on the back.

That left just one item—the most important of all. Once he found that, he could call in the evidence techs to dust everything for prints and look for tracks that matched the tires on Raymond Long's truck. The tracks would have to be nearby. Erie turned around to look.

Raymond Long was walking toward him.

"This what you looking for?" Long said.

He was holding a shotgun. It was pointed at Erie.

In the time it took Long to take two more steps, Erie had considered five different responses. He could dive and roll and draw his gun; charge Long and go for the shotgun; put up his hands and feign ignorance; put up his hands and try to talk Long into surrendering; run like crazy.

Erie didn't like any of his options, but he picked one anyway.

He put up his hands and started talking.

"Don't do anything dumb, Ray. A lot of people know where I am. If anything happens to me, they're going to know exactly who to point the finger at."

Long stopped about seven yards from Erie. At that range, there could be little doubt what outcome a shotgun blast would have.

"Yeah, well, maybe by the time they're pointing fingers, I'll be hundreds of miles away."

Long's voice was full of spiteful good ol' boy bravado. But Erie could see the sweat shining on his face, the damp rings that were spreading under the armpits of his T-shirt.

Erie shook his head. "You won't make it, Ray. Cop killers don't get away. Other cops take it too personally. You'd end up right back in Indiana facing a capital murder charge."

"Don't you mean *two* capital murder charges?" Long sneered. He had a good face for sneering. It looked like he'd done a lot of practicing over the years.

"You should stop talking, Ray. You should put down the shotgun and let me take you in. That's what a lawyer would tell you to do. You haven't crossed the line yet—you haven't doomed yourself. If you put down the gun now, this could all still work out for you and Candace."

Erie knew instantly that he'd made a mistake. As soon as he said the word "Candace," Long's sneer turned into a scowl of rage. Erie had pushed the wrong button. Now he had to get out of the way.

Erie threw himself to the left, twisting his body in mid-flight so he would take most of the buckshot in the back, buttocks or legs instead of the face and chest. There was a boom, and a searing pain lanced Erie's side. But it wasn't bad enough to stop him. He rolled over and came up with his gun pointing toward Long.

But Long wasn't standing there anymore. He was lying on the ground. Erie watched him for a second, stunned. Long wasn't moving.

Erie stood up and winced as a lightning bolt of agony struck in a familiar place: His gymnastics had strained his cranky lower back. He limped toward Long, each step sending pain shooting up his spine.

Long was a mess. And he was dead.

He'd probably bent the shotgun's barrel or jammed the chamber when he bludgeoned Joel Korfmann. He might have even used the stock to bust up the TV, VCR and stereo. So when he tried to shoot Erie, the shotgun had exploded, sending shards of metal and wood in all directions—but mostly into Long's body.

Erie checked the right side of his abdomen, where he'd felt the sting a moment before. He'd been wounded, but not by buckshot or shrapnel. His shirt was torn and a short, shallow gash was bleeding onto the clean white cotton. When he'd jumped, he'd landed on something sharp.

He began walking very, very slowly to his car, trying to remember the last time he'd had a tetanus shot.

3:55 p.m.: A patrol car was waiting for him at 1701 O'Hara Drive when he arrived, as he had requested from the dispatcher.

"Geez, Larry, where did the tornado touch down?" one of the officers asked Erie as he limped up to their car.

"Right on top of me. Can't you tell?"

"So what's the story?" the other cop asked.

"I need to pick somebody up for questioning. I'm not expecting any trouble, but I wanted a little backup just in case. You two just hang back and observe."

"Hang back and observe," the first cop repeated, giving Erie a salute. "That's what I do best."

Erie walked up to the house and rang the doorbell. Candace Korfmann opened the door almost immediately.

"I've been waiting for you," she said. She was wearing jeans and a River City Community College sweatshirt. "I'm ready to go."

She stepped outside, closed the front door and brushed past Erie.

"That's you, right?" she said, pointing at Erie's car.

"Yes."

She walked to the car quickly. Erie followed her.

"Do you want me in the front or the back?" she asked.

"The front is fine."

Korfmann opened the door and climbed in. Erie eased himself gingerly into the driver's seat and started the engine. He gave the cops watching from their patrol car an "Everything's O.K." wave.

"I hope you weren't hurt," Korfmann said as Erie put the car in gear and pulled away from the curb.

"You're not under arrest, Mrs. Korfmann. I'm taking you in for an interview, that's all. You don't have to say anything if you don't want to."

"Is he dead?"

Erie took his eyes off the road for a moment to watch her. "Yes. Raymond Long is dead. He was killed about half an hour ago."

Korfmann grunted. A long stretch of road slid past in silence.

"It's his own fault," Korfmann eventually announced. "He killed himself when he pulled that trigger."

She didn't look at Erie as she spoke. She stared straight ahead, unblinking.

"What do you mean?" Erie said.

"I filled the barrel with caulk last week." Korfmann was still staring at nothing, but tears had begun to trickle over her cheeks. "I was afraid he was going to use it on me."

"He was abusive?"

"Yes."

Erie stole another glance at her. The tears were still flowing, but her face was impassive, blank.

"He was your lover," he said.

"Yes."

"He killed your husband."

"Yes."

"He used a van from DeRogatis Ford to fake a burglary."

"Yes."

"He kept the things he took from your house and brought them with him when he moved in with you."

"Yes." The woman spat the word out this time. "That idiot."

"Will you repeat all this when we reach police headquarters? In a formal statement?"

"Yes."

Another mile rolled under the wheels before Erie spoke again.

"Why did you go along with it?" he said. "Did you love him?"

Korfmann finally turned to face Erie. That morning, she had reminded him, just a bit, of Nancy. But whatever resemblance he'd seen was gone now, crushed along with the rest of her spirit.

"Joel used to beat me, too," she said. "Ray promised to protect me."

5:25 p.m.: Korfmann repeated everything on the record, as she said she would. Erie stayed in the interrogation room just long enough to make sure it was all on tape. But he left Sophie Rogers to prepare the statement and get a signature. He simply stood up and said, "I'm tired, Sophie" and walked out without looking back.

Hal Allen was waiting for him outside. "I never would have guessed it," Allen said. "You've been holding out on us all these years. If I'd known you could wrap up a murder case every day, I never would have let you retire."

"Too late now, boss," Erie replied. "Alright if I go home?"

"In a second. I wanted to talk to you at the end of the day, remember?"

"Oh, right. I guess you need this." Erie slipped his badge-clip off his belt and handed it to Allen. "And this." He unholstered his revolver and handed that over, too.

"Well, yeah, we need those. But that's not what I wanted to see you about. Do you still carry cards for Julie Rodes, the grief counselor?"

"Yes."

"Good. Could I have one?"

Erie pulled out one of the cards. He handed it to Allen, who looked at it a moment before handing it back.

"Here," Allen said. "I think you should use this."

5:50 p.m.: Erie stopped at a grocery store on the way home. He found the cheapest red wine in stock and put four bottles in his cart.

But on the way to the register he changed his mind. He found the aisle marked Pet Supplies and threw a bag of kitty litter and a dozen cans of cat food into his cart. He left three bottles of wine on the shelf, beside the dog treats.

When he got home, he opened one of the cans of cat food and dumped its contents onto a small plate. He took the plate out to the front porch along with the wine, a glass and a bottle opener. He placed the plate on the walk that led to the driveway, then eased himself down onto the first step of his porch.

He opened the wine and waited.

FRED MENACE,
COMMIE FOR HIRE

It was July in Los Angeles, and my little one-room office was hotter than the glowing steel foundries of Minsk that were busy pouring out the molten foundation of a worldwide workers' state. A woman walked through the door, and things got even hotter.

She was dressed plainly in a brown shirt and matching slacks, with a mannish jacket wrapped around her broad shoulders. Steel-toed boots covered the sturdy feet at the end of her stout legs. Her dark hair was cut severely, barely reaching her thick neck. But most enticing of all were her hands. They were big and calloused, the hands of a woman who wasn't afraid she was going to break a nail when she wrestled the controls of production from the withered claws of the bourgeoisie.

I was in love.

"Are you Fred Menace?" she said, and she didn't purr like those soft, dime-a-dozen starlets who pop up in a P.I.'s office every ten minutes. Her voice was hard and strong, yet still unmistakably feminine. She was all business, so to speak, but all woman, too.

"I ain't Joe McCarthy," I drawled back at her.

I instantly regretted it. Cynicism is a decadent pose, a façade of apathetic ennui that's antithetical to the committed idealism of the true internationalist. But when you're a private eye, it sort of gets to be a habit.

"Yes, I'm Fred Menace," I said, dropping the hard-boiled routine. "Please have a seat, Miss…?"

She sat in one of my rickety old office chairs and locked eyes with me across my desk. She regarded me coolly for a moment before speaking.

"Smith. Mary Smith," she said. "My brother is missing, and I want you to find him. His name is John Smith. He's a screenwriter. He's been gone for four days."

No flirting, no innuendo, just the facts. I liked that. I like that a lot. I knew immediately that I was going to take the case, whether she could pay or not.

"My fee is $30 a day, plus expenses," I said anyway, just as a formality.

She nodded brusquely. "Fine. That seems reasonable."

It was reasonable. Maybe too reasonable, but what could be done about it? I'd tried to organize the other private investigators in Los Angeles into a collective so that we could create a sliding scale tied to the means of our clients and the needs of each individual dick. Unfortunately, I hadn't gotten very far with the idea. The other P.I.s in L.A. don't talk to me anymore.

"Do you have some reason to suspect foul play?"

"Foul play?" Mary raised a thick black eyebrow. "I don't know. I just know that my brother has disappeared."

"Did he have any reason to skip town in a hurry?"

"Yes, I suppose so," she said, still icy cool. "But that's not John's way. He's a very brave, committed man. He wouldn't just run away."

"He wouldn't just run away from what, Miss Smith?"

That finally warmed her up a degree or two. "The House Committee on Un-American Activities," she said, spitting the words out as if they were a mouthful of rotten borscht. "John's been subpoenaed. He was supposed to testify yesterday. He never appeared."

I leaned back in my chair, my mind spinning back to the years before the war. John Smith. Screenwriter. Pinko. Sure, I remembered him now. I'd met him through the Hollywood Anti-Nazi League. He was a squirrelly little knobby-kneed guy with all the sheer animal magnetism of a paper cup. His sister had fifteen pounds on him, easy.

I hadn't seen him since 1945—six years ago. Like so many Tinseltown Communists, his passion for revolution cooled once Hitler was out and Red-baiting was in.

"I know what you're thinking, Mr. Menace," Mary said, and her voice was softer now, almost pleading. "Everybody in town knows about you. You're a proud Marxist through and through. When it comes to the fight against bourgeois capitalism, you won't back down an inch."

I knew she was stroking my ego, but what the hey, I liked it. The way her lips caressed the words "Marxist" and "bourgeois" was enough to get Lenin up out of his tomb.

"You got that right, sister," I said.

"My brother...he was a true believer, really he was. But he couldn't just throw away his career. He had to make a living."

"I thought you said he was a brave, committed man."

Her expression turned cagey. "Keep waving the flag of the proletariat from the mountaintops, Mr. Menace," she said, the vulnerability gone from her voice. "But don't think that it's the only way to serve the cause."

"What do you mean?"

"My brother planned on confronting the Committee. He wasn't going to name names. He was going to throw their fascist grandstanding back in their fat faces."

"That's what a lot of these weekend revolutionaries say. Fifteen minutes under the spotlights and they're coughing up names like a talking telephone directory."

Mary reached into the pocket of her slacks—she didn't carry a purse—and pulled out a small wad of bills. "Believe what you like, Mr. Menace," she said as she counted out three tens. She held them out across my desk. "Just find my brother."

I looked at the money. Sometimes it really eats me up that I run a business. But until the day an American workers' state nationalizes private investigation services, what can I do? Like the lady said, a guy's gotta make a living.

I took the money.

೧෴

These days, you're not a real American—which is to say a member in good standing of the dominant consumer culture— unless you own a car. So I don't. That can be a little tough on a guy in my racket. Tailing somebody without being seen is rough enough. Tailing them when you're relying on the Los Angeles public transit system is next to impossible. But I manage.

After picking up a bus from Wilshire to Culver City, I hitched a ride with a fruit truck and a moving van before hoofing it the last twelve blocks or so to 545 Venice Blvd.—the home of John Smith, screenwriter. It only took me three hours to get there.

Some Hollywood types go in for shabby chic—homes where a little peeling paint and crumbling stucco add a touch of faux bohemian ambiance. But the rotting wood and weed-choked yard of Smith's little bungalow weren't there for show. His place was just plain shabby.

I let myself in with the key Mary had given me—her stubby, muscular fingers brushing my tingling palm all too briefly—and headed straight for the refrigerator. I didn't hope to find any clues there. I was drenched with sweat and I needed a cold beer. And I found one. Property being theft and all, I felt free to help myself.

Beer in hand, I gave the place the once-over. It wasn't exactly neat—dirty plates were piled up in the sink, clothes were scattered across the floor, the sheets on the pull-down bed looked like they hadn't been made since the Battle of Stalingrad. But I didn't see any signs of a struggle. A plain, wooden dining table was wedged into one of the bungalow's dark corners. A typewriter sat on it next to a stack of white paper and a dictionary. I sat down at the desk and tried to put myself in the mind of John Smith, hack. I stared at the typewriter, searching for inspiration. I didn't have to search long.

The typewriter wasn't empty. A small wedge of white was still wrapped around the cylinder. I pulled it out. It was about a third of a sheet of typing paper, ripped. Somebody had been in a hurry to pull the page out of the typewriter—too much of a hurry. I read what was on the paper.

D'ARTAGNAN
Thou hast erred, fiend! At this moment, Athos nears!

CARDINAL RICHELIEU
Ahhh, ridiculous rubbish, I vow!

[Zontak strikes Richelieu with the butt of his ray gun, sending him to the floor.]

ZONTAK
Earth scum!

CARDINAL RICHELIEU
(cowering)
A terrible mistake, I declare!

ZONTAK
No, I g

That was it. For a second there, I considered dropping the case. A writer this bad needed to stay lost for the good of mankind. Then I remembered his sister. And her thirty bucks. And my rent. I slipped the scrap of paper into my jacket pocket and got back to work.

Somebody had nabbed Smith's screenplay, but they hadn't done a very thorough job. Maybe they'd left even more behind. I leaned over Smith's typewriter and pushed down the shift key.

Bingo. The typewriter ribbon was still there. I carefully removed it and put it in my other pocket. Then I turned, ready to nose around some more.

I didn't get far. Before I'd taken two steps, I heard voices outside. Someone was walking up to the front door.

"So this guy was some kinda Pinko?" voice number one said.

"Not a Pinko—a Red to the core," voice number two replied gruffly.

Voice number one I didn't recognize. Voice number two I did. I started looking for a place to hide.

I threw myself on the floor and slid under the bed just as the front door opened.

"Not locked," said voice number one.

Voice number two—a.k.a. FBI special agent Mike Sickles—just grunted.

The two men stepped inside.

I began sweating worse than Henry Ford at a union rally. Sickles and I have a little arrangement: If he doesn't see me, he doesn't shoot me.

I was anxious to keep my end of the bargain. But if Sickles or his flunky looked under the bed, this comrade would be headed to the big workers' paradise in the sky. "Pretty lousy dive, ain't it?" said the first FBI agent.

"I dunno," Sickles replied absently. I could see his big feet moving slowly toward the sink, then to Smith's desk. He needed new shoes. "Makes my place look like the Ritz."

The other agent moved over to the desk next to Sickles. "Say, what's that?"

They stood side by side for a moment, silent.

"Nothing," Sickles finally pronounced. His feet moved in my direction, then suddenly swiveled.

I braced myself. His weight came down on the flimsy bed frame like the Battleship Potemkin. The mattress sagged under him, pinning me to the floor. A bed spring poked my back. Somehow I stayed quiet.

"You think he skipped town? Maybe the country?" Sickles's partner asked.

"Could be," Sickles mumbled. "Dirty Reds. Turn on the lights and they scatter like roaches."

"So what's our next move?"

"Well, there's that producer he was working for—Dominic Van Dine. We should lean on him a little, see if he knows anything." Sickles leaned back and sighed. The spring gouged my back like a shiv. "Tomorrow."

"Tomorrow? Why tomorrow?"

Suddenly the crushing weight on my back was gone. I could breathe again. Sickles's scuffed shoes shuffled toward the door.

"Because I've got an itch to play the ponies today, knucklehead," Sickles said. "And Dominic Van Dine's not going anywhere."

The other agent followed Sickles out the door like the loyal lapdog he was. I waited a minute, just in case Sickles was toying with me. There's not much to do when you're stretched out underneath a bed, so naturally my eyes started to wander. Having a rat's-eye-view of the place gave me a whole new perspective.

I caught sight of a bright yellow ball on the floor under Smith's desk. I slid out from my hiding place and groped under the desk for it.

It was another piece of paper, balled up tight. I flattened it out.

It was notebook paper from an oversized steno pad. Covering it top to bottom, back and front, was a list of scribbled words. It started with "t" words: tacky, tantalizing, tardy, tedious, tempting, tender, terrible, tiresome, etc. Then the list switched to "m" words, then "i" words, "d" words, "n" words and finally a few "g" words.

I folded the list and stuck it in my pocket. There would be plenty of time to puzzle over it later. Right now, I had to get moving.

So Sickles was going to visit Smith's producer tomorrow. Good. That meant I could drop in for a chat today. But first I wanted to pay a call on an old acquaintance of mine—a safecracker known as Benny the Bat. He had good fingers and tight lips and bad habits. He owed me a favor.

I left Smith's bungalow and started looking for a ride.

About four hours later, I was standing in front of Dominic Van Dine's house in West Hollywood. I'm using the term "house" a little loosely here. It was actually something half-way between a house and a mansion. It was big alright, but it had the wide, flat roof and squat, squashed look of those ultra-modern boxes they've been throwing up all over Southern California since the war. I figured at least three families could live in there comfortably. And after the Revolution, they would.

I rang the doorbell. It played the first five notes of "We're in the Money." That would have to change, too. Maybe it could be set up to play "There Is Power in a Union."

The door opened just enough for a head to poke out. It was a good head, if you go in for long, golden locks of purest sunshine and big, blue eyes like two bottomless lagoons and soft, sensuous lips just waiting to be kissed and kissed hard. Me, I don't cotton to blonde bombshells. The only bombshells that strike my fancy are the ones that will free the proletariat from the shackles of wage slavery.

Her baby blues devoured me. "Yes?" she said, making it sound more like an invitation than a question.

"I'd like to speak with Mr. Van Dine," I replied flatly.

"He's not home today. But I'll tell him you dropped by, Mr....?"

"Menace," I said. "Fred Menace, P.I. I have a feeling Mr. Van Dine *is* home today. And I have a feeling he *will* speak with me once you scoot your pampered caboose inside and tell him a private dick's nosing around asking questions about John Smith and the House Committee on Un-American Activities."

She didn't bat an eyelash—which was a good thing, since her eyelashes were so long and heavy batting one around would probably hurt somebody.

"Wait here, Mr. Menace," she said.

Her head disappeared. The door closed. I waited.

A minute later, the door opened again.

"Come inside," Blonde And Beautiful said, holding the door just wide enough for me to slip into the house. I had to brush against her lightly as I stepped inside. B And B smiled. "Follow me." She turned and walked across the foyer toward what looked like a study.

I followed. I had an unobstructed view of B And B as she moved. I could have charged admission for a view like that. She had curves, lots of them, just the way a pencil doesn't.

But such decadent sensuality couldn't hold my eye. I was more interested in the dimestore opulence of Van Dine's home. Glass chandelier and scuffed tile in the foyer, a faded Diego Rivera print on the wall, imitation mahogany desk and shelves in the study, row after row of dust-covered books that had never been read and never would. Van Dine was making a stab at class that wouldn't fool a poodle. Everything was fake. I took another look at Miss B And B, wondering how much of her was real.

"Please make yourself comfortable," she purred. "Mr. Van Dine will be with you shortly."

She left the study, closing the door behind her. It's every working man's right to do a little freelance redistribution of wealth, so I took her advice, pouring myself a cognac and lighting up a cigar I found in a box on the desk. I was just leaning back in one of the room's ridiculously overstuffed chairs when the door opened and a middle-aged man greeted me with the kind of welcoming smile hungry spiders flash at fat flies.

"Ahhh, I'm glad to see you're making yourself at home," he said. He closed the door and walked over and offered his hand. "I'm Dominic Van Dine."

I shook his hand without bothering to rise. "Fred Menace."

"Yes, yes. I've heard of you, Mr. Menace," he said as he slipped behind his desk and took a seat. The chair he sat in was at least half a foot taller than any of the others in the room, making him seem a bit like a kid in a high chair. Except this kid was fifty or so years old, had a Van Dyke and was wearing a red silk smoking jacket. He looked like Leon Trotsky masquerading as a debauched playboy. "People call you 'the Red detective,' correct?"

"Some do."

"You know, I've always thought there was a movie in that. *The Red Detective.* Communist sympathizer, private eye. Explosive. Ripped from today's headlines. It would be perfect for Brian Dunleavy."

He was a producer all right. Nobody in Hollywood would put a plug nickel in a picture like that. But he thought he could snow me with visions of movie stars and royalty checks. I blew a big cloud of cigar smoke up over my head.

"Sounds boffo, Mr. Van Dine," I said. "But I'm only interested if you get Paul Robeson to play me. And I want a Russian director. Is Sergei Eisenstein still alive?"

Rigor mortis set in on Van Dine's smile.

"So you're looking for John Smith," he said, his tone suddenly brittle.

"Why, yes. I am. How did you know he's missing?"

"Because I've been trying to find him myself. He's working on a script for me. Production's set to begin in three weeks. If he's left the country because of this witch-hunt in Congress, I need to know."

"This script Smith's working on—it wouldn't be a Three Musketeers picture, would it?"

Van Dine's eyes bulged out so far I thought they were going to hop out of his face and slap me. "Yes. *The Three Musketeers vs. the Moon Men*." He blinked, and a curtain of false calm dropped over his features. "Have you seen it?"

"I haven't just seen it, I've read it. Well, not all of it. It's not done yet. But I skimmed enough to know it stinks."

I was trying to shake things up, and it worked. I shook up a bona fide earthquake.

"I don't care if it stinks," Van Dine said. "A man in my position can't afford to care. I've got actors signed, costumes and sets being made, a studio that wants this picture in theaters by Thanksgiving. 'Stinks' or 'doesn't stink' doesn't enter into it." He smiled his spider smile at me again. "I would be very interested in knowing how you got your hands on a copy of that screenplay, Mr. Menace."

The fly smiled back at the spider. "It was handed to me wrapped up in a ribbon."

A moment of silence passed before Van Dine realized that was all he was going to get. He chuckled and reached toward the cigar box.

"Despite your reputation as a revolutionary, I see you're really just a businessman like the rest of us," he said. He stuck a cigar between his curled lips and lit it with a gaudy, faux crystal lighter. "You expect to be compensated for your efforts. Of course. I can make it worth your while to bring me the script."

I took a big puff on my own cigar and tried to blow a smoke ring toward Van Dine. All I got was a misshapen cloud that fanned out over his desk. It turns out I'm not as good at blowing smoke as I thought.

"You've got the basic idea," I said. "Except I don't want money. I want your help. You use your industry connections to open doors for me, help me find Smith, and you'll get your script."

Van Dine nodded. "I understand." He pushed a button on an intercom set on his desk. "Miss Bellevue, send Mr. Grey in, please. I'd like him to have a word with our guest." Van Dine leaned back in his chair and blew a smoke ring of his own. It was a perfect circle that floated up toward my head like a dirty halo. "My assistant Mr. Grey will get you started. He's the last one of us to have seen John Smith."

As he was talking, the door opened behind me. Before I could turn to see who'd entered, a sudden, crunching bolt of pain shot through my skull. I came to my feet clutching my head and spun around to see a hulking man in a dark suit that could barely stretch itself around his massive body. He was standing behind my chair with a blackjack in his hand and a look of surprise on his broad face.

"I'm not your usual soft-headed gumshoe," I spat at him. "I've got a head harder than Siberian granite. It's going to take a lot more than a love tap from a blackjack to—"

Another explosion of pain echoed through my head. I looked over my shoulder. Van Dine stood behind me, the crystal lighter in his hand. It was smeared with blood. My blood. I laughed bitterly.

"Careful there, Van Dine. You're going to break your pretty bauble trying to use it as a nutcracker. Next time, try a—"

A heavy weight crashed into my back, sending me spinning to the ground.

Mr. Grey had smacked me with a chair.

This time I shut up and stayed down.

I passed out, too.

Laughter echoed through my mind. It was John Smith, giggling maniacally.

"Smart boy, aintcha?" he said. "A real smart boy."

His head tilted back as he let out another roar of laughter, and suddenly his face was frozen, the mouth open wide. Light bulbs twinkled in his hair, and a neon sign flashed on and off on his forehead. "Funhouse," the sign said. The wind began to howl, and I was pulled screaming into Smith's huge, oval mouth. The wind stopped, replaced by the clanking of chains and gears. I found myself strapped in a cart, jerking through the darkness one tug at a time. A spotlight stabbed through the gloom to my right, pinning Dominic Van Dine and his apelike lackey Mr. Grey in a harsh cone of light. They stared at me with huge, multifaceted eyes that sparkled in the light like diamonds. Poison glistened on their fangs. Another spotlight snapped on to my left, revealing Mary Smith dancing the tango with a black bear. A third light broke the dark directly in front of me. In its glare, I could see Sigmund Freud juggling monkeys. He was dressed like Carmen Miranda, with a tight skirt and fruit piled high on his eggy head. "Talk, smart boy," Freud sang to me. "Wake up and talk."

"Wake up," I sang back dumbly. "Talk."

"That's right. Wake up and talk, Mr. Menace."

Something about the voice swept the visions from my mind. Maybe the fact that I wasn't dreaming it.

I blinked hard and shook my head, and a wave of nausea washed over me. When it passed, I could see where I was.

I didn't like it. I was in the center of a small, dank, dungeon-like room, sitting in a chair, my feet strapped to the legs, my hands tied behind me. A single light bulb hung a few feet above my head, blinding me with its bright, unfiltered light.

Dominic Van Dine and Mr. Grey stood a few feet away, watching me. Van Dine leaned in close and smiled.

"So you're back among the living at last. Let's see how long that lasts. Mr. Grey."

Van Dine moved back, and his gorilla stepped forward. I heard a sharp cracking sound, and my head jerked to the side. Pain knocked on the door of my addled brain. It forced its way inside and made itself at home.

I'd been slugged on the jaw. Hard.

"I hope ya' like them apples, smart boy," Grey said in a wheezy, high-pitched voice. "Cuz I got me a bushelfull."

There was another crack, and my head jerked again. The pain in my brain had company.

"Alright, alright! Enough with the rough stuff," I barked with as much force as I could muster—which wasn't much considering the blood in my mouth and the ringing in my ears. "Why don't you ask me some questions already?"

Grey glanced over his shoulder at Van Dine, who looked thoughtful for a moment before nodding his head. Grey moved away, rubbing his knuckles.

"Very well, Mr. Menace. Let's see if any more 'rough stuff' is necessary," Van Dine said. "Tell me where your copy of the script is."

A new sensation joined the party in my skull. It was hope. If there's one thing a guy needs when he's been tied to a chair by people of less-than-sterling virtues, it's leverage. Or a free hand and a .45. I was happy to have the leverage.

"Why are you so desperate to get your hands on that script?"

"Mr. Grey," Van Dine said blandly.

Grey stepped toward me, a smirk on his heavy, simian face.

"Hold on there, King Kong. You don't have to bother," I said before he could belt me. I looked past him at Van Dine. "You were going to remind me that you're the one asking the questions here."

"Exactly. How did you know what I was going to say?"

I tried to shrug. "I've been to the movies."

At this point, Monkey Man got tired of all the talk and slugged me anyway.

"Buddy," I said to Grey after my head stopped spinning on my neck like a top, "I realize that you're just a humble working man trying to survive in this dehumanizing Darwinian jungle we call the capitalist system. But one day you're going to find those knuckles of yours jammed down your thick throat."

Grey turned to Van Dine. "He just threatened me, right?"

Van Dine nodded. "That's right."

"That's what I thought."

Grey raised his fist. It was time to use that leverage, but fast.

"I'll give you the script."

"Wait!" Van Dine snapped.

Grey unclenched his fist and backed off. He looked disappointed.

"I'm glad you've decided to be reasonable, Mr. Menace," Van Dine said. "Now tell me—where is it?"

I licked my lips. I was about to see how much leverage I had.

"I'll do better than tell you. I'll show you…if you untie me and let me out of this rat hole."

That got a good chuckle out of Van Dine.

"What kind of fool do you take me for? I don't even know for certain that you really have a copy of the script and I'm supposed to let you walk out of here and stir up who knows what kind of trouble? I think not."

"I think so. I'm guessing you sent your primate playmate here over to Smith's bungalow to grab the script. But Mighty Joe Young didn't get the job done. He left a copy of Smith's script behind."

"Awww, applesauce!" Grey broke in. "There wasn't no other copy. I looked all over."

I graced Grey with a pitying smile. "But you didn't look in the right place, Cheetah. This copy wasn't sitting around nice and neat and double-spaced on white paper. It was inside the typewriter."

"Phooey!" Grey spat. "This is a buncha bunk."

"Shut up, you oaf," Van Dine snapped. His oily confidence was dripping away before my eyes. "You're talking about the ribbon," he said to me.

I nodded. "That's right. Everything John Smith has typed for the last week or two or even three, who knows? It all hit that ribbon. And it's still there, just waiting for someone with the time and the patience to get it. In fact, I've got a friend—a friend with very bad eyes and very, very sensitive fingers—who's going over that ribbon right now. I gave it to him just before I came here. I'll bet he's half-way through the script by now."

Van Dine stared at me. Or, more accurately, he stared through me. I could practically see the wheels in his mind turning, spinning faster and faster like pinwheels. And then they stopped.

"You have failed me, Mr. Grey."

"What? Don't tell me you believe this two-bit gumshoe," Grey protested, crooking a thumb at me.

"You know the penalty for failure," Van Dine replied coldly. His left hand slipped toward one of the big silk pockets of his smoking jacket.

Fear twisted the thick flesh of Grey's face. "No! Don't!" he cried. "Please!"

"I'm afraid you leave me no choice."

Van Dine pulled out his hand slowly. In it was a slip of thick paper.

"No screening pass for you this weekend," he said. "If you want to see—" He glanced at the paper, then began tearing it up. — *Bedtime for Bonzo*, you'll have to wait a month and pay your fifty cents like the rest of the little people."

Grey's whimper turned to a snarl as he whipped around to face me. "This is your fault, shamus! I'm gonna—"

"Untie him," Van Dine broke in.

"But—"

"I said untie him!"

Grey glared at Van Dine for a moment before moving his bulky body behind me and fumbling with the ropes. My hands came free first. Within seconds, they were stinging with the pain of a thousand needlepricks as the blood flow returned. A moment later, my feet felt the same way.

"Smart move, Van Dine," I said, buying time while my hands

and feet recovered. "You're playing this the right way."

"If he double-crosses us, kill him," Van Dine said to Grey.

Grey leaned in close to my ear.

"With pleasure," he said.

But the pleasure was all mine. Grey was a sloppy man. He'd done a sloppy job searching Smith's bungalow, and now he'd done a sloppy job untying me. He'd merely loosened the rope around my hands without bothering to take it away. And when he stuck his big ape head next to mine, it was simplicity itself to take that rope and wrap it around his neck.

It took all my strength to stand and take three steps forward, dragging Grey behind me. He toppled over the back of the chair. The chair pitched forward, and Grey came with it. The chair came down with a crash. Grey came down with a snap. His body went limp.

I turned my attention to Van Dine—but he was gone. For the first time, I got a good look at the room around me. Several black monoliths loomed in the darkness. At first, I thought they were bookshelves. But as my eyes adjusted to the gloom, I could see that they were loaded with bottles, not books. I was in Van Dine's wine cellar.

I heard a quick shuffle-step behind me. I whirled around just in time to see Van Dine rushing me, a champagne bottle clutched in his hand.

I wanted to meet him on equal terms, but there was no time to go looking for a bottle of vodka. So I ducked. The champagne bottle cut through the air just above my head. Van Dine's momentum carried him forward, and I gave him a good shove as he moved past. He stumbled, off balance, and slammed into the nearest wine rack. He hit the ground amid a shower of mid-range cabernets.

"Defeated by the trappings of your own decadence," I said, shaking my head. "Clifford Odets would pay me twenty bucks for a metaphor like this."

Van Dine groaned from beneath the pile of bottles. I gave him a moment to reflect on his predicament before I grabbed a foot and gave it a twist. Van Dine's groans turned into a yowl. I pulled the foot—and the body it was attached to—out to the center of the room.

"I want to thank you, Mr. Van Dine. You've given me the perfect setup."

I twisted the foot again. Van Dine howled again and kicked at me feebly. I twisted harder, then let go.

"I've been tied up. Beaten. Tortured. I've got the wounds to prove it." I walked around Van Dine's cowering form until I was just a step from his head. I placed the heel of one shoe on his face and gave it just a little bit of pressure. "So anything that happens now is purely self-defense. Because I'll be the only one left to tell the story. Get me?"

Van Dine was panting so hard I could barely make out his words.

"What was that?"

"I said, 'I get you,'" he rasped.

"Good. Now I want you to tell me what happened to John Smith." I put just a little more pressure on Van Dine's face. I could feel the cartilage of his nose bending almost to the snapping point. "And I don't want any fibs."

Van Dine talked. When he was through, I slipped the rope from around Son of Kong's throat. I left Van Dine lying face down, his hands tied behind him, in a puddle of cabernet and champagne. That wasn't very nice, I know. But if he got depressed waiting for the police to arrive, he could always slurp his cares away. Anyway, I could've left him in a puddle of blood.

Upstairs, I ran into Miss Bellevue. She gaped at me, stunned, from a sofa. A copy of *Film World Exposé* slipped through her suddenly slack fingers. I didn't have to be Criswell the Mindreader to know what thoughts were flying through her platinum-plated skull.

"Yeah, that's right, honey. All that screaming and yelling was your boss, not me."

"I...I...I didn't...."

"Save the smooth talk for the cops, glamour-puss." I went to the nearest phone—one of those old-fashioned gold-leaf and pearl jobs you always see Bette Davis gabbing on in the pictures—and asked the operator to give me police headquarters. Some lucky desk jockey was about to get the anonymous tip of a lifetime.

While I was waiting for the connection to go through, Miss Bellevue jumped off the couch and made a beeline for the front door. I took mercy on a poor working girl and let her go.

It was dark by the time I got back to my office. That was fine. It fit my mood.

I'd been settled behind my desk all of five minutes when my client came through the door. My heart went pitter-pat. My head told my heart to get lost.

She sat down across from me.

"Have you found my brother?"

Oh, that voice. It didn't purr like a kitten. It didn't caress me like a silk glove. It chipped away at me like a jackhammer. It was a husky, no-nonsense, "¡Viva la revolucion!" kind of voice. I loved her even more. But….

There's always a but when you're a private dick. And my but was as big as they come.

"I've found John Smith," I said. "Up until this evening, he was in a flower bed at the home of a movie producer named Dominic Van Dine." I glanced at my watch. "By now, I'd bet he's on his way to the Los Angeles County morgue."

I watched her for a reaction. She didn't disappointment me. She didn't have one. No false hysterics. No crocodile tears. Just a cocked eyebrow and a single word.

"Explain."

I obliged.

"Van Dine knew about Smith's ties to the Communist Party. That's why he hired him to work on a script. Not because Van Dine's some kind of sympathizer. He's just greedy. Smith's past made him vulnerable: It meant he'd work cheap. But when the House Committee on Un-American Activities started tossing around subpoenas, Van Dine got nervous. If it came out that he'd knowingly hired a Red, he'd be finished in this town. So he sent a muscle-bound messenger boy out to collect Smith and his script. Smith told Van Dine he *wanted* to appear before the committee. He wanted to…how did you put it this morning? 'Throw their fascist grandstanding back in their fat faces'? But Van Dine couldn't have that. He's not one of those studio producers. He's an independent. He has to finance his projects himself. He already had a small bundle tied up in his next picture, and a small bundle's more than a guy like that can afford to lose. So he convinced Smith not to testify—convinced him with a piece of rope wrapped around his neck."

My client's grey eyes didn't fill with tears. Sobs didn't erupt from her thin, colorless lips. Such displays would be beneath her— beneath *us*. Because we were both players on the same team. Maybe you've heard of us. The Los Angeles Reds.

"And the script?" she said.

I nodded. "Yes. The script. That's what you're really interested in, isn't it, comrade? Smith wasn't your brother. He was your stooge. And you need to get that script back to cover your tracks."

I finally saw her smile. It broke up the marble smoothness of her face, revealing the animal cunning beneath.

"Yes, comrade. You recovered the copy from Van Dine's residence?"

I nodded again. "I had time to do a little nosing around before the cops showed up. I found it."

"Good. Give it to me, and our work will be done."

No more nodding for me. I shook my head.

"I don't think so. Not until I get an explanation."

Her face turned to stone again.

"If you are a true revolutionary, you will give the script to me."

"Why don't you let me decide that? Now tell me: What's in that script that's so important?"

She shrugged with a nonchalance so transparent you could call it outright chalance.

"Nothing. As you said, I'm just trying to tie up loose ends."

I grunted unhappily. I don't like being lied to, even by women I'd like to run off and make little proles with.

"Then why is it written in code?"

"I don't know what you're talking about."

A deep, sad sigh rose and fell in my chest.

"Nobody in this town writes dialogue that bad on purpose. Not unless they've got a hidden agenda…or maybe a contract with Universal. I spent quite a few hours on buses today, so I had plenty of time to work out Smith's system. Take the first letter of each word of dialogue, add them together and voila. It's Western Union time. But I still don't know what it all means. 'Rosenberg says no.' 'The fluoridation is working.' 'The Roswell prisoners are ill.' It's all Greek to me."

As Spymaster Mary listened to my little speech, the smile I'd seen earlier started to return. I was hoping it would be a warmer smile, a more human smile, a throw-herself-into-my-arms-and-declare-her-undying-love kind of smile. But it was none of the above. It was a smug smile.

"And it will stay Greek, for the good of the cause," she said. "All I can tell you is this: That screenplay is the key to America's greatest secrets. It represents the accumulated work of our entire spy network here. How fitting it would have been to deliver it to our comrades overseas in the form of a Hollywood film—the ultimate symbol of Western foolishness. That can't happen now. But the script can still be smuggled abroad. With the information it holds, the Soviet Union will finally crush the United States like an insect."

Under different circumstances, I would have swooned. Mary Smith—real name Maria Smithostovovich or somesuch—really knew how to get a red-blooded Red worked into a lather.

But I'm not just Red. I hate to admit it, but under the surface I'm white and blue, too.

"Since you put it like that, it's no dice, sister." I wanted to bite my tongue off with every word. Somehow I managed to keep going. "I'm a traitor to my class, but not my country. I'm not giving you that script."

I didn't even get a raised eyebrow out of her, let alone a wistful tear. She simply pulled a revolver from her jacket and leveled it at me. My heart was broken. And in a second, it was going to be filled with hot lead.

"Now hold on. We can still talk this out, comrade."

"You are no comrade of mine," she spat back at me. "You call yourself a Communist, yet you let nationalist loyalties come between you and your duty to the revolution. I should shoot you down like a dog."

"But then you wouldn't get the other copy of the script."

"Other copy?" The barrel of the gun wavered just a bit—from my heart to my gut. It wasn't much of an improvement, but I wasn't in a position to be choosy.

"When a typewriter key hits the ribbon, it leaves an impression," I said. "And I've got the ribbon from John Smith's typewriter. Or, to be more exact, a friend of mine has the ribbon. A blind friend. I gave it to him this afternoon after I left Smith's bungalow. He's had plenty of time to go over it. I'm sure he's got the whole script transcribed by now."

It looked like my little visit to Benny the Bat was going to pay off for the second time today. Looked like that for about two seconds, that is.

"But as you said yourself, it's written in code," Mary sneered. "Your friend won't know what it means or who to take it to…so long as you're dead."

What could I say? "Good point"?

She thumbed back the hammer on her revolver. "Now give me Van Dine's copy of the script."

"Like I said—no dice. And if you shoot me, you'll never find it. Looks like we've got us a stalemate."

Mary waved the gun at a corner of my desk. "But isn't that the script sitting right there?"

She sounded amused. At last, I'd gotten a little warmth out of her. It didn't help me feel any better.

"Well, I guess that was the dumbest bluff I ever tried to put over."

"I'll have to take your word for that, Mr. Menace."

The barrel of her gun moved again. Now it was pointed squarely at my forehead.

"*Dasvidaniya.*"

I sighed again. "Yeah, O.K. So long, sister. Tell the boys in the Kremlin I said—"

A shot rang out before I could finish. I thought that was pretty rude. Not only does she kill me, but she's got to interrupt me, too. Some people ain't got no manners.

Then an amazing thing happened: The woman who'd just killed me toppled off her chair. The back of her head looked like a lasagna. Even more shocking: I was alive.

"Boy, am I gonna regret that in the mornin'," a familiar voice said.

FBI special agent Mike Sickles was standing in the doorway of my office, his gun in his hand. He was shaking his big, bald head.

"If I'd just waited two more seconds—*bang*. You'd have been out of my hair forever, Menace."

I wanted to say something like "What hair, cueball?" But I wasn't about to push my luck. He could still change his mind and let her shoot me retroactively. It was just a matter of how he wanted to write up the report.

Sickles stepped into the room and bent down over Mary Smith. He was followed quickly by the lackey I'd seen him with earlier in the day. At least it looked like the same guy from the shins down.

"She dead, Mike?" Sickles's partner asked.

"Naw, she's just hibernatin'. Now call the meatwagon, knucklehead."

Knucklehead scooped up the phone on my desk and asked the operator for the coroner's office.

Sickles waved his meaty hand back and forth before my eyes. "Hey, anybody home? Snap out of it, Menace. She scare you to death or somethin'?"

I blinked, maybe for the first time in a good minute.

"Thanks," I said.

Sickles grimaced. "Don't thank me. I handed you a break because you wouldn't give the broad the script. Next time I might not feel so merciful."

"How long were you there in the doorway?"

"Not long. I only moseyed over when things started to heat up."

"Moseyed over?"

"Sure. Knucklehead and me, we were next door listening to the whole conversation. It was mighty entertainin', too. Like *The Bickersons* and *Suspense* rolled into one."

"You've got my place bugged?"

Sickles tilted his head and gave me a don't-ask-stupid-questions frown. "Course not. We had tin cans pressed up against the wall."

I didn't push it. Besides, I had other questions on my mind. I nodded at Mary Smith's body without letting my eyes move that way.

"So what's her real name, anyway?"

Sickles ran his hands over his smooth, sweaty skull. He was obviously trying to decide whether or not to tell me the truth. The truth won out. What a day for sworn enemies. Around the world, cats and dogs stopped fighting and kissed each other on both cheeks.

"Beats me, Menace," Sickles said. "I didn't even know she existed until she walked in here and started gabbin' with you."

He saw my confusion and went on.

"You were the one we were following. Ever since we walked in on you at John Smith's place." He cracked a cockeyed smile. "You were hidden O.K., but that beer you were guzzling wasn't. It was still cold when we came in. All the windows were closed and bolted, so I knew somebody was still in there somewhere. I dropped a little hint about Dominic Van Dine—the next stop on my hunt for Smith—then stepped back to see what happened."

I grunted with grudging admiration. "You amaze me, Sickles. You played this one better than Machiavelli himself."

Sickles glared at me. "He some kinda Commie?"

I shook my head.

The G-man let it slide.

"Well, if I'm so smart," he said, "how come I've got boils on my butt the size of grapefruit from all the hours I spent sittin' in the car today? I tell ya' Menace, tailin' you is like gettin' in a high-speed chase with a three-legged turtle."

What a charming development. Sickles and I were so thoroughly bonded now he felt free to tell me about his carbuncles. I stifled a sigh.

My eyes drifted back to the body of Miss X, the Unknown Communist. I hadn't killed her, but I hadn't helped her, either.

What kind of revolutionary was I? What kind of detective was I? What kind of man was I?

"All that is solid melts into air," Marx wrote. That was me alright. Fred Menace, the Red Detective, had melted. I'm just vapor now, part of the smog that chokes L.A.

I still charge $30 a day plus expenses, though. Even vapor's gotta make a living.

STRAYS

It had been just four months since Larry Erie had retired, and already he was turning into a cat lady. At least, that's what his new friend William "Bass" Anderson kept telling him.

"How much do you spend on 9 Lives every month?" Bass would ask. "Eight, nine hundred dollars?"

"I've only got two cats, Bass," Erie would say, knowing it was hopeless to argue.

"That's where it starts!" Bass would reply, waving whatever he had in his hand at the time—usually a doughnut, sometimes a muffin. "Two hungry little strays you just had to take in off the street. But there's always two more and two more and two more."

"They were running around the neighborhood without anyone looking out for them. What was I supposed to do?"

"You call Animal Control is what you do."

"You know what would happen to them if I did that."

Bass would shake his head with infinite sadness. "You're still throwing your old newspapers away, aren't you? Cuz that's what happens next with you cat ladies. You start stacking newspapers up to the ceiling and then they fall over on you and they find your bones a month later, picked clean. It'll be in one of those grocery store papers. 'Retired Cop Eaten By Starving Cats.'"

And then the Survivors session would start and Erie would get an hour-long respite from Bass's haranguing. Altho͟ ͟ ͟ wasn't really much of a break. Erie didn't think of himsel͟ group kind of guy. Seven men sitting on metal fo͟ a church basement talking about death and fear it seemed strange to him. He never knew what to say. That was part of the tragedy of losing Nancy. She was the one who handled emotions for both of them.

Bass was about the same age as Erie, but he took to the support group concept right away. A young social worker named Julie Rodes was supposed to be their "grief counselor," but sometimes it seemed like Bass was really the group's leader. He was the first one to open up about his feelings, the first one to run over and give another group member a hug when tears started to flow, the only one to take Erie aside after meetings and say things like, "You gotta pull that stick out of your butt, Larry. Let your feelings out. It'll be good for you."

Bass was full of advice for Erie. Feel, talk, *do*.

"You can't stay retired, Larry," Bass would say. "You used to catch murderers for a living. Cleaning the litter box all day ain't a worthy use of your skills."

Bass even knew exactly what Erie should do. He came to one of the group's Tuesday morning meetings with a stack of paper, which he handed to Erie with a commanding, "Alright, grab a pen and get started."

Erie looked at the papers. Printed across the top of the first sheet were the words "State Form 43777: Application for Private Detective License."

"I don't think so, Bass."

Erie tried to hand the forms back.

Bass crossed his arms. "Just think about it."

Erie kept his arm out. "I don't have to think about it. I know. I'm not interested."

"Give it a little time. Let the idea sink in."

"I don't need a little time."

Erie was starting to feel silly holding the forms out, so he began leafing through them, looking for something he knew was in the fine print. When he found it, he pointed to it and tried to show Bass.

"Look at this. I've got to get a $7,000 surety bond. And I'll need extra insurance, too. This isn't something you just do on a whim. It's expensive."

While Erie had been talking, Bass had sauntered over to the snack table and picked up a cup of coffee and a jelly doughnut. His hands now full, he smiled at Erie with smug self-satisfaction.

"You just hold onto those forms. See what you think in a few days." He peered past Erie at the circle of folding chairs. "Excuse me, Larry. I wanna go see how Dave's holding up before the meeting starts."

Bass walked over and sat down next to a paunchy, sixtyish man with hollow eyes. They began talking quietly, and Bass handed him the coffee and the jelly doughnut. The man smiled.

I'm taking in cats, Erie thought to himself, *and Bass is taking in widowers.*

He tossed the application forms into the trash can next to the snack table.

The next week, Bass didn't mention the forms. Not that he'd given up on his project.

"I've got a case for you," he told Erie.

"A case?"

"You know what I'm talkin' about," Bass replied, sounding peevish. "A detective case."

"Darn. I thought you meant a case of beer."

"Don't use that one in your act, Bob Hope. It ain't funny," Bass snapped back.

The emotion in the little man's voice caught Erie off guard.

"What's going on, Bass?"

"I've got one of those crack houses right across the street from me, that's what."

Erie needed a moment to let that sink in.

"A crack house?"

"That's right. A crack house," Bass declared.

Erie stifled a sigh. He knew Bass's neighborhood well. It was predominantly working class, leaning toward redneck—the kind of place where you'd find more than your average share of domestic squabbles and exploding mailboxes, but no crack houses. Of course, that didn't stop self-appointed neighborhood watchdogs from reporting them to the police every now and then, especially after *America's Most Wanted* or *Law & Order* or some other TV show did a story about them.

"Have you called the police?"

Bass nodded, agitated. "You bet I did. Talked to some young gal who made me feel like a crazy man. I saw a patrol car cruise by once or twice, but that's all that came of it."

"Well, if you're still concerned, call again."

"I *am* still concerned, but I know the cops aren't gonna do doodley until I've got some proof."

"If there's any 'proof' to be found, you need to let the professionals find it."

"That's why I'm coming to you."

"Bass, I used to be a detective. *Used to*, as in 'not any more.'"

Erie hadn't meant to raise his voice, but he had. The other group members looked up from their coffee and muffins. Erie felt embarrassed, ashamed, the way he always felt when he lost his temper.

"O.K., I get it," Bass snarled before Erie could apologize. "You don't help people anymore. Just cats."

He stalked away and sat down next to Julie Rodes and instantly started up a conversation about the importance of regular exercise. He didn't look at Erie for the rest of the session.

Erie worried about his spat with Bass for the next week. He hated disagreements with his friends—even friends as meddlesome and stubborn as Bass. Squabbles like that made him feel emotional, vulnerable. But what could he do? Go off and play cops and robbers like some delusional old man who couldn't let go of the past? No, not him. He rehearsed a sincere but firm apology to Bass while hoping that his friend had come to his senses about his neighborhood "crack house."

But the following Tuesday morning, Erie didn't get his chance to apologize. Bass never showed up. The meeting went on with him. It was the first session Bass had missed in the group's three-month history.

Erie didn't say or hear a word for the next hour. The second Julie was finished saying "I'll see you all next week," he was on his feet heading toward the door. He'd been to Bass's place once before—Bass had invited the group over to watch the Super Bowl the previous month. Twenty minutes later, Erie was there again.

He could tell something was wrong a block away. Bass's rusty pickup was nestled on the cement like a cat with its legs tucked up underneath it. All four tires were flat. A garbage can near the curb had been knocked over, its contents spilling out onto the driveway.

Erie parked next to the pickup and walked toward Bass's squat, orange-brick ranch house. As he approached, he noticed the curtains in the front picture window swaying in the breeze. There was a large, jagged hole in the glass.

Erie rang the doorbell. Nobody answered. He pushed the button again. This time, he caught a glimpse of movement back near the driveway. He turned and saw Bass leaning around the side of the house peering at him.

"Oh. It's you," Bass said. He waved Erie over irritably. "Come on. This way. Quick."

He ducked out of sight.

Erie followed. When he got to the driveway, he saw an arm propping open a side door to the house.

"Come on, come on," came a whisper from inside.

Erie obeyed.

When he got inside and got his first good look at Bass, he didn't like what he saw. The little man was haggard, with tousled hair and bags under his bloodshot eyes. He was wearing a heavy parka over a blue pajama top and wrinkled trousers. His right hand stayed jammed into one of the pockets of his coat. The pocket bulged ominously.

"Bass, are you all right? What's going on?"

"I'm fine. Everything's fine."

Erie waited for more. It didn't come.

"What happened to the window?" he prompted.

"Got broke."

Silence again.

"And the tires on your truck?"

"Went flat."

More silence.

"Bass, come on. If there's been trouble, I want to help."

Bass narrowed his eyes. "Really? You mean that?"

"Of course."

"You'll help me out—my way?"

Erie opened his mouth to say, "That depends on what your way is." He quickly substituted a firm "Sure." Equivocation wasn't going to go over well with Bass.

Still, he did have one condition he had to mention.

"Just take your hand away from that gun," he said.

Bass looked down, surprised. He yanked his hand out of the parka pocket.

"I didn't even realize I was...." He stopped and stared at Erie. "What makes you think I've got a gun?"

"I'm a detective, remember?"

Bass's shoulders dropped, and his face loosened into a tenuous smile.

"You want some coffee?"

"Sure."

Bass moved into the kitchen and pulled two mugs down from a cabinet. One had "Truckers Do It for the Long Haul" printed on the side; the other had a pink heart circled by the words "World's Greatest Grandma." He filled them both from a Mr. Coffee on the counter top.

"Sit down, Larry," he said. "This story's gonna take a while."

Erie took a seat at the kitchen table without taking off his coat. The broken window out front was letting in plenty of chilly February air.

He watched his friend pull out a bowl of sugar and a carton of milk and a box of miniature powdered doughnuts. The little smile still curled the edges of Bass's mouth as he moved around the kitchen. He seemed almost cheerful now that he had an audience.

Finally, he spread everything out on the table and sat down across from Erie.

"O.K., where do you want me to start?"

"Tell me about the window and your tires. Any idea who's responsible?"

"Any idea? Any idea?" Bass erupted. "I don't just have an idea. I know!" Bass opened his mouth to go on, then picked up a doughnut instead, suddenly philosophical. "But I guess that's getting ahead of the story."

"Alright. Why don't you just start at the beginning, then?"

Bass nodded. "Good idea."

He threw down another gulp of coffee, then leaned forward and slapped his palms on the table. He looked like he was warming up for a performance.

"So here's the deal," he began. "Across the street there I've got this fella. He's maybe thirty five, forty years old. Not the sociable type. He's lived over there a year or so, and all I know about him is he's got the name 'Smith' on his mailbox and he doesn't give a gosh darn about keeping up his property. A couple months ago, this young hellraiser moves in with him. His son, I assume. Smith's not around 99 percent of the time, and this kid, he takes advantage of it. Plays his rock'n'roll loud enough to wake the dead in three counties. Which didn't bother me much at first. Bootsie and I raised three boys in this house, so I know a little something about noise. But then I started noticing all the kids comin' by in the afternoon. In and out in less than five minutes. It started out slow. Maybe I'd see one or two in a week. But now he's getting' sometimes five or six in a day."

Of course, Erie thought. *The "crack house."*

He kept his face neutral.

"How old is this boy?"

"Maybe eighteen. That's another peculiar thing. Until yesterday, he could've been thirteen or thirty for all I knew. I've only seen him clearly once cuz he never comes outside. He's like the Phantom of the Opera over there."

"And the kids who come by the house—how old are they?"

"All ages. I've seen ten-year-olds and twenty-year-olds go in together."

"That is strange," Erie had to admit.

"You could even say 'suspicious,' am I right?"

Erie nodded. "Yeah, you could call it that."

Bass bounced a fist on the tabletop. "See? If only somebody'd listened to me sooner. But who's gonna pay attention to some nobody spying on his neighbors? 'Oh, he's just a senile old kook. Next thing you know he'll be saying Bigfoot's out back eating his dog.'"

"I'm listening now, Bass."

"Right. *Now* you are. But it looked for a while there like it was up to old Bass to save the day himself. I figured I was gonna hafta come up with some evidence. So I pulled out my—"

"Wait, Bass, wait. Why didn't you just go talk to the father?"

Bass scowled. "Why didn't I? Because I *did*, that's why. Saw him drive up a couple nights ago and ran over to have a few words. Know what he said to me?" Bass's eyes went cross-eyed, and he leaned over the table and poked Erie in the chest with a crooked finger. "'Mind yer own bish-nish, ya ol' sho-and-sho. That boy ish my re-shponsh-ibility, and I'll be damned if shome little blankety blank ish gonna tell me how to raishe him.'" Bass straightened up again. "He wasn't two sheets to the wind—he was four or five. If I hadn't hauled my butt out of there, he probably would've called for his son to come out so they could kick it family-style."

Erie nodded grimly. It wasn't a new story to him. He'd been poked and yelled at and even kicked and punched plenty of times over the years. "Blame the Messenger" was the international motto of lousy parents.

"O.K.," he said. "So yesterday you decided to take matters into your own hands."

"That's right."

Bass pushed his chair away from the table and hustled off into the living room. He returned a moment later with a handful of Polaroid pictures. He dumped them on the table before Erie.

"There you go. See that?"

Erie picked up one of the photographs. All he saw was a white circle of light. Bass snatched the picture away.

"That was before I figured out not to use the flash." He spread out the other shots—there were about a dozen of them—and pointed. "But look there. And there. And there."

The photos clearly had been taken from Bass's living room, through the big (now broken) front window. Each shot featured two or three kids walking to or from the house across the street. The time had been written in blue ink across the white border at the bottom of each picture. Bass separated two shots from the pile.

"See? This boy arrives at 4:15 p.m. and then leaves at 4:21 p.m. You notice anything about the second picture?"

Bass had been too far away to get good shots with a Polaroid camera: The image of the boy was only about an inch tall. Erie had to pick up the picture and hold it up close to his eyes. But he saw something.

"A package? Maybe a plastic bag?"

"That's right! A bag!" Bass bellowed triumphantly. "And you know what's in it!"

Erie shuffled through the other pictures. But the photos didn't capture many details, and most of the kids were wearing heavy parkas with pockets big enough to hold just about anything.

"Something *is* going on over there," Erie said.

"What'd I tell you?"

"*But*," Erie went on, "these pictures don't prove anything. Those kids could be walking away with Girl Scout cookies for all we know."

"I had that selfsame thought yesterday," he said. "Obviously I wasn't close enough to get the goods. So I decided to move in a little closer."

"How close is 'closer'?" Erie could see where the story was

heading. "Maybe close enough to peek in a window?"

Bass smiled sheepishly. "You could say that."

"How about if *you* say it?"

"O.K. Yes, I sneaked across the street to see if I could get a look inside. That would be proof positive, right?"

"Not in court. And it's trespassing."

"For a good cause!"

"And I guess you didn't 'sneak' too well, right?"

"I did alright. For a minute or two, anyway. Got close enough to see money changing hands."

"Really? What else did you see?"

"Just that the Smith home isn't gonna be popping up in *Good Housekeeping* anytime soon. That place is an unholy mess."

"The boy, Bass. Did you see what he was selling?"

Bass waved his hands in disgust. "Proof proof proof! You really were a cop, weren't you? Can't do a blessed thing without proof. Well, no, I didn't see what he was selling. And, no, I didn't see his customers give him the secret crackhead handshake, either. But I'll tell you what I did see: I saw them see me and I saw myself running like hell."

Erie nodded. The story was working out as he expected.

"And the tires and the window—that was last night? A message?"

"That's right." Bass got up from the table again and returned a moment later with a brick and a folded piece of paper. "This is what came through the window at three in the morning."

He spread out the paper in front of Erie. There was a message on it written in black magic marker: "STOP PEAKING IN PEOPLES WINDOWS PREVERT OR NEXT TIME IT WILL BE YOUR HEAD THAT GETS BUSTED NOT YOUR CAMRA!"

"Not exactly spelling bee material, is he?" Bass said.

Erie pointed at the note. "His fingerprints are probably all over this. The brick, too. You might have enough for a vandalism charge right here."

Bass grimaced. "Vandalism? What would that get me? He'd

still live right across the street, wouldn't he? He'd still be selling his junk. And he'd have more reason than ever to slit my throat. No thanks. This thing has to be finished once and for all."

Bass had a point. Press charges and the boy wouldn't be away from home more than a few hours. And when he got home, he'd be madder than ever. He certainly didn't seem like the type to lay low until the feud with Bass blew over. He was hot-headed and none too bright and had a business to protect. There'd be more trouble.

And it could be big trouble. Erie didn't like the angry gleam in his friend's eyes when he said "once and for all." He was a scared, lonely man with a gun in his pocket. Bad things were going to happen...unless someone did something about it first.

But was Erie that kind of someone anymore? He'd only been retired a few months, but it seemed like years. The old Erie—the one who solved problems, the one who served and protected—was long gone. Maybe he'd died with Nancy. The Erie that had been left behind was just a cat lady. You couldn't expect him to help *people*, could you?

"O.K., Bass, I'll help," Erie heard himself say. He wasn't sure where the words came from. They seemed to ring out from someplace far away.

Erie finally picked up his coffee and took a sip. The coffee had gone cold, but the bitter shock of it helped ground him in the here and now. He pushed his feelings aside. They were too confusing. It was time to focus on facts.

"It's garbage day, right?" he said.

Bass slapped the tabletop again. "That's the spirit!" he declared, beaming. "It's time to take out the trash across the street—and you're just the fella to do it."

Erie took in a deep breath. "No, Bass. I mean isn't this the day the men in the big truck come and take everyone's trash away?"

"Well, you don't have to be sarcastic about it," Bass mumbled. "Yes, it's garbage day."

Erie stood up and walked into the living room, crushing bits of broken glass that still littered the floor near the front window. He parted the fluttering curtain and peered outside. "There are ways to collect evidence that don't involve trespassing or a search warrant," he said. He let the curtain drop and walked back into the kitchen, to the side door of the house. "I'll be back in a minute. Why don't you get that glass cleaned up while I'm gone?"

For a moment, Bass seemed to be torn between annoyance and excitement. But then he hopped up, saluted and went to grab a broom.

Erie walked to the end of the driveway and pulled Bass's garbage can upright. As he collected the trash that had spilled out—mostly TV dinner boxes and fast food wrappers—he stole a few glances at the Smith house. He didn't see any movement. When he was done picking up, he put the lid back on the trash can and walked briskly across the street. Smith & Son might be lousy neighbors, but at least they put out their garbage on time. Erie flipped up the lid of the big plastic trash can at the edge of Smith's driveway, reached inside and pulled out two white garbage bags. Then he closed the trash can again and moved quickly back across the street toward Bass's house. To his relief, no one shouted "Stop!" or threw a brick at his head.

Bass was waiting for him in the kitchen. "Evidence?" he asked, pointing to the bags with a grin.

"Could be. Where do you want to open these up?"

"This way."

Bass lead him downstairs to a dank basement with faux wood paneling and dingy grey carpet that might have been white once upon a time. A folded-up ping-pong table had been pushed into one corner, and a bumper pool table was covered with piles of unfolded laundry. Posters for old rock bands like KISS and AC/DC hung on the wall along with a dartless dart board.

"I haven't seen one of these in a while," Erie said.

"Yeah. A 'rumpus room' they used to call it. Course, not much rumpusing went on down here after the boys left home."

A large box sat in the middle of the room. It had a picture of a computer on the side. Bass slid the box along the carpet into a corner.

"Is that really a computer?" Erie asked.

"Maybe. Might be an electric paperweight for all I know. I could never get it to work right." Bass pulled a wrinkled sheet off the bumper pool table and began spreading it out on the floor. "Bill Jr. gave it to me for Christmas. Said we could keep in touch by 'e-mail.' I don't see what's wrong with the telephone, myself." He smoothed out the last corner of the sheet. "O.K., let's find us some evidence."

Erie put the bags down on the sheet and tore one of them open. A rank stench swirled out into the room.

"Good Lord!" Bass gagged.

"Welcome to the glamorous world of detective work," Erie muttered, pressing a hand over his nose and mouth.

"Hold on there a second." Bass hopped up the stairs. When he came back down a moment later, he was ripping open a small plastic bag. "Playtex Living Gloves," he explained. "Been under the sink since 1989." He handed a pair of the blue rubber gloves to Erie, then pulled on another pair himself. "I don't know why Bootsie kept 'em after we got the dishwasher. That woman couldn't bring herself to throw out anything. Boxed up in the back there I've got every scrap of schoolwork the boys ever did. Probably got all their dirty diapers, too. I've got canned hams in the cupboard that still have the price on 'em. Fifty cents. What year you figure that was? 1975?"

"Why don't you throw it all out?"

Bass frowned. "Well, I couldn't do that." He slapped his rubber-covered palms together. "Alright, chief. I'm ready when you are."

Erie up-ended the opened bag and poured its contents out on the sheet. The resulting pile was composed mostly of TV dinner boxes with some pizza boxes, coffee grounds and crumpled aluminum cans mixed in.

"Looks like they're on the Bass Anderson Diet," Erie said, spreading the trash out with his shoe. Small chunks of dark goo were stuck to everything. Underneath a fish sticks box he found something black and soft and lumpish. "I think that's where our smell's coming from." He knelt down and picked it up. It crumbled in his hands.

"What is it?" Bass asked, keeping his distance. "Some kinda drug...uhhh...thing?"

Erie pinched a chunk of the stuff between his fingers and gave it a cautious sniff. "I think someone was trying to make meatloaf."

He dropped what was left of the black lump and began sifting through the boxes and bags again. After a minute, he grabbed the empty garbage bag and began refilling it.

"Nothing in here. Let's take a look at the other one."

Bass set the other garbage bag on the edge of the sheet.

"Feels pretty light," he said.

"I noticed that." Erie picked up the bag. Something inside made a rustling, crinkling sound. "Loud, too."

He untied the bag and turned it over. Wads of cellophane and paper spilled out onto the sheet.

Bass and Erie stared at the pile for a second, puzzled.

"Whadaya make of that?"

"I don't know what to make of it," Erie said. "But at least it doesn't stink." He pulled off his rubber gloves and let them drop to the floor. "I don't think we'll need these anymore."

He bent down and started spreading the pile out. This time, Bass helped.

Erie picked up one of the crumpled scraps of paper and straightened it out. It was a standard, white, eight-and-a-half by eleven inch sheet. A box about five inches by six had been cut out of the middle.

"Maybe that's his rolling paper," Bass suggested. "You know. For making reefers."

"I don't think so. Wrong kind of paper. It would burn too fast."

"Yeah, but he don't get out too much," Bass persisted. "Maybe he was hard up. Some customers were comin' over and he had to make a few jays out of whatever he had lying around."

Erie measured the cut-out box with his thumb and forefinger. "That's awfully long for a joint." He shook his head. "Too long."

He picked up another piece of paper and flattened it out. It was exactly the same as the first: There was a five-by-six rectangle missing from the middle. He looked at another sheet. The same.

"There's another possibility," Erie said, "but I don't think it fits."

"What is it?"

"Could be blotter paper for LSD." Erie snorted and shook his head. "No. I'm reaching. It doesn't make sense. Why cut the box out of the middle? Why not use the whole sheet?"

Erie folded up the paper and slipped it into his pocket. He reached down and picked up a crinkled piece of cellophane.

Bass did the same thing. "Looks like…whadaya call it?" he said, spreading the material out on his knee. "Shrink wrap?"

Erie straightened out the wad in his hands as much as he could. There were straight lines in the cellophane. Maybe even corners.

"You're right. This is off some kind of package."

Bass looked around at all the cellophane spread across the floor. "Off a really big package, I'd say."

"Or a lot of small ones."

Erie knelt down and spread the cellophane and paper out some more. A flash of color caught his eye. He plucked a crumpled piece of paper out of the pile. It was dull yellow—a shade that looked strangely familiar. He straightened the paper out.

"Hey, that's a letter," said Bass, peering over Erie's shoulder.

"Not just a letter." At the top was a symbol Erie knew well: the seal of the state of Indiana. "It's a notice. It looks like a certain 'Andrew Allen Smith' has a hearing in juvenile court in a few weeks."

Bass clapped his hands together. "There we go! He's a drug dealer!"

"Not necessarily."

"What do you mean, 'not necessarily'?"

"The notice doesn't say what the charge is. They never do. For all we know, he could've been caught jaywalking."

Bass threw his hands in the air. "Sweet Lord, Larry," he groaned. "What do we need to find to convince you once and for all? A thank you note? 'Dear Andy, I just love your crack cocaine. It really hits the spot. You'll be seeing me again after I've stolen a few more purses from helpless old ladies. Signed, A Loyal Customer.'"

"Yeah, that would just about do it," Erie said. He was rummaging through the pile on the floor again. "Why don't you see if you can dig one up for me?"

Bass bent down to help, grumbling under his breath. After a minute of pawing through plastic and paper, he handed Erie two oversized envelopes.

"This look like anything?"

They were from a mail-order music club. Standard junk mail. Erie was about to say so when a glance at the address stopped him.

"Let me ask you a dumb question, Bass," he said. "Has a 'Sid Vicious' or a 'Johnny Rotten' ever lived across the street from you?"

"A what?"

"Not whats. Whos. Has anyone named 'Sid Vicious' or 'Johnny Rotten' ever lived where the Smiths live now?"

Bass shook his head. "Before Smith moved in, Joe and Thelma Weingartner lived there for twenty some-odd years. And I never heard anybody call either of them 'Sid' or 'Johnny.' Or 'Vicious' or 'Rotten,' for that matter."

Erie held up one of the envelopes and tapped the see-through address window. "That's funny. Because according to the National CD & Tape Clearinghouse, Sid Vicious lives across the street." He waved the other envelope. "And his roommate is Johnny Rotten."

Erie opened one of the envelopes and pulled out a letter and a small catalog. He unfolded the letter and scanned it quickly.

"Sid just joined the National CD & Tape Club," he told Bass. "He's already received his seven CDs for a penny. Now he just needs to order four more at full price to fulfill his obligation." He tore open the other envelope. The contents were identical. "Johnny's in the Club, too."

"Well, good for Johnny and Sid. But what does that have to do with the crack house across the street?"

Erie pulled the scrap of paper out of his pocket. The box cut out of the middle was just the right size. He got the old tingle in his hands, the one he got when the pieces were starting to fit together.

So Erie's intuition was still working—at least well enough to make a few wild leaps of logic. That made him either a gifted old pro or a silly old fool, depending on how close to the truth he'd landed. If he were the latter, he preferred to keep that knowledge to himself.

"All I can do is make guesses," he said. "How about if we go across the street and get some answers?"

"From the kid?"

"From the kid."

Bass stiffened. "Alright. If you're ready, I'm ready." His hands slipped into the pockets of his parka.

"Good." Erie held out his right hand. "But first, give me the gun."

"Well now, Larry, I'd feel a whole lot better about this if—"

"And I'd feel a whole lot better if we left it here."

Bass's eyes popped in surprise. "Left it here? You want us to walk right into the lion's den without a—"

"Give me the gun!"

Erie's words were hard, loud. But he wasn't yelling. This was different. He was using his cop voice—the one that left no room for debate, that reminded people that he was The Law. Erie hadn't tried it in a long time. He was almost surprised to hear it now. But he was glad he hadn't forgotten how to call it up. He was going to need it today.

Bass pulled a Smith & Wesson .32 out of his pocket and handed it to over. Erie walked to the computer box in the corner of the room and placed the gun on top.

"Let's go," he said.

As they passed by the kitchen table, Erie picked up the hand-written note—the one warning the "PREVERT" to stop "PEAKING" in windows—and slipped it into his pocket.

They left the house and walked up the driveway without saying a word. The bitter February chill sent a shiver through Erie as they reached the street. At least he hoped it was the cold that did it.

"Sorry I raised my voice," he said.

"Aww, don't worry about that," Bass said without looking over at him. "But I'm gonna be awful mad at you if we end up dead."

They marched up the steps to the Smiths' front porch. Erie reached out and pressed the doorbell. They heard the chime echo through the house.

Nothing happened.

Erie rang the doorbell again.

"Well, I guess that's that," Bass announced. "It's up to the police now."

He turned to go.

"Hold on."

Erie rapped on the door three times. They weren't polite knocks. They were like punches. That's how cops knock on doors.

"Andrew Allen Smith!" Erie was about to say, "This is the police!" He stopped himself just in time.

"We know you're home! Open the door!"

Still, nothing. Erie bent an ear toward the door, listening for movement inside the house. He didn't hear a thing.

"Maybe he's really gone," Bass said. "He could've slipped out the back."

"He's home," Erie said with more confidence than he really felt. He rapped the door four more times. "Open the door or we'll be back with a search warrant! We know about your little operation!"

"We do?" Bass whispered.

Erie ignored him. "We'll go to the police if we have to! Then you're looking at a real sentence! B.J.C.F, Andrew! Bloomington Juvenile Correctional Facility! That's where you're headed if you don't talk to us!"

Something stirred inside the house. A door opened and closed. Tentative footsteps grew gradually louder.

"I hope you know what you're doin'," Bass told Erie.

"Me too," Erie said.

The front door opened.

"What do you want?" said Andrew Allen Smith.

He didn't fit the profile of a ruthless drug kingpin. He was skinny and short—maybe five feet, four inches tall. A limp mass of dark hair flowed over his head and ears. He was wearing a black T-shirt with a picture of a grinning skull above the words "The Misfits." The pale green eyes that peered at Erie through cheap, plastic-rimmed glasses were filled with defiance.

Erie guessed he was sixteen years old.

"Let us inside and we'll talk it over," Erie said.

"I'm not letting you in," the kid shot back. "I don't know you. I don't have to do a thing you say."

Hollow bravado. It sounded to Erie like the kid was trying to convince himself more than he was trying to convince them.

"You're right," Erie said. "You don't have to listen to us. But you will if you're smart, Johnny Rotten. Or should I call you 'Sid'?"

"What are you talking about?" the kid sneered. But Erie could see the recognition in his eyes. The fear. He was bluffing.

"We've talked to some of your customers, Andrew," Erie bluffed back. "We know everything. So you'd better come clean with us or we're headed straight to the police. And that's something you can't afford with a court date coming up."

Andrew's eyes narrowed, his lips twisted. Something defiant and probably vulgar was about to come out of his mouth.

"Hey," the kid began.

His voice was trembling so badly he couldn't get out whatever he'd planned to say.

"Come in," he said instead, his voice barely above a whisper.

He moved away from the door and led them into the house.

As Erie stepped inside, he turned to glance back at Bass. A look of dismay hung on his friend's face. This obviously wasn't the kind of confrontation he'd been expecting.

Andrew led them into a tiny living room. The floor was covered with cigarette butts, empty beer cans and carryout bags from fast-food restaurants. Erie had to move a few porno magazines off the couch before he could sit down. He signaled Bass to sit next to him.

The kid stood before them nervously, shifting his weight from one foot to the other, then threw himself suddenly into a ratty green easy chair on the other side of the room. His demeanor still vacillated between terror and "Screw you!"

"What do you want?"

His right foot began bouncing rhythmically, sending his knee up down, up down, up down. It was a nervous tic Erie had seen hundreds of times in interrogations and jail cells and court rooms.

Just above the kid's pumping foot was a slight bulge, a place where his jeans swelled out to cover something about the size of a fist. It could have been an ankle holster, but Erie thought he knew better.

He put his intuition to the test.

"You were lucky to get house arrest," he told the kid.

Andrew's foot—the one with the electronic monitor strapped to the ankle—stopped bouncing.

"What were you busted for?"

The kid gaped at him a moment before recovering what was left of his nerve. "If you know so much, why don't you tell me?"

"Well, if I had to guess, I'd say it had something to do with computers. Maybe you're a hacker, but I doubt that. It's more likely you got caught doing what you're doing here."

"And what's that?"

He was going to make Erie say it. That was smart. If Erie wasn't right, he had no power over the kid, and the kid knew it.

"You're bootlegging CDs," Erie said. He made sure there was no question mark in his voice, no doubt. "It's pretty easy to do, if you've got the right software—and you obviously do. You get the CDs free from the music clubs, then make copies and sell them to kids in the neighborhood. They look pretty professional, too. You're able to print out covers for them and everything."

Andrew's lips creased into a smile, and for a quick second Erie expected to hear the words, "Wrong, old man." But it wasn't that kind of smile.

"So what? The Backstreet Boys lose a few bucks. They can afford it."

Erie had to tamp down the wave of elation that came over him. He'd been right! But this wasn't over yet.

"Have you made much money selling CDs?"

Andrew shrugged guardedly. But his smile widened just a bit, grew cocky. He was itching to brag about his little business. He was smart enough not to, though.

"Well, you'd better have some of your profits handy," Erie said to him. "Because you're going to pay Mr. Anderson here back for the damage you and your father did."

The kid's smile faded. "What do you mean?"

"I mean you two sent a message last night, and we're sending a message right back," Erie snapped. The cop voice was back. "You're going to pay Mr. Anderson for his window and his tires and you're going to stop pirating CDs, or I'm going to have a talk with my friends over in Juvenile Court. Judge Hinckle just happens to be a friend of mine." Erie pulled the "PREVERT" note out of his pocket and held it up for the kid to see. "You do *not* want her to see this. Because I guarantee you: A kid who threatens his neighbors is going to get something a lot harsher than house arrest."

Andrew leaned forward and stared at the note, wide-eyed. "I-I-I've never seen that before," he sputtered. "I don't know what you're talking about."

"This," Erie said, shaking the paper in his hand, "was tied to a brick and thrown through Mr. Anderson's front window last night. You couldn't have done it: You can't leave the house because of your electronic monitor. But your dad could've done it for you. And I think he did."

The kid's lips began to tremble. "It's not what you think! I told my dad about yesterday, about seeing this guy—Mr. Anderson—looking in our window. I just thought it was weird and kinda funny, but my dad got real mad about it. Sometimes he just freaks out about stuff. You never know what he's gonna do when he's like that."

Erie waved the "PREVERT" note again.

"You expect me to believe you had nothing to do with this?" he said, his voice dripping sarcasm.

Tears began to flow down Andrew's cheeks. He turned to face Bass.

"I'm sorry. Really sorry. Please believe me. I didn't know," he said. "This is my last chance. My mom kicked me out when I got house arrest. That's the only reason I'm here. If my dad finds out he'll...he'll take away my computer...and...and it's the only thing I...I don't want to go to jail!"

The kid was choking out his words between sobs.

"Listen to me, Andrew," Erie began, his tone still prodding, badgering.

He felt a hand on his shoulder.

"This ain't his fault," Bass said softly. His eyes were wide and watery. The anger and fear in them was gone, replaced by something new...or maybe something old. "A boy needs someone looking over his shoulder. He doesn't have anybody like that."

For Andrew's benefit, Erie looked unconvinced.

"That's just an excuse," he said. "I think we should still go to the police."

"Please! Don't!" the kid begged.

"We don't really have to do that, do we?" Bass said. Either he was a better actor than Erie would've expected or he didn't even know he was in a Good Cop-Bad Cop routine.

"Well...." Erie turned to face Andrew. "Maybe we could make some kind of deal."

The kid took a deep, shuddering breath and wiped his eyes.

"What do I have to do?" he said.

A few weeks later, Andrew got started. His ankle monitor was off by then, thanks to a visit Erie paid to Judge Hinckle's office. The CD bootlegging had stopped by then, too—or at least it wasn't run out of his father's house anymore. Bass kept an eye on the place and was sure of that.

Erie dropped by and caught the last few minutes of Andrew's second session with Bass.

"Now hit the 'Send' button," the kid was saying.

"Uhhhhh, O.K." Bass hunched over the computer keyboard. "Where's that?"

"It's on the screen. See? Use the mouse."

"Oh, yeah. The mouse."

"You don't have to double-click it. Just click once. With the left button."

The kid spoke slowly, patiently, without a hint of condescension. Erie was impressed.

"O.K.," Bass said.

He dragged the arrow on the screen over to the little box marked "Send" then pushed the mouse button down hard, as if he were launching a missile. The computer pinged, and the words "Your mail has been sent" appeared on the screen.

Bass turned to flash Erie a grin. "Look at that! I sent my first e-mail."

"Wow. What's next for you two?" Erie said. "Hacking into the Pentagon?"

"This is just our second lesson, Mr. Erie," Andrew replied dryly. "We don't hack the Pentagon until lesson twelve."

Bass laughed. "I think there's hope for this kid yet."

"I think there's hope for all of us," Erie said.

THE CASE OF THE UNFORTUNATE FORTUNE COOKIE

As the waiter went off to get the check, a silence fell over the table. Burt planned to make use of it.

The silence wasn't so much a lull in the conversation as a lull in the *lecture*. As was his way, Burt's friend J.P. had been talking non-stop ever since they'd met in front of the Golden Dragon Restaurant fifty minutes before. J.P. wasn't just a Renaissance man. He was an Enlightenment, Atomic Age and Postmodern man, as well. He knew—or pretended to know—enough about absolutely everything to dominate any social interaction he might have.

He'd talked about football as they were led to their table. He'd talked about the films of François Truffaut as they looked over the menu. He'd talked about the films of Don Knotts as they waited for their hot and sour soup. And from the first bite of their appetizers through the last bite of their entrees, he'd talked about chaos theory, string theory, g-strings, Hooters, *Atlas Shrugged*, the Republican Party, the Spanish Inquisition, the Norman Conquest, Norman Mailer, Norman Fell, Hungry Hungry Hippos and the proper way to poach an egg.

The facts, figures and quotations spewed out so fast, Burt's ears could barely catch them all. He strongly suspected that much of what J.P. said was bunk, but he could never get a word in edgewise to say so. The only times he was allowed to speak came when J.P. decided to take a bite. But even then J.P. controlled the conversation, asking Burt a question before shoveling a few forkfuls of kung pao shrimp or General Tso's chicken into his mouth.

So, Burt—how's the baby?

Chew chew swallow.

Enjoying the new job?

Chew chew swallow.

How'd the skin grafts go?

Chew chew swallow.

Doing alright with the artificial leg?

Chew chew swallow.

Any more trouble with those Japanese gangsters?

Slurp swallow chew BURP.

Burt felt that some of his answers were pretty interesting—perhaps even downright fascinating. But he never got more than five words into them before J.P. was off again.

"Yeah, those Yakuza guys gave you a pretty rough time—but you should've seen what the Reds did to the Braves last night. I don't think there's been an upset that shocking since the Turks sank the Duke of Medina's armada off Tripoli in 1560! There's an interesting story behind that, by the way. You see, the Duke suffered from a morbid fear of dachshunds, and the Turks knew it, so...."

Eating lunch with J.P. was like watching someone else channel surf: You never knew what was going to pop up next. But now Burt was going to make a grab for the remote.

"You know what annoys me?" he said, and there was no pause after he said it. He was far too smart to wait for an answer. "Fortune cookies. They used to actually tell you your fortune. 'You will meet a tall, dark stranger.' 'You will receive an important letter.' Stuff like that. Nowadays all you get are compliments or pseudo-Confuciusy truisms. 'You have many friends.' 'An open heart is a happy heart.' That kind of thing. It really—"

"There's a reason for that," J.P. cut in, and he didn't need an "Oh?" or a "Tell me" from Burt to continue. He just did.

Burt didn't mind. He was basking in the glory of his achievement. He'd managed to slip a thought into the conversation, in the process blurting out the most consecutive words he'd spoken in J.P.'s presence since the early 1990s. And now his reward would be an explanation for one of life's little mysteries. He'd decide later if he believed it.

Burt settled back into the plush booth he and J.P. were sharing and listened.

There used to be this famous defense attorney named Terry Dixon (*J.P. said*). The man never lost a case. He once had a client who was found passed out in a hotel bed with a bloody axe in his hands and the bits and pieces of his wife stuffed in the pillowcase under his head, and Dixon got the guy off. It turned out the maid who'd called the cops did it. Dixon picked up on two things no one else noticed: She'd come into the room despite the "Do Not Disturb" sign hanging from the doorknob, and the welcome mints smelled of bitter almonds. He threw that at her on the stand, and she just fell apart—broke down and admitted everything. The last time the couple had stayed at the hotel they'd stolen enough towels to start their own Turkish bath, and the maid was out for revenge. She got the chair instead.

Anyway, Dixon used to do that kind of thing all the time. He was the king of lost legal causes. His bread and butter was accused murderers. He used to save some poor slob's neck just about every week, it seemed like. But he handled civil cases on the side…if they were hopeless enough.

Now there was only one thing Dixon loved more than browbeating people into nervous breakdowns on the witness stand, and that was Chinese food. He ended up eating so much Szechwan and Mandarin he had to hire assistants to pull him around Chinatown in a wheelchair shaped like a little rickshaw. This was a few years before that, though, when he could still get around the buffet tables under his own power. But his obsession with sweet and sour shrimp and dim sum was already plenty famous. So it made perfect sense that the Fortunes would come to him.

The Fortunes, of course, invented what we know today as the "fortune cookie." Before the Fortune family came along, you'd get your *bill* in the cookie when you ate Chinese. That had to go when credit cards came in—no one could figure out a way to get carbon paper into a cookie without ruining it. But people still expected a tasteless, stale, folded-up wad of overbaked dough stuffed with *something* when they were done with their moo goo gai pan. The Fortunes dreamed up the fortunes, and it made them a fortune.

And that made them a target. This was long before frivolous lawsuits replaced baseball as the national pastime, but there are always bold men of vision who are ahead of their time, and one such man had found the Fortunes...and a lawyer. The man's name was Burl Oliver Butler, and this was his story.

One day, Butler was eating lunch at a restaurant very much like this one. When he finished his meal, the waiter brought the bill and a fortune cookie. Inside the cookie was this fortune: "Today is your lucky day." Overjoyed, Butler went straight to the bank, withdrew every penny in his possession, and proceeded directly to the dog track. There he bet everything he had on a greyhound named "Dogzilla." The race was a photo finish. Unfortunately for Butler, Dogzilla wasn't even in the picture: She finished fourteenth out of a field of twelve. When Butler returned to work, he was immediately fired. He'd been a quality control inspector on a G.I. Joe assembly line, and while he was playing hooky at the races a misaligned mold had resulted in more than 3,000 action figures that appeared to be so anatomically correct they were unsellable except as adult novelties. When Butler returned home and told his wife about his "lucky day," she flew into a rage and attacked him with the nearest weapon she could find. Butler only survived because that weapon was a grapefruit spoon, and though viciously spooned he lost no major organs and only one pint of blood. He did, however, lose a wife, for that very night she was committed to an institution for the criminally insane.

In short, it was not Burl Oliver Butler's lucky day. It was, in fact, the worst day of his life. In his suit against the Fortunes, he accused the family of fraud, false advertising, willful negligence and infliction of emotional distress.

He was asking for one million dollars.

"We can't afford that!" Amos Fortune, the head of the Fortune family, told Dixon when he came to plead for the great lawyer's help. "We're comfortable, yes. Maybe even well off. But a million dollars? Mr. Dixon, the profit margin on a fortune cookie is one cent! *One measly cent*! Do you know how many cookies we'd have to sell to make up for that kind of loss?"

As rhetorical questions go, it was pretty weak.

"One hundred million," Dixon said.

"If you don't help us, we'll be ruined!" Fortune moaned. "We'll have to close down our factory, lay off our cookie rollers, our cookie folders, our cookie stuffers. And what about our customers—the Great Walls and Happy Pandas and Peking Gardens and Mr. Eggrolls of this great land? What will they do? Offer their customers *almond* cookies? Orange slices? Mints? Preposterous! There's only one way to end a fine Chinese meal, Mr. Dixon, and that's with a genuine Fortune family fortune cookie! Take those away, and you've dealt ethnic dining in America a blow from which it will never recover!"

"Enough!" Dixon bellowed. "I'll take the case!"

Dixon wasn't a huge fan of fortune cookies himself, since they took valuable stomach space from more important things like sauce-smothered shrimp and fried won tons stuffed with cream cheese. It was the principle of the matter he cared about. No one was going to dictate the terms on which he enjoyed Chinese food. *No one.*

"This time it's personal," he whispered to himself.

"It's always personal with you, ain't it?" said Saul Swann, the investigator Dixon used for dirt-digging and keyhole-peeping, when he heard about the case.

"We've only got one chance to win, Saul," Dixon said. "Cheap irony."

"I don't get you."

"Maybe Butler would've been shot in a stick-up if he hadn't run out of that Chinese restaurant," Dixon explained patiently. "Maybe he would've been crushed by a crate of G.I. Joes if he'd been at the factory on time. Maybe one of the doctors cured him of a rare tropical disease when he came into the emergency room with that spoon sticking out of his—"

"Oh, I see. Maybe it really *was* his lucky day!"

Dixon nodded. "Get out there and prove it, Saul. If it wasn't Burl Oliver Butler's lucky day, this is my *unlucky* day...because I've just accepted my first losing case."

Two weeks later, Swann handed in his report.

"Dear Boss," it began, "you have just accepted your first losing case."

Swann had scoured Butler's life for signs of irony. He'd found none. Butler was just an ordinary schmo whose ordinary life had been extraordinarily screwed by bad advice from a pastry.

It was the night before the trial, and Dixon went out to his favorite Chinese restaurant and enjoyed what very well might be his final becookied Mandarin meal. His fortune was not helpful.

"This is your lucky day," it said.

Now there's cheap irony for you.

The trial did not go well. An astrologer testified that Butler's moon sign was in the house of Sagittarius on the day he received the cookie in question, meaning Butler—a Leo—was sure to have a *bad* day. Under intense badgering on the witness stand, Amos Fortune admitted that his family didn't employ a single psychic: The predictions they stuffed into their cookies were written by Fortune's 15-year-old niece. And as the *coup de grâce*, Butler's attorney called a surprise expert witness—the famed baking impresario Mrs. Fields, who told the shocked jurors that in her professional opinion fortune cookies weren't even cookies at all.

"Not...even...a...*cookie!*" Butler's lawyer thundered in his summation, his eyes already flashing with triumph. "You can't believe a thing these 'fortune' 'cookies' say! Perhaps they should be called 'lie pies'! Or 'fake cakes'!" He tossed a fortune cookie on the floor and began jumping up and down on it. "Here's how these cookies ought to crumble, ladies and gentlemen!"

Dixon was fond of courtroom theatrics himself. He'd given summations using hand puppets, interpretive dance, the Mormon Tabernacle Choir and psychedelic drugs. But this was going too far. Or so he thought until the jury began applauding. Some of the jurors even sprang from their chairs and began stomping cookie crumbs themselves.

Dixon got the uneasy feeling the jury was not favoring the Fortunes. His first legal loss was at hand.

He turned to look at Burl Oliver Butler across the aisle. A bottle of champagne was already chilling in a bucket of ice at the man's feet, and behind him was a cooler of Gatorade which he no doubt planned to dump over his attorney's head when the jury's judgment was read. Butler noticed Dixon's scrutiny and gave him a broad wink. He looked utterly and completely confident.

And why shouldn't he? Dixon thought (choosing out of a sense of propriety not to return the wink). *In a few minutes, he's going to be a millionaire.*

In a flash, Dixon saw his mistake. He smacked his forehead so hard he concussed himself. As he sank into unconsciousness, he whispered his revelation to Saul Swann.

Swann stared back incredulously. "Alright, boss. If you think it'll help." He hopped up and bellowed at no one in particular. "Get this man a pair of ducks—*now!*"

But Swann had misunderstood. Dixon explained it to the jury the next day from his hospital bed. The bed was in the courtroom at the time, having been wheeled in for Dixon's summation. Of course, by that point Dixon felt well enough to do cartwheels, but he wasn't going to miss an opportunity to win sympathy points. His forehead was wrapped with gauze, a tangle of tubes ran from his arms to brightly colored bags dripping mysterious fluids and three doctors and a nurse hovered by his side, all of them instructed to shake their heads and look troubled, as if any further trauma— such as, for instance, a defeat in the courtroom—would send Dixon spiraling toward death.

"Ladies and gentlemen of the jury," Dixon croaked. He'd spent half the night sucking on saltines and swallowing unchewed

Cracker Jacks in order to get the dry rasp just right. "This is really a simple case. Mr. Butler received a prophecy from one of my client's cookies, and he took action based on that prophecy. He now says that the prophecy was wrong, he suffered dire consequences as a result and he is entitled to compensation. But I ask you...*was* the prophecy wrong?"

A low murmur arose from the packed courtroom, the only clearly audible words being a half-whispered "Hell yes!" from one of the jurors.

"Think carefully, good people," Dixon chided with a small, paternal smile. "The cookie told Mr. Butler that his lucky day had arrived. The day that followed *appeared* to be quite *un*lucky. Yet now, as a result of that, Mr. Butler might be given one million dollars. I don't know about you, but I'd call that pretty lucky. In fact, I'd say the day he got that fortune cookie was the luckiest day of his life...if you find in his favor."

The jurors all began rubbing their chins and furrowing their brows.

"What we have here, ladies and gentlemen, is what's known as a *paradox*," Dixon went on. He paused just long enough to turn and raise an eyebrow at Saul Swann, who shrugged back apologetically. "If you decide the cookie was right, the cookie was wrong. But the second you decide the cookie was wrong, the cookie was right— and *you* were wrong! As Confucius once said, 'The fault lies not in our cookies, but in ourselves.' Truer words were never spoken. And do you want to know where I first encountered those words? *In a fortune cookie.* Thank you, my friends, and god...bless...Amer... ic...aaaaaaahhhhhh..."

Dixon swooned dramatically, and the jurors—who'd all taken to scratching their heads in unison—gasped as he collapsed into the spongy folds of his bed. While the judge and jury were distracted, one of Dixon's doctors pushed a button that created an alarming "beep-beep-*beeeeeeeeeeeeep*," and the medical team began pushing the lawyer's bed toward the exit shouting "Code mauve! Code mauve!"

What the judge and jury didn't know was that "code mauve"

means "time for lunch," and Dixon was rushed, still in bed, to the nearest Chinese restaurant, where he was immediately revived by the smell of garlic sauce and hot mustard. Saul Swann showed up just as Dixon was polishing off a plate of sesame chicken.

"Have they reached a verdict?" asked a pale Amos Fortune. He and Dixon had been at the restaurant for nearly an hour by that time, but he'd been too nervous to eat anything other than one of his own cookies.

"Still deliberating," Swann reported. "And by 'deliberating' I mean 'yelling, screaming and clawing each other's eyes out.' I tell ya', boss—that 'paradox' of yours really did a number on 'em. The jury just sent a note out to the bailiff asking for aspirin, Alka-Seltzer, a hot water bottle, a cold compress and six bottles of Southern Comfort."

Fortune looked like he could use all of the above himself. He buried his face in his hands and wept. Yet Dixon hardly seemed to be paying attention. Instead he was frowning at the slip of paper Fortune had removed from his cookie a moment before.

"You have many friends," it said.

"Who wrote this fortune, Fortune?" Dixon asked.

The cookie magnate wiped the tears from his eyes and glanced at the fortune in Dixon's hands.

"I did," he said. "We fired my niece. Her material was too edgy. Those predictions of hers got us into this mess, and the Chinese Anti-Defamation League was giving us trouble over the 'Confucius say' stuff we tried out. So I thought, 'Who's going to argue with a compliment?'"

Dixon nodded, his thick, sesame-smeared lips curling into a grin as he asked the question that would save the fortune cookie industry.

"Saul—has the jury had lunch?"

Half an hour later, a deliveryman arrived at the courthouse, bowlegged under the weight of box upon box of Chinese food.

"Compliments of the Mandarin Palace restaurant," the deliveryman told the bailiff. "With all the publicity this case is getting, business has tripled. The manager wants to show his appreciation."

Dixon had picked the most aromatic dishes the restaurant had to offer, knowing the sweet/spicy scent of orange beef and lemon chicken and walnut prawns would be more than anyone could resist—even a no-nonsense bailiff or an irritable, headachy juror swilling Pepto-Bismol straight from the bottle.

And Dixon was right. Minutes after the moveable feast was brought to the jury room, it was gone. And when the jury had licked up the last drop of sauce, they began cracking open their fortune cookies. Inside, they found the fortunes Dixon had hand-picked for them.

"People admire your looks, but they covet your brains," one said.

"Goodness flows from you like water from a spring," said another.

"Give advice freely—your wisdom is a treasure that grows with the giving."

"You possess great intelligence."

"You rock."

And so on.

Less than an hour later, Dixon, Fortune and Swann were back in the courtroom to hear the verdict. The jury looked a little sleepy, having recently consumed vast quantities of MSG, but they also looked very pleased. They were smiling like twelve happy Buddhas. As were Dixon, Fortune and Swann when they walked back out of the courtroom a few minutes later.

As Dixon had hoped, the jury couldn't bring itself to declare that fortune cookie fortunes are pure malarkey—not when the last examples they'd seen were so obviously, demonstrably *true*.

"On behalf of the entire food service industry, I thank you," Fortune said, shaking Dixon's hand on the courthouse steps.

"Don't thank me, thank...." Dixon's face went blank for a moment, then his grin returned. "Well, yes. You should be thanking me. Those fortunes of yours could've done some serious damage to a great American tradition: Chinese food. I hope you've learned your lesson."

"Oh, absolutely!" Fortune replied. "A man with burned fingers knows not to play with fire. We're dumping the prophecies and predictions for good. It'll be nothing but platitudes and pleasantries from now on!"

"Good," Dixon said. "Now what say we celebrate over at the Sizzling Wok? They've got pot stickers there that'll melt in your mouth...."

The check arrived when J.P. was barely a minute into his story, and it sat before him on the table, untouched and apparently unnoticed, as he unwound the rest of his tale at a leisurely pace. As always, J.P. remained oblivious when the waiter returned once, twice, three times to hover quietly nearby. And, again as always, it was Burt who finally gave in and pulled out his wallet. J.P. acted as if he knew the story behind everything, but there was one explanation Burt had yet to hear: why his friend could never pick up a tab.

After throwing some cash on the table, Burt managed to get in a quick announcement. He was going to the restroom. This was the kind of input J.P. would actually allow, and he graciously paused while Burt slid out of the booth and walked toward the back of the restaurant. When Burt returned a few minutes later, J.P. launched right back into his tale without so much as an "As I was saying...."

"'A man with burned fingers knows not to play with fire,'" J.P. said. "'We're dumping the prophecies and predictions for good.'"

Burt's change had arrived by then. With it were two plastic-wrapped fortune cookies. Burt picked one up and toyed with it as J.P. concluded his ludicrous story. It was the biggest load of shitake mushrooms J.P. had ever shoveled his way, and for once Burt planned to say so.

As J.P. was coming to the final words of his yarn, Burt unwrapped his fortune cookie and broke it apart. "You know, J.P.," he planned to say. "I believe you about as much as I believe this fortune."

The fortune stopped him.

"A man with burned fingers," it read, "knows not to play with fire."

Burt heeded the cookie's advice and kept his doubts unvoiced, even when J.P. supplied the perfect setup by reading out his own fortune.

"You have a vivid imagination."

Burt figured if the fortune in his cookie meant anything, the story was true, which meant fortune cookies aren't even *supposed* to mean anything, which meant the fortune was false. If *J.P.'s* fortune meant anything, the story was false—but only if Burt *believed* the fortune, and why should he do that if what it said was true, since it was implying that what it said was false?

Burt suddenly had a pounding headache. Yet he still managed to squeeze one more thought into the conversation before J.P. could spin off into another rambling round of free associations.

"Next time," Burt said, "we're going out for Italian."

MINOR LEAGUE

There are three detective agencies listed in the River City, Indiana, phone book. Two have ads with pictures and slogans and big logos. The third just has a line of text: "Erie Investigations, 1451 Hart Road," then the phone number.

Larry Erie's friend Bass thought that was a mistake.

"It pays to advertise," Bass said. "No one's gonna hire you to find their car keys when all you've got's that dinky little line there."

Erie just shrugged. He wasn't so sure about this private detective thing anyway. He was a retired cop living alone. Wasn't he a bit old to be playing Sam Spade?

He framed his detective's license and hung it in the living room—a room he almost never went in anymore—and tried to forget it.

So when a man pulled into Erie's driveway in a silver Cadillac, Erie assumed he was an insurance salesman. Or lost.

Erie's cats told him someone was coming. Erie didn't get many visitors. When he did, Mae and Goldie would jump up on the couch near the bay window at the front of the house to watch what was going on in the driveway. Erie walked over to the window, and he and the cats watched the man together.

He just sat in his car for a while, the engine running. He looked confused. From time to time he'd glance at a piece of paper in his hand, then look back up at the house.

Eventually, he shut off the engine and got out of the car. He was a tall man, fortyish, thin and balding. He wore gray slacks and a white shirt with pinstripes and a wide blue tie.

Erie stepped out of the house, careful to keep the cats from slipping out with him.

"Can I help you?"

The man still looked confused. He glanced at the piece of paper again, then looked back up at Erie, who stood there watching him in his sweatpants and wrinkled, ketchup-freckled shirt.

"Is this 1451 Hart Road?"

"That's right."

"Is there another Hart Road around River City?"

"No."

The man looked at Erie's house. He seemed baffled by what he saw.

"Why don't you tell me what you're looking for, and maybe I can help you find it?" Erie said.

"No, that's O.K. Thanks," the man said. "I'm just…I'm looking for a business."

He was backing up as he spoke, starting to turn and hurry to his car.

Erie wondered what kind of business this nervous-looking man could be searching for. A porn shop?

And then it hit him.

Oh, my God. I have a client!

"You wouldn't be looking for Erie Investigations, would you?"

The man stopped and gaped at Erie, obviously calculating some noncommittal answer.

"What makes you ask that?"

"I'm Erie. If you want to come inside, we can discuss whatever it is that brings you out here today."

The man looked both relieved and skeptical.

"Alright," he said.

Erie opened the door for him.

"Be careful," he said. "Don't let the cats out."

❧

"I'm Frank Ault," the man said.

The pause after his words told Erie he was supposed to recognize the name.

He didn't.

The pause continued.

Ault shifted his weight on the living room couch. Mae the cat sat on the floor nearby, staring up at him. It seemed to make Ault nervous.

"I'm one of the owners of the River City Brewers."

"Oh, really?"

Erie went to see River City's baseball team play four or five times each summer. They were part of a tiny Midwestern league called the Pioneer Association. The players were twentysomething wannabes and kids fresh out of high school, most of whom would never make it to a real farm team, let alone the major leagues. But it was enough for a town like River City.

The team was owned by a couple lawyers and an orthodontist. Erie pegged Ault as the mouth man.

"So then it's *Dr.* Ault, right?"

Ault smiled. It was a half-hearted smile, but his teeth were straight and white.

"Yes," he said. "The team's just a sideline—something my partners and I do out of love of the game."

"So what's the problem?"

Ault's wan smile crumbled. "We've had a theft. A major one. If word gets out, we've got a public relations nightmare on our hands. We're going to look like fools. The Brewers aren't exactly making money hand over fist, and a blow like this could—"

"Dr. Ault," Erie cut in. "Maybe you'd better just begin at the beginning."

They were words he'd said many times before in offices and interrogation rooms and victims' homes. It felt strange to say them in his own house, sitting in a rocking chair, a cat curled up in his lap. What had he gotten himself into?

Ault leaned forward on the couch. "You have to understand

something, Mr. Erie," he said, his voice low, as if he feared that the cat at his feet was eavesdropping. "My partners and I expect discretion. That's why we want to hire a private investigator to look into this. It's very important that we avoid publicity."

"I understand," Erie said. But it felt wrong. If this involved a felony, it was a matter for the police. He shouldn't go playing cops-and-robbers without a real badge...should he?

Ault leaned back on the couch, looking a little more relaxed.

"Good," he said. "Do you go to many Brewers games?"

Erie assumed that this, somehow, was the beginning he'd asked for. People have to tell their own stories in their own way. So he just said, "Sure."

"So you've seen the River City Wall of Fame?"

Ault noticed the blank look on Erie's face.

"At Lloyd Field?" he prompted.

That didn't help.

"By the main concession stand?" Ault said.

Still nothing.

"Between the Men's Room and the Women's Room?"

Now Erie got it. The Brewers played their home games in a stadium built in the 1940s, back when River City had a farm team for the Cincinnati Reds. Inside, not far from one of the entrances, there were maybe a dozen autographed pictures on the wall and a glass case about the size of your standard dining room table. The pictures were of local sports heroes. The case contained mementos from their careers. A basketball used in the state high school championships in 1963, a football helmet worn by an All-American running back, stuff like that. Erie didn't know that this little shrine had a name. He suspected that no one else did either, other than the team's owners.

"Sure, I know what you mean," he said, thinking, *Is that what this is about? Somebody stole some forgotten quarterback's old jock strap?*

"Well, the Wall of Fame has never been all it could be," Ault said, "because we've never had anything from Stormy Weathers."

Erie knew the name. "The old Negro Leagues player," he said.

Ault smiled. It was a bigger, truer grin this time. Clearly, the man loved baseball.

"That's right," he said, his eyes lighting up with excitement. "The greatest ballplayer River City ever produced. I've always felt it was a shameful oversight, him not being on the Wall of Fame, and I've been working to correct it. And finally, I did. A few days ago, Stormy Weathers's daughter sent me the bat he used in the 1946 Negro Leagues World Series. He hit five home runs with it in that series alone. It's a piece of baseball history."

"And now it's been stolen."

Ault nodded, suddenly somber. "That's right. It didn't even spend one full night in the display case."

"It was taken last night?"

"Yes."

"*Mrrrrrrrow,*" Goldie the cat said to Erie.

He looked down at his lap.

You aren't petting me, Goldie was telling him. *What gives?*

Erie began stroking the overweight tabby's broad back. She purred.

"Tell me the specifics," he said to Ault.

"Well, Federal Express dropped the bat off at my office around 2. I left there a little after 6 and took the bat over to Lloyd Field. There wasn't a game yesterday, so the place was empty except for two of our players: Del Johnson and Lee Wolfe."

"The players can get into the stadium whenever they want?"

"No. They don't have keys. Johnson and Wolfe stayed behind after that afternoon's practice."

"Is that normal?"

"Yes. Just about every night, you'll find a few players staying late, putting in a little extra time on the field. We've always trusted our boys like that."

"And maybe you shouldn't."

Ault sighed. "No, maybe we shouldn't. But you've got to understand something about the Brewers. We're not just minor league. We're *minor* minor league. We can barely afford to pay our players $75 a week. Most of them don't even have their own apartments: They live with host families in the community. One of the small perks we can give them is the chance to play in a real baseball stadium. And for these boys, that's worth an awful lot, because most of them know it's the only chance they'll ever get."

"How about the players who were there last night? Johnson and Wolfe? Tell me about them."

"Johnson's got real talent. He's a pitcher. Got a mean slider—at least for our league. I wouldn't be surprised to see him get snatched up by a farm team by August. Wolfe's got hustle, but I don't think we'll be seeing him on any bubblegum cards. This is his fourth summer with us. That's about as many summers as we get from anyone before they take a real job and move on with their lives."

"So what were Johnson and Wolfe doing when you saw them? Working on Johnson's pitching?"

Ault nodded.

"And you put the bat in the display case and left?"

"That's right. With a little plaque I've had ready for weeks."

"And this morning?"

"The case had been smashed open and the bat was gone."

Goldie meowed loudly. Erie had stopped petting her again.

"Quiet, you. I'm working," he told her. He looked up at Ault, suddenly embarrassed. "I don't always talk to my cats."

But he did. That's why it was so embarrassing.

Ault gave him a neutral "Umm-hmm." Obviously, he wasn't a cat person.

"So who knew about the bat?" Erie asked, his voice a little too loud. Goldie hopped from his lap and trotted off to the kitchen to look for new developments in her food dish.

"Lots of people. Me, my partners, our publicist, a writer over at the *Herald-Times*." Ault stared down at his feet, looking miserable. "He was going to do a story about us. Me and the bat. I don't know what I'm going to tell him now."

"What about the players?"

Ault looked up again, his gaze hazy, still focused on headlines he'd never see. "The players?"

"Did they know about the bat?"

"Oh. Yes, I guess. There was never any kind of formal announcement, but word gets around."

"Right."

Erie gazed past Ault, out the window, thinking. He'd had his private investigator's license for months now, but he hadn't done anything with it but dust it a couple times. Did he *really* want to be a P.I.? There was so much moping around the house to do, and the cats weren't going to pet themselves....

"What do you think?" Ault asked.

Erie bought himself another few seconds with a long "Welllllllll." Then he made up his mind. Sort of.

He'd leave it up to his client.

"I'd advise you to go to the police. That's your best bet, if you want the bat back," he said. "But if it's more important to you to avoid publicity, I'll look into the matter. I can't promise that I'll recover the bat, but I can promise a discreet, professional investigation."

"How much do you charge?" Ault said.

To Erie's surprise, the man hadn't hesitated for a second.

Erie *Welllllllllll*ed again.

He didn't have rates. He'd never had a client, so why should he need them?

"One-hundred dollars a day," he said. Then he added, "Plus expenses." Because that seemed to be what someone said in this situation.

"That seems reasonable."

"Good. Has the crime scene been tampered with?"

Ault blinked. The phrase "crime scene" seemed to bother him.

"Tampered with?" he said.

"Cleaned up."

"Yes. Well, some of it. Maybe. I don't know."

"I'd like to see it. Please make sure it's not disturbed any further before I look at it."

"Of course."

"I also need more information on Johnson and Wolfe. Full name, place and date of birth, that sort of thing."

"Are they…suspects?"

Ault's voice trembled as he said "suspects."

Erie was glad the man didn't have to say "police" or "robbery" yet. He'd probably have a stroke.

"I just want to be thorough," Erie said.

"I see. Well, I guess I can call you back with all that later."

"I'd like to talk to them, too. Can you arrange something? For today? When I come over to the stadium?"

"Sure. We've got a home game tonight. Why don't you come to Lloyd Field a few hours early? I'll let you know an exact time."

"That'll work."

"O.K., then." Ault reached into his back pants pocket and pulled out a small black book. A checkbook. "I assume you'll need a retainer?"

"Yes," Erie said. The customer is always right. "I usually ask for three days' pay in advance."

"Three-hundred dollars then." Ault pulled a pen from his shirt pocket and wrote out the check, the checkbook balanced on one knee.

Mae the cat, mesmerized by the back-and-forth motion of the pen, hopped onto the couch and crept towards Ault, ready to pounce. Erie walked over, scooped the cat up and dropped her to the floor.

Ault tore out the check and handed it to Erie, who stared at it for a moment as if it were some mysterious artifact from a long-long civilization. Then the two men shook hands and said awkward goodbyes as Erie walked Ault to the door.

Mae jumped onto the couch again, bouncing up to the back so she could watch Ault climb into his Cadillac and roll backwards down the driveway toward Hart Road.

"So, what do you think, buddy?" Erie asked her. "Am I crazy or just senile?"

The little black cat didn't reply.

Ault called back an hour later. Delmonte Octavio Johnson was born in Fort Wayne, Indiana, on July 3, 1981. James Lee Wolfe was born in Lafayette, Indiana, on November 14, 1977. Erie should show up at the ballpark at 4 p.m.

Erie thanked his client, hung up and called Bass.

"A client? You mean you've got a *case*? Well, yeeeeeeha!" Bass whooped when he heard the news. "So what are we talkin' about here? Murder? Blackmail? Some kinda sex scandal?"

"No, nothing like that. Someone just wants me to make a few inquiries."

"A few inquiries? What does that mean? You're gonna be asking old ladies how the weather's treatin' 'em today?"

"I can't talk about it, Bass. It's confidential."

"Confidential? So confidential you can't even tell *me*?"

"Yes. That confidential."

"Well, be that way then, James Bond."

Bass had a habit of taking offense to things and then instantly forgiving them—which he did once again.

"I tell you what I'm gonna do," he said, suddenly sounding amused. "Onea these days, I'm gonna convince you to hire me on as your assistant. I'll follow you around and help you out on cases. Then you won't have to worry about being confidential, cuz I'll be working with you. I'll be like your Dr. Watkins."

"Dr. who?"

"You know—the tubby fella with the moustache. British. In those movies."

"Oh. Right."

Erie didn't feel like getting into a debate about old movie characters. He was on the clock for a client.

"So what's Andrew up to today?" he said.

(While Erie had filled his empty house with cats, Bass had filled his with a teenager: Andrew had lived across the street from Bass until he couldn't take one more day with his alcoholic dad.

He'd been living in Bass's basement for the last month.)

"Oh, he's downstairs doin' what he always does—playin' with his computer and listenin' to that head-banger music. I've been tryin' to find him a summer job somewhere. I saw a 'Help Wanted' sign over at the Hardee's on 41, but when I tried to tell him—"

"I've got some work for him."

"Well, that's just great. I'll go and...hold on there. Does this have anything to do with your case?"

Erie stifled a sigh. "Yes."

"So you can't tell me about it, but you can tell Andrew?"

"I'm not going to tell him any more than he needs to know to help me out."

"Well, I'll go tell him you want to talk to him, then. I guess playing messenger boy's all this old man's good for."

There was a thud as Bass put the phone down hard, and Erie could hear him stomp away, grumbling. A minute later, Andrew came on the line.

"Hey, Larry. What's up?"

Erie filled the kid in, editing as much as he could. He didn't mention the Brewers and he didn't mention the bat. But he gave him the information on Johnson and Wolfe and told him he was interested in any recent activity involving rare sports collectibles with a River City connection.

"Yeah, sure, I can check on all that. Do you want credit reports on these guys or just public records?"

Erie wasn't sure if Andrew was joking or not. The kid was pretty good with computers, but not *that* good. He hoped.

"Whatever's legal, Andrew," he said. "Will ten dollars an hour be enough?"

"I'm getting paid for this? Bonus. I was gonna do it just for the fun of it. Yeah, ten bucks an hour is great."

"Good. I'll be by to pick everything up around 3:30."

"No prob. It'll be ready."

Erie heard a muffled voice on the line, and Andrew said, "Hold on, Larry. Bass wants to say something to you."

Erie steeled himself. He heard the phone being passed from hand to hand.

"Hey, Larry, buddy," Bass said. "Are you sure you don't need backup with you? In case you run into some rough stuff? You know, I'm pretty handy with my fists."

"Tell you what, Bass: If there's any 'rough stuff,' you're the first person I'll call."

"Alright, then," Bass said, sounding pleased. "That's all I needed to hear."

The greater River City metro area has more baseball card shops than detective agencies—five in all. Erie spent the rest of the afternoon driving around to each of them, making small talk with the men behind the counters about this, that, the Brewers, Stormy Weathers. There wasn't much scuttlebutt about this year's Brewers lineup. Just the usual crop of kids and dreamers. And no, no one had seen any Stormy Weathers collectibles recently. Negro Leagues stuff was pretty rare. "Not much interest in that kind of thing around here," one bearded, overweight man told Erie. Erie knew what he was saying.

Andrew had a more productive afternoon sitting in Bass's basement. When Erie showed up, the teenager had a small pile of printouts for him.

"This is everything I could find about those baseball guys," he reported, handing the papers over to Erie on the front step of Bass's house. "I cruised around eBay and some of the sports auction sites, but I didn't find any Stormy Weathers stuff posted."

Erie tried to look confused. "Baseball guys? Stormy Weathers? Who said anything about baseball guys or Stormy Weathers?"

"The kid ain't dumb, Larry!" Bass shouted from somewhere on the other side of the screen door.

"I know that!" Erie called back. "Now stop eavesdropping!"

Bass didn't answer, but Erie could hear him grumbling something to himself.

Erie started flipping through the pile of papers. The first few were printouts from a newspaper's website.

"High School Hero Headed to Big Leagues?" was the headline on one story. It was a recent article from the *Fort Wayne Journal Gazette*. It was about Del Johnson.

Erie kept flipping and came across a sheet of paper overflowing with tiny print. He had to squint to make out what was on the page. He looked back up at Andrew.

"Is this what I think it is?"

Andrew nodded, obviously proud.

It was Del Johnson's high school transcript.

"I don't want to know how you got this."

"And I wouldn't tell you if you did."

The kid flashed him a wise-ass smile. Erie went back to flipping through the sheets of paper. It was mostly more *Journal Gazette* articles that mentioned Johnson. "Redskins Eye Regional Pennant," "Redskin Pitching Overpowers Indy Champs," stuff like that.

"You're getting close to the James Lee Wolfe section now," Andrew said.

After a few more flips, Erie saw what he meant. The stories changed. He wasn't looking at sports page features anymore. Now the articles were no more than 40 or 50 words long. They had headlines like "Area Youths Admit Vandalizing Library" and "Duo Arrested After Church Break-In." The name James Lee Wolfe popped up in all of them.

"Johnson looks like just another jock to me. But this other dude—he's my kind of guy," Andrew said.

"I thought Bass and I were helping you reform."

"Oh, sure, you are. Crime does not pay. I've learned that." Andrew held out his hand. "By the way...you owe me twenty bucks."

Half an hour later, Erie pulled into the parking lot in front of Lloyd Field. The lot was almost deserted. It wasn't the kind of place where you could watch players pull up in their SUVs and Lamborghinis. You were more likely to see them getting off buses or being dropped off by middle-aged women in minivans. Weeds sprouted from cracks in the pavement.

Erie spotted Ault's silver Caddy in a reserved space. It was the fanciest car in sight.

Erie walked to the main entrance, a bank of turnstiles under a brick archway. A chain link fence on rollers was pushed to one side, unused. It wasn't exactly Fort Knox. No one was around to officially let him in, so Erie just scooted over one of the turnstiles.

The only light inside streamed in through the entrance and down the ramps that led up to the seats. But there was enough for Erie to see by. Barely.

The Wall of Fame was less than 20 yards away. It looked as unremarkable as ever in the shadowy gloom except for the jagged hole in the glass case beneath the pictures. Erie moved towards it, hoping to hear the sound of glass crunching under his feet. No such luck. The concrete floor around the Walk of Fame had been swept clean.

Erie bent down and peered into the case. Something inside shimmered.

The lights came on with a loud clack, bathing everything in a sickly yellow fluorescent glow. Footsteps echoed off the walls, and a voice said, "Can I help you?"

"It's me, Dr. Ault. Larry Erie."

"Oh. I didn't recognize you in the dark," Ault said as he came closer. He looked Erie up and down. "You changed your clothes."

Something about the way he said it made it seem like he didn't like the idea.

"You caught me in my puttering-around-the-house stuff," Erie said. He glanced down at his suit and tie. "This is what a private investigator ought to look like, don't you think?"

Ault attempted a polite smile. He didn't quite pull it off.

"So," Erie said, turning back to the Wall of Fame. "The scene of the crime."

Ault nodded stiffly. "Yes."

Erie crouched down and looked inside the case again. There were various mementos inside—a football helmet, a catcher's mitt, a basketball—each with a little bronze plaque explaining the item's significance. The space next to one plaque was empty. "Bat used by River City baseball great James 'Stormy' Weathers, Negro Leagues World Series, 1946," the plaque said. Shards of glass were spread evenly over the faux-velvet lining around it.

"The inside of the case hasn't been touched?"

"No. But we need to board it up before the game tonight. And I'm taking the plaque out, of course."

Erie was disappointed in himself. It hadn't occurred to him to bring a camera, and of course there were no evidence techs to snapshots of the shattered case for the files. Erie resolved to dig out his camera—he hadn't used it in more than a year—then instantly reconsidered. He didn't know if he'd ever have another case, so why bother?

"How does this open?" he asked.

Ault stepped over and pointed to a small, circular lock mechanism built into the wood paneling on the left-hand corner of the display case.

"I'm the only one with a key," he said. "The Wall of Fame is my responsibility."

Erie examined the lock for a moment, then pulled his keys out of his pocket. Attached to his keychain was a small Swiss army knife. He flipped out the smallest blade—little more than a sliver of metal—and gingerly worked it into the lock.

"What are you doing?"

"Just…"

Click.

The broken glass panel swung out on a hinge.

"…experimenting."

Erie pocketed his knife and pushed the glass panel back into place.

"So are Johnson and Wolfe here yet? I'd like to talk to them," he said as he stood up.

BLARNEY

"They're out on the field practicing with the rest of the team. This way."

Ault led him up the nearest ramp into the sunshine. Down below them, about 20 blue-uniformed men were stretching, sprinting, taking batting practice, throwing balls around. The sights and sounds of it brought a smile to Erie's face. Maybe it was only minor league players in a run-down old stadium in southern Indiana, but it was still baseball. He'd never been much of an athlete, but he could understand why young men would want to put off a real job, a real life for just one more summer of this.

Ault pointed out a wiry black player pitching in a bullpen near right field. "There's Johnson," he said. He pointed to another player who was leaning against the brick wall next to one of the dugouts, waiting for his turn in front of a pitching machine that was hurling balls over home plate. "That's Wolfe. Which one do you want to talk to first?"

With a loud *crack*, the player at the plate sent a ball deep into the outfield. It didn't quite make it to the warning track before dropping into the left fielder's glove, but the batter got a few cheers from his teammates just the same.

Erie couldn't help but wonder how he'd do out there. He'd played baseball in high school, then softball in a church league until his bad back retired him from sports altogether. But there was a part of his soul that was still itching to hit the field. What red-blooded American male wouldn't get that feeling watching the players down below? Who wouldn't want to load up the pitching machine, grab a bat and swing for the fences?

The pitching machine....

It was little more than a spinning rubber wheel with a box on top to hold the balls. It didn't look very heavy at all. One man could easily move it into position and load it.

"You know, Dr. Ault...I think I've got a whole new angle on this case," Erie said. He kept his eyes on the players. Lee Wolfe was stepping into the batter's box. "Johnson doesn't make any sense as a suspect. He's got a future—or at least a chance for a future. Would he risk throwing that away by stealing something out of his own home field?"

"So you think it's Wolfe?"

Wolfe fouled off the first pitch. The second he sent bouncing down the third base line.

"Well, like you say, he's probably not bubblegum card material. And he's no stranger to petty larceny," Erie said. "But that's part of the problem."

"What do you mean?"

Wolfe finally got a solid hit—a line drive that shot through the infield between second and first.

"I mean he knows how to pick a lock. If I could open that case in ten seconds, he could do it in three. So why pull a smash-and-grab?"

"You think it's someone else then? Someone who broke in at night? It can be done. We've known that for a long time. My partners have never wanted to spring for new gates, though."

"But—"

Ault was talking so loud and so fast he didn't even hear Erie.

"Every other weekend we've got kids running loose in here trying to find where we keep the beer. It's been a disaster waiting to happen, and I guess it finally happened. If only we'd—"

"*But*, Dr. Ault."

This time Ault stopped.

"There's something else," Erie said. "The shattered glass in the trophy case is spread evenly around the plaque for the bat. That suggests something very strange."

Erie waited for Ault's "And what would that be?" but it didn't come. So he pressed on.

"You'd expect to see some kind of pattern to the glass—an outline around the spot where the bat was mounted. But there's nothing like that. Which means maybe the bat wasn't in the case when the glass was broken. Maybe it was never there at all."

Erie waited again for a prompt from Ault. A "What are you saying?" or perhaps a "You're crazy."

What he got instead was a quiet "I didn't steal it."

"Why would you? You're the one who got it for the Wall of Fame. No. I think you broke it." Erie nodded out at the pitcher's mound. "With that. After Wolfe and Johnson left for the night."

Ault sighed, slumped, seemed to wither before Erie's eyes.

"I just wanted to feel what it would be like to get one hit with Stormy Weathers's bat in my hand. Just one hit."

"And that's all it took."

"Yes, damn it. One measly little blooper, barely out of the infield, and the bat split right in two."

A bitter grimace twisted Ault's long, lean face. He still couldn't believe the cosmic injustice that had been done to him. One good hit, that's all he'd wanted. One moment of stolen glory.

Erie didn't judge the man. He just felt horribly embarrassed.

"Where is it now?"

"Hidden in my garage. I couldn't admit what happened to my partners or Stormy's daughter. It's...it's...oh, god. I feel so *stupid*."

Erie started to say something, then stopped himself. He started again, then stopped.

"It was an accident," he finally got out. "But you control what comes next. Admit what happened before this goes any further and someone gets blamed for something they didn't do. That's my advice to you."

Ault nodded quickly, then slapped a hand over his eyes and turned away. He was crying.

Erie left without asking his final question: "Why did you hire me?"

He knew the answer.

Ault had been trying to hide his mistake. He had to play out the theft scenario all the way. But he couldn't go to the police. That would be too dangerous. So he'd convinced his partners to hire a private investigator—to avoid bad publicity, of course.

And who do you turn to if you've got a mystery you don't want solved? Just flip open the yellow pages and find the cheapest nickel-and-dime detective agency in town.

How about one that won't even pony up for a real ad? One run by an old man out of a house that smelled of must and kitty litter?

Perfect.

The only job Erie was good for was one he supposed to botch. Except he'd botched botching it.

It wasn't much consolation.

Driving home, Erie tried to push all this out of his mind by turning on the radio.

"...count is three and one. Gonzalez winds up annnnnnnnd blows one right by LaRue."

"That was a beautiful pitch. Right across the chest. We should be watching that one drop into the Ohio."

"Three and two is the count now."

It was a Reds game.

The big leagues.

Erie turned the radio off.

BURL LOCKHART'S IN TOWN

"Lucas Harte," someone said. Behind, close. Practically whispering in Harte's ear. "Why, you thievin' bastard...you're still alive after all these years?"

Harte put down his beer and looked into the mirror behind the bar. It was a dirty little mirror for a dirty little saloon, and a crack ran through it from top to bottom. The break in the glass split the man standing behind Harte in two, making his features seem crooked, the halves mismatched. He was a thin man, gaunt even, dressed as Harte was—for the saddle, rough. But that was all Harte could tell.

"My name ain't 'Harte,'" Harte said.

"Oh, yeah? Why don't you say that to my face?"

Harte's right hand was still on the bar, near his beer glass. But as he turned around, he pulled the hand in toward his body—and the Colt holstered to his hip.

"My name ain't—"

There was no use finishing. The man behind Harte knew it was a lie.

"Shit," Harte said when he saw the man's face. "You son of a bitch."

And they both laughed.

"Gunther Tietzmann." Harte clapped a hand on the man's shoulder. "I'll be damned."

"You got that right," Tietzmann said. "But *my* name ain't 'Tietzmann.'"

They laughed again.

"How long's it been?" Harte asked, his hand still on Tietzmann's shoulder. He could feel the tendons taut as rope beneath the lean man's shirt and skin. "Ten, fifteen years?"

"I can't even remember. When was it they...?" Tietzmann's grin wilted, his shoulders sagged. "When was it Frank and Smokehouse passed? Sixty-seven? Sixty-eight?"

Harte nodded, somber. "Yeah, something like that." He gave Tietzmann's shoulder a squeeze, then pointed at a table at the back of the room. "You wanna?"

"Now ain't a good time, but...hell, how could I not?"

"Glad you feel that way." Harte scooped up his beer and guzzled it down to the foam. "First round's on you."

A minute later, Harte and Tietzmann were seated side by side in the corner, both turned to face the batwings at the front of the saloon. The Phoenix was a small, dingy place, little more than a shack really, and there were only three other customers there. Two were hunkered at another table, conducting business in angry whispers. The third was stooped over at the bar, sullenly draining glass after glass as if there were a fire in his gut he could never put out.

The light that streamed in through the warped slats of wood that served as walls was slowly changing from twilight-orange to dusky-gray. The day was dying.

"So," Harte said, "what you been up to?"

Tietzmann shrugged. "Same ol' thing. You?"

Harte smiled slyly. "Same ol' thing."

"I figured as much. What do you call yourself while you're at it?"

"These days? This and that. Tommy Taylor, mostly."

Tietzmann's eyes popped wide.

"So...you heard of me," Harte said, his smile stretching, pushing his puffy cheeks practically over his eyes.

"Course, I have." Tietzmann hung his head. "Goddamn it."

"What?"

"I got bad news...Tommy."

When Tietzmann looked up, he flicked his gaze over to the saloonkeeper wiping glasses with a greasy rag, the huddled whisperers hissing at each other, the drunk doing his damnedest to get drunker. Then at last he looked at Harte again. Looked *into* him.

"Burl Lockhart's in town," he said.

"Burl Lockhart...the Pinkerton?"

"I ain't talkin' about Burl Lockhart the Pope."

Harte picked up his beer and took a long drink.

"I just rode in this afternoon. Found me a room at a boardin' house," Tietzmann went on. "And the lady I rented a bed from, she says to me, 'Don't miss dinner, Mr. Adams—you'll be dinin' with a celebrity. *The* Burl Lockhart came in just before you did today. Why, he's in the room right next to yours, in fact. Two hotels in town, and he chooses to stay here. It's a real honor, don't you think?'"

Tietzmann spat into the dirt at their feet.

"'A real honor.' Shit," he said. "At first, I figured Lockhart was after *me*. I was gonna get myself a bottle of rye for the trail and clear out. But now that I know 'Tommy Taylor' is in town...?" Tietzmann shook his head. "I'm sorry. He's here for you."

Harte took another drink. He was staring off at the mirror behind the bar, the crack that seemed to split the world in two. He said nothing.

"You know what?" Tietzmann said. "You oughta come with me. We'll put some miles between us and Kansas. Head up to Montana maybe. Then we can get back to work. Together. 'Same ol' thing,' just like in Texas after the war."

Harte tore his gaze away from the mirror.

"I ain't runnin'," he said.

Tietzmann sighed like he'd just lost a game he never thought he could win. "You always was the brave one, weren't you?"

"The smart and handsome one, too."

Both men made noises that were supposed to be laughter. It sounded more like they were coughing, gasping.

"Look," Harte said, "do you know who the town marshal is here?"

"I ain't never even been in Jetmore before."

"Well, you remember Beak Fitzhugh, don't you? Rode with Cal Harper's bunch?"

Tietzmann nodded. "He'd still be wanted for killin' them Rangers, wouldn't he?"

"Yeah. But George Thornton's not—and that's what he calls himself now. *Marshal* George Thornton."

Tietzmann grunted out another dry, mirthless chuckle. "Damn. They'll pin a badge on anybody, won't they?"

"I don't know...kinda makes sense to me." Harte tipped his seat back on two legs, his back against the wall. He was a burly man, and the chair beneath him groaned in protest. "Outlaws and lawmen, we're just two sides of the same plugged nickel, ain't we? A little thievin', a little bullyin', a little lyin', a little killin'. It's all in a day's work."

"Yeah, maybe. But that don't mean you can count on Beak to stand with you against Burl goddamn Lockhart."

"Badge or no, Beak still hates the big outfits and the Pinks," Harte said. "He's not gonna let the Cattlemen's Association send some assassin in here to gun me down. And the town'll back him up, too. Hell, half the squatters in this county are rustlin' themselves. It's safer to be a brand artist around here than a range detective."

Tietzmann shook his head. "That won't stop Lockhart. You've heard the stories. Just look at how he done Little Billy LaFollette. Tricked him into drawing first—right in front of the kid's own damn *church*! Almost got Lockhart lynched, but after the inquest he rode out free as a bird."

Harte leaned forward, bringing his chair down on all four legs again. He spread his hands flat on the table, too, as if bracing himself for something—a punch, a cyclone, an earthquake, worse.

"I ain't runnin' with you, Gunther," he said.

"Alright. I suppose that's just as well." Tietzmann took a prim little sip of his beer. "Lockhart would track you down soon enough, anyway."

The two men sat in silence for a moment. Over at the bar, the drunk was still drinking, the saloonkeeper still spit-polishing dirty glasses that never got clean. The whisperers had left to do whatever it was they'd been whispering about doing. No one else had entered the Phoenix. It was a dive so low-down even the whores didn't bother with it.

"Did you see him?" Harte finally said, his voice low. He didn't look at Tietzmann. He was glaring at the drunk. "Lockhart?"

Tietzmann shrugged stiffly. Now he was giving the boozehound the eye, too. "I don't think so, but that don't mean nothin'. You know how he keeps his face out of the papers."

The souse at the bar noticed their stares. He was a nondescript man of perhaps fifty years dressed in the manner of a clerk or small-time merchant. He squinted at Harte and Tietzmann as if he couldn't quite make out their faces, was straining to see if they were smiling or frowning. He played it safe and flashed them a shit-eating grin.

He had half a dozen teeth left, at most, and those were as worn-down and brown as old tree stumps.

"Gentlemen," he croaked.

Tietzmann saluted him with his beer glass.

Harte slumped back into his seat.

"I know this much," Tietzmann said. "Burl Lockhart doesn't have to gum his mush."

"And that's about all we *do* know."

"Well, I bet you he doesn't have a peg leg, either. Or an eyepatch. Or green hair. Folks'd say so."

Harte turned his glare on Tietzmann.

"Sorry. It ain't funny," Tietzmann said. "How do you keep a feller from shootin' you in the back when you wouldn't even recognize him face to face?"

"The lady at your boardin' house has seen him. You could ask her what he looks like."

"Sure, I could. And what do you think would happen next?" Tietzmann pursed his thin lips and spoke in the warbly, high-pitched voice of an old woman. "'Ooo, Burl—remember how you told me to let you know if anyone started askin' nosy questions about you? Well, guess what Mr. Adams just did. And him with the room right next to yours!'"

"I know it's risky. But, dammit, we know where the man's beddin' down. There's gotta be some way we can...."

Harte's voice trailed off but his mouth kept moving, curling at the edges, dimpling his round face.

"I remember that look," Tietzmann said. He sounded wary, as if Harte's smile were a hat on a bed or boots on a table. A bad omen.

"We don't need to know what Lockhart looks like," Harte said. "Cuz we know where to find him."

"Us...find *him*?"

Harte nodded.

"You can't be serious."

"We'd do it quiet," Harte said. "With knives. Two on one, it'd be easy."

"You...can't...be...serious."

Harte's smile grew wider, becoming not just a toothy grin but a prod, something with which he could push, steer.

"Now, come on, Gunther. Show a little backbone. You don't know Lockhart's after me. You've still got a hand in the game. He might be trailin' *you*. Either way, you or me, we could end it tonight...if we do it together." Harte waggled his bushy brown eyebrows. "Just like old times."

Tietzmann played with his glass a moment, tilting it this way and that, watching the suds rise up and slide down, rise up and slide down. Then he made a sound that was part sigh, part growl.

"Yeah...you always was the brave one. Shit."

He threw back his head and practically poured what remained of his beer straight down his throat. When he was done, he pounded the glass on the table.

"I'm in. But the next round's on *you*."

Over the course of the next three hours—and the next six rounds—there was no talk of Burl Lockhart. Instead, Tietzmann and Harte swapped gossip. Where the wire was going up, where the easy pickings still were, which outfits were sending herds up which trails, who was buying cattle with blotched brands. And every so often one or the other would make a reference to the "old times" in Texas. "Frank would've laughed himself sick at that." Or "Now ol' Smokehouse, there was an artist. Give that man a runnin' iron, and he could turn a Bar 6 into a Diamond 9."

But there was no mention of the day the old times had ended. The day Tietzmann and Harte rode in with supplies and found their friends hanging from the oak behind the cabin, each with a sign around his neck as well as a rope. "RUSSLER" on Frank. "THEEF" on Smokehouse. Two other signs had been left propped up against the tree's trunk. They each said the same thing: "KILLER."

Harte and Tietzmann never even dismounted. They spoke for all of half a minute then wheeled around and galloped off without the packhorses, headed in different directions.

"So long, Gunther!"

"Good luck, Lucas!"

And they hadn't seen each other since.

"Well, Mr. Adams," Harte said after finishing yet another beer, "it ain't gonna get any darker."

"I reckon you're right, Mr. Taylor." Tietzmann drained the last drops from his glass. "It's time decent folks was in bed."

In the ten minutes it took to walk to the boarding house, Tietzmann pissed once, Harte three times. They made their plans between stops.

"You do have a knife on you, right?" Harte asked.

"Of course. You?"

"Of course."

And then:

"What if he's not in his room?" Tietzmann asked.

"Then we settle in and wait for him to come back."

"Well, I'm gonna hope it don't play out like that. If I have to go up against Burl Lockhart, I'd rather do it when he's asleep."

And then:

"We oughta go in through the window," Tietzmann said. "The floorboards and doors in that place creak loud enough to wake the dead."

"The old lady'll get to test that out tomorrow mornin'. On Lockhart."

And then:

"This is it."

The house was small but pretty. One story, crisply painted, neat, with flowerbeds along the front porch and vegetables around back growing in lines as straight as soldiers on review. Even the water pump had been whitewashed. It seemed to glow eerily in the moonlight.

There was no light at all in the windows.

"Over here," Tietzmann whispered, leading Harte to the back of the house. "Me." He pointed at a window, then crept on toward another. "Lockhart."

Tietzmann crouched down beneath the second window. Harte knelt beside him.

A black strip of nothingness about three inches tall ran along the sill. The window was open just enough for a breeze to slip in. Or fingers. The room beyond was a void, the kind of dark so deep it hurts a man's eyes to look into it.

Harte and Tietzmann stared up at the window, then at each other. Neither moved. Their plan was incomplete—one question remained.

"Who first?" Tietzmann said.

Harte swallowed spit. He looked like he wanted to piss again.

"You," he said softly. "You said the floorboards creak. You're skinnier than me. It should be you."

Tietzmann shook his head. Not like he was arguing. More like resigned.

"And you the brave one," he sighed.

"Me the smart one," Harte said.

"Right."

Tietzmann stood, slid his hands beneath the window and lifted. It rose four, five, six inches silently, smoothly— then suddenly jerked upward with a clatter.

Harte and Tietzmann jumped to either side of the window, both men reaching for their guns. They stayed pressed against the house for a full minute before Harte spoke.

"You hear anything?"

"I...I can't tell. Maybe...maybe snorin'?"

"Yeah. Maybe." Harte jerked his head at the window. "Alright, let's get this over with."

Tietzmann nodded slowly and holstered his forty-five. The window was open high enough for him now. He took a deep breath and slithered through it.

Then he was gone, swallowed by the blackness beyond the sill. Harte waited a moment, then hauled himself in, too.

"Just hold still for a second, Gunther," Harte whispered as he got to his feet inside the room. His words came out so quiet he could barely hear them himself. "We'll do this together."

He drew his knife and took a step into the dark. The floorboards didn't creak.

"Lucas," Tietzmann said, his voice hoarse, strangled.

Harte turned toward the sound, seeing nothing.

Then Tietzmann spoke again. One more word. It sounded different this time, coming out hard, low, like the bitterest of curses—a curse he was aiming at himself.

"Tommy."

Harte saw the flash of light, heard only the beginning of the thunderclap. By the time it registered, the bullet was already tearing its way through his brain. After that, there was only oblivion.

The body toppled back against the window then crumpled to the floor in a shower of shattered glass. Yet Harte never dropped the knife.

Tietzmann shot him again, twice. Because that's what startled men do. Not that Tietzmann was startled.

He walked over to the bed, pulled off his boots and got under the covers.

Down the hall, he could hear the old lady screaming. In a moment, he'd calm her down and send the other lodger off to fetch Marshal "Thornton." Beak would be pissed, but what could he do? It was self defense. Obviously.

There was a soft knock on the door.

"H-hello?"

It was the Yankee drummer who'd rented the next room over.

"Are you alright, Mr. Lockhart?"

"I'm fine," Tietzmann said. "But I can't say the same for the other feller in here."

ANIMALS

Peter Lorre was melting before Larry Erie's eyes. The soft-voiced, sad-eyed actor was Turner Classic Movies' "Star of the Month." In the span of 48 hours, Erie watched more than a dozen Lorre films.

The movies progressed chronologically, so Erie saw the young, lithe Lorre of *The Maltese Falcon* gradually give way to the puffy, middle-aged Lorre of *Beat the Devil* and finally the hunchbacked, basset-faced Lorre of *The Raven*. As the actor got older, he seemed to curl in on himself, as if he were shrinking into a ball like a pill bug trying to protect itself from time and age.

Erie found watching another man's deterioration sad but strangely compelling. His cats enjoyed it, as well. Or at least they enjoyed his enjoyment. They liked it when he stayed still. One curled up on his lap, one between his feet. Erie obliged them by moving as little as possible. He critiqued the weaker films for them, saying things like, "Geez, would you look at that?" and "Is that the dumbest thing you ever saw or what?" The cats never disagreed with him.

The doorbell rang about twenty minutes into *The Comedy of Terrors*. The cats ran to the front of the house to investigate, but Erie already knew who it was—his friend Bass, come to repeat in person the conversation they'd had on the phone twice in the past four days.

Bass: "Let's go fishing."

Erie: "I hate fishing."

Bass: "Me too. Let's go."

Erie: "I don't think so."

Bass: "Come on, Larry. You gotta do something. You can't just keep moping around here."

Erie: "I'm not moping."

Bass: "Yes, you are. You've been moping for weeks. You're depressed."

Erie: "Goodbye, Bass."

Bass: [Sigh.] "Bye."

Erie reluctantly turned off the TV. Potato chip crumbs fluttered to the floor like snow when he stood up. The bell rang again as he shuffled toward the front door.

"Alright! Calm down! I'm coming!" Erie bellowed.

He pulled open the door expecting to see Bass standing before him, a fishing rod in one hand and a tackle box in the other. The "I don't fish!" was already forming in Erie's mouth when he noticed his mistake.

Bass was a wrinkled, small-boned man. The person on Erie's porch was a young, chubby-cheeked girl.

Not Bass. Not even close.

"Oh," Erie said. "I'm sorry. I thought you were someone else."

"That's O.K."

The girl stared up at him with her hazel eyes opened wide.

"What can I do for you?" Erie asked. He steeled himself for a pitch for Girl Scout cookies or magazine subscriptions.

"Are you Mr. Erie?" the girl asked. She seemed to find it hard to believe.

"Yes."

"The detective?"

Erie smiled grimly, shrugged.

"From time to time," he said.

Erie Investigations, his one-man detective agency, hadn't had a case in three months.

"Well, I'd like to hire you," the girl said.

Erie's smile sagged.

It was going to be just like in the old days, before he'd retired, when he was still a cop. Every so often a neighborhood kid would drop by and say, "Mr. Erie, can you help me? Someone stole my bike." Or "My daddy doesn't come to our house anymore. Can you find out why?" Erie wondered which it was going to be this time. The girl would probably offer to pay him with the nickels and dimes in her piggy bank.

Erie suddenly wished he'd stayed in his La-Z-Boy.

"What do you need a detective for?"

The girl's mouth glittered silver with braces, and her lips seemed to catch on the metal as she spoke, giving her a slight lisp. So when she answered, the words came out like this: "Shomebody shtole my dog."

A sigh heaved up in Erie's chest. A missing pet. Classic. And he was supposed to roam the countryside with a leash and a box of Milkbones shouting, "Lassie, come home!"

The girl was young, eleven or twelve by the look of her. But she was old enough to read Erie's body language.

"She didn't just run away," she protested. "There were these people in a van driving around the neighborhood real slow yesterday and my dog was in our backyard and then she was gone and so was Mr. and Mrs. Wingate's dog, and David Greek's cat got stolen, too."

One of Erie's cats, Mae, was slinking along the wall toward the open door. Erie put up a slipper-covered foot to block her. Mae turned and walked away, feigning indifference for the door that had her hypnotized a moment before. The girl kept talking.

"We called the police and this detective called us back and talked to us but I could tell he didn't care. He didn't even come out to look around and he didn't call the Wingates or the Greeks like he said he would. He's not even going to try."

There was a slight tremor in the girl's voice, and for a moment Erie was terrified that she'd start crying—and that he would have to comfort her. But no tears came. She was more outraged than sad. The tears would come later, when she got the bad news that almost always ended stories like hers. For now, she still had one hope to cling to.

Erie.

The thought of being a little girl's knight in shining armor made him squirm.

"I heard you became a private detective—that you help people for money. Well, I can pay you. I've been babysitting. I've got my own money. I'd pay anything to get Ginger back."

Mae returned, creeping along the wall again. The front door was open, and she was going to get through it. It was her mission in life.

Erie blocked her, like he always did. It was *his* mission to keep her inside. This time Mae protested with a piteous meow. Erie looked down into her wide, owlish eyes and felt the push of a sudden impulse. He acted on it instantly, knowing somehow in that split second that if he thought about it he wouldn't do it.

"Don't worry about the money," he said to the girl. "I'll take the case. Come on in."

The girl flashed him a metal-studded grin and stepped inside.

Limber, long-haired Mae and lumbering, short-haired Goldie quickly joined the girl on the couch in the living room. She stroked one cat then the other as she told her story.

Her name was Jodi Marksberry. She lived five blocks away. Her dog, Ginger, was a ten-year-old chocolate Lab. Jodi always put Ginger out when she got home from school so the dog could "do her business" and have some time outside. Yesterday was no different. But when Jodi checked on the dog an hour or so later, she was gone.

Jodi went looking for her. She asked some of the neighborhood kids if they'd seen her. They said no, but they had seen a rusty brown van—or a brown truck, some said, or a black van—driving up and down the street "super slow." In school they'd all been taught how to spot potential abductors, so the unfamiliar brown/black van/truck had struck a nerve. Some of the boys went off on their bikes to look for it, determined to see who was inside, but they couldn't find it.

Later that night, Jodi and her parents went door to door, asking more neighbors if they'd seen Ginger. No one had. But the Wingates, who lived four doors down from Erie, reported that their dog Sweetie had been gone for hours. Sweetie was a beagle/collie mix the Wingates allowed to roam the neighborhood. The Greeks, who lived a few blocks over, hadn't seen their cat Buster since he'd gone out that morning.

None of the animals returned later that night or the next morning or the next afternoon. Jodi had checked. Ginger, Sweetie and Buster were all missing.

"And they all disappeared the same day there's this weird van driving around. That can't just be a coincidence," Jodi concluded, her voice and bearing deadly serious, like a little prosecutor summing up for a jury of one. "They were stolen by those people in the van."

She brushed a long, stray strand of auburn hair out of her face, and her confidence seemed to evaporate.

"I mean…at least that's what *I* think," she said. "What do *you* think?"

"Well, for one thing, I think you might make a good detective one day. That was a very thorough report."

The girl shyly shrugged off the compliment.

"And I think you're right about the animals," Erie continued. "They were probably stolen."

"So there are guys who steal people's pets just like stealing cars and bikes and stuff?"

"That's right."

"That's so weird. So who do they sell the animals to? Pet stores?"

Erie saw the hope in her eyes. Ginger had been spirited off to a crooked pet shop. Getting her back was just a matter of finding it, right?

Erie nodded. "Sometimes," he said.

It wasn't true. But he wasn't ready to share the truth with her. Not until he knew he had to.

"So do you have a picture of Ginger I can have?"

"Yeah, but I didn't bring one. There's a ton at my house, though."

Erie stood up. "Good. I've got some things to do here. How about if I come by a little later and get one?"

Jodi picked up on the cue. She stood as well. "O.K."

Erie started for the door, and Jodi followed. So did Mae.

"What's your address?"

"1412 Hamilton Drive."

"Alright. I'll be there in a couple hours. I'd also like to talk to your parents while I'm there. You know—interview them."

"Sure." Jodi nodded as if the ins and outs of an investigation were old hat to her. When they reached the door, she held out her hand. "Thank you, Mr. Erie."

Erie wrapped his hand around hers and gave it two solemn shakes.

"You're welcome."

What he really felt like saying was, "Don't thank me yet."

Jodi said goodbye and walked to a bicycle lying in the grass near the driveway. She hopped on it, waved and pedaled away.

So he had a new client. A kid looking for her dog. Should he feel noble or pathetic?

Erie didn't know. He wasn't even sure why he'd agreed to do anything at all.

Maybe it was because a little girl had asked for his help. Maybe it was just because someone—it didn't matter who—thought there was something he could do. Maybe it was because he suddenly couldn't stomach the thought of another minute with Peter Lorre.

When Erie closed the door, Mae looked up and gave him another frustrated meow.

"Forget it, knucklehead," he said to her. "You're better off in here."

And then again, maybe he'd taken the case because he'd started talking to his cats. Maybe it was time to try talking to people again.

☙

The first thing Erie did now that he had work to do was sleep. In his bed. For the first time in two days.

Sleep came to him easily now. There was no hint of the smothering mix of insomnia and lethargy that had left him stranded in front of the television. He simply got under the covers and slept. And when the alarm went off ninety minutes later, he got up. It was that easy.

He brushed his teeth and showered and shaved. He put on a suit. Then he took it off, replacing it with jeans and a knit shirt and sweater. He was looking for a dog, not the crown jewels.

He stepped in front of a mirror, hurrying through a quick inspection—hair in place, zipper zipped, clothes free of stains and cat fuzz. He checked himself without really looking at himself. He was ten pounds heavier and a few dozen hairs grayer than he'd been the year before. He knew that. He didn't need to see it again.

When he felt ready, he began his investigation by picking up the phone and calling Bass.

"It lives!" Bass declared when he heard Erie's voice.

"Yeah, I'm alive. And I need your help."

"You got a case?"

"Yup."

"Well, alright then! Whadaya need me to do? Tail somebody? Go out on a stakeout with ya? Whatever it is, I'm your man!"

Bass was so excited he was practically panting.

"I've got a very important role for you to play," Erie told him.

"What kinda role?"

"Bait."

There was a pause.

"What now?"

Erie explained, trying to make it sound as exciting as possible. Bass bit.

"Oh yeah, I could do that. I'm a natural-born actor. People've always said so."

"That's why I came to you," Erie said. Which was half-true. Erie was reasonably certain Bass wouldn't screw up. And he was even more certain Bass was the only person he knew who'd do it.

"So when do we get rolling?" Bass asked.

"Soon. I'll let you know."

"Alright, chief. I'll start practicing."

It pleased Erie to hear Bass so happy. He figured it might be the only positive thing to come out of this case, so he basked in it.

"Yeah, good idea. You do that," he said.

After they'd said their goodbyes, Erie picked up the River City phone book. He looked up the numbers for *The Weekly Nickel Pincher* and the *River City Herald-Times*. He placed the same ad in each.

PETS

FREE TO GOOD HOME

2 beautiful choc. labs, both 5 yrs old.

Moving to FL, can't take them. Great with

kids, cats. Call before they're gone!

Erie ended the ad with Bass's name and phone number. *The Weekly Nickel Pincher*, a smudgy black-and-white collection of classified ads and coupons, wouldn't come out for another four days. But the *Herald-Times* ad would appear in the next morning's edition.

That was good news. Erie recalculated his chances of finding Ginger alive. They moved from "no way in hell" to a simple "unlikely."

Erie sat in his car for a minute and stared at 1412 Hamilton Drive. Jodi Marksberry's house.

The backyard was fenced in. But it was a simple, low, chain-link fence. Good—*maybe*—for keeping a dog in. Not so good for keeping a person out.

The fence had a latched entrance on one side of the house. It faced the street.

When Erie finally went to the front door and rang the bell, he was greeted by a fortyish man with graying red hair and a bushy moustache. The man looked vaguely familiar. Erie had probably seen him at some long-ago block party or Christmas pageant. Erie had stopped going to things like block parties and Christmas pageants after his wife died. He'd stopped doing a lot of things.

"Oh, hello...."

Erie could see that the man was groping for his first name.

"Larry," Erie prompted.

The man smiled and nodded. "Yeah, of course. Larry. Thanks for coming over."

The two men shook hands.

"My pleasure...."

"John."

"My pleasure, John."

"Jodi tells me you're going to help us look for Ginger."

"I'm going to do what I can." Erie peered over Marksberry's shoulder into the house. The lights were on in the kitchen, and he heard the murmur of conversation and the clinking and scraping of silverware on plates. "Am I interrupting dinner?"

"Oh, don't worry about it."

For a moment, Erie expected—or maybe hoped or maybe feared—that Marksberry would invite him inside to join his family at the dinner table. But he didn't.

"So do you really think some kind of dognapping gang stole Ginger?" the man said instead.

Erie took a step back from the door and lowered his voice. "Would you mind stepping out here with me for a moment?"

"Oh. O.K. Sure."

Marksberry followed him onto the porch, looking confused and a little nervous. Erie had seen that look plenty of times before he'd retired. When you're a cop, people are always expecting you to accuse them of something.

"Look, John—I just wanted a chance to talk to you without Jodi overhearing. You understand?"

"Sure," Marksberry said glumly. He obviously wasn't looking forward to hearing what Erie had to say.

"I'm going to be honest with you here. It doesn't look good. There *are* people who steal pets."

"To sell to pet stores?" Marksberry broke in, sounding skeptical. He had good reason for that.

"I sort of let Jodi jump to a conclusion there. The truth's a little harder to hear," Erie said. "Ginger's ten years old, right?"

"That's right."

"That makes her too old to be much use to your run-of-the-mill breeder or dealer. And…well, the other possibilities aren't very pleasant."

Erie paused, giving Marksberry the chance to say, "I don't know if I want to hear this." Marksberry didn't take it, so Erie pressed on.

"One of the possibilities," he said, "would be ritual sacrifice."

"What? You mean like devil worshippers?"

Erie shrugged. "You could call them that. That's a longshot, though. That kind of thing's never popped up around here, except for teenage boys stirring up trouble on Halloween. Another longshot's a dogfighting ring. They've been known to steal animals. They use them to train their dogs."

Dusk was settling in, but there was still enough light for Erie to see Marksberry's face growing more and more pale as the world receded into shadow.

"But it's a lot more likely these guys are bunchers," Erie went on. "People who grab pets and sell them to research labs. There's a place down in Missouri called Calkins Life Sciences. They put out the call sometimes for certain kinds of dogs, certain kinds of cats. When they do, people's pets start disappearing all over the Midwest."

"My God." A flash of color returned to Marksberry's cheeks. Anger was mixing in with his fear. "What kind of scumbag would do a thing like that?"

"One who wants money and doesn't care how he gets it. Unfortunately, it's not exactly an exotic breed."

"My God," Marksberry said again. "I can't believe they'd steal a dog right out of someone's yard and do that to her."

"They would. But we don't know yet that's what happened to Ginger. Still…now you see why I didn't want to have this talk in front of Jodi."

"Of course. Thanks, Larry." Marksberry glanced back at the front door of his house. He took a deep breath. "She really loves that dog. They grew up together. They're practically like sisters."

"I understand."

"I've got to tell you—I was a little miffed when I heard Jodi had gone to you. Last night I told her not to. I was sure Ginger would turn up today. But now, after hearing all that…? Look, I know Jodi offered to pay you, and you said no. But I'd like to—"

Erie brought up a hand and shook his head. "Don't worry about it. Just think of it as one neighbor helping another."

Marksberry's gaze dropped for a moment, and something flickered across his face. It took Erie a second to recognize it.

Guilt.

Here was this sad, lonely old man—practically the neighborhood hermit—coming to offer help. And yet how many times had Marksberry dropped by to help *him*?

The man's transparent pity annoyed Erie. "You weren't the neighbor I was talking about," he wanted to say. But he didn't.

Jodi rescued them from the moment by charging out the door with a handful of snapshots.

"Hi, Mr. Erie! I got some pictures of Ginger for you."

Marksberry took the opportunity to fade back a few steps toward the door.

"She's looking right at the camera in this one, so you can really see her face," Jodi said. "Her eyes are dark brown, see? And in this one she's kind of looking off to the side, so you can see that. And then here she is when she puts her ears up, like when she hears a siren or something. She almost looks like another dog. And in this one—"

Erie left with more than a dozen shots of the dog.

"Thanks, these will be a big help," he told Jodi as he slipped them into a pocket in his cardigan. But he didn't know if he'd end up using the pictures at all. He wasn't looking for Ginger. Not to begin with.

He was looking for a brown van. Or a brown truck. Or a black van. Or a black truck. And it was time to start.

He said goodbye to the Marksberrys, promising to update them when he had some news, and left.

As he drove away, the futility of his task dragged behind him like an anchor. More than 100,000 people live in River City, Indiana. Erie remembered hearing one of the detectives in Auto Theft say that there were nearly that many cars. How many brown/black van/trucks could there be?

A lot.

Erie thought about his house, his cats, his La-Z-Boy. He wondered what was on TV. But he kept driving. And driving. And driving.

If he was looking for a needle in a haystack, at least this particular needle didn't just lie there like all the others. The van—and it had to be a van, really, if someone was using it to haul around stolen pets—was going to be doing what he was doing. Prowling through River City's west side neighborhoods, searching, hunting.

In three hours behind the wheel, he saw eleven roaming cats, five dogs, one brown van and no black vans. The brown van was parked in front of a church. Erie didn't even bother to slow down and get a good look at it. The words "Shepherd of the Hills Methodist Church" were printed on both sides in white. Even kids who couldn't tell the difference between a brown van and a black truck would've noticed that.

When Erie got home, Mae and Goldie met him at the door. As always, Mae tried to dart past his feet and get outside. Erie snatched up the little black cat and cradled her in his arms.

"No way, Jose. It's not safe out there."

Mae complained loudly, obviously unconvinced.

It was almost ten o'clock. Erie went straight to bed. Mae and

Goldie went with him. They'd spent the day in the TV room. Now it was time to spend the night in the bedroom. That had been the routine of their days for months. For all three of them.

It took Erie a long time to fall asleep this time. Goldie was curled up near his feet. Mae was snuggled up under the sheets with him, her small chest moving up and down, pressing against him with each breath. That motion, the in and out of life, both comforted and haunted Erie. If it were to stop—just *stop*—there would be nothing he could do about it. He knew that because it had happened before, fourteen months ago, in a different bed. A hospital bed. All he could do when his wife died was watch. Maybe all he could do now was wait.

And somewhere out in the night, maybe somewhere nearby, Ginger was lying, maybe dead, maybe sleeping, but either way *waiting*.

Waiting for him.

By eight the next morning Erie was back in his car driving up and down the same streets he'd toured the night before. Nothing had changed, except now instead of flickering blue-white TV light in every window he saw moms and dads going off to work, kids going off to school. And still no brown or black vans.

He tried to fight off frustration by switching on a talk radio station and looking on his fruitless circling as a chance to catch up on current events. After half an hour, he grew so angry with the mean-spirited idiots he heard on the radio he switched over to an oldies station. That got him through another hour. For some reason, he'd always hated the song "Bad, Bad Leroy Brown," and when it came on he turned off the radio rather than subject himself to it.

For a few minutes, the only things he heard were the steady purr of his tires rolling over pavement and the voice in his head telling him he was wasting his time. The voice was interrupted by the burping blare of a police siren.

Erie looked in his rear-view mirror. A patrol car was gliding along behind him, the officer at the wheel stony faced behind his sunglasses. Erie pulled over. He turned off the engine and sat there the way he knew a cop would want him to—perfectly still, hands on the wheel where they could be seen.

He was in Briarwood Grove, a newish neighborhood crammed with large, boxy, nearly identical homes. The curtains fluttered in a nearby window. You didn't hear sirens much around here.

The cop stayed in his patrol car for a minute, checking Erie's plates. When he finally got out, the lips beneath his sunglasses were twisted into a smirk.

Erie rolled down his window as the cop approached. He recognized the man as he drew closer. His name was Reggie Loftus. He was a young guy, not around long enough for Erie to know well, just another one of the uniforms on the street, neither friend nor enemy.

Loftus put his hand on the top of the car and leaned over to shine his leering grin at Erie like a flashlight.

"Good morning, Mr. Erie."

"Good to see you, Reg."

"Why didn't you just get out and let me know it was you?"

"I couldn't see who it was back there. I didn't want to spook some rookie and get my head blown off."

Loftus nodded, still amused but not laughing.

"So is there some kind of problem?" Erie asked him.

"We got a call from one of the local soccer moms. Seems a mysterious stranger's been spotted checking out the neighborhood."

"Driving a brown van?"

"No. Driving a tan Toyota Corolla."

"Oh," Erie said.

His car.

"So what's the story, Mr. Erie?" Loftus asked. His smile stretched wider, a dam barely able to hold back laughter.

Erie finally understood. He felt his face flushing.

River City's cops, his old comrades, knew he'd started a

detective agency. And they thought it was funny.

"There's no story. I'm just house hunting."

Loftus looked skeptical. "House hunting?"

"Sure. I'm thinking about buying something bigger."

"Oh, yeah?"

"Yeah. My daughter might be moving back to town, and we're thinking about sharing a place. You know—top floor for me, bottom floor for her. That kind of thing."

"Sure you're not looking for a brown van?"

It was Erie's turn to smile. The grin felt wobbly, as if it might topple right off his face at any moment.

"Oh. That. Just the old instincts acting up, I guess. I saw a brown van creeping around, and it seemed a little suspicious. No one's called in about it?"

Loftus shook his head. "Nope. Not that I've heard. Mr. Erie, are you sure you're not up to something else here?"

"What do you mean? What would I be 'up to'?"

"Oh, working a case maybe."

Loftus was practically snickering.

"Just house hunting, like I said."

"Ooooookaaaaaay," Loftus said, stretching the sounds out, making them musical and sardonic. "Well, if you're going to keep at it around here, you might want to pick up the pace. A lady called in thinking you were some kind of perv."

"No problem. I was just about done for today anyway."

"Alright then. You take care, Mr. Erie. Don't get into any trouble now."

"Same to you, Reg."

Loftus gave him a little two-fingered salute and walked back to his car. Erie didn't have to look in his rear-view mirror to know the cop was still smirking. What a great story he had to tell over lunch with the troops at Peppy's Diner. He got a call about a molester cruising the streets of Briarwood Grove...and it was old Larry Erie, private eye! Probably out trying to crack The Case of the Missing Metamucil, or maybe The Adventure of the Lost Dentures.

Erie started his car and drove straight to Bass's place. He was through roaming aimlessly around River City like one of those senile coots who goes out for toothpaste and ends up running out of gas in Alaska. Maybe he was through with everything. He'd bumped into a real cop and all Erie had done was *amuse* the son of a bitch. He hadn't accomplished a thing—except get a little girl's hopes up.

"Forget it, Bass," he was going to say when he got to his friend's house. "Let's go fishing. Isn't that what old farts like us are supposed to do?"

But when Bass came to the door, the slender little man was in such a dither Erie's words died in his throat.

"Well, *there* you are!" Bass proclaimed rapturously, as if Erie himself wasn't aware of that fact. "Finally! I've been trying to get you on the phone all morning!"

"I've been out looking for that van I told you about."

Bass waved his hands dismissively. "Awww, don't worry about looking out there. They're coming right here!"

"What do you mean?"

"The ad in the paper! I got three calls about it this morning! One of 'em had to be from the bad guy."

Bass's enthusiasm was not infectious.

"Yeah, well, maybe," Erie said. "And maybe we're going to have three families drive out here and then drive away crushed because they had their hearts set on a couple dogs we don't have."

"Well, we'll find out soon enough!" Bass countered, unwilling to let his glum buddy suck the thrill out of his first undercover operation.

Erie cocked an eyebrow at Bass. "How soon?"

"Any minute now! That's why I was so desperate to get a hold of you. The first guy's comin' 'round at ten."

Erie looked at his watch. It was nine fifty-six.

ℰℐ

Erie had just enough time to jump back in his car and circle the block. As he pulled to the curb five doors down from Bass's house, a red pickup truck rolled up the street from the opposite direction. It stopped across from Bass's place, and a pot-bellied, gray-haired man got out. He walked to the house slowly, taking small steps, as if he didn't want to scuff the blindingly white sneakers that covered his feet.

He rang the bell, Bass answered, and the two of them chatted for a moment. Then the gray-haired man shuffle-stepped back to his truck and drove away. Erie didn't bother following him. Instead, he got out of his car and walked to Bass's house. Bass met him on the porch.

"Well?" Erie said.

Bass shrugged, looking chagrined. "Oh, he was a retired fella, like us. Said he wanted the dogs for his grandkids. You believe that?"

"Um-hmm."

"Yeah, me too. When I told him I'd already given the dogs away, I thought he was gonna cry."

"Um-hmm."

"You see the way he walked? I can't see him grabbin' animals off the street. The man could barely walk a dog, let alone steal one."

"Um-hmm."

Bass peered into Erie's tight, grim face. "Oh, now don't be like that. Come on in and have some coffee. The next suspect isn't supposed to show up for another half hour."

Erie followed Bass into the house without saying a word.

"You hear that?" Bass said as he poured their coffee. He looked up, put a hand to one ear, grinned. "Nothin', right? Peace and quiet. Beautiful, wonderful peace and quiet."

Erie nodded, humoring Bass with a small smile.

Earlier that year, Bass had turned his basement over to a neighborhood kid who'd been having problems with his father. The kid had the typical teenage boy's love for industrial-strength rock'n'roll blasting from nuclear-powered speakers. But now the summer was over and school was back in session, so during the day Bass got a temporary reprieve from the musical stylings of The Misfits and The Suicide Machines.

"So how are things with Andrew these days?"

Bass plunked the coffee cups on the kitchen table and sat down across from Erie. "Oh, fine. I don't see him much anymore now that he's back in school. When he is here, he's usually downstairs messin' around on his computer with the stereo cranked up to 'Earthquake.'"

"Ever regret taking him in?"

Bass blew on his steaming black coffee, looking thoughtful. "I don't know. We don't always talk a lot, me and Andrew, but it means somethin' just havin' him around. It feels like there's a family here again, even if it's just the two of us. You could use a dose of that, Larry. Creepin' around that house of yours all alone ain't healthy."

"I'm not alone. I've got Goldie and Mae."

Bass made a sour face.

"I'm serious," Erie said.

"I know you are. That's why I'm disgusted. They're just dumb animals, Larry. It's not the same as havin' people around."

"You're right. It's a lot easier."

Bass rolled his eyes, but didn't challenge Erie further. They'd already had this debate too many times. Erie changed the subject to politics, and twenty minutes later he was back in his car, waiting.

It wasn't a brown van that pulled up in front of Bass's house. It was an ancient white Buick Skylark. The woman who got out looked to be about forty years old. She was wiry, with long, stringy black hair. She was wearing faded jeans and a denim jacket.

She rang Bass's bell, he came to the door, they talked, she left.

It was quick, but not exactly painless. The woman looked annoyed. Bass looked disappointed. Erie felt guilty.

Their next "suspect"—Erie was beginning to think of them as

their "victims"—wasn't coming until six o'clock. What was Erie supposed to do until then? Drive in circles the rest of the day? Frighten more housewives?

The white Skylark lurched from the curb. Erie watched it roll away, wondering why the woman had come. Maybe she wanted the dogs for her kids, maybe for her lonely old mother, maybe for her lonely not-so-old self. He wished her happy hunting.

He was just about to climb out of his car to go commiserate with Bass when the Skylark slowed to a halt. It began to back up, and for a moment Erie was afraid the woman had changed her mind about leaving quietly. She was going to come back and throw some kind of fit on Bass's porch. But her car stopped before it reached the house.

The woman got out, moved quickly to the side of the road and leaned down over something dark and lumpy nestled against the curb. She picked it up, carried it to her car and put it in the trunk. When she started the engine and pulled away, Erie followed her.

He got a good look at the thing she'd stopped to grab as she hustled it to her car. She held it by the tail, the torso and legs dangling, stiff.

It was a dead cat.

There was little danger Erie would lose the woman. She was heading out to the edge of town, into the farmland that corralled River City on three sides. The roads out there were narrow and straight. Perfect for a nice, easy tail, if you knew what you were doing. Every so often, Erie even let a car or two get in between him and the Skylark. He wasn't worried. If the woman turned, he'd see it.

Whenever he was directly behind her, he kept his eyes on her rear-view mirror, waiting for that long look, that twitchy squint that would tell him he'd been spotted. He never saw it. She wasn't looking for him. She was looking for something else.

About ten miles outside town, he saw what it was. The woman

hit her brakes and craned her neck to look at something in a ditch by the road.

It was a doe, a big one, lying there looking perfect, beautiful, except that her tongue was hanging out, and she was dead. The woman took the next half mile slowly, as if she were trying to burn that stretch of road into her memory.

She was going to come back after dark. That told Erie something. And she was going to need help with that deer. That told him something else.

This wasn't what he thought it was. Bunchers, pet thieves, they have clients. And those clients want their animals alive. You can't test drugs on a dead dog. And you can't keep a fighting dog sharp with a dead cat.

This woman was involved in something he'd never seen before. And she wasn't alone.

For the first time since he'd retired, Erie missed his gun.

About ten minutes later, the woman finally turned. A field of corn ran along one side of the new road. Trees and houses and mobile homes dotted the other side. Erie kept going straight.

The woman was home, Erie could feel it. It wouldn't be smart to stay stuck to her bumper all the way to her doorstep. He drove another hundred yards, pulled into a farm's dirt access road, circled around, headed back.

He turned where the woman had turned, taking it slow, but not too slow. He spotted the Skylark about a quarter mile up the road. It was perched on top of a low rise next to a dilapidated ranch house the color of a month-old lime. Broad, scruffy pine trees circled the property, swaying in the breeze like a lineup of tipsy green giants. A wilting paper NO TRESPASSING sign was nailed to the mailbox.

Erie drove a little further before pulling over. He sat in his car for a moment, reviewing his options. Or, as he quickly came to see it, his *option*. He was there, she was there. What choice did he really have?

Before starting toward the house, Erie propped up the hood of his car. Anyone driving by was supposed to think, *Car trouble? Ha! Good luck gettin' a tow out here!*

The woman's neighbors to the east didn't seem to be home. There were no cars parked in the driveway next to the house, and as Erie got closer he didn't hear the tell-tale clamor of daytime television. There were no neighbors in back, just trees and, beyond that, more farmland.

Somewhere nearby, an engine roared to life. Erie froze. A dog began barking, then howling. Another joined it, then another, then another.

"Shut up!"

A man's voice. Close.

A car door slammed shut.

Erie crouched down and slowly pushed his way through the pine trees' clinging branches. He stopped when he could see into the woman's yard.

There was the Skylark. Beyond it, parked on the grass in back of the house, was a mud-brown van. It had no side windows. The paint along the side was scratched and discolored where some corporate logo had resided long ago. No one was behind the wheel, but the engine was running.

The van was sitting next to a crude structure made from cement blocks and corrugated metal. It was only slightly longer and broader than the van, and not as tall. The howling was coming from inside.

A long black shape curled between the van and the cement bunker. Erie pushed a little closer, knowing he was getting too close. But he had to see what the black thing was. He had a hunch. And he didn't like it.

He reached the edge of the trees, took a step beyond. He was close enough now to hear scratching coming from the other side of those cement blocks. And close enough to see that his hunch was right.

A length of black plastic pipe had been tied tight to the van's exhaust. The other end disappeared into the ground next to the bunker. Erie was sure that it reappeared on the inside.

It was a do-it-yourself gas chamber.

A year before, Erie could have simply pulled out his gun and his badge, called in backup, put an end to this. But he had no gun or badge or backup. What could he do now?

He didn't let himself think about it. There was no time to work through his choices, no time to dream up a plan. He'd left his hiding place. He was in the open, where he could see and be seen. He couldn't hide again—not from what he was facing now.

He stood and walked to the bunker. There was a latch on the flimsy wooden door. A small combination lock hung from it. The woman and her partner hadn't bothered to bolt it. They were going to be back in a few minutes to check on their handiwork.

Erie opened the door.

A cloud of gray vapor billowed out, swirling past his face. A foul smell came with it. The stench of ammonia and feces. The howls turned to barks—lots of them.

As the exhaust fumes cleared, Erie could see cages, one stacked on top of the other along the sides of the building. Inside were dogs and cats, more than twenty, all staring at him. The end of the black plastic hose jutted from the ground near the door, puffing out a steady stream of deadly fog. At the far end of the bunker was a small mound of loose coiled shapes, like a pile of dead snakes.

Collars. Dozens of them.

Erie felt something he hadn't felt in a long time. Raw, animal rage. He whirled around, not sure what he was going to do next but almost hoping the woman and her helper would get in his way.

He got his wish sooner than he'd expected. A squat, thick-armed man was facing Erie. The shovel in his dirty hands was already swinging toward Erie's head.

Erie instinctively threw up his left arm and pivoted away from the blow, but it was too late. The shovel's handle cracked into his forearm, and the flat surface of its metal blade smacked against the back of his head.

Erie stumbled a few steps, his feet willing to run but his knees not cooperating. He was unconscious before he hit the ground.

୯ର

There were no hallucinations or fever dreams for Erie as his mind clawed its way out of the darkness. Just pain. And more darkness.

He was lying face down in the dirt, that he could tell. But when he opened his eyes, he saw nothing.

He pulled his hands under his chest and tried to push himself up. His left arm protested with a bolt of searing pain, and he dropped back down to the ground.

He blinked hard, but no vision came. Sounds and smells registered, though. The whining and whimpering of dogs, the hum of an engine, the nauseating odor of animal waste mingled with a whiff of rotting flesh.

Erie stopped worrying about whether the blow had blinded him. He had other things to worry about. He knew where he was now—inside the little cement bunker. He forced himself up on his right elbow and craned his neck around, scanning the void that surrounded him.

He saw what he was looking for just beyond his feet—a faint rectangle of light glowing in the darkness. The door.

One of the dogs began panting heavily. Another retched. The sounds came from up high, a few feet above Erie's head.

The cages were stacked up to the ceiling. Carbon monoxide rises. The animals on top would be affected first.

It was beginning. Erie didn't have much time.

He wriggled around and began crawling slowly toward the doorway, the throbbing in his head growing worse every second. Was it because of the blow he'd taken? Or were the fumes starting to affect him? The first sign is a headache....

He made it to the door, reached up for the knob. And stopped.

The lock. Surely it had been bolted now.

The door was little more than plywood. He could easily kick through it if he had all his strength back. But how long would he last outside? The man and woman would be just beyond the door, waiting, watching. Stumble out groggy and weak and they'd just use the shovel to finish what they'd started. He needed time to recover, think.

More animals were wheezing now, hacking and fighting for breath.

Erie groped along the floor, his hand brushing over loose soil, the cool metal of a cage, the warm fur of a dog or cat pressed up against the bars. Then he found it—the end of the black tube that was filling the shack with fumes. He sat up and pulled off his cardigan, wincing as the movement sparked fresh pain in his left arm. When he had the sweater off, he stuffed as much of it as he could down into the tube. The soft material of the sweater packed in firmly.

He turned and crawled to the opposite end of the shack, where the air would be a little clearer—he hoped. He spread out his hands and put his head down low, his forehead resting on the ground. He breathed in deeply, trying to suck up as much oxygen as possible. He would need all his strength when he got outside.

Something moist and rough raked the back of Erie's right hand. He pulled the hand back, startled. Then he thought for a moment and pushed the hand out to where it had been.

The tongue found his hand again. He stretched the hand out further, reaching a cage and the panting muzzle just beyond the bars. The dog licked his hand harder, whimpered, pleading.

Let me out.

Erie petted the dog as best he could. "Hold on," he whispered. "Hold on."

Somehow it seemed to comfort him as much as it comforted the dog.

A few yards away, on the other side of the cement blocks, the van's engine sputtered. It revved, coughed, revved, coughed.

The van's exhaust was blocked. The engine was choking on its own noxious fumes.

Erie heard cursing, arguing just beyond the door. The engine hacked, roared, then died. The curses grew louder, moving.

They were going to check the van. Erie had to move *now*. He stroked the dog one last time, then groped in the dark for the one weapon he could find. When he had it, he took two deep breaths and pushed himself to his feet, fighting a wave of dizziness and nausea as he stood. When he felt steady enough, he walked to the door.

The van's engine screeched, grinding, then whimpered and died. They were trying to start it up again. Perfect.

Erie waited for them to turn the key again. It didn't take long.

The engine screamed in protest. Erie kicked. The door flew open.

There was no one on the other side. The engine rattled into silence.

A woman's voice: "Did you hear that?"

A man's voice: "Hear what?"

"I heard somethin'. From the shed."

No answer. Then footsteps.

They were close. The trees, Erie's car—too far away. Erie still felt woozy. He knew he wouldn't make it if he ran. It would have to be fight, not flight.

He pressed himself back into the darkness, against the cement blocks next to the door.

The footsteps grew louder.

"Awww, hell!"

It was the man. Erie could see his shadow in the doorway. He was so close Erie could smell the man's sweat, feel the electric crackle of his anger.

"He's gone!"

"You sure?"

Erie heard noises—the rustling of clothes, the scrape of boot leather over gravel—that told him the man had turned around to face his partner.

"What do you mean am I sure?"

Something buried deep in Erie's soul screamed *"Now!"*

Erie obeyed.

He stepped out behind the man, bringing up the dog collar he'd grabbed in the dark. He wrapped it around the man's thick neck, crossing the leather in back, forming a crude noose. He pulled tight.

The woman screamed. The man staggered back a step, gurgling, clawing at his throat, trying to work his fingers under the collar. The woman rushed forward, bringing up her hands like claws. But the man was struggling, kicking in the doorway, and she couldn't reach Erie.

"I'll kill you!" the woman shrieked. "I'll kill you!"

Her snarling face disappeared for a second, breaking into a million tiny black dots. Erie's wounds, the fumes, the smell, the fight—they were all taking their toll. Erie was blacking out. His fingers loosened on the leather strap.

The man bucked hard, throwing all his weight back at once. Erie lost his footing, and the two men tumbled to the ground. Erie's left hand lost its grip on the collar.

The man rolled to the side, away from Erie, retching. Erie was stretched out on his back, stunned by the fall. The woman stepped into the doorway and spat an obscenity at him. Erie lifted his head, blinked her sneering face into focus and threw the collar at it. He knew it was pretty feeble as a last act of defiance, but she was too far away to spit on.

The woman batted the collar away with another curse, then repeated her threat, quieter now, making it a promise. "I'll kill you."

"I don't think so, lady."

The woman froze.

The voice had come from behind her.

"I've got me a gun in my hand, so I think I get to say who kills who around here."

When the woman turned around, Erie caught a glimpse of Bass Anderson a few yards beyond her. He was clutching a snub-nosed revolver in his right hand.

Erie recognized the gun immediately. He'd been trying to talk Bass into getting rid of it for months. He'd been afraid his friend would hurt someone with it.

When Bass got a glimpse of Erie and the dogs and cats in their filthy cages, he suddenly looked like he wanted to do just that. His jaw jutted out and his brow furrowed, the way they did whenever he lost his formidable temper. He brought his other hand up to steady the gun. It was pointed at the woman's chest.

"It's O.K., Bass." Erie sat up slowly. "I'm fine."

He grabbed a nearby cage and used it to pull himself up. A broad tongue lapped at his fingers. Erie looked down at the dog he'd been petting in the dark a few minutes before. It was a chocolate Lab.

"Ginger?" he said.

She wagged her tail.

Erie had two questions. He got the answer to one almost immediately. The other didn't come so easily.

"How'd you find me?" he asked Bass after he called the police. He'd used the phone in the cluttered, smelly ranch house. There were more dogs and cats inside, roaming free. Maybe they were pets. Maybe they were patiently waiting their turn in the bunker.

"I followed you," Bass answered, not taking his eyes—or his gun—off his prisoners. They were huddled together in the half-dark next to the cages, glaring sullenly at Bass and Erie. "When I saw you take off after Miss Sunshine here, I figured you might need some backup."

Erie nodded, not letting himself feel annoyed. Yes, Bass could've blown the whole thing. But he hadn't. The woman hadn't spotted him. And, to his shame, neither had Erie.

"You know, followin' people's a tricky business. It's not as easy as you'd think," Bass mused. "I lost you when you turned around at that farm back there. I had to go a little further up the road before I could turn around too, and by the time I got back I didn't know where you'd disappeared to. I was drivin' up and down all these side roads out here maybe twenty minutes before I saw your car. When I got out to take a look, I heard this Screamin' Mimi sayin' she was gonna kill somebody. Well, naturally I grabbed The

Peacemaker and came to take a look."

That was the first time Erie had heard Bass refer to his gun as "The Peacemaker." Bass was really enjoying himself.

"You did good, Bass," Erie said. "Thanks."

Bass tried to give him a dismissive, manly shrug, as if he saved lives every day and didn't need any thanks for it. But he couldn't keep the grin off his face.

"Can ya' believe this?" the woman hissed at her partner. "It's Matlock and Barney Fife."

Erie turned to face the man and the woman again. The sight of them made him sick with rage. He asked his other question, spitting it out, not expecting an answer.

"Just what kind of monsters are you?"

The woman swore at him again. The man didn't say anything.

Erie knew that was all he was going to get out of them. He'd have to wait for someone else to supply the answer.

He closed the door to the bunker, leaving them in the little hell they'd created until the police arrived.

There were several reunions in the days that followed. First came Erie's reunion with the River City Police Department. There were handshakes and slaps on the back and promises to "crucify those sickos." That was the first day. But after that, the camaraderie became strained, tentative as Erie pushed for updates on the investigation—and didn't get any.

Happier and simpler were the family reunions. Erie's neighbors Buster the cat and Sweetie the dog soon went home with their owners, who called to thank Erie, tell him he was a hero. When it came time for Ginger to leave the shelter where the impounded animals were being kept, Erie was there to see it. He said he just couldn't miss the sight of Jodi Marksberry together with her "sister" once again. But that was just an excuse. He really wanted to see Kent Cox, the police detective handling the case. They'd never been friends, but they'd been friendly. And now he wasn't returning Erie's phone calls.

Cox and Erie were a step behind Jodi and John Marksberry as they walked through the shelter, down the row of cages, past one wagging tail after another. An impatient bark echoed down the corridor, and Jodi broke from the herd, dashing to one of the last cages.

"Here she is! It's Ginger!" She got down on her knees and pressed her face up against the bars. "Hello, baby! Hello! I'm so glad to see you!"

Out came Ginger's tongue, slapping against Jodi's chin. The girl giggled.

"You sure that's your dog?" Cox asked Marksberry, smiling.

Marksberry smiled back. "Yeah," he said. "I'm pretty sure."

There were forms to fill out, a statement to make, a quick, quiet conference with Cox away from Erie, but then it was over for Jodi and John Marksberry. On their way out, Jodi's father offered again to pay Erie. Erie again refused.

"Neighbors, remember?"

Marksberry nodded. "Right."

They shook hands.

Erie nodded his head toward Cox. "So what did he have to say to you over there?"

"Oh, not much. He just asked us to be 'discrete.' You know. While the investigation's still going on."

"Discrete?"

"That's what the man said."

"You know," Erie was about to reply, "he told the Greeks and the Wingates the same thing. And I don't know why."

But before Erie could get the words out of his mouth, Jodi Marksberry ran up and gave him a hug. Then she was dragging her father toward the door, anxious to get Ginger home. Marksberry chuckled and let his daughter haul him away.

When they were gone, the sound of laughter went with them. The Marksberrys had left with one animal out of forty three at the shelter. Erie recognized several of the dogs and cats still in cages. He walked up to one, a cat, and waved his fingers at her. She watched him with big, yellow, impassive eyes. She looked exactly like his cat Goldie, minus Goldie's substantial girth.

"What about these guys?" Erie asked Cox.

Cox shrugged. "We haven't been able to track down all the owners. We went through that pile of collars, but a lot of 'em didn't have tags. The ones we can't place...I guess they stay here."

"Why don't you make some kind of announcement? The press would eat up a story like this. I'm surprised they haven't been all over it already."

Cox shrugged again, looking uncomfortable.

"Come on, Kent. What's going on?"

"What are you talking about? Nothing's 'going on.'"

Cox tried to put some snap in his voice, but his heart didn't seem to be in it.

"This investigation's screwy somehow. I can smell it," Erie said. *"What is going on?"*

Cox scowled and shrugged and shook his head all at once, resentment and frustration and regret swirling together.

"Just drop it, Erie. Drop it."

The snap was really there this time. So Erie dropped it.

For a couple hours.

Erie didn't have to get out of his car and flag down Hal Allen. He didn't even have to watch for his old boss too closely. He simply parked across the street from Allen's house and waited.

Allen had been doing his police work from behind a desk for almost a decade, but he'd still have the eye. Without even trying to, without even wanting to, he would notice something different in his neighborhood—something like a man sitting in an unfamiliar car in the dusky gloom alone.

Allen pulled into his driveway a little before seven. Erie watched him get out of his car, walk around to the back, pretend to look for something in the trunk. He was trying to get a better look at the strange car across the street.

Erie brought up his right hand, the back of the hand to Allen, and curled his fingers twice—the international gesture for "come 'ere."

Allen's eye was sharp indeed. He slammed the trunk closed and walked over to Erie's car. Erie rolled down his window. Neither man spoke until Allen was just a few feet from the car.

"Larry. It's you. Hi." Allen's expression was pleasant, his voice soft. But something underneath was neither. "Sorry I haven't gotten back to you. You wouldn't believe how crazy things have been downtown the last few days."

"Maybe I would."

Allen tried to give him a puzzled look, as if he had no idea what Erie was taking about. Erie didn't buy it. Allen wasn't a game player by nature. It was one of the reasons Erie liked him.

"Come on, Hal. Let's not B.S. each other. I want talk to you about this case of mine."

Allen smiled quizzically. "What? The dog thing?"

His acting wasn't getting any better.

"You know it's 'the dog thing.' Just get in the car and talk to me about it for five minutes. That's all I'm asking."

Allen acknowledged defeat with a sigh, then walked around the car to the passenger door. It was already unlocked. He slid in next to Erie.

"Listen, Larry," he said, "everyone was hoping this conversation wouldn't have to happen. And as far as the rest of the world is concerned, it *didn't*. Do you understand?"

"Of course, Hal. I'm not trying to get anyone in trouble here. I just want to know why you guys are acting like these nickel-and-dime bunchers shot Kennedy or something."

"Don't 'you guys' me on this, Larry. This isn't Homicide's show. It's Special Investigations in the hot seat."

Erie groaned. "Oh, geez. Is that what this is about? Politics? Did I embarrass somebody in S.I. by doing his job for him?"

"Yeah, it's politics. But not inside the department. It's bigger than that."

Erie was getting wound up, ready to rail about egos and petty rivalries in the RCPD, when Allen's words sunk in.

"Bigger? Over a couple redneck psychos? How could they have any political juice?"

"They don't. They don't need any."

Erie frowned. "I don't get it."

Allen stared out the window, obviously debating whether to go on or simply go.

"You might as well tell me, Hal. If you don't, I'll just dig it out some other way."

"I know you would. That's why you should've been brought in on this. But some people aren't sure if you're still...trustworthy."

Erie rewound the words in his head, played them over, unable to believe he'd heard them right.

"What do you mean?"

"Look," Allen said, his voice softer now—so soft Erie knew his next words were *really* going to sting. "After you retired, you dropped off the face of the earth. Nobody saw you or heard from you for months. Then you pop back up calling yourself a P.I., driving around chasing lost dogs. I guess people aren't sure what to make of you anymore."

"People don't have to make anything of me. I'm still *me*."

"Larry, you are still a friend, O.K.? But you're not a cop. Not anymore. That changes things."

The words stabbed Erie so deeply he almost winced.

You're not one of us now, Allen was saying. *You're one of* them.

"Forget the excuses," Erie snapped. "I just want to know if this case is gonna get buried."

"Not entirely."

"For God's sake, talk straight."

"Shut up for a second and I will!"

Erie opened his mouth to say something, closed it, nodded.

Allen took a deep breath before speaking again. "Believe me, a couple days ago, S.I. was all pumped up about nailing these creeps. Kent Cox kept hammering away at 'em until one of 'em—the guy—opened up, blabbed out the whole scam. That's when things got screwy."

Erie raised his eyebrows. *Scam?* the gesture said.

"They were grabbing animals, whatever they could find," Allen explained, "and selling them to the zoo."

Erie stared at Allen for a quiet moment, his brain unable to make the leap.

"The Hoosier Zoo was buying dogs and cats?" he said.

Allen nodded wordlessly, letting Erie work it out.

The Hoosier Zoological Garden and Wildlife Refuge was River City's one and only tourist attraction. But there wasn't much that was attractive about it. Run down, perennially strapped for cash, it had been on the verge of closing for years. So many corners had been cut there it was a wonder anything was left in the middle.

Erie had heard a hundred stories about the place. Every cop in town had. After all, it was the cops who had to come chase down kangaroos when they hopped over fences that were too low. It was the cops who had to root out the teenage vandals who ran wild through the place every other weekend because it was so easy to break in. And it was the cops—by unspoken order of the mayor—who stayed quiet about all of it.

And now the zoo was buying dogs and cats? *Dead* dogs and cats? It didn't make any sense. Unless....

"Oh, no. You've gotta be kidding."

Erie looked at Allen. He wasn't kidding.

At first, Bass couldn't believe it either. Erie waited a while to talk to him about it, unsure if he was going to tell anyone that his last question about the case had been answered. He finally decided to tell two people, and Bass was the first.

Erie could've timed it better. Bass was behind the wheel of his pickup when Erie told him. He took his eyes off the road to stare in disbelief at Erie for an uncomfortably long time.

"Am I hearin' what I think I'm hearin'?"

Erie wrapped his arms around the cat carrier in his lap and

stomped on the invisible air-brakes on the passenger side of Bass's pickup. Bass turned back to his driving and stepped on the real brakes just in time to avoid rear-ending a semi trailer. When they'd come to a complete stop, Erie lifted the carrier and looked inside. Goldie's miniature doppelgänger from the shelter meowed at him. Bass checked the rear-view mirror. The dog tied up in the back of the pickup—*his* dog, the one Erie had browbeat him into adopting at the shelter—was fine, too.

"Sorry 'bout that," Bass mumbled. "So you're sayin' the zoo's feedin' all them lions and tigers and such people's *pets*?"

"Apparently they're buying all the roadkill they can get their hands on," Erie said. "Twenty five cents a pound."

"And those two blankety-blank unmentionables we met— roadkill just wasn't bringing in enough money for 'em?"

"That's it. Their contact at the zoo didn't ask a lot of questions. He was desperate. Another budget crunch. The zoo can't afford all the slaughterhouse meat it needs, so he had to supplement. As long as it was an animal and it was dead, he bought it."

Bass shook his head in disgust. "That's…it's…I can't even think of a word for it. If people found out about this—"

"It would finish the zoo for good. Exactly. That's why no one's supposed to find out. The D.A.'s working on a quiet little deal right now. There'll be no animal cruelty charges, no attempted murder charges. Those two psychos'll plead no contest to everything else, so there won't be a messy trial. They'll do their two years while everyone else forgets this ever happened."

"Well, maybe not *everyone*. We're goin' on this little detour for a reason, am I right?"

Bass looked over to give Erie a significant look. Erie acknowledged it with a nod, then tilted his head toward the road.

"Yeah, yeah, I'm drivin', I'm drivin'," Bass grumbled.

A few minutes later, they were pulling into the parking lot of the Hoosier Zoological Garden and Wildlife Refuge.

Erie wasn't supposed to be there. He was supposed to keep his head down and his mouth shut, show that he could still be trusted, that he was still a team player. That's what Hal Allen had implied.

But Erie didn't particularly care if the RCPD saw him as a team player. He wasn't on that team anymore.

There were only about a dozen cars in the parking lot. Another slow, uneventful day for the Hoosier Zoo. Well, Erie was about to change that. He was going to have a word with the executive director.

Maybe the cops and the D.A. were going to shut their eyes, but Erie was keeping his open. He was going to keep on looking. And if he saw something he didn't like, he was going to do more than watch.

"This won't take long," Erie said as he climbed out of the truck.

"You want me to tag along?"

Erie gave his friend a small, grateful smile. "I'll be fine."

"O.K., then. I'll be waitin' for you right here."

"Thanks."

Erie closed the door and started to walk away, but the sound of whimpering drew him to the back of the truck. Bass's new dog was staring at him, whining. Erie reached out and stroked the sad-eyed mutt's sleek fur. She tried to jump up to lick his face.

She wasn't one of the animals he'd saved. She'd already been at the shelter for nearly two weeks. If she'd gone unadopted one more day, she would have been euthanized.

"Alright, settle down, we'll have you home soon," Erie told her.

She wailed mournfully when he headed toward the entrance to the zoo.

"Calm down! I'll be back!" he called to her over his shoulder.

Talking to animals again. Crazy.

The dog was watching him intently, her tail wagging.

No, it wasn't so crazy. She understood him. Not the words maybe. But friendship, kindness, compassion—that she understood. Better than some people.

Erie told the sleepy-eyed woman behind the ticket window that he was there on business. She waved him on, uninterested, and he pushed his way through the turnstile into the zoo, not worried about being alone when he came back out.

Who needs a team? He had a pack.

148

DIDN'T DO NOTHING

Every day, Scottie Crocker walked past Jayzee's corner on his way to the store for a Coke. And every day, one of Jayzee's guys would waddle after him, imitating him, babbling, maybe even drooling. Scottie had learned to ignore them.

Then one day Jayzee himself actually spoke to Scottie. Jayzee you couldn't ignore.

"Hey, Crackhead!" Jayzee said. "Come here!"

All the young people in the neighborhood called Scottie "Crackhead." Some of the older people, too. When it first started, Scottie tried to argue.

"I ain't no crackhead!"

He always got the same answer.

"No, you just act like one!" And laughter.

So Scottie stopped fighting it, and when Jayzee said, "Hey, Crackhead! Come here!" Scottie walked over and said, "What?"

"You know Goldfinger, right?"

"You...you mean Michael Gra-...Graham? D-down on 81st St-...Street?"

It was hard for Scottie to get words out when he was nervous—and Jayzee made him nervous. Jayzee was a few years younger than Scottie, no older than eighteen or nineteen, but he had a confidence, a fierce fearlessness, that Scottie knew he'd never have no matter how long he lived.

"Yeah, yeah, *him*," Jayzee said.

"I...I know him. I went to school wi-wi-...with his sister."

Jayzee's guys snickered.

"Didn't know you ever went to school, Crackhead," one of them said.

"Sure he did," another cackled. "Crackhead went to retard school."

"Oh, yeah," the first one said. "Used to see him ridin' the short bus."

"I ain't no retard!"

Scottie knew immediately that he'd made a mistake. That was his problem. People would lay traps for him, the same traps over and over, but he never recognized them until it was too late.

The guys' eyes lit up, and it was just a matter of who would say it first.

No, you just act like one.

Jayzee spoke first. But he *didn't* say it.

"Hey, hey, back off," he told his guys. He snaked an arm around Scottie's neck. "Crackhead's my man—ain't you, Crackhead?"

"Sure," Scottie said. Because his mistake had reminded him to be cautious.

"Good. Cuz I need you to do somethin' for me. And if you do it right, I'll give you twenty dollars."

The guys whistled and whooped.

"Twenty dollars, Crackhead!" one of them said, punching Scottie's arm. "That's a lot of money!"

"Wh-what I gotta do?"

Jayzee smiled. "Nothin'. Just go over to Goldfinger's corner— 81st and Langley—and take a walk around." He reached into his jacket pocket and pulled out a cell phone. "Then push this button—this one right here. See it? 'Redial'? Can you read that?"

"Sure."

"What I tell you?" Jayzee said to his guys. "My man here ain't no retard." When he turned back to Scottie, his smile had grown even bigger. "When you push that button, the phone'll call me. And when I pick up, you just tell me who over there with Goldfinger and what they doin' and what side of the street they on. But don't let Goldfinger see you, understand?"

"Sure."

"Good. That's it. That's all you gotta do. Can you do it?"

"Yeah, I...I guess."

"Alright! That's my man!" Jayzee slapped Scottie on the back. "I give you the money when you get back."

"O.K."

"Alright then."

Scottie stood there a moment, confused by this break in his daily routine of watching TV and going to the store for Cokes and heading home for more TV.

"Well, *go*, Crackhead," Jayzee said, still smiling.

"Ri-...right now?"

"Yeah, right now. Go on."

Jayzee's guys laughed as Scottie walked away. Certain people were always laughing when Scottie was around. He didn't know why. He didn't think he was funny.

It took Scottie fifteen minutes to walk to 81st Street. In that time, he left his neighborhood and entered another. There were no border checkpoints, no men in uniform asking for passports, but most men Scottie's age would have been unwelcome foreigners there. They would have seen the warnings—graffiti, glares, posture, gestures—and they would have left. Quickly.

But Scottie was different. He didn't see the danger signs, and because he didn't see them, they had no power. And because they had no power they had no reason for being. The slouch of his shoulders, the perpetual bend in his knees, the trudging rhythm of his gait, his breathy mumbling and unfocused eyes—it charged him like a magnet. He didn't attract attention here. He repelled it. He wasn't a threat, so he could be ignored.

Michael Graham—"Goldfinger"—ignored him, too.

"I saw Mi-Michael with his little br-...brother Ronnie and another guy," Scottie told Jayzee over the phone. He was in an alley a half-block from Goldfinger's corner. "A man pulled up in a car and th-they talked and then he drove a-...away."

"Which side of the street they on?"

Scottie thought hard. "The closer side."

"Closer to our neighborhood? You mean the north side?"

"Yeah. I g-guess."

"And it was just the three of 'em?"

"Yeah."

"Who went up to talk to the guy in the car?"

"Michael."

"You sure about that? *Goldfinger* walked up to the car?"

"Yeah. I'm su-sure."

"By himself?"

"Yeah."

"Damn," Jayzee said. He didn't sound angry, though. He sounded surprised and pleased. He even laughed. "You my man, Crackhead. I see you later."

Scottie stuffed the phone into his pocket and headed home. When he got back to his own street, Jayzee was still on his corner. But only one of his guys was with him—a skinny kid called "Freak." Jayzee's other guys were gone.

Jayzee held out his hand.

"Phone," he said.

Scottie dug the cell phone out and handed it over.

Jayzee didn't look at the phone as it slid into his palm. His eyes stayed locked on Scottie, piercing him, pinning him in place.

Scottie couldn't hold the gaze. He looked down at his shoes.

When he looked back up, Jayzee was smiling.

"You did good, Crackhead," Jayzee said. He turned to Freak. "Give the man his money."

Freak guffawed.

"What are you laughin' at?" Jayzee snarled. "I said give my man Crackhead twenty dollars."

The laughter choked to a stop, and Freak slowly pulled a wad of money from his jacket and counted out twenty ones and gave them to Scottie.

Scottie couldn't believe how light and small and dry the bills were. He didn't expect twenty dollars to feel that way. He thought it would be heavier.

"You did good," Jayzee said again. "Maybe I'll need you to take another walk for me sometime."

"O.K.," Scottie said.

"Hey, Crackhead," Freak said as Scottie turned to go. "Gimme that money back and I'll give you somethin' good."

Scottie kept walking. He already knew what he wanted. He had to take the bus and walk six blocks and then take the bus again, and by the time he got back he only had a few pennies and dimes left, but it was worth it.

When Scottie's aunt Nichelle came home from her night job, she found him in front of the TV with his ten-year-old cousin Keesha. They were playing *Super Mario Bros. 3* on the battered old Nintendo Scottie had purchased that afternoon at a Funcoland on Cicero.

"Where'd you get that?" Nichelle asked. There wasn't much snap in her words. She worked three jobs to support herself and Keesha and Scottie. She didn't have the energy for snap.

It took Scottie a few seconds to answer. Mario was jumping, grabbing magic coins out of the air.

"I bought it."

"Where'd you get the money?"

"Jayzee Clements gave it to me."

"Jayzee Clements? Why would he give anything to you?"

"I did somethin' for him."

A giant plant snapped at Mario, almost swallowing him, and Scottie grunted and cursed. Keesha giggled and said, "Hey!"

"What'd you do for Jayzee?"

Scottie shrugged without turning to look at his aunt. "Nothin'."

"Make up your mind, Scottie. Did you do *somethin'* or did you do *nothin'*?"

Scottie began to breathe hard, almost panting. It was the sound he made when he couldn't make words, when the circuit between his brain and his mouth overloaded, shorted out.

On the screen, Mario hopped and ran and hopped and ran until he ran when he should have hopped. He plummeted off a cloud, disappearing from the screen, and Keesha shouted, "My turn! My turn!"

Scottie handed her the controller and finally looked around at Nichelle.

"I bought McDonald's, too," he said. "We saved you some fries."

He wasn't panting anymore. He was smiling.

Nichelle didn't return his smile. Instead, she took in a deep breath and held it for a moment, as if unsure what to do with the air in her lungs—talk, yell, scream, sigh.

In the end, she did none of these things. She simply turned and walked into the kitchen. It was almost ten o'clock, and she hadn't had dinner.

Scottie found out Goldfinger was dead nearly a week later. Scottie was in church with Nichelle and Keesha, and some of the ladies were shaking their heads about that poor Michael Graham, had so much promise once. Scottie thought it was sad, too.

A few days after that, Jayzee stopped him on the street again.

"Hey, Crocker!" Jayzee called out.

Not "Crackhead." *Crocker.*

"I got another secret mission for ya', C," Jayzee said when Scottie got close. "You know Marcus Dillard?"

He did. Scottie spent the next day following him, just as Jayzee asked. It was like a game, watching Marcus, trying not to be seen, and Scottie enjoyed it. He found himself moving more quickly, *thinking* more quickly than he had in years.

He reported back to Jayzee the next morning. He stammered at first, fighting with the words. But for once Scottie won that fight, and the words started to come quickly, obey him.

"...and then he went to the building where Ricky Thompson lives and he talked to Ricky outside and Ricky gave him somethin' in a brown bag and they looked at me so I went around the corner. And when I came back Marcus was gone so I looked for him and I found him walkin' up Calumet and he stopped and got a burrito and then he started walkin' again. And Dion Baker was drivin' by in a car and he got out and Marcus gave him the thing he'd been

154

carryin' and...."

By the time Scottie was finished, Jayzee and his guys were laughing. But Scottie could tell it was a different kind of laughter this time, a kind he rarely heard. He didn't understand it until Jayzee, shaking his head, said, "Damn, C. You really got you some eyes, don't you?"

It was good. Scottie had done *good*.

Jayzee gave him another twenty dollars, and Scottie bought more old games for his Nintendo and a frozen pizza and a birthday present for Keesha—a pink Dora the Explorer backpack he found at Goodwill—even though her birthday had come and gone two months before. Scottie hadn't worked in years, not since he'd lost his job sweeping up at McDonald's because he forgot to show up sometimes, and he yelled at the customers when they called him "retard" and "Crackhead." So for once Scottie had his own money to buy Keesha a gift, and it didn't matter to him if it was her birthday or not. Aunt Nichelle didn't ask any questions this time, and Scottie felt something he hadn't felt in so long he'd forgotten he could feel it. Pride.

A few days later, Marcus Dillard and Ricky Thompson were dead.

They were found together in a dumpster, both of them shot in the chest. Scottie's pride turned sour, bubbling in his stomach as if he'd swallowed something rancid. He wasn't sure why he felt that way. No one knew who'd killed Marcus and Ricky, and *Scottie* certainly hadn't hurt anybody. But the pain in his gut wouldn't go away.

There was a memorial service for Marcus at Scottie's church, and Scottie and Nichelle and Keesha went. The body was there, in an open casket, and Scottie almost expected Marcus to sit up and say something to him, say something *about* him.

But just looking at a dead man can't bring him back to life, Scottie told himself. Just like looking at a living man can't kill him.

Scottie avoided Jayzee's corner after that, going blocks out of his way when he went to the store. He avoided certain thoughts in the same way—sidestepping them, not taking the most direct route from point A to point B. He didn't think about why he was staying away from Jayzee. He didn't think about why he'd stopped playing his Nintendo games. He tried not to think about any *whys* at all.

But it wasn't easy to avoid Jayzee—not if *he* wanted to see *you*.

One day when Scottie was in the store buying himself a Coke, he turned to find Freak behind him, blocking his way out.

"Hey, Crackhead," Freak said. "Whatcha doin'?"

Scottie shrugged. "N-n-...nothin'."

"Good. Then you can come with me."

Freak wrapped a hand around Scottie's arm and pulled him toward the door. Even after they were outside, the hand remained, steering Scottie to Jayzee's corner.

Jayzee greeted them with a big smile. "C! Where you been, my man?"

"I...I b-been...I been around."

"Not where *I* could see you."

There was still a smile on Jayzee's face, but Scottie couldn't hear any smile in his voice.

"I...I j-just...I...."

Words abandoned Scottie, and he began to huff out hard puffs of air in their place.

"Hey, C! Don't get like that," Jayzee said, sounding friendly again. He threw an arm around Scottie's shoulders and pulled him in tight. "I was just worried somethin' was wrong, that's all."

Scottie's breathing slowed. Jayzee's smiling face was just inches from his own, so close they were inhaling the same air. Scottie tried to smile back.

"N-nothin's wrong," Scottie said, unsure if his words were true or not.

"Yeah?"

"Yeah."

Jayzee's hand squeezed the flesh between Scottie's shoulder and neck. It felt reassuring at first, but the pressure increased, began to pinch, swaying on the line between pleasure and pain.

"You'd tell me, wouldn't you?" Jayzee said. "If somethin' was wrong?"

Scottie nodded. "Y-yeah. Sure."

Jayzee let go of Scottie and took a step back.

"Good. Cuz I need you again."

"N-need...me?"

"That's right, C. You know Antoine Miller, right?"

Everyone knew Antoine Miller—knew to stay away, unless they were in the market for something he could provide. He had a corner of his own, guys of his own, just like Jayzee.

Just like Michael Graham.

"Sure," Scottie said.

"Go do your James Bond thing on him. See what he's doin' and how he does it." Jayzee slipped a hand into his jacket pocket and pulled something out. "Then use this."

Scottie looked down.

The cell phone.

Scottie didn't take it.

"I...I...."

"You *what?*" Jayzee said. He was still holding his hand out to Scottie. The phone hung between them like a bridge.

"I...I wanna know. Wh-...what's gonna happen?"

Freak and the rest of Jayzee's guys had been snorting, snickering, whispering. But suddenly they were totally silent. Totally still.

Scottie wasn't sure what he expected Jayzee to say until Jayzee didn't say it. Scottie expected a laugh, he realized. He expected "Whatta you mean, C? Nothin's gonna happen."

But what Jayzee said was, "Why you wanna know that?"

The way he said it, it didn't sound mean or angry. It didn't even sound like a question. It sounded like advice.

"Well, what...what if—?"

Jayzee cut Scottie off with a sigh. "What am I askin' you to do, C? Look a little. Talk a little. Well, lookin' and talkin' don't hurt nobody, right? Whatever else happens—" Jayzee shrugged. "That ain't you."

Scottie hesitated, thinking it over.

"B-but what if—"

"You afraid somebody might get hurt?" Jayzee snapped. He did sound angry now. He was losing his patience.

Still, Scottie nodded.

"Well, stop worryin' about people you don't even know. You oughta be worried about *Keesha.*" Jayzee's gazed flicked over to Freak for a split second. Freak's eyes brightened. "You oughta be worried about your aunt. *They* could get hurt. You hear what I'm sayin', retard?" He pushed the phone into Scottie's belly like a knife. "I ain't gonna explain anymore. You gonna do this thing."

Scottie took the phone.

Jayzee put another grin on his face, and Scottie saw for the first time how stiff and unnatural Jayzee's smile really was, like a plastic mask strapped to his face with a rubber band.

"That's my man," Jayzee said. "Don't worry, C—this is the last time I'll ask you to help me." His eyes connected with Freak's again, flashing some silent message. "The last time. I promise. Now go."

He sent Scottie on his way with a pat on the back. Jayzee's guys joined in as Scottie shuffled away, each of them slapping him between the shoulder blades as they giggled at some private joke.

"Thanks, Crackhead."

"You can do it, Crackhead."

"Yeah, go get 'em, Crackhead."

And the last words, from Freak.

"See ya' later, Crackhead."

It took Scottie ten minutes to walk to Antoine Miller's corner. Houses and apartment buildings and cars and people slid past unseen as he shambled along. He was thinking about what was going to happen to Antoine—and anyone standing nearby when it happened. He thought about how he'd never meant to hurt anybody, and how that didn't matter. You could hurt someone by doing practically nothing at all. He thought about the people he would hurt if he did nothing now—Keesha and Aunt Nichelle, maybe even himself. And when he saw Antoine Miller, he knew what he had to do.

"He's on the west side of Eb-Eb-...Eberhart Avenue," Scottie told Jayzee over the phone. "There's another guy wi-with him who goes up to the cars and talks to the dr-dr-...drivers. Then he calls Antoine over and Antoine g-g-gives him something in a bag."

"Antoine comes to the car with the stuff?"

"Yeah."

"And it's just him and one other guy there now?"

"Yeah."

A muffled rumble came over the line, the sound of Jayzee putting his hand over the phone and saying something to his guys. Then the rumbling stopped, and Jayzee was back, his voice clear and bright.

"Go home. Right now. Stay there."

"O.K."

"We shouldn't be seen talkin' to each other today. Freak'll give you your money tonight. Meet him in the alley behind your building at midnight."

"O.K."

"Don't tell anybody you're goin' to see him. It's a secret, right? Just between us."

"O.K."

There was a long pause, and just as Scottie began to think Jayzee was gone, Jayzee spoke again.

"Goodbye, C," he said.

"Bye, Jayzee."

Jayzee hung up then, so Scottie turned the phone off and put it back in his pocket.

"S-see?" he said to the burly man who'd been leaning in close, his ear just inches from the phone while Scottie and Jayzee spoke.

"How do I know that was really Jayzee Clements?" Antoine Miller asked. He was glaring at Scottie skeptically, like someone might look at a unicorn or an angel—something too good to be true. It was the same expression he'd been wearing ever since Scottie crossed the street and walked up to him and his guys and said, "I g-got to tell you s-somethin'."

"I d-don't know. It just...is," Scottie said with a shrug. "He'll send Tommy and...B-Boost. They're probably on their way now. Jayzee'll stay on his corner a-a-...alone with Freak."

"If this is some kinda trick, retard, I swear I'll hunt you down and mess you up," Antoine growled.

"I ain't l-lyin'."

Antoine went on staring at Scottie for a long time, his guys gathered silently around him, waiting for his signal, ready to sneer, laugh, kill.

"Naw," Antoine finally said, "you're too dumb to lie this good, ain't you?"

Then he turned away and started barking out orders.

"T.T., Ray—go get Tonio and have him drive you down to Jayzee's corner. You know what to do—just like we done with Jon-Jon and McNeil. Monk and me'll take care of things here. Monk, when that car pulls up, you go around behind it and I'll start toward the driver...."

They were ignoring Scottie, too absorbed in their war plans to waste any more time on the "retard." So he left.

Scottie took his time walking home. He was hoping he'd miss it all—return to find a quiet street, a deserted corner. Whatever he'd brought into his neighborhood, he didn't want to see it.

Not that he should feel guilty. None of it would be his fault. Jayzee said it himself: Lookin' don't hurt nobody. Talkin' don't hurt nobody. Whatever else happens, that ain't you, right?

When Scottie got back to his block, he saw the flashing lights of police cars and ambulances. A woman—someone's mom or aunt or sister—was out by Jayzee's corner, screaming. A crowd was gathered around, people pulled from in front of their televisions by the drama outside their doors. Some were trying to comfort the hysterical woman. Most simply stood nearby, watching.

Scottie didn't join them. Instead he went upstairs and switched on the TV and the Nintendo.

He turned the volume up loud.

TRICKS

No tricks. That was Larry Erie's goal for Halloween. No toilet paper in his trees. No soap on his car. No rotten eggs splattered against the side of his house.

The year before, Erie had been in a daze. Newly widowed, newly retired, he hadn't even realized it was Halloween until the doorbell rang and he found Batman, Yoda and a Powerpuff Girl on his front porch. The only "treats" he had on hand were Oreo cookies, so that's what they got. When those ran out, he tried giving away bananas, but most of the kids refused to take them. After a while, Erie just turned off the lights and stopped answering the doorbell.

The next morning, he had to hose down the front of the house, drive to a carwash and pick long sheets of Charmin from the branches of his elm trees.

So this year, Erie was prepared. He'd asked Andrew Smith, one of the few teenagers he knew, what kind of treats kids really want.

"Everybody loves Snickers," Andrew told him. "And Reese's Peanut Butter Cups. What you don't want to give out is that cheap chewy crap in the orange and black wrappers. Or fruit. Man, that'll get you egged before midnight!"

Erie figured Andrew knew what he was talking about: He was the kind of kid who would've thrown a few eggs himself over the years. So he followed Andrew's advice, and the day before Halloween he'd bought enough Snickers and Reese's Peanut Butter Cups to feed a small army—which was exactly how Erie thought of trick-or-treaters. They were like little Vikings who invade once a year, sacking and pillaging the villages that don't give in to their demands for candy.

Come Halloween morning, Erie was sitting in his kitchen sipping coffee and munching on a mini Snickers, figuring he had more than enough to get him through the day unscathed. Then the phone rang.

"Hello?"

"Morning, Larry! Cy Reed here. I was wondering if you were up to anything just now."

"Uhhh...no. Not really."

"Good! Why don't you come over to the zoo then? I've got a little problem that could use the Larry Erie touch."

"Oh. What kind of problem?"

"I'll fill you in when you get here. So I'll see you in—what? Fifteen minutes?"

"Well, I—"

"Alright, twenty then. It's a bit of an emergency, so the sooner the better. And of course I know I can rely on your legendary discretion."

"Oh. Sure. But I—"

"Great! See you soon!"

Click.

Erie hung up, then simply stood there, staring at the phone. After a few seconds, he turned away and poured himself more coffee. Caffeine, that's what he needed. Because he wasn't sure if that phone call had been real or a dream.

The first and last time Erie had spoken to Cy Reed had been six weeks before. A neighborhood girl had asked Erie to track down her dog, and the trail led to a couple of hardcore rednecks who picked up beer money selling roadkill to the local zoo. When they couldn't find enough dead deer and half-flattened skunks, it turned out, they supplemented their haul with people's pets. So Erie had marched into the Hoosier Zoological Garden and Wildlife Refuge, cornered the man in charge and announced that if he found out any more dogs and cats were being turned into Tiger Chow he was going to take the story straight to the *Herald-Times*.

The man in charge was Cy Reed, and his reaction wasn't what Erie had expected. He didn't deny everything. He didn't throw around words like "slander" and "libel" and "lawsuit." He didn't call for security guards to drag Erie away. Instead he nodded sadly and said, "Don't worry, Larry. It won't happen again."

They were in Reed's office, and around them on the walls were pictures of the zoo director with local politicians and celebrities and well-dressed men and women Erie assumed were big donors. Reed had been a River City fixture for years, showing up on call-in shows and at street fairs and parades, usually with a parrot on his shoulder or a lion cub in his lap, always shilling for the Hoosier Zoo.

A man like that had to be smooth. He had to know how to tell people what they wanted to hear. Erie fixed him with a hard gaze, unwilling to let his guard down.

"*Really?*"

"Really," Reed said. He was an elderly man, somewhere north of seventy, and he seemed to shrivel even more before Erie's eyes. "I'm not as sharp as I used to be. The details around here—they're getting harder to keep track of every day. So I rely on my people. And...you know we're a small zoo. We don't have money just lying around. So people look for ways to cut corners. Sometimes they—"

Reed slammed the palm of his hand onto the desk before him, and suddenly he seemed years younger.

"But those are excuses. Here's what you want to hear: I've been told all about that 'meat' we bought, and it sickened me as much as it sickened you. The appropriate parties have been disciplined, and new rules have been put in place to ensure that nothing like this ever happens again."

"Good," Erie said. "That *is* what I wanted to hear."

"So we can consider this matter closed?"

Erie knew what that meant. Reed wasn't really asking whether "the matter" would stay closed. He was asking about Erie's mouth.

"Like I said before, as long as I don't hear about anything else like this...." Erie shrugged. "Sure. It's closed."

Reed stood up and reached a withered hand across the desk to Erie. Erie took it, and they shook.

"I'm glad we understand each other," Reed said. He stepped around his desk. "You're a private detective, you say."

It didn't sound like a question, so Erie didn't treat it like one. If he had, the answer would have been "Occasionally," which always led to follow-up questions Erie didn't like. He was retired and he had nothing better to do and sometimes things happened, that's all. It always sounded dumb to say it.

Reed pointed at one of the framed photographs on the wall. "So tell me, Mr. Private Eye. Who do you think that is?"

Erie squinted at the picture. "That would be you. With Marlin Perkins."

Reed grinned. "You're good. I'd say that young man up there looks as much like me as an egg looks like a pile of chicken bones. You know, I worked for ol' Marlin at the Lincoln Park Zoo up in Chicago. A fine man. He told me something once I've never forgotten...."

"Ol' Marlin" had said a lot of interesting things, it turned out. Erie politely listened to Reed spin yarns for almost half an hour before a portly, bearded man walked in without knocking and started handing Reed papers to sign.

"Sorry, Larry. Duty calls," Reed had said, and Erie left the zoo actually liking the man.

And now, a month and a half later, he was going back to see Reed again. On his way to the zoo, Erie wondered exactly what kind of problem would require "the Larry Erie touch."

When he walked up to the front gate, a zoo employee was washing something that looked like blood off the turnstiles.

"You Leary?" the woman asked him.

"Not quite. Larry Erie."

"Yeah, you're the guy. Overbeck said you could take a look at this if you got here before I was done."

She slapped her sponge into a bucket of pink suds. The water sloshed, sending the smell of ammonia into the air. The woman leaned against the ticket booth nearby, pulled off her rubber gloves and lit a cigarette.

"Who's Overbeck?"

"Assistant director," she said. "Go on. Have at it."

"What exactly am I having at?"

The woman shrugged and blew out a cloud of smoke. "I don't think I'm supposed to have an opinion," she said.

Erie leaned in close to the metal bars of the turnstiles. There were three sets of three, rising from ankle level to waist level to shoulder level. They were wrapped in a cage of more bars, and the only way for a paying customer to get in or out of the zoo was to step up to the turnstiles, grab one and move forward, like using a revolving door. Most of the red smears were on one of the middle bars—where someone would take hold and push. The smears looked like they'd been fingerprints before the ammonia began working on them.

"Who told you to wipe this off?"

"Overbeck."

Erie had no idea who "Overbeck" was, but already he didn't like him.

He looked at the bars again, scowling. If some kind of crime had been committed, why destroy crucial evidence?

"It's 9:30," the woman said, answering the question she could read on his face. "We open in half an hour."

"I see."

"You done there?"

"Yeah, I guess."

"Then go on in. They're waiting for you in the Monkey House."

Erie moved through the turnstiles by using his foot to push the lowest bar. He didn't ask for directions. He could have found his destination blindfolded thanks to the unmistakable odor that pointed the way like a neon arrow.

The Monkey House was the first big building in the zoo, up a path past a ramshackle souvenir shop. The monkeys and apes were free to go in and out, moving from outdoor chain link cages to barred indoor habitats as they pleased. As Erie approached the entrance, he spotted a pair of lemurs swinging happily on ropes. Across from them, in another cage, sat a big, gray-bearded chimpanzee. There were other chimps roaming around listlessly behind the fence with him, but he was different. He was watching Erie.

The old chimp was perched on a large rock and had something clutched in the long, curled fingers of his right hand. The ape lifted the hand out toward Erie, as if offering him something. Curious, Erie stopped.

"Hello," he said.

The chimp lifted his right arm up over his head, then brought it back down.

Was that a wave?

Erie smiled.

"He wants you to come closer," someone said.

Erie turned to find a fiftyish woman stepping out of the Monkey House. Her salt-and-pepper hair was spiky short, and she had piercing green eyes that glared at him through wire-rimmed glasses. She was wearing a zoo uniform.

"Why?" Erie asked her.

"So he can hit you with that shit he's got in his hand."

Erie took another look at what the chimp was holding, then backed away from the cage. "Why would he throw feces at me?"

The woman gave him a "Well, *duh*" look.

"Because he thinks it's funny," she said. "So you're the detective, huh?"

Erie nodded, aware that he'd already failed to impress the woman with his keen powers of observation and deduction.

"Yes," he said. "Larry Erie. And you are?"

"Bea Huff. The curator."

She rushed over the words, not offering to shake his hand.

"Come on. You better a get a look at the scene of the crime before it gets hosed down."

She turned and headed into the Monkey House, pushing

through a pair of metal doors with glass window panes. One of the windows had been shattered, and the shards crackled under Erie's feet as he followed the woman into the building.

Cy Reed was waiting inside with another zoo employee—the bearded man who'd barged into Reed's office six weeks before. The man had wide eyes and sweat-soaked underarms, but Reed was all smiles.

"Larry! Thanks for coming on such short notice." Reed moved forward using an ornately carved cane—though he didn't seem to have a limp—and gave Erie's hand a firm shake. "This is Bill Overbeck, our assistant director."

The bearded man stepped up and gave Erie's hand a shake that was all the more limp and moist in comparison to Reed's.

"Hi...thanks...we appreciate this," he muttered without looking Erie in the eye.

Erie's opinion of the man didn't improve upon meeting him.

"And you've already been introduced to Bea, I take it," Reed said.

"I rescued him from Corny," Huff told him.

Reed chuckled. "That old devil. If only they'd kidnapped *him*."

"There'd be a hell of a lot more blood, that's for sure," Huff said.

Erie held up his hands. "Hold on, guys. Maybe you better tell me what's going on."

Reed nodded. "Right. Of course. Well, you see, Larry, we're a small operation without the budget to—"

Erie braced himself for a few minutes of familiar spin, but Huff spared him.

"One of our animals is missing," she cut in. "A capuchin monkey named Maggie. When I came in this morning, she was gone, and the capuchin habitat looked like that."

She pointed toward one of the cages nearby. Erie didn't see anything out of the ordinary at first, just faux rock walls and a jumble of ropes and tire swings. But then a red smear caught his eye, and he moved closer.

There were two doors in the cage—a big one for humans, and a smaller one for the monkeys. The monkey door led outside, to an enclosure identical to the one where Corny sat, luring victims closer like a hairy siren. The human door had two bloody streaks near the knob.

Erie wanted to find out where that door went. He wanted to get a closer look at those streaks of blood. He wanted to get to work. But he stopped himself.

"Call the police," he said.

Reed smiled grimly and shook his head. Huff glared at Overbeck. Overbeck turned pale and stammered, "We've already... we can't...no. We decided. No police. Right, Cy?"

"We've already got problems with security, Larry," Reed said. "You've got to build zoos like prisons these days just to keep the real animals *out*. This place is nearly sixty years old. Any half-wit could break in with a ladder and a rope."

"Or less," Huff added bitterly.

Reed shot her a long-suffering glance before continuing. "And the truth of the matter is we simply don't have the funds to do anything about it. As you know, Larry, we've barely got enough money to keep the animals fed. We certainly don't have an extra hundred thousand to spend on motion detectors and silent alarms."

"That's too bad. But it still doesn't explain why you're not reporting a serious crime to the police."

"Copycats," Overbeck said.

"Excuse me?"

"Copycats," Overbeck said again, nodding emphatically in agreement with himself.

"Bill's concern—and I happen to share it—is that we'd be overrun by thieves and thrill-seekers if people realized how vulnerable we are," Reed explained. "Just last month we ran off a dozen college kids skinny-dipping in the duck pond. And last spring a couple of drunks broke in because they wanted to ride a zebra. One of them managed to shatter his pelvis, and now *he's* suing *us*. Can you imagine what would happen if it got out that you could actually get in here at night and steal a monkey? Our animals—all of them—would be in grave danger."

Reed was good. Oh, yes. Once the man found his footing, he could really shovel it out.

And it was working too. Erie found that the guilt and sense of responsibility Reed was shifting onto his shoulders actually had some weight.

"So you want me to investigate?"

"Yes," Overbeck said.

"Quietly," said Reed.

Huff fumed wordlessly. It was obvious who'd been overruled that morning.

"I'll do what I can," Erie said. "But if I think there's something more serious than monkeynapping going on, I'll have to go to the police."

"Of course, Larry. Of course," Reed said.

"It's not a 'monkeynapping,'" Huff snapped. "It's theft and it's cruelty and it's serious."

"Right. Sorry. No offense."

Huff didn't look appeased.

Erie turned away from her glare and pointed at the monkey cage. "So can I get up in there?"

"Follow me," Overbeck said. He headed for a door with the words "ZOO PERSONNEL ONLY" stenciled on it. Erie followed. So did Huff.

Overbeck pushed through the door into a small storage room and kitchen beyond, but Erie stopped to examine the knob. The metal around it was scratched and bent.

"Crowbar," Erie said. He looked back at the building's south entrance, the one he'd come in through. "Once they smashed the glass back there, they could reach around and unlock the doors by hand. This one they had to jimmy."

Erie looked at the other side of the door. As he expected, there were smears of blood there. There was blood on the floor, too—a trail of tiny droplets, dried to black. The droplets led to another door. On it was a sign printed from someone's computer.

"BE SURE TO SECURE DOOR BEHIND YOU!" it read. "SMART MONKEYS!!!"

"Whoever our bleeder is, he didn't cut himself on the glass breaking in," Erie said. "There's no blood on the outside of this door and no blood on the outside of the door into the monkey habitat. So he went in O.K. and came out not-so-O.K."

"It's obvious how the son of a bitch got himself hurt," Huff said. "The capuchins wouldn't let strangers just stroll in there and grab Maggie. They'd put up a fight. We don't need a detective to tell us that."

Erie almost started to explain that he was just trying to form a mental picture of the night's events, that it wasn't good to jump to any conclusions—even the seemingly obvious ones—until there was physical evidence to back it up. But he didn't. For whatever reason, Huff didn't like him. An explanation wouldn't change that. So he decided to form his mental picture more quietly while she was around.

"Just how big are capuchins anyway?" he asked.

Huff held her hands a little over a foot apart. "Yea big, not counting the tail. An adult male weighs about ten pounds, a female a little less. But don't let the size fool you. They can mess you up if they want to."

"And they're all outside right now?"

"Yeah. We closed off the access chute, so they can't get back in till we want 'em to."

Overbeck opened the door to the capuchin habitat. "It's safe, Harry. Come on," he said, his voice quivering with fussy anxiety.

Huff gestured toward the cage.

"Yeah, better get a move on, *Harry*," she said to Erie.

She was inexplicably hostile, but at least she seemed to know that his name was *Larry*.

Erie ignored her. If he could get away with it, he'd make that his permanent policy.

He followed Overbeck into the monkey habitat. For a few

seconds, he *really* regretted it.

Even from a distance, the zoo's apes and monkeys had a smell that was less than appealing. On the other side of the bars, the stench was downright appalling.

It was a struggle to keep his Snickers bar and coffee down, so he kept his tour of the habitat brief. There were more bloodstains on the floor, including the red outline of a footprint. Someone had stepped in blood, and it left behind the kind of print detectives love. It was so clear Erie recognized the brand (Nike) and could make a good guess on the size (twelve at least, fourteen at most—big).

The footprint was in a back corner of the habitat, where the concrete floor met the fake rock wall. There were more bloodstains concentrated there than anywhere else. Erie crouched down and examined the wall. Caught in its rough, yellow surface, about a foot off the ground, was a tuft of fuzzy white fabric the size of a quarter.

"You're not really going to hose all this down, are you?" Erie said.

"Well...yeah. We are," Overbeck told him. "I mean, we don't have any choice. We can't keep the monkeys outside forever. And we certainly can't have them sitting around in blood. It's a...a health issue."

"A P.R. issue, you mean," Huff scoffed.

Erie glanced back at the two of them. Overbeck was hovering nearby, the moist stains under his armpits growing larger by the second. Huff was leaning in the doorway giving Overbeck the kind of look most people reserve for insects in their food. Erie figured the Hoosier Zoo had some bumpy days ahead if Overbeck and Huff were the only ones waiting in the wings for Reed to retire.

Erie turned back to the white fluff on the wall, debating whether or not he should take it. On the one hand, it wouldn't do him much good. He didn't have a crime lab in his garage. On the other hand, it would be a shame to let a high-pressure hose blast potential evidence down the drain. After a few moments of indecision, he reached out, plucked the material off the wall and put it in his wallet.

"Anything else I need to see?"

"No, that's it," Overbeck said. He checked his watch, obviously eager to get the place cleaned up before the general public started strolling in.

"Nobody saw or heard anything out of the ordinary?"

"No. Nothing. I mean...other than what you've looked at already." Overbeck was backing toward the door as he spoke, trying to draw Erie out of the habitat. "We just came in this morning and Maggie was gone."

Erie followed reluctantly. A part of him felt like he was betraying something by leaving. He was abandoning a footprint, blood samples, maybe fingerprints, all kinds of evidence that he should have been protecting. But he had no badge to protect it with. So he left it behind.

"Don't you have security guards?" Erie asked as they rejoined Reed. "A nightwatchman or something?"

Huff snorted. "We've got a 'something.'"

"Percy Williams is our night keeper," Reed said without looking at Huff. "Unfortunately, he must've been in another part of the zoo when Maggie was stolen."

"Yeah," Huff said. "The part where he keeps his TV and beer."

Overbeck fidgeted and eyed Reed warily, gauging his reaction. He didn't have one. Reed just kept smiling at Erie as if Huff hadn't said a thing.

If they'd been a family, Erie would've told them to go straight into therapy.

"So what kind of person steals a monkey?" he asked.

"I'm afraid you're going to have to tell us that," Reed said.

"You don't have any ideas? I mean—is there a black market for zoo animals?"

"No," said Overbeck.

"Yes," said Huff.

"Not really," Reed said, talking over both of them. "Not for capuchins. Not around here. Maybe if we were in Costa Rica...."

Reed chuckled. No one else joined in.

"I'm sorry we can't give you more to go on, Larry," Reed continued. "But you're a resourceful man. I'm sure if anyone can bring Maggie home, it's you."

Pep talks were all well and good, but Erie preferred leads. He eyed Huff, but she wasn't saying anything more. She was too busy impaling a squirming Overbeck on another nasty glare.

Erie knew all too well that there were few things less pleasant than stepping into the middle of a family argument. That's just what this felt like, and he hated it. He missed his job sometimes, but not crap like this.

Why had he picked up the phone that morning? Why had he gotten out of bed?

"You'll hear from me," he said, and after another handshake and more rah-rah from Reed, he left.

When he was outside, he passed the lemurs and chimpanzees—careful to keep his distance from the chimps, just in case Corny decided to take a potshot at him—and walked around to the next cage. The weathered, faded information plaque there identified the animals on the other side of the fence as capuchin monkeys. There were seven of them, and Erie recognized them immediately.

They were organ grinder monkeys. Not that Erie had ever seen a real organ grinder. But he'd seen enough in movies to know they always had the same little sidekick—monkeys with slender bodies and long tails and white faces with large, expressive eyes. Seven sets of those eyes were staring back at him now.

"Wraa!" one of the capuchins screeched as Erie got closer.

"Wraa!" another one answered, and then the rest joined in, all of them screaming and scrambling up into branches. Out of reach.

Erie couldn't blame them for being jumpy. He imagined men—one of them giant-sized, to judge by his footprint—chasing and grabbing at them inside the Monkey House. The animals' shrieking would've been even louder in there, bouncing off all that cement and metal. The thieves must've had nerves of steel. Or stomachs of Budweiser.

Erie lingered just long enough to glance at the plaque. For him, it was more informative for what it didn't say than what it said. There was nothing about capuchin monkeys being rare or endangered. Which meant, Erie assumed, that they weren't particularly valuable.

There could be no argument, however, that they *were* particularly loud.

"O.K.! I'm going! I'm going!" Erie told the monkeys when he was through. They didn't stop screaming until he was almost to the front gate.

The turnstiles at the entrance were gleaming clean when Erie reached them. The woman who'd been wiping them down was in the ticket booth now, reading a paperback novel.

"Excuse me. How are these locked up at night?"

The woman looked up from her book slowly, as if reluctant to leave its reality and re-enter the one with the zoo and the guy asking nosy questions.

"What?" she asked.

"These turnstiles. How are they locked?"

"There's a lever around the side there, close to the ground. Push it down all the way and the bars lock up."

"Go ahead, Erie. Try it," Huff said.

Erie turned to find her walking down the path toward him.

"That's the lever there. Step on it."

The lever had a pad on top, like a brake pedal. Erie put his foot on it and pushed, and the lever clicked downwards.

"Now watch." Huff stepped up to the turnstile, grabbed one of the bars and gave it a shake. "Locked, right?"

"If you say so."

"I don't."

Huff leaned into the turnstile, pushing against the direction it was designed to rotate. The lever popped up with a loud *clack*, and Huff moved slowly through the barred cage that surrounded the turnstile, pushing herself out of the zoo.

"That's all it takes," she said to Erie through the bars. "Except why bother when there's twenty places you can get in over a wall and twenty other places you can get in under a fence?"

"But this is the way they went last night."

"Obviously."

If Huff had been a little less of a smartass, a little less prone to jumping on people's words and stomping them into the dirt, he would've said something, maybe "Doesn't that suggest anything to you?" But instead he just walked through the turnstile—going in the right direction, unlike Huff—and headed for the parking lot.

"Thanks for the extra information. Every little bit helps."

"Wait!"

Erie stopped and looked back. Huff was following him.

"Where are you going?" she asked.

"To my car."

"And after that?" Huff said slowly, as if speaking to someone for whom English was a challenging new language.

"After that I'm beginning my investigation."

When Huff realized that was all she was getting, she closed her eyes and took in a deep breath.

"Look, Erie," she said, her eyes popping back open, "Reed wants me to go with you."

"He *what*?"

It was official now. For the second year in a row, Erie's Halloween was ruined.

"What do you know about monkeys, Erie? What do you know about *this* monkey? Squat, that's what. I'm the expert, so I'm coming along. Reed's orders."

Erie didn't snap very often, but he snapped now.

"What makes you think I take orders from Reed?"

Huff cocked an eyebrow at him. There might have been genuine surprise on her face. Erie couldn't be sure.

"You mean you don't?"

"I barely know him."

"You're working for him, aren't you?"

"Well, yeah," Erie said, realizing it for the first time. He hadn't even told Reed his rates. This whole private investigator thing was still too damn new. "That doesn't make me his slave."

"So you're refusing to work with me?"

There was a challenge in Huff's voice, almost as if she *wanted* him to say "Yes." And he was certainly tempted. But he knew the logical thing to do, even if he didn't particularly want to do it.

"Alright. You can come along. But because it makes sense, not because Cy Reed ordered it."

"Whatever," Huff said. She didn't seem particularly satisfied by her victory.

They got in Erie's car, left the parking lot, went north on Lamprecht Road and east on Highway 50 toward downtown, all without saying a word. It was Huff who finally broke the silence.

"Look," she said, and for a second Erie thought an apology might be forthcoming. It wasn't. "When you hit 41 head north."

"What for?"

"We need to go to Spencer. You can pick up 67 off 41."

"You think Maggie's in *Spencer?*"

Calling Spencer a dot on the map would be generous. It wasn't even a speck. Erie had driven through a hundred times on his way to and from Indianapolis. Spencer was easy to drive through. It was harder to stop there. If you didn't hit the brakes at the city limits, you'd cruise right out again in a heartbeat. Erie didn't think of it as the kind of town that would be crawling with wildlife—other than rednecks.

"There's an animal dealer up around there named Eyler," Huff said. "Runs his own 'sanctuary' for exotics. He'd just love to get his hands on a young female capuchin. Good breeding stock. The babies are what really bring in the money."

They passed a sign for Highway 41. The turnoff was a mile ahead.

"This Eyler guy—he steals animals?" Erie said.

"More or less."

"What does that mean?"

"It means it's complicated."

"It doesn't have to be complicated. When I say 'steal,' what I mean is 'sneak into a zoo, bust glass, pry open doors, chase monkeys around a cage, let one bite the hell out of him then wrap it up and haul it out the front gate.' He'd do that?"

They passed another sign for 41. The turnoff was coming up.

"You need to get over," Huff said.

"Would he do that?"

"You're going to miss the turn!"

Erie missed the turn.

"We're not going to Spencer," he said.

The look on Huff's face made Erie worry she might bite *him*.

"I knew it," she snarled.

"We can go to Spencer later," Erie said. "If this Eyler guy stole Maggie, she's safe. She's merchandise, right? He'll take care of her. We've got time. But if she was grabbed for some other reason, she could be in danger."

"*Some other reason*? Like what?"

Erie made an effort to speak slowly and softly, hoping it would rub off on Huff.

"I was a cop for a lot of years. I saw a lot of weird things. And the weirdest of all? Those were always on Halloween. Always."

"So what are you saying? Someone stole Maggie so they could dress her up like a ballerina and take her trick-or-treating?"

"It wouldn't surprise me."

"Well, I don't buy it."

Huff turned away and glared out the window.

Erie knew why she couldn't "buy it": She'd already made up her mind. The animal dealer did it, she was thinking. With help.

And maybe she was right. If so, it might actually be good news. A motive makes a perp predictable. But if the bad guy's just out for some dumb laughs, anything can happen.

After a few quiet miles they reached downtown River City, and Erie zigzagged through the streets to the first stop of his investigation: St. Mary Mercy Hospital. When he parked, he told Huff to wait in the car.

"Yeah, right," Huff said as she unbuckled her seatbelt and opened the door.

Erie didn't try to fight it. But as they walked toward the emergency entrance, he slipped off his windbreaker and handed it to her.

"Put this on."

Huff scowled back at him as if he'd just taken off his pants, not his jacket.

"I'm not cold," she said.

"I'm not trying to keep you warm. I'm trying to keep you anonymous."

Huff looked down at her shirt, with its Hoosier Zoo patch and the plastic tag with her name and title on it.

"Oh," she said.

She put on the jacket.

Erie needed to find a familiar face inside. He got lucky. There were two. He kicked his memory into high gear and came up with names to go with them. Then he glued a smile on his face he was far too irritated to feel.

"Jackie. Lee," he said as he walked up to the admissions desk. "How you been?"

The women smiled back.

"Detective Erie! It's been a long time!"

"We heard you retired."

"You heard right."

There was a brief flurry of chitchat about retirement, the cop who'd taken Erie's slot in Homicide, Jackie and Lee's complaints about supposedly arrogant doctors Erie could barely remember. Huff observed it all silently, ignored, until Jackie turned to her and said, "And who do we have here? Mrs. Erie?"

Erie managed to launch into his response before Huff could open her mouth (or roll her eyes).

"No, no. This is my friend Bea. I'm helping her out with a private matter. That's what brought me in today actually. I was hoping you could tell me if anyone came in last night with any serious bite wounds."

"Or scratches," Huff added.

"Yeah. Bites or scratches. Like from a small animal."

Jackie and Lee exchanged a quick glance of the "I hope *you* know what he's talking about cuz *I* sure don't" variety.

"All we had last night was the usual—drunks puttin' their fists through windows and folks with the flu and no insurance," Jackie said.

"The big excitement was a guy with a kidney stone," Lee added, chuckling. "He was back there for hours carryin' on, screamin', callin' the doctors every filthy name you can think of."

"Oh, yeah," Jackie said. "You shoulda heard what he called Dr. Adad. I've been thinkin' of sayin' the same thing to the man for months!"

Erie forced out a hollow laugh. He'd struck out, and now he had to extricate himself smoothly before anyone asked about—

"So what's with the bites and scratches?" Lee said. "We got us a werewolf on the prowl?"

"Yeah. Or is it vampire?" Jackie threw in.

Erie laughed again to buy himself a little time. He didn't want to admit he was working a case as a private investigator.

"Well," he said. "Uhhh...."

"It wasn't a werewolf or a vampire," Huff said. "It was my Chihuahua. He sure as hell sank his teeth into *somebody's* butt last night." She leaned in over the admissions desk and dropped her voice to a just-between-us-girls whisper. "Fortunately, I'm pretty sure the butt belonged to my ex."

Jackie and Lee ate it up. Erie took advantage of their laughter to throw out his goodbyes and steer Huff toward the door without any further conversation.

"Good save back there," he said once they were in the parking lot.

"So what now?"

"You're a smart lady. Guess."

"Knox Memorial Hospital."

"Very good! You ever moonlight as a detective?"

Huff didn't even crack a smile.

River City's other hospital was twenty-five minutes away. The first ten minutes passed in silence. Erie had plenty he could say, most of it in the form of questions. But he didn't feel like sticking his head into the lion's mouth. So it was Huff who spoke first, and when she did Erie knew the words had already been echoing through her brain for hours.

"What if it's her blood? Maggie's?"

Erie looked over at Huff. Her face had changed. The cynical "Screw you" mask was gone. Now Erie saw anguish.

"You tell me," he said.

"Even if she was barely hurt, she might go into shock. Capture trauma, it's called. She could be dead already."

Huff tried to punch out the words, make them hard and clinical. But by the time she reached the word "shock" there was a tremor in her voice, and the last few words barely came out at all.

"*Do* you think it's her blood?" Erie asked.

Huff sucked in a long breath that seemed to fill the emptiness inside her.

"Hell no," she said firmly. The other Huff, the tough one, was back in charge. "She's a capuchin monkey. You think they're cute, just wait till one tries to scratch your eyes out. Anybody who'd try to snatch one out of a group like that's gotta be nuts."

"Well, if that's really true...?" Erie said, letting his inflection ask the rest of the question.

...why would your prime suspect do it?

He saw in Huff's eyes that she heard the question. He also saw that she didn't have a good answer—and that it enraged her.

He stopped talking. She did, too.

When they got to Knox Memorial, they went through the same routine at the admissions desk. With the same result: no bites, no scratches, too many questions. They escaped as quickly as they could.

"You ready for Spencer now?" Huff asked as they walked back out to the car.

Erie shook his head. "I'm ready for Hart Road."

"What's on Hart Road?"

"My place. I need to make some calls. And if we're gonna drive up to Spencer, I'll need to feed my cats."

"Catsssss? Plural?"

"Yeah."

"How many?"

"Three."

Huff swiped a hand dismissively. "Is that all?"

"'Is that all'? I've got friends who say it's three too many."

"They don't know what they're talking about. Wanna know how many cats I have?"

"Sure."

"Five."

Erie shrugged. "That's only two more than me."

"Yeah, but then there's the dogs, the rats, the pig and the parrot."

"Geez. Do you work in a zoo or live in one?"

"Yeah, yeah, I've heard that one before," Huff said. But for a second it almost looked like she was capable of smiling.

When they got to Erie's place, Goldie and Mae met them at the door. Huff was a lot friendlier meeting new pets than new people, and she bent down to introduce herself to the cats with ear scratches and tummy rubs.

"Where's number three?"

Erie pointed across the living room. His newest cat, Phoebe, peeked at them from around a corner, her yellow eyes wide and unblinking.

"A shy one, huh?"

"Yeah. I don't blame her. She's been through some rough stuff. She almost ended up an hors d'oeuvre at your zoo, as a matter of fact. Excuse me."

Erie walked into the kitchen and checked his answering machine. There was one new message. He pushed PLAY.

"Hi, this is Bob calling from 21st Century Travel Plus. I'm really sorry I missed you today, because I've got some great news. You've—"

Erie erased the message. He'd heard Bob's "great news" twenty times. Apparently, Erie had been specially selected—by virtue of having his phone number dialed—to become a member of the 21st Century Travel Plus Luxury Living Timeshare Program. All he needed to do to activate his membership was begin handing over his life savings in simple monthly installments.

One of these days Erie was going to really put his detecting skills to the test and track Bob down. He hadn't made up his mind what he was going to do when he found him. He was torn between a pie in the face and a kick in the ass.

Huff stepped into the kitchen, and Erie asked her if she wanted any coffee or water or juice or candy bars before they headed out again. She looked so lost in thought Erie wasn't even sure she heard the question. But then her eyes refocused on him, and she shook her head.

"So," she said, "you had phone calls to make?"

"Actually, the first one's yours. I think you should give the zoo a call. Maybe there's been some kind of development."

"Such as what?"

"A ransom demand. Or maybe they found Maggie hiding in a tree. I don't know. That's why I need you to call in."

"O.K.," Huff said. "Makes sense."

Erie moved away from the phone, and Huff picked it up and dialed. He had the feeling she'd wanted to check in with the zoo anyway but felt obligated to run everything he suggested through a B.S. X-ray.

She didn't call Reed or Overbeck, Erie noticed. Instead, she chatted with someone she called "Dave." She asked if anything had happened since they'd left and how the remaining capuchins were acting. She also asked what Overbeck had been up to, and Erie noticed that she tried a little too hard to make the question sound like a casual aside. Then she gave "Dave" a gruff goodbye, hung up and said, "Nothing. What next?"

Now we try a long shot, Erie thought. *And I swallow my pride.*

"One other call," he said, reaching out to take the phone. He dialed the number from memory.

"Lt. Zirkelbach, please," he told the dispatcher who picked up the call. She didn't recognize his voice, and he was thankful.

Erie's friend Bass kept telling him he'd had "a thing" about the River City Police Department ever since he'd applied for a private detective's license.

"It's like you're embarrassed every time you're around 'em," Bass would say.

"I am embarrassed."

"Well, get over it!"

But Erie couldn't. Whenever he took a case, he felt like a kid dressing up as a cop for Halloween.

"East Sector, Zirkelbach."

"Mike, it's Larry Erie."

This was the moment Erie dreaded. If he got through the first few seconds, he'd be O.K. He just needed Zirkelbach to say something other than "So how's River City's toughest gumshoe these days?" or "Hey, Rockford! How are the files comin'?"

"Larry! How ya' been?" Zirkelbach said.

Yet even in those words Erie thought he heard something. A snicker maybe. A sneer. Or maybe that was just Erie's "thing" about the RCPD playing tricks on him. He did his best to ignore it.

"Oh, you know. This and that. Raking leaves, watching too much TV. The usual old fart stuff."

"Sounds good to me. Four more years and I'll be out there rakin' leaves with ya'. I can't wait."

"Yeah, it's the life alright," Erie said. Because it was the kind of thing he knew he was supposed to say. "So, Mike, I'm just looking into something for a friend. It's no big deal. But I was wondering—did anything weird go down last night?"

"Weird? Like how do you mean?"

"You know. Out of the ordinary. Noteworthy. Something that would have people talking."

"Nope. Not that I heard."

"How about the other sectors? Same thing?"

"Yeah, same thing. Nothin' weird. Just the usual perps and pervs."

"O.K. One other thing. Do you know if that Mojo kid is still in town?"

"Oh, yeah. We ain't rid of him yet."

"He have any known hangouts?"

"Hold on. DeYoung's right here. I'll ask him."

Erie heard Zirkelbach's thick hand wrap around the receiver.

"Hey, DeYoung!" Zirkelbach called out, his booming voice only slightly muffled over the phone. "Where'd you buttonhole Birdboy last time?"

Erie couldn't hear the response, just Zirkelbach's "Uh-huh."

"Know where he lives?" Zirkelbach asked, his hand still smothering the mouthpiece. "Really? That figures. Larry Erie. I don't know. Yeah. O.K."

Zirkelbach brought the receiver back up to his mouth.

"He works in a coffee shop on Sherman. The Daily Grind. You know it?"

"I know it."

"No known place of residence. The landlords in town talk to each other, y'know. Last time DeYoung checked in on him, he said he was living in a VW van."

"You're kidding."

"Nope. DeYoung says to say 'Hi,' by the way."

"Right back at him."

"So, Larry...."

Erie's shoulders tensed, his jaw clenched. Here it came.

"I gotta ask. You callin' up with questions about the East Sector and Dr. Dolittle and all...well, I can't help but put two and two and two together. There somethin' else goin' on out at the zoo we should know about?"

Erie glanced over at Huff. She was watching him warily, eyes full of distrust.

"Like I said, I'm just looking into something for a friend."

Zirkelbach chuckled. A part of Erie wanted to chuckle right along with him. Another part wanted to ask him what was so goddamn funny.

"O.K., Larry," Zirkelbach said. "I hope you find whatever you're lookin' for."

"Me, too. Thanks for the help, Mike."

Erie hung up. He wanted a minute to think, scroll back over the conversation, dissect it. But Huff didn't give him the chance.

"What was that all about?" she asked.

"Acquiring information."

Erie walked over to the refrigerator and pulled it open. The shelves inside were brimming with almost every condiment known to man—and almost nothing to put them on. After a little scrounging, Erie found a package of hot dogs buried beneath a loose pile of individually wrapped slices of cheese.

"You sure you don't want something to eat? It's almost one."

"I'll eat after we go to Spencer."

Erie sighed. "Suit yourself. But it could be a while. It's a long drive, and we've got another stop to make before we hit the road."

Huff cursed so explosively Mae threw herself off the kitchen counter and streaked out of the room. Erie put the hot dogs back in the fridge, his appetite suddenly gone.

"Let's just go," he said.

He tried to explain once they were in the car.

"Have you ever heard of Animal Freedom Now?"

"No. Did you just make it up?"

"No. But you're probably going to think I did. It's supposed to be an animal rights group, but as far as we can tell it's just one guy."

"We?"

She'd caught him there.

Not we. *They.*

"The police," Erie said. "Last summer, somebody 'liberated' a bunch of chickens from a farm outside town. There was a message left behind—a nutty manifesto from 'Animal Freedom Now.' It spooked certain people, and the case got a lot of attention."

"Then how come I never heard of it?"

"*Internal* attention. The RCPD, the county sheriff and the state police were all in on the investigation. It got cracked on a lucky break though. A noise complaint."

"Let me guess. Crowing."

"Pecking and scratching, actually. The guy took more than fifty chickens, but he didn't know what to do with them. So he just kept them in his apartment. By the time the police showed up, the place was covered wall to wall in—"

"I work with animals. I know."

"Yeah. Well, all the chickens were recovered, and nobody wanted to give this Animal Freedom kid any publicity—because that's all he was really after in the first place. He calls himself 'Major Mojo,' and he figured he needed some ink to attract recruits. I think he was actually looking forward to a trial. So certain interested parties talked the farmer into dropping charges, and—"

"And the whole thing was kept quiet," Huff snapped.

It wasn't just a statement of fact. It was some kind of accusation. Erie couldn't figure out he was being accused of, though.

"That's right," he said. "Now every time anybody so much as crank calls a farmer, an officer has a few words with Major Mojo. I don't think he's been up to much since then beyond handing out flyers in front of McDonald's, but who knows? Maybe he thought up another way to make a name for himself."

"You said you think this kid works alone?"

Erie nodded.

Huff shook her head.

"There's no way in hell anybody could grab Maggie without help. Not with seven other capuchins there, too. No way."

"Maybe there's a Sgt. Mojo now," Erie said.

It didn't get a laugh. Of course. Erie wasn't sure why he'd even tried.

The Daily Grind was one block from the Midwest's most awkwardly named campus: Indiana University-Purdue University River City. The locals shortened that to IUPURC, but it was still a mouthful.

Before he'd even parked, Erie knew Major Mojo was there. The VW van out front told him that. He gave it a good look as they walked up to the coffee shop.

The van was covered with flaking orange paint and enough

bumper stickers to wallpaper a small house. "I DON'T EAT MY FRIENDS," one of the stickers said. Another was a picture of a little cartoon boy relieving himself on a pair of golden arches.

Erie tried to move quickly, glancing down to check all the door handles as he circled the van. They looked grimy, but free of blood. He'd told Huff to wait on the sidewalk, but she stayed a step behind him, peering in through the windows.

"You're being conspicuous," he said under his breath.

"Oh, really?"

One of the windows was cranked down a few inches, and Huff pushed her nose up against it and gave the air inside a sniff.

"Oh, man," she said, grimacing.

"What?" Erie's heart beat a little faster. "Does it smell like Maggie?"

"No. It smells like doobie. A lotta doobie."

Erie almost asked her how she knew what "doobie" smelled like, but he thought better of it.

"Come on," he said instead. "Let's go inside before—"

"How can I help you today, officers?"

Erie turned and found himself facing Fidel Castro circa 1959: a young man wearing combat fatigues and big black boots and a thick beard that threatened to grow over his smiling face like kudzu.

"Do you want a signed confession? Or were you hoping to beat it out of me?" Major Mojo asked.

"We're not cops," Erie said, but Huff was already talking over his words, drowning them out.

"What do you have to confess?"

Major Mojo shrugged happily. "What you got? It don't matter. You're gonna hassle me anyway, right?"

"We're not cops," Erie repeated.

Major Mojo winked at him. "Hey, I understand. It's Halloween, right? You wanna say you're not cops, fine. So what are you then? Tourists?"

"We're just—"

"Where were you last night?" Huff asked.

Erie groaned. If he ever took another case—*if*—he would have an unbreakable rule: Clients never, ever take part in an investigation.

"I was just hangin' with some friends. You know—startin' a bonfire with Old Glory, plottin' acts of sedition. The usual."

"Look," Erie sighed.

That was as far as he got.

"You say you like animals?" Huff said.

Major Mojo nodded. "Love 'em all, big and small."

"And you want to help them?"

"That's what I'm all about."

"Then here's your big chance."

Huff stomped up to the young man, getting so close she was almost standing on his toes.

"There's an animal out there somewhere," she said, her voice dropping low but the intensity dialed up high. "She's scared. Alone. Maybe hurt. Maybe *dying*. And every second I waste here on your bullshit is a second I'm not out looking for her. So stop playing games and answer me *right now*. Where were you last night?"

Major Mojo blinked, and for a moment he seemed strangely dazed and distant.

It wasn't fear and it wasn't too much "doobie." He was thinking. Considering. Maybe inventing.

The pause that followed was over so quickly most people wouldn't even notice it. But a cop would.

"I worked here till eight, then I went to my girlfriend's place," Major Mojo said. "We watched a movie and went to bed. That's it. Really."

"I believe him," Huff announced without hesitating. "Let's go."

She stalked away, heading for Erie's car up the block.

So much for the quiet investigation Reed had asked for. Another scene like that and they'd end up on the evening news.

Erie didn't follow Huff right away. He lingered, waiting for Major Mojo to say "What the hell's she talking about?" or "Who are you people?" But he didn't. Which meant Erie had more questions for *him*.

Now wasn't the time and place, though. Huff had seen to that.

Their conversation had turned a few heads on the sidewalk, and everyone inside the coffee shop was staring at them. It was time to go.

"Thanks," Erie said. "Happy Halloween."

Huff was already in the passenger seat when Erie got to his car, her seatbelt buckled. She was ready to travel. Erie wasn't.

"Listen," he said as he slid in behind the steering wheel.

"Just drive."

"*Listen.* I think that kid knows something."

"Oh, please. Just because he's a little fringy doesn't make him the bad guy."

"It's not just that. I've got a feeling—"

"*You've* got a feeling? I've had a feeling from the beginning! But no. We had to waste the day touring beautiful River City! Do you even want to find Maggie? Or are you just dicking around so you can collect a per diem?"

"Hey, lady—I don't know anything about your petty squabbles at the zoo. But I do know they've got you so twisted around you can't see facts when they're staring you in the face. Whoever stole Maggie, they're amateurs, and that means they're probably right here in town."

"What facts am I not facing, Erie? Because you're right—I don't see 'em. All I see is a 'detective' who's bending over backwards not to follow up his best lead."

"You want to see my best lead? Here's my best lead. In fact, it's the only damn evidence I've got."

Erie pulled out his wallet and showed Huff the piece of fabric he'd tucked there earlier.

"I found this in the monkey habitat. Do you know what it is?"

Huff gave her shoulders an angry, jerking shrug. "Some lint you just pulled out of your pocket?"

"I think it's a piece of a blanket. Do you get what that means? These guys didn't bring a net or tranquilizer darts or whatever. They showed up to catch a capuchin monkey with a *blanket*. Whoever they are, they're not just amateurs—they're idiots."

"Or maybe that's what it's supposed to look like."

"What?"

"Maybe it's a trick."

"If it's a trick, it got taken pretty far. The zoo's got a back entrance, right? It must. There's no way you bring animals in and out through the front gate."

"Yeah? So?"

"So if these guys were pros or had any brains at all, why would they take an angry monkey out through those turnstiles?"

"We don't know they did."

"The blood—"

"Doesn't prove a thing. It could have been planted."

"Oh, god. That's your answer? There was some kind of brilliant plot? A conspiracy?"

"Why not? At least the people I'm thinking of had a *reason* to steal Maggie. Money. Why would these mythical idiots of yours do it? And another thing…."

Huff kept going, barking at Erie about animal dealers and the black market for exotic pets and Overbeck and his supposedly cozy relationship with that "scumbag son of a bitch Eyler" in Spencer.

Erie sighed, spent, and let her rave.

She was right about one thing. The blood, the fuzz, everything he'd seen at the zoo—it could be part of an elaborate ruse.

It could be…but it wasn't. That's what Erie's gut told him. He'd spent three decades looking people in the eye while they lied to him. He'd listened to a thousand bogus accusations and ten thousand phony alibis. People had tried to con him from the day he put on his uniform to the day he handed in his badge. And this didn't feel like a con. It felt like a stupid, stupid joke.

But why should he trust his instincts? They can fool you, too. Huff was proof of that. She kept jabbering at him, growing angrier and angrier as it became more obvious he was only half listening.

At least her instincts gave her ready-made bad guys. Erie's left him with a whole city of suspects. You never heard a cop say, "Somebody's pulled a dumb-ass prank on the East Side—round up the usual suspects."

Wait.

Erie *had* heard cops say that. Lots of times.

"Of course," he said. "Them."

"Let me guess. There's just one more place we've got to check before we go to Spencer."

"Yes."

Huff rolled her eyes and coughed out a scoffing laugh.

Erie pretended not to notice.

"This morning," he said, "Reed mentioned that your night watchman recently chased off some college kids who were skinny-dipping somewhere in the zoo."

"So?"

"He didn't catch them?"

"No, they got away."

"How did he know they were college kids?"

"He said they were frat boys and their girlfriends."

"But how did he *know*?"

"One of them had a sweatshirt with, you know...Greek letters."

Erie shook his head. "IUPURC doesn't have fraternities."

A scowl twisted Huff's face, but it was different than all the scowls Erie had seen there before. It wasn't bitter or angry. Just confused.

"Let me show you something," Erie said.

He started the car. Less than two minutes later, he was shutting it off again. They were on a quiet street just a few blocks from the coffee shop. One side of the street was lined with the kind of low-rent apartment complexes favored by college kids living off campus. Facing them was a row of houses that, judging by the gleaming Jeeps and SUVs out front, catered to students with a little more money. Over the doorway to one of the homes hung three twinkling horseshoes—the Greek letter Omega done up in white Christmas lights.

"They call themselves 'The Omega Men,'" Erie said. "Or at least they did last I heard. They've lived in that house for more than 20 years. Not the same ones, of course. Different guys coming and going. Just like a frat, which is exactly what they'd be if the school were a little bigger and they could get picked up as a chapter of one of the national fraternities."

Spider-Man strolled by the car, and both Erie and Huff did a double-take. Walking with him were a hobbit and an adolescent girl who was either dressed as a streetwalker or Britney Spears. They were chattering loudly and swinging plastic buckets shaped like pumpkins.

"They're getting an early start."

"Erie, why are we here?"

It wasn't just another jab this time. Huff was actually prepared to listen. Maybe she could sense the presence of idiots.

Erie began counting with his fingers.

"One: If your nightwatchman's right, they've probably been in the zoo before. That explains how they knew their way around in there at night. Two: There's a 24-hour student clinic on campus, which is why whoever got hurt wouldn't have gone to a hospital. Three: These guys have a reputation for crazy stunts and parties. The RCPD has to send a car out here at least once a month, and I could tell you stories about homecoming that would curl your hair. And four: There's what they call their headquarters over there."

"What's that?"

"Animal House."

Huff nodded silently and stared off at the house for a moment. Then she turned back to Erie.

"If Maggie's not in there, we go to Spencer. Immediately."

"Whatever you say, boss. If these guys don't have her, I'm just your chauffeur from here on in, because I'll be out of ideas."

Huff didn't crack a smile, but Erie could tell she liked the "boss" part.

As they marched up the walk to the front door, they passed Spidey and his friends, who were grumbling about the "candy" they'd just been given: fried eggs.

"Real comedians," Huff said sourly.

"Unzip your jacket," Erie told her.

They were almost to the porch.

"Why?" Huff said.

"I want to see what they think of your costume. And *please* let me do the talking this time. We don't have any real authority. We'll have to bluff our way in."

"I can bluff," Huff muttered. But she unzipped her jacket and zipped her lip.

Erie reached out and rang the bell and put on his own costume. His cop face. Stern, stiff, dry, unforgiving.

When a brawny Omega Man came to the door with a pan of fried eggs in one hand and a spatula in the other, Erie got the reaction he was hoping for. First a bad boy grin, the kid assuming they were neighborhood parents furious about the "treats" he was giving out. Then, once he got a look at Erie's expression and Huff's uniform, the grin lost its balance, tipping over into a lopsided grimace.

The kid had something to hide.

He recovered quickly. His smile righted itself, and he snaked a foot around the door and pulled it tight to his side, blocking Erie's view into the house.

"Aren't you two a little old to be trick or treating?" he said.

"You know why we're here," Erie told him.

"You came for the Grand Slam breakfast?"

"You boys are in a lot of trouble."

"What? Because of this?" The kid waggled the pan. "Hey, eggs are delicious *and* nutritious. A hell of a lot more healthy than candy bars. You ought to be thanking us."

He was smooth, Erie had to give him that. A political science major probably. Pre-law. He had the bland, doughy good looks of a state politician. He'd go far—assuming Huff didn't kill him.

"We don't want to call the police," Erie said. "But we will if we have to. It'll be a lot better for everybody if it doesn't come to that."

The kid furrowed his brow in mock confusion. "Man, what are you smoking? You are making no sense."

"If you deal with us, this'll all be over in minutes. But the cops…." Erie shook his head and shrugged. "We'll have to press charges. We won't have a choice."

"O.K., man," the kid said, forcing out an unconvincing chuckle. "Whatever."

Erie saw what was coming next. He could read it in the college boy's eyes.

Close the door and get rid of the evidence. Get rid of it fast and without pity.

"Enjoy the rest of your crack," the kid said as he started to push the door shut.

It had been a long, long time since Erie had stuck his foot in a closing door. You have to do it just right or you end up with a shattered ankle or crushed toes or a thigh the color of grape jelly. Fortunately, with his hands full, the kid couldn't slam the door hard, and Erie's foot stayed on the end of his leg.

"Don't be stupid," Erie spat.

He was pressed up against the door, glaring in at the kid like Jack Nicholson in *The Shining*. One "Herrrrrrrrre's Johnny!" and the guy would probably wet his pants.

"Back off, man!" he said. "Back off or I'm calling the cops!"

"Do it," Erie said. "Please."

"Get out of here!"

The kid poked at Erie with the spatula, wiping dried bits of egg on his face.

The last drop of Erie's considerable patience finally evaporated.

"Hey!" someone yelled. "Stop him!"

It took both Erie and the kid a moment to realize the shouting wasn't about them. Something else was going on inside the house—something involving running and scuffling and finally a series of piercing, inhuman shrieks.

Erie looked back at Huff.

"Maggie?"

"Go!" Huff said.

Erie went, giving the door a shove that sent it smacking into the college boy's face. The kid and his frying pan went down in a messy, clattering pile.

Assault? Trespassing?

Erie didn't care anymore.

The screams were coming from the second floor. Erie hopped over the kid and headed for the stairs. Huff quickly passed him, bounding up three steps at a time.

A guy dressed as Tarzan met them at the top. He actually looked relieved to see them.

"You from the zoo?"

"Yes," Huff said.

"Some guy got in the house and now he's in my room with the monkey and I think it's killing him!"

"Which room?" Huff asked, but another scream told her exactly where to go.

She and Erie pushed past more young men in the hallway, most in costume. Erie noticed that one of them, a hulking redhead dressed as Frankenstein's monster, had real stitches over his forehead and across his chin. Fresh ones. Erie glanced down at the young man's feet. Size twelve, at least—just like the footprints in the monkey house.

The shrieks were coming from a closed door just beyond him.

"I don't think you wanna go in there," the redhead said.

Huff stepped around him and opened the door. The Omega Men ran for cover.

Huff didn't open the door all the way, but it was enough. A familiar odor assaulted Erie's nostrils, and an involuntary "Ewwww" slipped past his lips. Eyes watering, he peered over Huff's shoulder, looking for the source of the smell.

The room—someone's bedroom—looked as if it had been picked up by a giant, shaken like a snow globe and put back in place upside down. Lamps and chairs had been overturned, posters torn off the walls, beer and wine bottles shattered, clothes and magazines and notebooks strewn about the floor, viscous brown clumps splattered over just about everything.

A tattered blanket lay crumpled in a corner next to a length of stained rope. Hunched nearby was a panting, wild-eyed monkey. Maggie.

She shrieked and scrambled up on top of a stereo speaker,

knocking over the bong that had been perched there.

"Is somebody out there?" asked a trembly, muffled voice. "You gotta help me. Please. I'm trapped."

"Where are you?" Erie said.

"Down here. In the corner."

Protruding from under one of the beds was a pair of combat boots and fatigue-covered ankles.

"Major Mojo?"

There was a pause, then a pitiful, "Yes?"

Erie wasn't sure what to do. Would they have to get tranquilizer darts from the zoo? Chase Maggie around with the blanket? Given the wounds he'd seen on Frankenstein, he wasn't anxious to play monkey in the middle himself.

He turned to Huff. "What now?"

Huff simply stepped into the room and said, "Hi, sweetie."

Maggie launched herself off the speaker and charged toward the door. Erie brought up his hands, sure that within seconds he was going to be pulling a clawing, screaming monkey from his face.

Instead, he watched as Maggie leapt onto Huff, scrambled up her side and huddled in her arms.

"It's O.K., baby," Huff cooed. "Everything's fine."

Maggie wrapped her long arms around Huff's neck, suddenly looking like a very skinny, very fuzzy child.

"You two get out," Huff said, still in a low, soft, sing-songy tone even though she was talking to Erie and Major Mojo. "I need a few minutes to make sure she's totally calm before I try to move her. And keep those morons out the hallway. I don't want them scaring her on the way out."

Erie walked over and nudged the bottom of Major Mojo's boot with his foot.

"Come on. You're safe now."

The young man slithered backwards out of his hiding place and rolled over to peep up at Erie, revealing a large purple-blue bruise across the left side of his face. He looked a little sheepish about being caught cowering under a bed, but by the time he and Erie were out in the hallway he'd managed to straighten his spine and plaster a haughty/defiant grin on his face.

"You want to tell me what you were trying to do in there?" Erie asked him.

"The right thing. You ought to try it sometime."

Erie wished he'd left him under the bed.

Frankenstein's monster poked his head out a nearby doorway.

"So you're taking it back to the zoo?" he said.

Erie nodded. "That's right."

"Thank god."

The other Omega Men began stepping cautiously into the hallway again. When they saw Major Mojo, their expressions soured.

"O.K., so you're from the zoo," one of them said to Erie. "But what the hell is *he* doing here?"

"Good question." Erie turned to Major Mojo. "Why don't you answer that for us while I escort you out of the house."

Major Mojo got it right away. He'd just lost a fight with an eight-pound monkey. He wouldn't do any better against a dozen two hundred-pound wannabe frat boys.

"Suits me," he said.

"The rest of you follow us. We need the hallway clear if we're going to get your other guest out of here." Erie held out his hand toward the stairs. "Alright, Major. Walk and talk."

That's just what he did.

"I've got my sources, you know," Major Mojo said. "Everybody around here knows I'm Mr. Help-the-Animals. So I had three different people come into the Grind today to tell me these guys had a stolen monkey. Not. Cool. So I planned an action for tonight. But then—"

"Wait. 'An action'?"

"Yeah. An operation."

"Oh, right," Erie said. "You mean you were going to steal the monkey."

"Liberate, man. I was gonna *liberate* the monkey. Later tonight. But then you guys showed up and, you know, I had to speed things up."

"Why not just help us?"

"I thought about it. But hey—zoos are prisons, man. And this one we've got here is like...like...? What's a really bad prison?"

"Alcatraz?"

"Yeah. Like Alcatraz. It's the worst."

"So what were you going to do with Maggie?"

"With who?"

"Maggie. The monkey."

"It's a she? Wow." Major Mojo rubbed the side of his face. "Well, I hadn't planned things out that far. I thought I'd just liberate her and then take it from there."

"Only she didn't want to be liberated."

"No way, man. She wanted to take my damn head off."

They were outside now, on the back porch.

"Alright," Erie said. "I guess that's that."

"I can go?"

Erie nodded. "Consider yourself liberated."

"Oh. O.K."

Major Mojo walked away slowly. He seemed disappointed to be getting off so easy. Some police brutality might have cheered him up, but Erie didn't feel like obliging.

The gaggle of Omega Men had dutifully followed Erie and Major Mojo to the back of the house. They peeked at Erie through the screen door, their anxious expressions asking *What about us?*

"Alright, guys," Erie said to them as he stepped back inside. "If you want this story to have a happy ending for yourselves, you're going to tell me everything."

There wasn't much to tell, really. The Omega Men were having a Halloween party that night, and they wanted to make it "something special." After all, as residents of Animal House, they had a reputation to live up to. They already knew how easy it was to break into the zoo, so why not borrow one of the animals—just for Halloween? They settled on a monkey because "monkeys are funny."

"When you see 'em on TV they're just like little people. You know, they're just goofy and cute," said the kid Erie had dealt with at the front door. He was pressing a red-stained paper towel to his nose. "But they're not."

Frankenstein's monster pointed at his stitches. "That one we caught was one of the smallest ones in there, and she still managed to do this to me."

An Omega Man dressed as Abe Lincoln showed Erie a black eye. "I got this from her *tail*."

"Yeah," Tarzan said. "And there was this big one that got hold of my hair—"

There were footsteps on the stairs, and the room fell silent.

"You guys stay here," Erie said. He pushed through the crowd in the kitchen to the foyer. Huff was waiting for him with Maggie still snuggled in her arms.

"Let's go," Huff said.

Erie walked her to the car, both of them trying to move fast but not too fast. Fortunately, the block was free of costumed kids for the moment, and they managed to get to Erie's Corolla without being spotted.

Once Huff and Maggie were in the car, Erie started around for the driver's side. But he stopped himself as he rounded the trunk. There was one more bit of business to attend to. He went back to Animal House.

It was like trick or treating in reverse. The Omega Men were inside, all of them done up in ridiculous costumes, peering at the stranger outside their door who had the power to hand them something nice or something nasty.

Erie knew they had nothing to be nervous about. Reed would want everything kept quiet. Which meant no criminal charges.

Which meant they would get away with it.

Erie could tell them that, give them a little speech about how they'd be fine as long as they kept their mouths shut. He pictured their relieved smiles, heard how'd they'd tell the story around the keg that night, and he said to himself, *No.*

He stepped onto the porch, crossed his arms over his chest, and took a moment to think of the most bone-chilling, spine-tingling, hair-raising words he could.

"You'll be hearing from our attorneys," he said.

"What was that all about?" Huff asked as he scooted into the driver's seat.

Erie told her, and she grinned in a way that said she'd have burst out laughing if she didn't have a freaked-out monkey in her arms.

"To the zoo?" Erie asked.

"To the zoo."

On the way, Erie filled Huff in on Major Mojo and the Omega Men. She shook her head once or twice, frowned a bit, but now that she had Maggie back she seemed almost unflappably relaxed.

"Looks like you two are pretty close," Erie said.

Huff beamed down at Maggie. "Oh, yeah. When she was barely a year old, she caught pneumonia. Almost died. I nursed her back to health by hand. She pretty much lived with me for three months. Monkeys don't forget something like that."

"Neither do people."

Huff looked at Erie again, her expression turning curious.

"Let me ask you something," she said. "Back at your house, you made a crack about one of your cats. What did you mean?"

"What crack?"

"Something about one of them almost ending up an hors d'oeuvre at the zoo."

"Oh. She was one of the animals I rescued," Erie explained.

Huff didn't nod or say "I see" or make any indication she knew what the hell he was talking about.

"From the people who were selling roadkill to the zoo."

Huff still looked bewildered.

"The ones who were stealing people's pets."

"*Stealing people's pets?*" Huff said. "I think you'd better tell me this story from the beginning."

So he did. As he talked, the confusion left Huff's face, replaced first by horror, then rage, then shame.

"You didn't know any of this?" he asked when he was done.

"Just bits and pieces. I knew Overbeck was buying roadkill on the sly. And I heard that got us into some kind of hot water with the police...and a private detective got us out of it."

"What?"

And then Erie knew why the woman had been so hostile from the moment he'd met her. She thought he was a cheap fixer, someone who swept dirt under the rug for a living.

"I'm so sorry," Huff said. "I know I've been a real bitch today."

Erie didn't contradict her.

"I assumed you were someone else, you know what I mean?" Huff went on. "I was so convinced you were hooked in with something skanky that I...well, I made up an excuse to tag along."

"You mean Reed didn't tell you to come with me?"

Huff shook her head. "I wanted to keep an eye on you. See if you were really going to look for Maggie or just jerk me around."

"So instead you spent the day jerking *me* around."

"But it all worked out, didn't it? And really—I am sorry I was so nasty. If it hadn't been for the rumors I'd heard, I would've known you were a good guy."

"How would you have known that?"

"Well, come on. *Three* cats? You had to be O.K."

Huff was smiling at him again.

It had been a very strange, stressful day, but Erie didn't have a talent for holding grudges. He smiled back.

By the time he dropped Huff off at the zoo's rear entrance, she'd promised to make it all up to him by taking him out for dinner sometime. He wasn't sure how he felt about that—he could tell she was a lady with edges even on a good day—but he said yes all the same. It seemed like the safest thing to do.

It was growing dusky by the time Erie left the zoo, and he quickly realized two things: He hadn't eaten since the little Snickers bar that morning, and he'd earned a better dinner than cheese slices and hot dogs. So he picked up a pizza and a bottle of wine on the way home.

He was feeling pretty good as he turned onto Hart Road. His old instincts had come through for him. The badge was gone, but the cop remained.

His satisfaction evaporated when he was half a block from his house. Up ahead, he could see long strands of white waving like ghostly tentacles from the branches of his elm trees.

His house had been egged, too.

THE MACGUFFIN THEFT CASE

Burt was twenty minutes late for lunch, but it couldn't be helped—he'd been marked for death by a Yakuza kingpin, and it had taken him all morning to eradicate the latest team of ninjas sent to do him in.

When Burt finally limped into Luigi's Slice o' Heaven Pizza Parlor, his friend J.P. didn't bother asking about his tardiness. He didn't even ask why Burt had blood on his clothes, nunchucks in his hands and a poison dart sticking out of his artificial leg.

J.P. *never* asked questions. J.P. provided answers—usually to questions that hadn't been asked. An overturned shaker of salt might inspire a five-minute lecture about the medieval spice trade, leading into a ten-minute lecture about why the game "Marco Polo" isn't an Olympic sport, leading into a fifteen-minute lecture about the 1980 Bruce Jenner/Village People disco musical *Can't Stop the Music*. J.P.'s stream of consciousness was a roaring river capable of sweeping away anyone within earshot.

When Burt walked into the restaurant, J.P. was exhaustively explaining the difference between "farther" and "further" to a desperate-looking waitress who was slowly inching *farther* from the table mumbling, "Yeah...uh-huh...alright, gotta go...umm-hmmm...well, work to do...uh-huh."

"Hello, Ray," Burt said. "Sorry I'm late."

J.P. turned toward his friend, and the waitress shot away from the table like the cork from a bottle of champagne.

"Better late than never," J.P. said as Burt dropped wearily into the seat across from him. "Do you know who first said that?

Herodotus of Halicarnassus, the ancient historian. Some say he was talking about the Greeks' victory over Xerxes at Mycale, which finally stopped the expansion of the Achaemenid Empire. Others speculate that he was referring to a plate of feta cheese that was brought to him just as he was about to pass out from hunger while completing Book Nine of *The Histories* in 430 B.C. Did you know you can make feta in your bathtub? All it takes is some milk, the right yeast culture, a lot of brine and a little patience."

J.P. went on to explain the feta-making process while Burt reset the shoulder he'd dislocated while dispatching a particularly deadly ninja in hand-to-hand combat just minutes before. The pain of popping the shoulder back into place made Burt swoon, but even when his face dropped within inches of the red-and-white checkered tablecloth, J.P. didn't slow down.

"If you don't have yeast," J.P. was saying, "just throw in a loaf of Wonder Bread. The yeast cultures in underbaked white bread are still active enough to serve as a coagulant in milk. You might have to keep the feta in your tub an extra week or two, but it'll come out tasting *wonderful*."

Somehow J.P. managed to lick his lips and kiss his fingertips and rub his tummy all at the same time. But Burt didn't plan on trying J.P.'s feta recipe anytime soon. His wife surely wouldn't appreciate a bathtub full of milk, bread and brine—and she was already pretty steamed about all the dead ninjas around the house.

And there was another, equally important reason Burt wouldn't be following J.P.'s advice: Burt didn't believe a word J.P. said. Not that he *disbelieved*. J.P. wasn't a liar. He just had a way of twisting Truth's arm until it screamed "Uncle!"

"So," Burt said, picking up a menu.

That was as far as he got.

"I already ordered for us," J.P. cut in. "There's only one thing to get at Luigi's Slice o' Heaven. Did you know this is the last pizza parlor in the state that still serves pizza classico?"

"Pizza—?" Burt began.

"Classico. Old school pizza. The kind you could get back in the day, before pizza lost its *edge*. You mean you don't know the story?"

Before Burt could even draw a breath to answer, J.P. was spinning his tale.

Burt didn't mind. He was bruised and bloodied and bone-tired—in no shape to keep up his end of a real conversation. Which made J.P. the perfect person to be with. Burt wouldn't even have to bother with the occasional nod of the head or "No way!" or "Then what happened?" J.P. wouldn't stop talking until his tale was told—and he wouldn't stop then, either.

Burt didn't even have to listen, so long as he didn't snore too loudly. He leaned back, closed his eyes and tried not to think of ninjas....

Pizza's a lot older than most people think (*J.P. said*). The first Pizza Hut was an actual *hut* just outside the hanging gardens of Babylon, and a mummified deep dish with pepperoni was found in King Tut's tomb, presumably because he'd need comfort food in the after-life.

But these early pizzas were different from modern 'za in two important respects: They were square, and they were never sliced. People simply grabbed hold, tore off a strip, rolled it up and ate it like a burrito. Which is why the popularity of pizza dropped off considerably after Louis Pasteur started warning everybody about little invisible things called "germs." Who wants to eat food that's been pawed by every person at the table? I mean, you know *you* washed your hands the last time you were in the bathroom, but can you be so sure about Uncle Walter?

Still, pizza hung in there as a food on the wane with a small but loyal fanbase, sort of like cow-brain sandwiches, haggis, Pop Rocks and fresh vegetables today. It didn't make its big comeback until geopolitics and crime collided to create the modern "pizza pie."

Here's what happened.

Back in the twenties and thirties, becoming a "gentleman sleuth" was about the most fashionable thing you could do. If you were upper crust, you spent your ample free time either playing polo or catching murderers. Probably the most renowned of these dilettante detectives was the brilliant amateur scientist/ psychologist/art critic/winemaker/horse breeder/palm reader/ lion tamer/monkey trainer/florist/philanthropist/philosopher/ philatelist/Egyptologist/meteorologist/ethnomusicologist/ mixologist/hairstylist Phyllo Doe. Doe and his "companion" (*J.P. winked*) Cyrus Pherman filled an entire wing of Sing Sing with killers, cracking famous mysteries like "The Purple Poodle Murder Case," "The Spatula Murder Case," "The Dust Bunny Murder Case" and "The Little-Piece-of-Felt-at-the-End-of-a-Pool-Cue Murder Case."

Unfortunately, World War II took the fun out of death for a lot of people, even Doe, and after working tirelessly to keep Greenwich Village free of Nazi saboteurs during the war, he and Pherman slipped into quiet semi-retirement. Doe spent his days reading, writing and cataloguing his vast collections of wine, art, stamps and hair-styling products, while Pherman continued to do what he did best—look on admiringly.

But duty called for Doe one last time in the spring of 1950. In the past, Doe's cases had always started the same way: with a visit from his old friend, district attorney Dunsel. By '50, however, Dunsel was long gone, having been hounded from office after the citizens of New York finally realized the only thing he could do without Doe's help was collect a salary.

It wasn't Dunsel's replacement who came to Doe hat in hand now, though. It was a much younger, leaner man with buzz-cut hair and cold eyes and a frown that looked like it had been set in cement.

"My name isn't important, and you don't need to know who I work for," the man said by way of introduction when Doe met him at the door of his elegant penthouse apartment. "What is important is this: Your country needs you."

"Then by all means come in and have a seat, Mr. Hershey," Doe said, stepping aside and sweeping his arm out toward the study. "If the Central Intelligence Agency thinks I can be of some assistance, then of course I'm at your disposal."

Even though Pherman was in the kitchen cutting out radish florets to adorn Doe's lunch, his unerring sidekick radar gave off a *ping*, and he knew the great detective had done something impressive somewhere.

"Astounding, Doe!" he called out reflexively. "How ever did you do it?"

"Observation and analysis, Pherman! Nothing more!" Doe called back.

"On your jacket," he whispered to a glowering Hershey as the young man stepped into the apartment.

Hershey looked down. Stuck to the left breast of his drab gray overcoat was a nametag.

HI! MY NAME IS
HERSHEY—CIA

Hershey ripped off the sticky tag and crumpled it in a curled fist.

"I can't very well impress you with my genius if you don't make it hard for me," Doe said, his thin lips pressing themselves into a prim smile. He led Hershey into the study, eased himself into one of the room's plush armchairs and gestured at another seat nearby.

Hershey glared at the chair, practically sneering at it, as if he considered sitting an affectation of the decadent and effete. He stayed on his feet.

"So," Doe said, "I infer from your nametag that you were a visitor somewhere today. A government facility, I presume— perhaps a laboratory conducting work of vital importance to our national defense. A laboratory which has recently played host to… *murder*?"

"Great Scott!" Pherman yelled from the kitchen.

"Not quite," said Hershey. "Yes, I was at a secret government lab today, and a crime was committed there. But it wasn't murder. It was theft."

STEVE HOCKENSMITH

"Theft?" Doe said, looking slightly deflated. "My specialty's murder, you know. 'The Ping-Pong Paddle Murder Case,' 'The Flying Squirrel Murder Case,' 'The Unopened Tube of Preparation H Murder Case,' 'The—'"

"I know all about your career as a detective, Doe," Hershey snapped. "And believe you me—if you need deaths to pique your interest, then this could easily become the most fascinating case of your career."

Doe leaned back and stroked his neatly trimmed Van Dyke.

"Tell me more, Hershey," he said. "Tell me *everything*."

"If I told you everything," Hershey replied, "I'd have to kill you."

It was an old joke, even then…only Hershey wasn't joking.

"The government has secrets, and it has *top* secrets," the CIA agent explained. "And then there are secret top secrets—secrets so secret even the existence of the secrecy is top secret. Of all these secrets, one is the secretiest of them all. I can't confirm or deny its existence. I can't even confirm or deny that I'm having this conversation about it at this very moment. Secret? Conversation? I don't know what you're talking about! See what I mean? It's *that* secret. It's that explosive. It's—"

"The hydrogen bomb," Doe said.

"Gasp!" Pherman called out from the dining room, where he was setting out plates. "How could you possibly—?"

"Simple logic, my good fellow! Simple logic!" Doe shouted back.

"Been reading about it in the *Times* for months," he whispered to Hershey, who'd slipped his right hand into his coat pocket, where he obviously kept something bulky and loaded with bullets. "Oh, come now, Hershey. Surely you wouldn't kill me for 'knowing too much,' as they say. Not when half the world knows as much as I do. We're racing against the Soviets to create the first hydrogen-fueled superbomb. That's about as secret as J. Edgar Hoover's boyfriend Clyde."

"J. Edgar Hoover's *what*?" Hershey shot back, the gun in his pocket bulging ominously in Doe's direction.

"Never mind that," Doe said quickly, waving the matter away with a flutter of his long hands. "Let's stick to the case at hand, shall we? Something's been taken from a lab where scientists have been working on the most powerful weapon ever devised. I do hope you're not about to tell me someone's stolen an actual H-bomb."

Hershey slowly drew his hand from his pocket. "No, thank god. But it's just about that bad. A prototype is almost ready for testing—and the blueprints are missing."

Doe tried to leap to his feet, but he was pushing seventy by then, and it took him a good half-minute to hoist himself from the soft cushions of his armchair.

"There's no time to lose!" he announced when he was finally upright. "We must go to this secret laboratory at once! It's nearby, I presume—on the campus of NYU."

Hershey stuffed his hand back in his pocket. "How did you—?"

"Come come, Hershey. Your nametag. You could've forgotten you were wearing it long enough to travel a few blocks, but no more than that, I'm sure. And where else in Manhattan would such cutting-edge scientific research be conducted?"

"The lab could've been on the Columbia campus," Hershey pointed out.

"Yes, it could've. In which case you would've gone to Nero Wolfe—he lives closer to the Upper West Side than I do."

A muffled cry sounded from somewhere inside the apartment.

"What was that, Pherman?" Doe called out.

"Sorry, old bean! Just pulling your *croque monsieur* out of the oven!" Pherman yelled back. "I said, 'Brilliant, Doe! By Jove, you never cease to amaze me!'"

"How does he do that?" Hershey growled.

"Enough dilly-dallying," Doe announced, heading for the front door as quickly as his old legs would carry him. "We've got a traitor to catch!"

But Doe would have to catch that traitor without any help from his sidekick. Hershey refused to let Pherman come along.

"What's he good for, anyway?" Hershey asked. "Far as I can see, all he does is tell you how great you are."

"Precisely!" Doe shot back. "He's indispensable!"

But Hershey dispensed with him anyway, and when he and Doe left, Pherman was sitting alone at the dining room table glumly munching on a radish floret.

Within fifteen minutes, Hershey was leading Doe down a hidden stairwell in one of NYU's most unassuming classroom buildings. When they reached the bottom, Hershey gave the wall a shave-and-a-haircut knock. A brick in the wall slid aside, revealing a pair of steely gray eyes.

"Password?" a gruff voice barked.

"'Jeopardy,'" Hershey said.

"Code?"

"Omega."

"Clearance?"

Hershey heaved an annoyed sigh. "You want to know my clearance?" He made a V with his fingers and poked the gray eyes Three Stooges-style. "Don't be a dumb-ass, Powell. I was just here half an hour ago. Open up!"

The brick slid back into place and the wall swung open on hidden hinges.

"Sorry, sir. Can't be too careful these days," said a burly MP on the other side, rubbing his eyes. Behind him was a small table with a stack of "Hi! My Name Is" nametags and a magic marker resting on it. Beyond that stretched a short hallway with five doors—two on each side and one at the end.

"Welcome to the Chicago Project," Hershey said.

Powell the MP nodded at the nametags. "If you wouldn't mind, sirs…."

Hershey ignored him.

"Those are offices," he said to Doe, pointing at the two doors on the left and the one at the end of the hall. "The door at the far right leads to the records room. That's where the blueprints were kept."

Doe turned toward the nearest door. "And what goes on in here?"

He was answered by the sound of flushing water. The door

opened, and a stout, red-haired, heavily bearded man stepped out wiping his hands on his kilt.

"This is Professor MacGuffin, the project leader," Hershey said. "MacGuffin, this is Phyllo Doe."

"Ah, Mrrr. Doe! I canna tell ye what a rrrelief it is to see ye, sirrr!" (*Here J.P. switched to an accent that was half Long John Silver, half Scotty from* Star Trek.) "If any man can get those plans back, it's you. Well, you orrr Nerrro Wolfe. Come back to ma office herrre and I'll tell you the whole storrry."

MacGuffin's office was behind the central door at the end of the hallway. It was a small, dimly lit room packed with thick reference books and crumpled paper and broken abacuses. A caber the height and width of a man was leaning in one corner— "Forrr when I need a wee touch of exerrrcise," MacGuffin explained. A chalkboard dominated the far wall. It was covered with long strings of numbers and mathematical symbols. The last line was:

$(E = mc^2) - IQ = 1,000 \ TNT^{100} = BOOM!$

"You appear to be very close to your goal, professor," Doe said.

"Aye, *verrra* close. We'rrre just weeks away frrrom finishing the MacGuffin Device." The professor's lips twisted into a small, prideful smile. "That's what we've named the mechanism that trrrigerrrs fusion. If the Rrrusskies got those blueprrrints, they'll have theirrr own MacGuffin soon enough. And that'll give them the H-bomb within the yearrr, I guarrrantee."

"When did you notice the plans were missing?"

"This morrrning. I went into the rrrecorrrds rrroom to make a few changes, and they werrren't therrre. We checked the otherrr offices—even the loo! The plans couldna be found."

"How big are the plans?"

MacGuffin held his hands not quite two feet apart.

"About so."

"And who had access to them?"

"All of us herrre in this wing of the prrroject: maself and ma colleagues, Doctorrr Herrrrrring and Doctorrr Strrraw."

"'This wing'? You mean there's more to the Chicago Project than this?"

"Oh, aye. Underrrneath Brrronx Community College therrre's a—"

Hershey jammed his hand into his coat pocket, and the resulting bulge aimed itself at Professor MacGuffin.

"Ahhh, I meant to say, 'Oh, no! This is it, Misterrr Doe!'" the professor hastily corrected himself. "Therrre's nae anyone else. And even if therrre werrre—theorrretically speaking, you underrrstand—this is the only place plans for the MacGuffin Device would be storrred."

"I see. So isn't it possible someone who worked here simply walked out with the plans?"

"They could trrry, but Powell out therrre searrrches us everrry time we leave. Even *he's* searrrched when another soldierrr comes at the end of his shift. No. You couldna just walk out with the plans in yourrr sock."

"Yet there were no signs of a break-in, I take it."

"Nae. Nothing."

"But we do know the facility's cover's been blown," Hershey said.

Doe cocked an eyebrow. "Blown?"

"Aye, that was a surrrprrrise," MacGuffin said. "Yesterrrday just beforrre five p.m. Powell, the guarrrd, knocks on ma doorrr and tells me we've just had a pizza deliverrred!"

Doe cocked his other eyebrow. "A *pizza*?"

"Aye. From Uncle Joe's Pizzerrria. The deliverrryman knocked on the wall outside our secrrret entrrrance and wouldna go away till Powell opened up and paid him. He claimed someone inside phoned in the orrrderrr!"

Doe couldn't cock any more eyebrows, so he cocked an ear.

"Standard KGB psyops," Hershey explained. "The Reds have phoned in fake pizza orders for the Pentagon, the Treasury, the Justice Department. They ring-and-run the White House about twice a month. And just last week a Soviet mole left a flaming bag of dog poop on the Capitol steps. Of course, we run the same kinds of operations ourselves." Hershey's granite-stiff expression looked almost on the brink of breaking into a smile. "I got Stalin on the phone once. Asked him if his fridge was running."

"Yes, well...congratulations, Hershey," Doe said. He turned back to the professor. "So, you didn't actually *eat* any of this mysterious pizza, did you?"

"Ach! That's the most fiendish thing about it!" MacGuffin exclaimed. "Those Rrrrussian bastarrrds sent us an extrrra larrrge... with double anchovies and *pineapple*! I couldna brrring maself to so much as touch it!"

"Of course," Doe said. "I only have one more question, professor."

"Aye?"

Doe leaned forward, the intensity of his gaze pinning MacGuffin like a butterfly in a collector's case. Hershey leaned forward, too, sensing that the old detective's next words could be of literally earth-shaking importance.

"Tell me," Doe said, "were you wearing your kilt yesterday?"

MacGuffin blinked slowly, then smiled and let out a relieved sigh. "It's easy enough to answerr that, Misterrr Doe. Nae, I was not. I had on ma Aberrrdeen trrrouserrrs—rrred with grrreen and black checks."

"Sounds fetching," Doe said. "Come along, Hershey. I'd like to speak with Professor MacGuffin's colleague Dr. Herring."

"What was that about MacGuffin's kilt?" Hershey asked when the two of them were out in the hallway again.

"Have you no curiosity, Hershey? Don't tell me you've never wondered what a Scotsman keeps under his kilt."

"Pervert," Hershey mumbled under his breath as Doe brought up a hand to knock on Dr. Herring's door.

"There's nothing perverse about it," said Doe, who had sharper hearing than Hershey thought. "If you'd give a moment's thought... to..."

Doe's words trailed off and he froze in place, his knuckles hovering a fraction of an inch from the door.

"Do you hear that?"

"Hear what?"

Hershey moved his ear closer to the office door.

A faint sound could be made out through the muffling of the wood—the sound of someone whistling cheerfully.

"So Herring's a music lover," Hershey said. "So what?"

"So...."

Doe pursed his lips and began to whistle quietly, matching Herring's melody note for note. After a few bars, he stopped and rapped on the door.

Herring's whistling stopped, as well. A moment later, the door opened, revealing a fortyish woman with pale skin and thick lips and round, unblinking eyes. Atop her head was a massive tangle of graying hair so voluminously frizzy Tarzan could swing through it clinging to stray curls like jungle vines.

"Oh...it's *you*," the woman said to Hershey with undisguised contempt. "Back for another turn of the thumb screws, huh? Well, come in if you really have to."

Hershey and Doe followed her into her office, which was even more packed with bric-a-brac than MacGuffin's.

"You must be Doe, the big detective," Herring said as she took a seat behind her clutter-covered desk.

Doe smiled modestly. "Well, I am Phyllo Doe and I am a detective. Whether or not I'm 'big' I'll leave to others to decide."

Herring coughed out a raspy laugh. "I bet you will." She reached up and scratched her head, and when her fingers emerged from the thicket of salt-and-pepper locks they were clasping a cigarette. "Care to join me?"

Hershey and Doe both shook their heads. Herring shrugged and lit up her smoke with a lighter she fished from somewhere behind her ear.

"So," she said, leaning back and swinging her heels up onto the edge of her desk—revealing a set of surprisingly shapely gams in the process. "Let the inquisition begin."

"I only have a few questions, Dr. Herring," Doe said. "And there will be no thumb screws, I promise."

Herring shrugged. "Suit yourself."

"I usually do," Doe replied. "First off, did you have cause to enter the records room yesterday?"

"I not only had cause, I did it. I'm in and out of there all day. So are MacGuffin and Straw."

"And at the end of the day, when it comes time to leave, you're searched just like MacGuffin and Straw?"

"I wouldn't say 'just like.' I'm guessing Powell's a little more *thorough* with me. He seems particularly worried that I'm gonna sneak something out strapped to my caboose. Ever been groped by a man in uniform, Mr. Doe? Let me tell ya'—it gets old fast."

Doe gave her a cryptic smile.

"One more thing, Dr. Herring," he said, and he leaned toward her, his smile instantly replaced by a frowning glower. "How were you wearing your hair when you left yesterday?"

Herring gaped at him for a moment.

"What are you—a detective or a hair-dresser?" she finally scoffed.

"A person can be many things," Doe responded coolly. "Now answer the question."

"Alright." Herring pointed her cigarette at a small cluster of hairpins on her desk. "I had those in. My hair was in a bun. That's how I wear it when I'm outside." She ran the fingers of her left hand through her tresses, and a pencil, some paper clips, a wad of chewing gum and a heavy dusting of dandruff fell from her bushy locks onto her desk. "I only let my hair down here in the office."

"I see," Doe said. "Well, thank you for your time, doctor. Let's go, Hershey."

Herring didn't quite slam the door behind them, but she did close it quickly and firmly, missing their hindquarters by only the tiniest fraction of an inch. Doe lingered outside the door, listening intently.

"The good doctor doesn't appear to be in a whistling mood any longer," he said.

"So? What was the big deal about her whistling in the first place?"

Doe shook his head at Hershey, looking both saddened and disappointed, like a teacher who spots a student picking his nose in class.

"Really, Hershey—how are you supposed to protect America from Communists when you don't even recognize their fight song when you hear it?"

"Their *what?*"

"The Internationale, Hershey. The official anthem of the Communist Party."

Doe whistled the turgid tune they'd heard coming from Herring's office a few minutes before.

"Not exactly Cole Porter, is it?" Doe said. "Perhaps that's why you didn't recognize it. It's hardly *Your Hit Parade* material."

Down the hallway behind them, the phone on Powell's desk began to ring. The burly M.P. scooped up the receiver.

"Mandelbaum's Thin and Puny, clothing the runty man since 1931. Mandelbaum speaking. How may I help you?" Powell's slightly bored expression shifted quickly to surprise. "Why, yes—this *is* actually a secret government lab. Yes—Phyllo Doe *is* here. Uh-huh. O.K., I'll pass that along. My pleasure. Right. The same to you. And, sir—don't ever call here again."

Powell hung up the phone and turned to Doe.

"A Mr. Pherman just called. He left a message for you: 'Good heavens, man! You've done it again! Your powers of observation are positively supernatural!'"

Doe gave a modest shrug. "There's nothing supernatural about it. When one spends a lifetime accumulating and cataloging information, one simply acquires a certain—"

"Hold on, Doe, hold on!" Hershey spluttered. "All that stuff about 'the Internationale'...are you saying Herring's a Red?"

"Perhaps. Or she used to be. Or she has unusually bad taste in music. It's...*suggestive*, that's all. Communist sympathies would provide a motive for stealing the blueprints, but then again so would a simple bribe. I wager the KGB isn't so doctrinaire it doesn't recognize the persuasive power of cold, hard cash. No, it's the means not the motive that holds the key to this affair. Now come along. It's time we spoke with Dr. Straw."

The man who answered the knock on Straw's door would've made a perfect customer for Mandelbaum's Thin and Puny, if such a store actually existed. He was only slightly taller and broader than your average lawn jockey, and he had to bend back to look up at Doe and Hershey the way they would've had to crane their necks to see the top of the Empire State Building. He could've been mistaken for a child if he didn't have a smoldering pipe sticking from one side of his mouth.

"Well, if it isn't my favorite G-man," Straw said, his voice a surprisingly resonant basso profundo. "Back so soon. And you've brought a friend along. The great Phyllo Doe, perhaps?"

Straw stretched a tiny hand up over his head, and Doe reached down and took it.

"Indeed," Doe said as they shook. "If you don't mind, I have a few questions for you, Dr. Straw."

"Of course. Come in."

Straw's office was substantially tidier than his colleagues', partially because the furniture took up far less space. The desk and chairs and bookcases were all built to fit Straw's tiny proportions. The only bit of clutter in the room was a half-eaten pastrami sandwich and a kosher dill sitting on a crumpled bed of wax paper on one corner of the desk.

Doe wedged himself into one of the Lilliputian seats, his knees almost bumping into his chest. Hershey chose to stay on his feet.

"So tell me, doctor," Doe began. His long, thin nose twitched like a rabbit's, and the old detective seemed to lose his train of thought.

"Yes?" Straw said.

"Did you...go into the...records room...yesterday?" Doe asked, taking a discreet whiff with each pause.

"I did. I went in to look over the plans for the MacGuffin Device. I've been working on the—" Straw shot a quick glance up at Hershey, then chuckled softly. "I guess I shouldn't say. But the

Chicago Project is a team effort, and everyone's got their own little field of expertise, including me. Only Professor MacGuffin really understands the thing as a whole. I've been thinking about some alterations I was going to propose to him, and I wanted to look the plans over one more time before doing my final calculations."

"And...did...you?" Doe said, still sniffing at the air.

"No, as it turns out. Dr. Herring was already going over the blueprints, and I didn't want to disturb her. I figured I could just come back some other time." Straw shrugged his tiny shoulders. "I guess I was wrong."

"Was...Herring wearing...her hair...up or...down?"

"Gosh, I don't know. Dr. Herring's hair isn't something I pay much attention to, to be honest." Straw sucked on his pipe for a moment, looking thoughtful. "Down, I guess."

"Ahhhh," Doe said, nodding absent-mindedly. He took in one more deep whiff, then smiled broadly. "Of course! *Anchovies!*"

"What?" Straw and Hershey asked simultaneously.

"I've been trying to identify a scent I picked up when we walked into this room," Doe explained. "It was obscured by the smoke from Dr. Straw's pipe, but now I have it. Salt-cured fish. Anchovies, to be precise. Doctor, am I correct in thinking that the pizza that was delivered here yesterday ended up in your office?"

Straw gave an astonished nod. "That's right. I took the pizza. Turns out I'm the only one around here who enjoys anchovies. That's quite a nose you've got, Mr. Doe."

"For the true gourmand, smell is at least as important a sense as taste."

"Hold on!" Hershey barked. "Straw, are you saying you *ate* that Commie pizza?"

"Absolutely!" Straw declared with chest-swelling pride. "I figured if somebody was out to poison us, they would've sent us a pizza with pepperoni and mushrooms or sausage and green peppers—toppings people like. The pineapple and anchovies were just to taunt us. And I wasn't going to let some Boris or Ivan put one over on *me*. No, sir!"

The diminutive scientist pushed back his chair and climbed up onto his desk.

"They say we're in a 'Cold War' with these Bolshevik bastards," he went on, his deep voice booming. He stared up over Doe and Hershey's heads as if watching a fireworks display or an eagle in flight or bombs bursting in air while our flag was still there. "Well, if I'd been too scared to eat that pizza, then the Reds would have already won. So I took it home and I had it for dinner. And, friends, let me tell you something. That pizza tasted like America to me. It tasted like mom and apple pie and baseball. It tasted like amber waves of grain. It tasted like freedom. And damn it—it was *delicious*."

Hershey looked like he was about to salute.

"Yes, by god," the CIA agent said, wiping a tear from his eye. "What could taste better than a heaping plate of piping-hot liberty?"

"You stepped on your sandwich," Doe added.

Straw began wiping his foot off on the edge of his desk.

"So there you are, gentlemen," he said. "Any more questions?"

"Just one." Doe leaned forward, glaring at Straw melodramatically. He stretched out his long, thin arm and pointed at the bottom of the scientist's shoe. "What is that?"

"Uhhh...pastrami," Straw said.

"Yes, but it's more than that, isn't it, doctor? It's much, *much* more."

Straw flashed Hershey a quick, confused look that asked, "Is this guy senile?" Hershey shrugged.

"It's pastrami...on rye?" Straw said. "With a pickle?"

Doe nodded. "And...?"

"Uhhh...it's my lunch?"

"Exactly!" Doe proclaimed. He turned toward Hershey, a look of smug satisfaction stretching his wrinkle-creased features.

Hershey stared back at him as if he had an Airedale on his head.

Doe's gloating collapsed into a sigh.

"Means, Hershey. *Means*," he said. "MacGuffin, Herring, Dr. Straw here, even the guards. They're all searched when they leave this facility. So how could the plans be sneaked out? Why, in something no one would want to touch or examine too closely. Beneath a Scotsman's kilt, for instance. Or tucked away in a voluminous head of dandruffy hair. But MacGuffin wasn't wearing his kilt yesterday, and Herring had her hair pinned up when she left. Which leaves...?"

Hershey's brow was so furrowed his forehead almost bumped his nose.

Doe sighed again.

"'I couldna brrring maself to so much as touch it!'" the old detective said, imitating Professor MacGuffin's oatmeal-thick brogue. He turned toward Straw and shook his head sadly. "Really, doctor. No one likes anchovies on pizza. *No one*."

"I do!" Straw protested.

"Enough to eat an entire pizza all by yourself? Stand it on end, and an extra large would be taller than you."

"I didn't say I finished it."

"Then where are the leftovers? All true connoisseurs will tell you pizza's just as good the next day. Some say even better." Doe nodded at the mangled pastrami on rye. "Yet you bought your lunch from a deli today. Why would that be necessary if you had a refrigerator full of pizza at home?"

"I ate too much of it! It made me sick!"

"But here you are at work looking remarkably well. Perhaps it was the pastrami and the pickle that settled your stomach, eh?" Doe shook his head and chuckled. "No, I think not. The truth is, doctor, you couldn't hide the blueprints on your person: You don't have enough *person* on which to hide anything. But you could hide the plans under an extra-large pizza—especially if it was sure to disgust anyone who so much as glanced at it. So your KGB handlers sent in the pizza...and you brought out the plans."

Straw clenched his little fists in impotent rage. In the blink of an eye, his expression changed from incredulous to defiant.

"You don't have any proof, old man!" he sneered. "You'll never find the blueprints—and you'll never be able to pin the theft on me!"

"Oh, I beg to differ," Doe replied calmly. "When you hid the plans beneath a double-anchovy and pineapple pizza, you no doubt created the stinkiest blueprints in the history of drafting. All we need to do now is procure the services of any reasonably competent tracking dog. Why, with a trail of anchovies, cheese and diced pineapple to follow, *I* could probably sniff out the trail."

With a feral roar, Straw launched himself at Doe's throat. Before Doe could so much as gasp, Hershey stretched out a hand, snatched Straw out of the air and tucked the tiny traitor under his arm like a football.

"Why'd you do it, Doc?" Hershey asked. "How could you sell us out to the Commies?"

"That MacGuffin! Naming the device after himself when all of us helped build it!" Straw ranted, kicking his feet like a child throwing a tantrum. "He thinks he's so big! Someone had to cut him down to size!"

"Let me tell you something, doc," Hershey said, shaking his head. "There's nothing *smaller* than a man who betrays his own country."

Straw went as limp as a rag doll and began weeping quietly.

"Nicely put, Hershey," Doe said. "Now I suppose we'd best—"

There was a firm knock on the office door.

"Yeah? What?" Hershey called out.

The door swung open, and Powell leaned into the room.

"Pardon me for interrupting, sirs," the M.P. said. He paused for only a fraction of a second upon catching sight of Straw wedged under Hershey's armpit. "This just came for Mr. Doe."

He handed Doe a Western Union telegram and backed quickly out of the room.

"ASTONISHING, DOE!" the telegram read. "YOUR POWERS OF DEDUCTION ARE AS SHARP AS EVER! AMERICA CAN SLEEP EASIER TONIGHT KNOWING YOU'RE STILL READY TO HEED THE CALL TO DUTY!

SINCERELY, CY PHERMAN"

"Really, Doe—how does he do that?" asked Hershey, who'd read the message over Doe's shoulder.

"All I know is this," Doe said. "*I'll* sleep easier tonight knowing the Soviet Union will never have its own H-bomb. Let's go get those plans!"

And that's exactly what they did. One of New York's finest police dogs led them from the underground lab to Straw's apartment to a KGB-front bakery in Little Italy, where a Soviet spymaster/pastrymaker was about to smuggle the blueprints out of the country folded and baked into a pumpkin pie. So MacGuffin got back the plans, Hershey got the spies, the dog got the pie, Straw got the chair and Doe got to ease back into retirement with one more victory on his impressive roster of cases solved.

And the rest of us got something, too. The government quickly established a new security protocol for all federal offices and installations: Any pizzas brought in or out had to be round and pre-cut by at least four intersecting radial lines. That way, all a guard had to do was lift up one slice to see all the way to the middle, thus insuring that nothing could be smuggled underneath.

These new-fangled "pizza pies" caught on with civil servants, and soon they were ordering them even when they weren't at work. The practice spread to their family and friends, and through them to the rest of the country, and before long the sliced-circle-pizza fad was sweeping the globe.

Today, of course, square pizza is rare, and you'll only find unsliced pizza in the frozen food aisle. The pizza pie reins supreme as perhaps the most popular culinary dish in the world. But some of us—historians, gourmets, collectors of antique food—remember the way it used to be…and that we have a man named Phyllo Doe to thank for changing it all.

Burt hadn't been able to get much rest while J.P. told his story. For once, he wasn't just incredulous. He was furious.

As Burt saw it, he and J.P. had an unspoken covenant: J.P.

could go on whatever flights of fancy he wanted as long as he didn't insult Burt's intelligence. And this square pizza/Phyllo Doe/ MacGuffin Device story crossed the line. It didn't just insult Burt's intelligence. It spat in its face, kicked it in the groin and called its momma dirty names.

It was an extra-large serving of malarkey with a generous topping of balderdash and a side order of B.S. And Burt was going to say so.

Just as he opened his mouth to speak, the waitress returned.

"One-extra-large-need-anything-else-no-O.K.-enjoy," she mumbled quickly, tossing the pizza on the table frisbee-fashion before turning and dashing for the safety of the kitchen. Having once been trapped in the black hole-strength gravity generated by J.P.'s mouth, she obviously had no intention of being sucked in again.

Burt looked down at the pizza, which was spinning like a roulette wheel on the table before him.

No, he realized as it slowed to a stop. *Not like a wheel at all.*

The pizza was square. And it was unsliced. Just like in J.P.'s story.

And there was something else odd about it: Every inch was covered with heaps of small, brown, leathery-looking strips.

The pizza had been topped with an entire school of anchovies.

"No one likes anchovies on pizza," Phyllo Doe had said. "*No one.*" And that part of the story Burt had been almost willing to believe. To him, anchovies were about as appetizing as a deep-fried jockstrap.

Yet there was J.P. peeling off a particularly long sliver of fish and dropping it into his mouth. He chewed, smiling, then licked his fingers before grabbing a corner of the pizza and tearing it off.

"Ahhhh, the food of the gods," J.P. said with a satisfied sigh. He began rolling the pizza-scrap up, and sauce and cheese and grease and bits of fish oozed out to coat his fingers.

Burt moaned and put his head down on the table. Facing a ninja death squad had been easy. Watching J.P. mangle "pizza classico" with anchovies—*that* was hard.

"You know why they call them 'anchovies,' don't you?" J.P. said, the speaking of words doing absolutely nothing to slow his chewing of food. "They're named for the woman who first farmed them commercially: Anne Chovy. In the wild, they used to be known as *foedus salsus pisciculus*—or, more commonly, 'the salty little-pischer fish.' Ferocious creatures. Make piranha look like goldfish. It's pretty amazing how Chovy domesticated them, actually. 'The Fish Whisperer,' people called her…."

And on J.P. went, not pausing until half the pizza was gone—and Burt had picked up the bill, as always. Burt didn't eat a bite, except to nibble at a breadstick in a half-hearted attempt at calming his queasy stomach. When the waitress boxed up the leftovers and tried to give them to him, he nearly passed out.

"No," he managed to gasp, pointing at J.P. "*Him.*"

"Goody," his friend said, giving the waitress a cheerful wink as she handed him the box. "More for me."

And that, beyond a doubt, was true.

THE BIG ROAD

"Private eye." Sounds pretty exciting, don't it? Kinda macho. Probably makes you think of guys like Tom Selleck and Jim Garner and Mike Connors.

Mike Connors, I said. You know...Mannix.

You never heard of *Mannix*?

You sure you're old enough to be holding that beer?

Anyway, like I was saying, you think "private eye," you think "man of action"—some fella who'd rather throw himself through a window than just stroll in through an open door. Well, let me tell you, one of my best buddies is a private eye, and that just ain't him at all. He's more what you'd call a "man of *in*action," unless you want to say watching TV and scooping poop out of a litter box counts as action...which it don't.

This buddy of mine—Larry Erie's his name—he's got him an O.K. excuse for moping. Lost his wife a year or so back, right before he retired from the River City police. But heck—I lost my Bootsie just about the same time, and you don't see me shuffling around the house like a zombie in a bathrobe. It hurt...oh, it did hurt. But here I am with a beer in my hand and a smile on my face, you know what I'm saying? Life goes on.

That's what I keep telling Larry, and you know what he says? "Not for long." Can you beat that? The man makes Chicken Little look like a cockeyed optimist.

Seeing as how I've got a little more bounce left in me than old Larry, I've taken it upon myself to drag him out of the dumps whether he wants to come or not. In fact, the only reason he's a

226   226

private eye is I wouldn't shut up about it until he gave it a try. I thought it would be good for him—you know, therapeutic.

Well, he's had him a few cases, but nothing that would get anybody worked up enough to jump through any windows. The biggest mystery he's cracked is who stole some neighbor kid's dog, and even then I had to pull his fat out of the fire before it was all over. Mannix would've wrapped that one up before the first commercial.

All this had me just about ready to change my opinion on private eye-types. Being a *P.I.* didn't seem to be any more special than being T.P., O.J. or an A&P.

But Erie set me straight on that, and he didn't have to bust any glass to do it. Get me another beer and maybe I'll tell you what happened.

Thanks, kid. Gotta keep my throat moist if I'm gonna get through this story.

So here's the deal. I've got a son about your age—my youngest, David. Now he's "special," though not in the way a father might want. You know those bumper stickers that say "Proud parent of an honor roll student"? Well, I wouldn't have qualified for that. Mine would have said "Embarrassed parent of a juvenile delinquent." I was long-haul trucking in those days, so I'd call from Florida or New York or the moon or wherever and Bootsie would say "Do you wanna hear what your son did today?" and I'd know she wasn't talking about Bill Jr. or Pete. It was always Dave, and it was always trouble.

We kept hoping it was just a phase he was going through, and I suppose it was. Problem was, that *phase* lasted ten years. By the end of it Dave wasn't just blowing up mailboxes and doing doughnuts on the neighbor's lawn. He was drinking and toking and probably snorting too, and his friends weren't the sorts of folks who limit themselves to pranks.

It got so bad I almost had to take myself off the road just to keep a better eye on him, and it was a blessed miracle the boy never went to jail. He finally got himself turned around, but it didn't come cheap. The last time Bootsie went into the hospital, she got him to open his heart to Jesus. I thought at the time he was just trying to send his mother off happy, but after she passed away he kept right on going to church.

Now while Bootsie might have saved Dave's soul, it was up to me to do something about his wallet. A heart full of the Holy Spirit and a nickel won't get you a gumball these days, so I set out to give the boy a livelihood. I only had one to give, of course. My own. Trucking. Usually he'd treat advice from me like you'd treat a plate of cow patties at a potluck dinner, but he was flat-busted broke and one bounced rent check away from sleeping in his pickup, so he listened. I taught him all there is to know about eighteen-wheelers, saw to it he got himself a commercial driver's license and even sniffed him out his first job.

Well, times are tough, as I'm sure you know, so the only thing I could come up with was less than perfect: delivering Budweiser for the local beverage distributor. I was having nightmares that somebody was going to find my son floating face-down in a swimming pool full of Bud, but God bless him, Dave managed to resist temptation—or "keep Satan in a headlock," as he calls it. He was none too pleased about "doing the devil's work" though, and the first chance he got he jumped over to a new job.

It was a good one, too. Cross-America Freight's got a distribution center up around Indianapolis. They specialize in hauling TVs and PCs and DVDs and all those other high-tech blah-blah-blahs. Dave was going to be running gizmos all over the country. I was pretty darned proud, I tell you. My boy had become a long-haul gearjammer, just like his old man.

He called me from a motel outside Atlanta after his first day on the highway, and I don't think I'd ever heard him happier.

"There ain't a feelin' in the world better than takin' a rig down the big road," he said. "How'd you ever give it up?"

Of course, I could've reminded him what it was that tore my hands off the wheel—a sick wife and a son headed for a guest appearance on *COPS*. But I didn't dredge all that up. Dave was happy. Why say anything to spoil it?

Unfortunately, it all got spoiled soon enough anyway, because the very next day Dave called me again, and this time he was practically in tears.

"Somebody stole my load, Dad! I'm gonna get fired! I...I might even go to jail!"

"Now hold on, Dave, hold on," I said. "Nobody can blame you if your truck got jacked. Just get a hold of yourself and tell me what happened."

It took him maybe ten minutes to get out the whole story, and by the time he'd finished I'd changed my mind. He could and most likely *would* be blamed. All I could think of to say was "I'm so sorry, son. You're screwed."

But that kind of language isn't really my style—Bootsie had no tolerance for swearing, and she broke me of the habit on our first date. And it wouldn't have done Dave any good to hear such talk. So I did the fatherly thing, which is to sound cool and calm even when inside you're screaming, weeping and begging the Lord for mercy.

"You just sit tight," I said. "Me and Larry'll come down there and straighten this whole thing out."

Now volunteering Larry Erie for a quick trip down south qualifies as optimistic bordering on nuts. There are days I can't even drag the man out of his La-Z-Boy, let alone out of his house. He'll glue his butt in front of the idiot box and watch old movies from dawn to dusk and dusk to dawn. I told him one time he ought to just go ahead and move the toilet and the refrigerator in next to the TV so he'd never have to stop watching, and he looked at me like he actually thought it might be a good idea.

When you got yourself a couch potato buried that deep, a mere phone call ain't gonna pull him up into the sunshine. You gotta roll up your sleeves and *dig*. So I drove over to Larry's place and just walked right in the front door. One of his cats came out to say hello, but Larry was occupied in the back room. Like always, the volume on the TV was turned up so high it's a wonder it didn't bust out the windows. I could hear Cary Grant talking loud and fast, like he was in the back of the house calling a horse race through a megaphone. I went to the master bedroom and got to work.

Five minutes later I walked into the TV room with a suitcase in my hand.

"Alright," I said. "Let's go."

Larry jumped out of his recliner like the cushions were on fire.

"Bass! You just about gave me a heart attack!" He took a look at the suitcase—*his* suitcase—and my words began to sink in. "What do you mean, 'Let's go'?"

"Dave's in trouble down in Atlanta. He needs us."

"What? Bass, I can't just go running off to Georgia at the drop of a hat."

"Why not?"

I could see that threw him, but he's a quick-witted fella, and he recovered fast.

"There's the cats for one thing. They need—"

I shook my head. "I already set out enough food and water for two days. You won't be gone any longer than that."

"But they—"

"They're cats, Larry. They'll be fine. *Next.*"

"Well, I...I..."

A sort of sad horror settled over Larry's face as he groped around for words, and I knew exactly what he was thinking. There was no "next." He had no excuses because the only things filling up his days were three cats and Turner Classic Movies.

"What kind of trouble?" he said.

I explained as I drove us up to Indianapolis International Airport.

Dave's trailer had been loaded with TeleSonic flat-screen, high-definition, plasma-tube, nuclear-powered 3D TVs with diamond-studded remote controls and gold-plated extension cords. Or something like that. Anyway, they were televisions, the new kind, big and fancy. Just one of those suckers'll run you north of three-thousand dollars, and Dave was hauling a hundred of 'em.

Now the load being so valuable and Dave being so new and the dispatcher being what some folks would call a "control freak," Dave's every move on the highway was mapped out in advance. The dispatcher gave him a road plan telling him which route to take, how fast to take it and even which rest stops he could visit along the way. There's strict rules about how long a driver can stay behind the wheel, so Dave had to pull over after eight hours, and of course the dispatcher told him exactly where to do it: the Rest-Eaze Motel in Crabapple, Georgia. Once he was checked in, Dave looked over his trailer—which was sealed up tight with a cable and padlock—then settled in for the night.

The poor kid had a rough time of it. This being his first big haul and all, he couldn't get over the crazy idea that someone was going to snatch his freight, and twice he got up in the middle of the night to peek out the window at his rig. But it was safe and sound both times, and the next morning he found it sitting there waiting for him without so much as a scuff on the chrome. He got her in gear and fought his way through traffic down to a little burg called Douglasville, where the BigBuy SuperStores have their metro Atlanta warehouse. Dave gave the foreman there the keys to the lock, they threw open the trailer doors and the dock crew stepped inside to start unloading...*nothing*.

There wasn't a TV in sight. That trailer was as empty as a state trooper's skull.

Naturally people got to pointing fingers, and most of those fingers were pointed straight at my son. He'd left Indy with a hundred TVs and arrived in Douglasville with nothing—not even a notion as to what the heck might have happened. He'd spent most of the day being barked at by BigBuy brass, and all he could do was shrug and say, "I don't know. Them TVs was in there yesterday." The last I'd heard from him, the cops were on their way.

That Dave was going to be fired was inevitable. That he might get sent off to jail was entirely possible. That he was innocent...well, that we had to take that on faith.

"Maybe *you* can take it on faith," Erie said as I finished filling him in, "but everyone else is going to want proof."

"Exactly," I said. "That's why we're gettin' on the four o'clock flight to Atlanta. If there's proof to be found, you're the one to find it, am I right?"

Now a real man-of-action, Magnum-type fella would've answered me with "Darn straight" or "I'll clear Dave or die trying" or something like that—the kind of thing that'll give a worried father a little comfort. I needed Larry to be cocky and confident. Instead he just looked kind of embarrassed.

"I'll do what I can," he said.

I started to wonder then if Dave would be in prison in Indiana or Georgia. I was pulling for Indiana, of course, as I wasn't looking forward to an eight-hour drive just to pay him a visit.

A noble TV private eye would've offered to buy his own ticket too, I suppose, but Larry let me pick up the bill. As usual he let me do most of the talking as well, so I passed the time on the plane by reminiscing about Dave's teenage hijinks—the way he used to help himself to any alcohol or tobacco he could find in the house, the stubby reefer butts and girlie mags he left lying around his room, his collection of stolen street signs and newspaper vending machines, the time he "borrowed" Bill Jr.'s Pinto and left it three feet deep in the Wabash River.

My stories didn't seem to buck Larry up much, maybe because so many of them involved shenanigans that bent the law to the breaking point and beyond. I realized somewhere in there that I wouldn't make much of a character witness at my son's trial. He'd been trying to wear a halo ever since he'd been "saved," but I knew him too well to convince anybody he was an angel.

I called his cell phone number once we were on the ground, though I half-expected I'd get no answer. They take your possessions off you before they throw you in a jail cell, you know. But Dave picked up on the first ring. It turned he wasn't in jail or even a police station—he was right out front waiting for us.

We hooked up with him at baggage claim. It was Larry who spotted him first, though he and Dave had never met face to face.

The family resemblance was probably the first tip-off: Dave's a wiry little fella, just like his old man. But I think Larry would've known it was my son even if he were seven feet tall and four feet wide. The expression on his face would've given him away. Dave looked so downhearted it's a wonder complete strangers weren't walking up to offer him loose change and pats on the back.

"I'm sorry, Dad" was the first thing he said to me.

I clapped a hand on his shoulder, and the father in me said, "There ain't nothin' for you to be sorry about, Dave." I hate to admit it, but the trucker in me wanted to add, "Is there?" Fortunately, the father told the trucker to keep his trap shut.

I introduced Larry to Dave, and Dave said, "I've heard a lot about you" as they shook hands.

"I've heard a lot about *you*," Larry replied, and maybe I turned a little red thinking of just what he'd heard, seeing as how he'd heard it all from me and most of it wasn't exactly flattering.

"So you got your rig parked outside?" I asked.

Dave shook his head. "I don't *have* a rig anymore. Cross-America's sendin' another driver down to get mine and pick up my next load. I guess they think I'd drive it all off to Tijuana or somethin'. I'm supposed to fly back tonight and meet with my dispatcher in the morning. I figure first thing he'll do is fire me. Second thing he'll do is hand me over to the police." Dave shrugged and looked down at his feet, which were covered with gleaming-new leather cowboy boots. "I guess there ain't nothin' we can do about it now. Looks like you two came all this way for nothin'."

I wasn't going to say he was right, but I was sure thinking it. Those airplane tickets had put me out more than three-hundred dollars, and that was money I couldn't afford to set a match to just now. Dave sure as heck didn't have the cash to hire a lawyer, so it was going to fall on me to bankroll his defense. I was already cooking up a scheme to get some of my airline money back—it's amazing what folks'll do for you when you're a little old man with a weepy story to tell—but Larry stepped in before I could start weaving my web of fibs.

"How long did it take you to drive down here from Indianapolis?" he asked.

"A little over eight hours to Crabapple yesterday," Dave said. "Another two to Douglasville this morning."

Larry looked at his watch. "It's not even seven yet."

"Yeah. There's one more flight to Indy tonight, and it doesn't leave till eight thirty," Dave said, not seeing what Larry was driving at. "Dad, my credit card's still maxed out, so if you could—"

"Hold on there, Dave," I said, thankful for an excuse to sidestep the rest of the sentence he'd started. "Larry...are you thinkin' what I think you're thinkin'?"

"That depends. What do you think I'm thinking?"

"I think you're thinkin' we should *drive* back to Indiana."

"Drive? Blankety-blank! Why in the doodly-dee would we go and do that?" Dave blurted out. (Well, except for the "blankety-blank" and the "doodly-dee": That's just my translation. The words he used had a bit more hair on their chest.)

"Because somewhere between Indianapolis and Douglasville your cargo disappeared," Larry explained. "And it's going to be a lot easier to find out how if we're there where it happened, not 34,000 feet overhead."

"You want us to follow Dave's route?" I asked.

Larry nodded. "From beginning to end."

Dave had more to say to that, none of which I can repeat here without plugging a bar of Irish Spring in my mouth afterward. The gist of it was that we'd be in no condition to face his dispatcher, the cops or anybody else the next morning after an all-nighter on the highway.

Larry's plan made sense, though, and a rental car's a lot cheaper than three one-way airline tickets. Yet the prospect of a whole night cooped up in a car with Dave and Larry...well, one's my son and the other's like a brother, but that wouldn't keep me from strangling the both of them somewhere between the Georgia and Indiana borders. Long distances on the road will do that to a man, particularly if he's got some stress coming down on him. That's why I'd done all my hauls alone.

Still, what choice did we have? We might only get one chance to prove Dave was innocent. We had to take it.

"Where do you get rental cars around here?" I said with a sigh.

Larry smiled. Dave groaned.

Our first stop once we hit the road was the BigBuy warehouse in Douglasville. We pulled up in the only vehicle the airport's Rent-a-Heap-Cheap had to offer: a blue Chevy Metro no bigger than a Shriner's go-kart. Getting out of it we must've looked like three gorillas fighting their way out of a cereal box.

Except to give directions, Dave had gone sulky-quiet for the ride over. But he was the first to speak now that we'd arrived.

"I had to wait over there about forty-five minutes before a dock was free for me," he said, pointing off to the south end of the lot. There was another rig there now, in plain view even though darkness had fallen. Daylight or nighttime either one, nobody could have messed with that trailer without being spotted by the dock crew.

I guess Larry came to the same conclusion, because he didn't waste any time snooping around out there. Instead he turned toward another part of the lot, where a Mack truck sat alone, a Cross-America trailer hitched up behind it.

"Is that your truck?" he asked Dave.

"Yessir."

"Show it to me," Larry said, starting off toward the eighteen-wheeler. Dave and I tagged along behind like a couple of ducklings chasing their mother.

Larry hadn't exactly transformed himself into Tom Selleck, but he wasn't his old bump-on-a-log self either. He was moving a lot faster than his usual shuffle, and even in the dim light I could see a new brightness flashing in his eyes as he walked around that truck. I felt like the Larry Erie I knew back in River City had a dead battery, and this one had gotten himself a jump start.

"So you left Indianapolis with a full load, but when you pulled up here the trailer was empty," he said.

Dave nodded. "That's right. I was all bundled out when I got on the boulevard, but by the time I got my dry box to the dock I was dead-headin' without even knowin' it."

Larry threw a confused glance back at Dave. But he didn't ask my boy to repeat himself, so he must've put the pieces of the puzzle together without any help. Me, I just rolled my eyes. All Dave had done was repeat back exactly what Larry had said, only in trucker-talk. It happens to green drivers all the time. They feel like they've just joined some big club, so they're always trying to slip you the secret handshake even when you don't give a rat's ashtray.

"What?" said Dave.

He'd noticed the eye roll.

Instead of answering his question, I asked one of my own.

"What do you see there, Larry?"

He'd come to a stop by a bunch of dark scrapes along one side of the trailer. Once upon a time, a Cross-America driver hadn't been careful enough pulling in or out of somewhere.

"Did you notice that yesterday?" Larry asked.

I saw what he was getting at as Dave stepped up to take a look at the scratches. Maybe someone had pulled a switch on Dave, trading him an empty trailer for the one filled with TVs. It would be tough to do quickly and quietly, but if they got to it while Dave was asleep....

But no. It just wasn't possible without a lot of noise and a lot of trouble. I'd already tossed the idea aside by the time Dave said, "Yeah, that was there. I pointed it out to the dock foreman before I left Indy. I didn't want him or the dispatcher thinking *I'd* done it."

That light in Larry's eyes grew a little dimmer.

"Alright," he said. He started around toward the back of the trailer, Dave and me on his heels again. "Tell me about the trailer doors. How were they locked?"

"Just as you see there." Dave pointed at a steel cable wrapped around the door handles and secured with a padlock. "Usually the lumpers just slap a plastic tie wrap on the—"

Larry held up a hand. "'Lumpers?'"

"The loading crew," I explained. "Try to keep it in English for the man, would you, Dave?"

Dave gave me a sullen nod before picking up where he'd left off. He might have been born again, but he was every bit as touchy as he'd been the first time around.

"Usually *the loading crew* just slaps a plastic tie wrap on the door handles. There's no key. The plastic's cut off when you deliver your load. But if you're haulin' something worth real money, everybody likes a little extra protection."

"So who had a key for the lock?" Larry asked.

Dave let out a long breath. "Me."

"Nobody else?"

"No such luck."

"There's no spare back in Indianapolis?"

"Maybe." Dave shrugged. "I suppose Kuhlenschmidt or Sears might have one." Dave glanced at me, then added quick explanations before I could ask for them. "Kuhlenschmidt's the dispatcher. Sears is the dock foreman."

Larry leaned in closer and squinted up at the lock. It was pretty dark in that parking lot, but Larry's eyes seemed to pick out what they needed to see.

"The lock looks pretty banged up. It's definitely not new. Do you think any of the other Cross-America drivers might have used it before?"

"I guess so," Dave said.

"Good." And without bothering to explain, Larry got down on his hands and knees and crawled right under the trailer.

This came as quite as surprise to me, I can tell you, since the most physical exertion I'd seen Larry put himself through was picking up a cat and settling it on his lap.

"What's good?" I asked, squatting down to look at Larry. He was on his back now, staring up at the bottom of the trailer.

"Keys can be copied," he said. "Hmmm. Too bad we didn't bring a flashlight."

I still hadn't figured out what the heck he was up to down there, but Dave knew.

"No need for a flashlight," he said. "We checked under there this afternoon. There weren't any holes in the floor. No holes in the roof either."

"Oh. Alright," Larry said, popping out beside a couple of tires and hauling himself slowly to his feet again.

As he was standing, the sound of footsteps echoed across the parking lot, and we all turned to see a tubby, bald fella waddling toward us from the warehouse. He was wearing one of those generic black and blue outfits security guards always wear—the kind of thing that's supposed to look just enough like a cop's uniform to inspire some kind of respect. For me that never quite worked, maybe because truckers don't have what you'd call a warm and loving relationship with law enforcement in the first place. This rent-a-bear didn't look like he was going to turn that around for me either. Wearing a uniform brings out the bully in certain men, and I could tell I was facing just such a man simply from the way he swung his stubby arms and glowered at us.

"What are you doing out here?" he barked, stopping about fifteen feet from us. *He* had a flashlight, and he brought it up and shined it in my face though there were floodlights on the warehouse not too far off and he could probably see me fine enough.

Being confronted by a man in uniform must have triggered some old reflex in Dave, because he gave the guard the knee-jerk answer you'll always hear when you ask boys up to no good what they're doing.

"Nothin'."

"Nothing?" The flashlight beam swung over to Dave's face. "Hey, you're that trucker."

"No shirt, Shylock," Dave said. More or less.

"Look," Larry said to the guard, "I just wanted to examine the truck before we left town. I've seen it, so now we'll go."

"And just who the hell are you, anyway?"

Larry took a deep breath before speaking. "I'm a private investigator. I've been hired by Mr. Anderson here to look into the disappearance of his cargo."

The guard's flashlight did a quick up and down, shining over Larry's wrinkled sweater and coffee-stained pants and scuffed, worn-out sneakers. Larry had dressed to travel, not make a good impression.

The guard busted out laughing.

"Oh, man," he said to Dave. "If you get your lawyer from the same rest home you got this guy, you're really in trouble." Then he shut off his chuckles like you'd shut off a faucet and started waving his flashlight away from the truck. "O.K., fun's over. Get out of here."

Dave couldn't resist a parting shot, making a comment so nasty it would certainly have failed the "WWJD?" test he supposedly held himself to. Jesus might have had strong words for the Pharisees, but he would never have stooped so low as to insult somebody's mother.

"Come on. Let's go," Larry said, heading toward the car at a slow, stoop-shouldered shamble. The new, lively Larry was gone. Sad sack Larry was back.

We headed back along Interstate 20 after that, taking Dave's route from that morning in reverse. I drove while Dave sat next to me griping about pathetic little so-and-so's who need a uniform to feel big. Larry just slumped in the backseat like a duffel bag full of dirty clothes, not even bothering to disagree though he'd once worn a uniform himself. I knew my saying anything wouldn't do any good, so I finally turned on the radio to drown out Dave's ranting. Eventually he talked himself out and shut up.

It took us a little less than an hour to get up to the Rest-Eaze, the motel Dave had stayed at the night before. We were darned lucky it was almost nine o'clock by then, because to pick up the highway out there we had to wind our way through Atlanta's "Spaghetti Junction," the most tangled-up knot of cement and asphalt you'll find anywhere in the country. Get stuck in that briar patch at rush hour and you might not be seen for days.

Naturally Dave and I both voiced our opinions on the wisdom of the dispatcher's road plan—my son using saltier language than myself—and our complaints seemed to pull Larry out of his coma.

"You *had* to stay here, Dave?" he asked as we came to a stop in the parking lot.

"A driver's gotta follow Kuhlenschmidt's road plan, no matter how dumb it is."

"Really? Every step of the way?"

"That's what he says, anyway." Dave slipped into a thick, Gomer Pyle-style Southern accent. "'Mah road pla-in ain't no list uv su-gges-tions. It's a set of *orders*. You follow me?'"

"And you followed all his orders?"

Dave shrugged and smiled. "Well, I got creative here and there—took a shortcut or two. But when it comes to where you stay at night, that you can't get around. You gotta turn in your receipts sooner or later, and if you stayed at the Hyatt Regency instead of the Fleabag Motel, Kuhlenschmidt would know it, and there'd be hell to pay."

"Like you could find a Hyatt around here anyway," I said, gazing out upon the splendor that is Crabapple, Georgia.

The town has two things going for it: Southern Baptist College of Northern Georgia, a dinky little school that's got as many words in its name as it's got students, and an "antique mall" that could qualify as antique itself.

The Rest-Eaze certainly didn't give the Chamber of Commerce more to brag about. It sat on the edge of town like a pimple on a toad's behind. It wasn't just another of those seen-better-days motels you find so often off the interstate. It was hard to believe it ever had better days in the first place. It was built in the classic 1950s "motor lodge" style—a square, two-story fortress wrapped around a puddle-sized pool, with the guest-room doors accessible from outside. While such motels inevitably look rinky-dink, the Rest-Eaze looked even rinky-dinkier, like it was made from Tinkertoys and Lincoln Logs. I don't think the place would stand up to a good, strong sneeze.

There was a sign out front.

ROOMS AVAILABLE
FREE CABLE
GO LIONS

"Where was your room?" Larry asked.

"Right up there," Dave said, pointing to a door on the second floor—#206.

"And you were parked out here?"

Dave nodded. "Pretty much right where we're sittin' now."

Larry leaned forward and took a long look at #206. Like all the rooms at the Rest-Eaze, it had a picture window just to the left of the door.

"You could look right down on your truck from up there," he said.

"That's right. And I did, too. More than once. This place didn't strike me as the best place to leave a trailer full of big-money freight."

"How long would it take somebody to unload all those TVs?"

Dave scoffed at that. "No more than forty-five minutes—if they were at a loading dock with a forklift. Those TV screens may be flat, but they're danged big and heavy, too. Weigh more than a hundred pounds each when you add in the box and the packing foam. You'd need half a dozen pickup trucks and twice that many men to cart away all those TVs in less than two hours."

Larry eased down into the cramped backseat again, twisting his body so his head wouldn't press up against the roof of our little car.

"Did you notice any pickup trucks in the parking lot last night?"

Dave snorted again. "Shoot, man—we're in Georgia. Of course there were pickups."

I scanned the lot around us. "Ain't that many here tonight."

"Maybe the lions scared 'em off," Dave joked, nodding at the sign out by the road.

"How about other semis?" Larry asked. "Did you see any of those?"

"Sure. Two. Both Cross-America drivers—Ken Wells and Marty Manning. They parked their rigs right out here next to mine. Marty even asked me to keep an eye on his rig cuz his room was around the other side of the motel lookin' down on the pool."

Larry mulled that over like a fella looking for one last bite of meat on a gnawed-up sparerib.

"Well," he said after a long silence. "We may as well have a look around."

Seeing as we were only there because Larry thought it was a good idea, I would've hoped to hear a bit more enthusiasm from him now. But we did like he said, hoisting ourselves up out of the Metro and wandering around the parking lot for a while.

I felt pretty useless, and I could see by the look on his face that Dave did, too. Larry was walking this way and that like a man who'd just lost a quarter, his shoulders slumped and his eyes scanning the pavement. But all he'd say when I asked what he was looking for was "I'll know it if I see it." He even opened up some dumpsters nearby and poked around in the trash while Dave and I kept our distance from both him and the awful stink he'd released. If a cop had happened along, I'm sure he would've hauled Larry off to a homeless shelter.

When he finished with the garbage, Larry headed up to the second floor of the Rest-Eaze, stopping outside room #206. He leaned on the handrail and stared down at the parking lot a minute, looking like he was either going to make a speech or jump over the side. When he came back down, he just said "O.K., I guess that's it" and got back in the car. Dave and I looked at each other, I shrugged and we followed Larry.

"So?" Dave asked as I started up the car and got us back on the road.

"Yes?" Larry asked back.

"Did you see anything?"

"I saw a lot, Dave. Did I see anything I can use to help you...? I don't know."

"Cheeses Cripes," Dave groaned. "And now we gotta stop at every pickle park between here and Indy?"

"Pickle park?"

"Rest area," I explained.

"Oh." Larry nodded, a little smile tugging up one side of his mouth. "Just the ones you 'rested' at, Dave."

"Well, I...," Dave began. He took a lungful of air in through his nose, then let it out again with a gag. "Awww, fudge, man—what is that smell?"

A foul odor had invaded the car, as if we'd picked up a hitchhiking skunk or loaded up the trunk with rotten eggs. After some sniffing, we figured out where the smell was coming from: Larry's shirt. It had soaked up the stink from those dumpsters he'd been messing around in.

"Sorry, guys," Larry said, looking genuinely mortified. "I didn't know that was me."

We were on Interstate 75 by then, with about five-hundred miles of blacktop between us and the Indiana border. We wanted those miles behind us as quickly as possible, so we just rolled down the windows and suffered for the next two hours. Larry even took the shirt off and stuffed it under my seat, but there was no escaping the stench.

It was sweet relief to finally reach a rest area Dave had stopped at the day before. Of course, it was on the wrong side of the highway, so we had to go past it, turn around and come back. That added an extra ten minutes onto our drive, and we'd have to repeat the process all over again to get us back on I-75 North.

Yup, it was going to be a long, *long* night.

Now you'll see some strange things going on in "pickle parks" after dark. But probably the prize winner for this particular night was a paunchy, nude-from-the-waist-up, sixty-year-old man jumping out of the back of a Chevy Metro to stuff a shirt into a garbage can. Just to be on the safe side, Larry washed up in the men's room before putting on a new shirt. Larry's a quiet, sensitive kinda guy who embarrasses easily, so I'm sure it took a lot of effort to ignore the stares he was getting.

Once he was scrubbed clean of his dump-truck cologne, he came back out to the car and I pulled his suitcase out of the trunk. But the only shirts he found inside were wrinkled and a touch aromatic themselves. I'd snagged them from a massive pile of dirty laundry when I'd packed for Larry that afternoon.

"I thought you'd wanna look all official and businessy, and those were the best shirts I could find," I explained. "You know, you really oughta run your washing machine more than once a year."

Larry scowled at me for a few seconds before heaving a sigh and settling on a heavily creased blue button-down with a ketchup stain over the left breast.

"Hey, guys...could you wrap up the fashion show and get to it?" Dave said, looking at his watch. "I've only got eight hours before I'm supposed to get fired and arrested."

"Right," Larry said. "Show me where you left your truck."

Dave led us out to the middle of the truckers' lot.

"Here," he said.

There was little light to see by, but that wasn't really a problem. There was nothing to see but cement, cigarette butts and crushed cola cans anyway.

"What did you do after you parked?" Larry asked.

My son's reply was pretty blunt and pretty crude. Suffice it to say that nature called, and the resulting conversation kept him away from his semi for about ten minutes.

"And there were other trucks out here at the time?" Larry asked.

"Sure. Five or six. And before you ask—yeah, it was still light out, and no, nobody could've messed with my rig without doing it in plain view."

Larry nodded silently for a moment. Apparently, those *had* been his next questions.

"Alright then," he finally said. "Let's go."

"'Let's go?'" Dave and I repeated in unison.

Larry started toward the car. "Like Dave said, we've got a long way to go tonight and we don't want to miss his appointment in the morning."

"You don't wanna...." Dave waved his hands at the empty lot around us. "I don't know...*investigate* some more?"

"Not here," Larry said. And with that he ducked his head and stuffed himself back into the Metro.

Dave went stomping after Larry and laid claim to the driver's seat. I didn't object to riding shotgun, since it was obvious Dave needed to blow off some steam and driving hammer down for a few hours might do the trick.

We probably would've been feeding the bears—that is to say, picking up speeding tickets—if that little roller skate we were in didn't have about as much raw horsepower as a lawnmower. We took the next hundred miles with the speedometer barely pushing seventy and the RPM needle about to bust through the dashboard and poke Dave in the leg. But I didn't much mind the steady roar of the Metro's puny little engine. It did a fine job discouraging conversation. What was there to say other than "Larry—how the heck did you ever talk us into this?"

Our next stop was a gas station outside Knoxville, Tennessee, where Dave had filled up on diesel the day before. We quickly ran through the same routine as at the truck stop: Larry took a walk around and Dave told us where his truck had been and what he'd done when he was away from it (namely, buy himself a Mountain Dew and some Teriyaki jerky).

We hit one more rest area and a Burger King after that, running through the same motions with the same result. Nothing. Larry shrugged, Dave fumed and I realized how much I *didn't* miss life on the road. We'd been in that flippity-flapping car nearly seven hours at that point, and the sky in the rear-view mirror was going from black to orange. A new day was dawning—an *important* new day—and I was greeting it feeling like a bug on the windshield of life.

I was behind the wheel for the last stretch to Indianapolis while both Larry and Dave sawed logs. Dave didn't stay still for long, though. He spent a few minutes squirming around in his seat and sighing and mumbling under his breath before finally giving the floorboards a kick and sitting up straight.

"Dog gamn it," he said. "I can't sleep. I just keep thinkin' about what's gonna happen to me."

I ran through my possible responses.

"Don't worry—it'll be alright" seemed pretty empty. Dave was right to worry, and I couldn't see how things would turn out alright for him. "Put your faith in God" didn't seem much better. That's exactly what Dave had been doing the last year, and just look where it got him. If he thought too hard about that, he might end up not only a jailbird but an atheist to boot. So I steered things off in a different direction.

"Don't give up hope yet. Ol' Larry might not look like much, but what he's got workin' for him don't show on the outside."

I tapped a finger to my forehead to make it clear what I meant.

"Dad—from what I've seen, whatever Larry's got workin' for him *ain't* workin' for him. Or at least it ain't workin' for me."

"If there's an explanation for what happened to your load, Larry'll find it."

"What do you mean, '*if* there's an explanation'?" Dave shot back. "If there ain't an explanation, that means *I* stole those TVs."

"Now, Dave, I don't think you stole any—"

"Sure, you do! Just like always. You used to come back from wherever you'd been in that rig of yours and Mom would tell you some story about what I'd supposedly done while you were on the road, and you *never* believed me when I said I didn't do it."

"Well, Dave, that's because you *had* always done it. Am I right?"

"But you could've *believed* me. What did you know? You were never around. You could've had a little faith in me. But no. You never did. Not once."

"Gosh darn it, Dave!" I finally snapped. Only I didn't say "gosh" and I didn't say "darn." Somehow my youngest son is the only man alive who can get me to blaspheme. "Would I have crammed myself into this little shoebox for twelve hours if I didn't have any faith in you? No! I'd be asleep in bed at this very moment. But here I am, driving across the mother-lovin' country again in the middle of the diggity-dog night. That's what faith looks like, son. Now why don't you show a little faith in me and Larry, huh?"

Dave went quiet, and I let a few miles roll by in silence. When I finally glanced over at him again, I saw a small smile on his face.

Whatever he'd had stuck up his hoo-hoo, my conniption-fit had yanked it free. Dave's always seemed to like it when I lose my temper. I think it proves to him that I care.

"There's still a chance we'll find something, son," I said. "We ain't in Indianapolis yet."

Dave shrugged, still smiling but looking unconvinced, like that faith I'd asked him for couldn't quite kick in. He pointed at a road sign coming up on us.

"Speaking of Indy, get off up here and take 44 over to I-74."

"What? That'll add half an hour onto our drive."

Dave hooked a thumb back at Larry. "The man said go back exactly the way I came, and that's the way I came."

"Well, why'd you go and do that in the first place? I-65's a clear shot all the way to Louisville."

"Yeah, but there's a busy chicken coop on I-65 between here and Indianapolis. One of the other drivers told me I might lose as much as an hour just sittin' there in line. And if the lumpers sent me out with a heavy load—"

"Chicken coop?"

Dave and I jerked up straight. We'd both assumed Larry had slept right through our little family spat. Just how much of our conversation he'd heard, I can't say, but he looked wide awake now.

"A weigh station," I explained.

"Oh."

Larry sank back in his seat, his eyes going droopy. Just when I thought he was about to nod off again, he spoke up.

"Stay on I-65," he said.

"You wanted to follow my route all the way back," Dave reminded him. "What's the point of going somewhere I didn't even go myself?"

"Did you stop anywhere when you were doing your detour around the weigh station?" Larry asked in reply.

"Nope."

"Then there's no point taking that route now."

"Well, dang it—I'm still not sure I see the point of this whole unrepeatable word drive," Dave groused. But he let the exit for 44 slide on by without any more complaints.

We hit the weigh station twenty minutes later. The sun had come up by then, but the station wasn't open. That came as no surprise to me, since there's not a chicken coop in the country that operates on a schedule mortal man can predict. They're run by fellas called "station masters," and I used to think they just flipped a coin once an hour to decide whether to keep working or not. A station might be closed for a month then pop back open for business the very day I'd drive by with an overweight load. I'd get stuck with a two-hundred dollar fine—and of course I wouldn't see that station open again for a year.

I was grumbling about such ancient injustices as Larry wandered around the weigh station, peeking in windows and checking out the scales.

"What's that?" he asked, pointing at a large, black sign that looked a little like the scoreboard at a high school football field.

"Your weight flashes up there," I explained. "Most states don't even bother telling you what you weighed in at unless you're heavy, but for some reason Indiana puts it up for all the world to see."

"What happens if you weigh too much?"

"You get a fine you gotta pay then and there," I said. "But what's worse is they make you get legal—meaning you gotta dump off some freight. If you're hauling something big and expensive, you are truly up the ding-dang creek."

"So it's a pretty big pain to stop and get weighed."

I rolled my eyes. "Like having your teeth pulled and your prostate examined at the same time."

Dave had been uncommonly quiet as Larry and I strolled around the weigh station, but he spoke up now.

"Not only do you have to sit in line and worry about whether the dock crew back at the warehouse stuck you with a fat load, the station master can pull all your paperwork just for giggles," he said. "Your log book, your bills of lading, your permits. Everything. And if one little thing's not right—*blam*. Trouble."

"So you were nervous about stopping," Larry said.

My son shrugged. "Sure."

"Did you have any reason to be?"

"What do you mean?" Dave snapped.

"I mean was there something about your truck or your cargo or your permits you might not want the authorities to see?"

Dave's temper went from zero to sixty in one second flat, his face turning red and his mouth twisting into an ugly sneer. I expected him to lay into Larry with the crudest curses he could muster—and he can muster some doozies. But he didn't. I don't know if it was the faith I'd asked him for a few minutes earlier or he was simply too tired to throw a full-blown hissy, but all he said before storming off was "I didn't do anything wrong."

"He's under a lot of pressure, Larry," I said as my son stormed away. "Let's not push his buttons, huh?"

"I'm not trying to hurt your son's feelings, Bass. But I'm not here to spare his feelings, either. I'm here to save his butt."

"So...can you?"

Larry sighed, which answered my question as well as what he said next.

"Not yet."

"Not yet? Larry, we're thirty miles from Indianapolis. Dave's meeting is in less than an hour. If we're gonna nip this thing in the bud we gotta get nipping, cuz there ain't much bud left."

"I know, Bass. I know. I just...I...it hasn't...I...." Larry squeezed his eyes shut and rubbed his hands over his face. "You know what we really need to crack this thing?"

"What's that?"

"Coffee. Come on."

We got back on the road and picked up three jumbo coffees the first chance we got. By then, the signs were telling us Indianapolis was less than fifteen miles away, and Dave's mood had turned blacker than the truck-stop java we were slurping. That caffeine was supposed to be kick-starting Larry's brain, but if it was doing the trick it was doing it awful quiet. I decided to give things a kick myself.

"It happened at the motel," I said. "There's just no other way.

That's the only place anyone could get into your trailer without being seen. Right, Larry?"

Larry made a neutral kinda noise half-way between a "hmm?" and an "um-hmm."

"Maybe," Dave said. "But even in a little podunk burg like Crabapple you couldn't have a bunch of guys drivin' off with a hundred TVs without *somebody* noticing. And anyway, how'd they do it without cuttin' off the cable and the padlock?"

"Maybe they did cut 'em off," I said. "Maybe they had another cable and another lock that looked exactly like the old ones."

"We already went over that way the bleep back in Atlanta," Dave said. "Anyway, it don't matter how the lock *looked*, Dad. The key Kuhlenschmidt gave me opened it when I got to Douglasville. It had to be the same one."

All I could say to that was "Oh. Right." I'd been hoping Larry would jump in and spitball his theories with us, but he just took another slurp on his coffee and stared out the window. I couldn't even tell if he had any theories to spitball. I sure as heck didn't. That brilliant "identical lock" theory had been the best I could think up.

I turned on the radio and tuned in one of those "Christian rock" stations Dave likes so much. I figured he could use the inspiration. Me and Larry obviously didn't have any to offer.

Not long after that, we were there: the Cross-America warehouse. It was eight twenty, and the place was already hopping. Three semis were backed up to the loading docks, and another two were pulling in as we parked. The sight of it brought back plenty of nostalgic memories of my gearjamming days—memories I didn't have the time or the heart to savor, since we were there to see my youngest son's life destroyed.

As you might guess, we got some pretty funny looks when we came inside. Most of them were directed at Dave. Clearly word had spread that he'd "lost" his freight, and Dave being a new man there didn't appear to be much faith that the losing had been accidental.

Larry and I got our fair share of stares too. We probably looked so wrinkled and bleary-eyed people suspected we were a couple hitchhiking drifters Dave had picked up on the road.

Those stares went from curious to suspicious to downright hostile as Larry led us through the maze of merchandise stacked up in the warehouse. We walked past VCRs, DVD and CD players, stereo speakers, computers, washing machines, dryers and every other kind of big household gizmo you could think of, all of it in boxes piled up practically to the ceiling. Just what Larry was looking for we didn't know. I figured he was just doing what he'd done all night—wander around in the vain hope that some clue would jump up and wave a flare under his nose. Only he wasn't wandering around deserted parking lots now. He was in a busy warehouse, and twice we almost got run over by forklifts whipping quick around corners.

Larry took these brushes with death in stride, only stopping to make a comment once, as we were passing a bunch of refrigerator boxes in one corner of the building. They were tipped over on their sides and stacked on top of each other, their "THIS END UP" arrows pointing off to the west.

"Sloppy," Larry said, shaking his head disapprovingly. "Looks to me like someone's going to end up with a busted freezer."

"Yeah, and some trucker'll probably get blamed for it," I grumbled.

My remark drew a funny kind of stare out of Larry, but Dave just blew right past it.

"The dock crews don't pay much attention to what it says on the box," he said. "They've all got their own little theories about the best way to load and store merchandise. Kuhlenschmidt and the rest of the white shirts don't care as long as nothing gets busted... or lost."

That last thought left Dave looking pretty miserable, but Larry didn't let him wallow in it. He asked to see where the TVs had been loaded two days before, and Dave led us to one of the docks at the far end of the warehouse. Three lumpers were there, moving big pallets loaded with shrink-wrapped boxes into a trailer backed up to the dock. The men looked busy, but not so busy they couldn't shoot us a few glares. One of them peeled himself away from the work to come talk to us. He was a big, beer-bellied, fortyish guy with the swagger state troopers and dock foremen seem to share in common.

"Hey, Anderson, I heard what happened," he said. "That's a real shame."

There was more suspicion in his voice than sympathy.

"Yeah, it sucks alright," Dave mumbled in reply.

"You talk to Kuhlenschmidt yet?"

Dave shook his head.

"Well…good luck."

The man turned his cold eyes on me and Larry, and Dave launched into some half-hearted introductions. My trucker's instinct had been right: The man was Lee Sears, the foreman. He shook our hands like they were made from rancid hot dogs. I didn't much like being treated like a thief, but Larry didn't seem to mind one bit.

"Looks like you guys have a lot of work to do," he said cheerfully, nodding at the pallets and boxes piled up on the dock.

Sears shrugged. "Those trailers don't load themselves."

Larry gave that a good-natured chuckle. "So how about the morning you loaded Dave's truck? Busy?"

Sears gave us another shrug, this time throwing in a distrustful squint to go with it. "No more so than usual."

"So you didn't notice anything out of the ordinary?" Erie asked, still coming off all friendly and innocent, like he was just making polite conversation. "Anything strange?"

"Nope. Things didn't start getting 'strange' until after Anderson there left." Sears gave my son a smile that was only half-apologetic. "No offense. I'm not pointing any fingers."

"No offense taken," Dave said, though from the look on his face it wasn't clear if he meant it.

"So you don't have any theories about what might have happened to those televisions?" Erie asked.

Sears turned back to Larry, looking at him the way you'd look at a beagle that won't stop trying to mambo with your leg.

"No, I don't have any theories. I manage the docks. Once a trailer's on the road, it's none of my business."

He was about to say more when something behind us caught his eye and his face took on a look of smug pity.

"Good luck, kid," he said to Dave in a quick whisper. "Don't let that cracker so-and-so get you down. Just remember—he can't prove you did anything wrong...right?"

Heavy footsteps clattered up behind us, and we all turned to face a husky, round, red-faced fella wearing a short-sleeved work shirt and a big frown.

"You're early," he said to Dave. Only it sounded more like "Yo-ah uh-ly" on account of the man's peanut butter-thick Southern accent. It had to be Kuhlenschmidt, the dispatcher.

"Wouldn't want to be late for my own funeral," Dave muttered.

"What'd you say?" Kuhlenschmidt snapped.

"Nothin'," Dave said, not much louder than before. "Can we just get this over with?"

Kuhlenschmidt threw an annoyed glance down at his watch. "I'd rather stick to the plan. Nine o'clock. You can just wait outside until—"

"Let me guess," Larry said, a sudden smile curling his lips. "Matt Springer."

Kuhlenschmidt snapped his gaze over to Larry. "What?"

"Detective Matt Springer, Special Investigations Unit. He's supposed to be here already, isn't he?" Larry shook his head, still grinning. "Matt's never been a morning guy. Never been all that punctual, either. You won't see him till nine thirty at the earliest."

Kuhlenschmidt looked over at Dave. "Who the heck is he?" he said, hooking a thumb at Larry.

"Well...he's *Larry*. He's...uhhh...well...."

"Just a friend of Dave's dad, that's all," Larry said, nodding toward me. "I used to know a lot of cops, so he thought maybe I could help out somehow. I don't think it's worked out that way, to be honest with you. But I can tell you Detective Springer won't be here for quite a while, so you may as well do whatever you were planning to do."

Kuhlenschmidt crinkled up his hairy eyebrows and stared at Larry, obviously trying to decide if he should believe him or throw him out.

"Alright," he said. "Let's go, Anderson."

He jerked his head to the side, pointing the way to his office.

Dave turned and gave me the kind of look that breaks a father's heart. "Help, Dad," it said. But I had no help to offer. We'd stayed up all night and put five-hundred miles under our tires, and all we had to show for it were the bags under our eyes. I struggled to find the right words, asking myself what my own father or maybe Robert Young would've said in this situation. But my dad and Robert Young were never *in* this situation, and they couldn't help me now.

So I just said, "It'll be alright, son."

Dave nodded, took in a deep breath and started toward the dispatcher's office. Kuhlenschmidt went with him, and Larry and I followed up behind.

"You two wait out here," Kuhlenschmidt told us when we reached the office door. Then he guided Dave on through. The walls were glass, and we could see the two of them on the other side as they sat down. But we couldn't hear a word—or raise a finger. I could watch my son's life ruined, but I couldn't do a diddly-dee thing to stop it.

I was heartsick and I was tired and I was bitter, so naturally I turned on my best friend.

"Dang it, Larry—what were you thinking? You practically pushed Dave in there to get fired!"

Larry didn't bother turning to look at me. He was staring through the glass into the dispatcher's office.

"You heard Kuhlenschmidt," he said. "He was about to throw us all out until Springer shows up. We can learn a lot more right here than we could hanging out in the parking lot."

On the other side of the glass, Dave and Kuhlenschmidt had seated themselves. Dave was doing the talking, gesturing and shaking his head and shrugging all at the same time while Kuhlenschmidt looked unconvinced behind his desk.

"It's too late for that, Larry. You had all night to—"

"Bingo!" Larry blurted out.

His eyes had locked onto something on Kuhlenschmidt's desk. I followed his gaze, but what I saw hardly filled me with faith that my son was about to be saved.

Propped up against the Rolodex on Kuhlenschmidt's desk was a small stuffed lion in a blue sweater with five white letters across the chest: "SBCNG."

"Bingo?" I said, starting to wonder if sleep deprivation was doing funny things to Larry's head. "Bingo *what?*"

And at that moment I got to see how detectives really are different from you and me. I looked at Larry just as something behind his eyes went click-click-click, like bar-bar-bar coming up on a slot machine.

He'd hit the jackpot—only I couldn't understand how. I'd been everywhere he'd been, seen everything he'd seen, yet I was totally clueless. And there was Larry, so darned clued-up he broke out grinning and slapped me on the back.

"Come on," he said, and my meek man of inaction opened up the door and marched right on into that office just as Kuhlenschmidt was saying, "I don't believe you, Anderson."

"He's innocent," Larry said.

Kuhlenschmidt looked up, the surprise on his face quickly replaced by anger.

"I don't have time for any bull-shingles, mister." He snatched up the phone on his desk and started to dial. "You better get out of here before I—"

"I suggest you make the time," Larry snapped back, his grin gone and his voice harder than I'd ever heard it. "Because if you don't, I'll have to have a talk with your bosses about your little arrangement down in Crabapple."

Kuhlenschmidt's fingers froze mid-dial. "What the heck are you talkin' about?"

"The Rest-Eaze Motel," Larry said.

"What about it?"

Larry took the stuffed animal off the desk and turned it around so its black, beady eyes were facing Kuhlenschmidt.

"'Go lions,'" he said.

Slowly, reluctantly, Kuhlenschmidt brought the phone away from his ear and put it down.

"Close the door," he said to me.

I blinked at Larry for a few seconds, my jaw probably somewhere down around my knees, before I did as the man asked.

"It looks bad for you, Kuhlenschmidt," Larry said once the door was closed. "Steering your drivers to the Rest-Eaze—a run-down motel thirty miles off any major trucking route. I couldn't figure out why you'd do it—unless you were working with somebody down there to highjack one of your own trucks."

Dave sat up straight in his chair, like he was getting set to jump over the desk and sink his teeth into Kuhlenschmidt's throat.

"What?" Kuhlenschmidt choked out. "No, it ain't like that at all!"

"I know," Larry said. He put the lion back on Kuhlenschmidt's desk. "This is what I was looking for. Another explanation."

If my jaw had been around my knees before, now it dropped down to my ankles. The clue Larry had been looking for was *a stuffed lion*? I couldn't see the connection at all. Which is why I'm not a detective, I guess.

"You graduated from Southern Baptist College of Northern Georgia—SBCNG," Larry said, tapping a finger on the stuffed lion's fuzzy little sweater. "It must be convenient to know you can always get a free room in Crabapple. That's the deal, isn't it? You give them business, they give you a place to stay when you're back in town for a home game? Maybe even free tickets?"

Kuhlenschmidt had managed to swallow his first burst of panic, and with every second he listened to Larry he looked calmer and craftier.

"Don't try to make this about me," he said. "I didn't have anything to do with those TVs gettin' stolen."

Larry nodded. "I know. That's why the motel had me so confused until just a minute ago. It looked suspicious, but there were two things that told me you probably weren't involved. One, the Rest-Eaze put Dave in a room that gave him a view of the parking lot—something you would've told them *not* to do if you'd arranged to have cargo stolen there. And two, your road plan sent Dave past a weigh station."

From the confused looks on their faces, I could tell neither Kuhlenschmidt nor Dave had any more idea what Larry was talking about than I did.

"Huh?" I said for all of us.

Larry turned to Dave instead of me.

"You said one of the other truckers told you about the 'shortcut' around the weigh station."

"Yeah. Ken Wells."

Larry smiled at that. "There were two other Cross-America drivers at the Rest-Eaze the same night as you. He was one of them, wasn't he?"

Dave nodded, his eyebrows crinkled up like he was trying to figure some tricky arithmetic. "Yeah. But what does that prove? There's no way he could've moved all those TVs by himself."

"He didn't have to," Larry replied, and he spun on his heel and headed for the door. "Come on."

He didn't wait to see if we were going to follow, which is probably part of the reason we all did. The conviction and confidence of his stride just kind of swept us up, and I felt more like I was marching along behind a drill sergeant than droopy old Larry Erie.

That spirit seemed to be contagious, too. As our little platoon went past the loading docks, some of the lumpers fell in behind us, obviously sensing that something was up. When Larry came to a sudden stop, there was a small pile-up behind him, with six men walking into each other before they could skid to a halt.

"Bass," Larry said to me. "Could I have your keys, please?"

"My keys?"

He nodded, holding out his right hand.

I had no earthly notion how my housekeys could help us now, but Larry still had such an air of command about him I didn't ask any more questions. I pulled out my keys and slapped them in his palm like a nurse loading up a surgeon with a scalpel.

As it turned out, Larry wasn't really after those keys at all. He wanted something else he knew I kept fastened to my keyring— my Swiss army knife.

"Hey, wait a second," someone said as Larry flipped out the blade. I turned to see Sears, the foreman, behind me.

Larry didn't listen to him. He just plunged that knife into one of the boxes nearby and started cutting.

"Don't mess with the merchandise," Sears said, starting to move around me.

I stepped in front of him again. I wouldn't make much of a road block considering the man's size, but fortunately Larry didn't need much time to finish the job. Within seconds, he was peeling back the cardboard—cardboard with the sideways words "THIS SIDE UP" printed across it. Inside the box was something smooth and gleaming-gray. It sure as heck wasn't a refrigerator.

It was a TV screen.

"Well, I'll be...," Kuhlenschmidt said. His eyes moved to all the identical boxes stacked up nearby. "They never even left the warehouse."

"I don't understand." Dave was staring googly-eyed at the box Larry had opened as if Jimmy Hoffa and Bigfoot were in there sharing a pizza with Amelia Earhart. "I saw the trailer loaded."

Larry nodded. "You did. Loaded with empty boxes. That's why Wells told you to go around the weigh station. If you'd seen how light your truck was, you might have noticed something was wrong. Once you were at the Rest-Eaze, all he had to do was get inside the trailer and take the boxes apart. He could throw the cardboard into his own truck and get rid of it later. In the meantime, you'd head on to the warehouse in Douglasville—where you'd be blamed for the missing televisions."

"That means someone gave Wells the key to the deadbolt," Kuhlenschmidt said, turning to face Sears.

"And someone hid all those TVs and loaded me up with a trailer fulla nothin'," Dave added, turning in the same direction.

"And someone planned on slipping the TVs out of the warehouse quietly, after hours, a few at a time," Larry said. "Isn't that right, Sears?"

I turned to look at the foreman like everyone else, only noticing then that the two men who'd joined our little convoy with him a minute before were his buddies from the dock. Sears couldn't have pulled off his switcheroo alone—he would've needed accomplices in the warehouse. And from the mixture of fury and fear I saw in those lumpers' eyes, I knew I was face to face with those accomplices now.

Well, if you counted Kuhlenschmidt on our side, the man-to-man advantage was ours. But pound for pound the bad guys had us easy. Sears alone probably weighed as much as Dave and me put together, and his buddies formed a solid wall of muscle behind him. So if punches were going to be thrown, it was in our interest to start throwing 'em first—which was just what I was fixing to do when Sears grabbed me by the shoulders, tossed me out of his way and went for Larry. I got my balance back just in time to see Sears pull something long and gray from his back pocket.

A box cutter.

Larry was backed up against the refrigerator box, unable to run without putting himself in slashing distance and with nothing but a two-inch Swiss Army knife blade to fight with. Sears stopped a couple feet from him, set his feet and brought up his cutting-hand, obviously intending to lunge in and gut Larry like a fish.

That pause gave me all the time I needed. There's one surefire way to stop a fight in a hurry, and I'd practiced it in bars up and down the big road. I stepped forward and kicked my leg up like a Rockette, swinging my boot-covered foot into the inseam of Sears' jeans.

He tried to turn on me, but his body was curling up in a ball so fast his legs couldn't keep straight beneath him. The box cutter hit the floor just seconds before he did.

That took all the fight out of his friends, who'd been tussling with Dave and Kuhlenschmidt. One sank down to the ground and put his head in his hands, while the other just went still as a statue as the truth sunk in: They'd been caught, and nothing he could do would change that now.

"Thanks, Bass," Larry said. He kicked Sears' box cutter aside before stepping past Sears himself, who was too busy rocking and moaning on the cement to be any danger.

"My pleasure," I said. But there were probably too many gasps and shouts of "What the heck's goin' on?" for him to even hear me.

It's not every day you get a knock-down brawl in a warehouse, and lumpers and truckers alike had come running to see what all the hubbub was about. Mixed in with them was a clean-cut young fella in a suit and tie. The only thing that surprised him more than seeing Sears rolling around on the ground was the sight of Larry standing guard over him.

"Larry Erie?" he said.

Larry looked up and smiled. "Matt! Hi! You're right on time. You need to put out an APB on a trucker named Ken Wells. He should be down around—" Larry turned to Kuhlenschmidt.

"Miami," Kuhlenschmidt panted. He still looked shaken up from his little dance with our thieves. "Picking up a load of Italian massager chairs for Hammacher Schlemmer. I can give you the name and address of the warehouse."

"Larry," the young fella said. I'd figured out by now that it was the cop Larry had mentioned—Detective Springer. "What's this all about?"

"Oh, just a little grand larceny, criminal conspiracy, assault and a few other things I could mention."

Larry looked as happy as I'd ever seen him as he explained everything to Springer. The younger man stared back at him with something like awe. Ol' Larry had proved it beyond a doubt. He really is something special.

As pleased as I was for my friend, I was even more pleased for myself. Dave turned to look at me, and I saw on his face something I hadn't seen in years. It wasn't awe exactly, or respect, but it was something close enough to both to pump my heart up like a Goodyear tire. My son was thinking his old man was something special, too.

"Thanks, Dad," he said. "Thanks for being there for me."

"Where else would I be?" I said.

BLARNEY

Don't write a story that starts with a dream. Don't write a story that starts with a storm. Don't write a story about a writer. And never, ever, under any circumstances write a story about a writer in a bar.

I know the rules. And up to now I haven't had any trouble sticking to them, for all the good it's done me. I write mysteries—or try to—so the problem solves itself. I start with a dead guy. The dead guy could be a writer, even a dead writer in a bar, and I don't think I'd be breaking the rules. He'd be dead, and that trumps everything. He wouldn't be a writer anymore. He'd just be The Dead Guy.

But I'm not starting this story with The Dead Guy. I'm starting it with a writer. A writer in a bar. A writer in a bar with two other writers. So it's not just a cliché. It's a cliché times three.

Sorry. But what's a writer supposed to do when the truth is a cliché? What's a writer supposed to do when *he's* a cliché?

You see, I'm the writer in the bar. Did you see that coming? Is my story hackneyed? Predictable? That's my problem. That's why I'm in the bar: I'm not a very good writer. (Had you guessed *that* already?) I was looking for a mentor, a guru. And if you're a writer looking for a guru, you're going to end up in a bar sooner or later.

I'd been going to mystery conferences and fiction seminars and adult-learning writing classes for years, an apprentice in search of a master. I was on a quest for wisdom, insight, encouragement, truth. And what did I get?

Reams of Xeroxed handouts. Stacks of promotional bookmarks,

postcards, pencils, coasters, napkins, matchbooks, finger puppets, crap. Endless sales pitches. ("If you want to learn more about plot and pacing, you should pick up my book—*Giving Wings to the Writer Within*. It's on sale in the lobby.") Notebooks filled with useless scribbled "tips" and "secrets" and "rules."

"Show, don't tell."

"Write what you know."

"Writer stories bad. Bar stories worse."

So let me show you. Let me write what I know.

I'm a writer in a bar with two other writers: Russ, writer of Tolkienesque fantasy epics, erotic horror stories, *X-Files* fan fiction, crap; and Daniel, writer of Joycean word jazz, free-form poetry, post-modern metafiction, crap. They're the perfect companions for me, Robert Potts, writer of Jim Thompsonish noir, two-fisted detective stories, post-post-modern hardboiled crime fiction. All of it unpublished. All of it *crap*.

Russ I know from "The Write Way to Success: A Workshop for Pre-Published Authors." Daniel I know from "Fiction for Dummies: The Seminar" and "So You Want to Be a Novelist?"

The three of us are in a pub called O'Grady's that's about as Irish as a burrito and we're dissecting the way we've squandered our day. Six hours and two-hundred bucks blown on something called "Unlocking the Mysteries of the Storyteller's Craft."

Daniel and I are post-thirty/pre-forty, bloated, tired, cynical. But Russ, older than both of us, is still boyish, exuberant, full of hope. It makes me want to hug him. Like a snake. Squeeze him to death.

"That Susan Tracy lady was interesting," Russ says.

Daniel and I look at each other, become voices in each other's heads.

Interesting how?

Interesting "She's doable in a Mrs. Robinson kind of way"?

Or interesting "I can't believe we spent an hour getting advice about 'the storyteller's craft' from a woman who writes romance novels"?

All without speaking. Cynics are psychic, but only with each other. Contempt's always on the same wavelength.

"Remember when I went to the john? When they were having us write our own obituaries?" Russ continues, my conversation with Daniel passing through him harmlessly, unnoticed, like radio waves through a marshmallow. "I saw Susan in the hallway."

Daniel's eyebrow twitches.

"Susan"?

They're on a first-name basis now?

Screw that. She can stay "Mrs. Tracy" to me.

I smile at a joke never spoken.

"I went up and talked to her, and she was really nice. Look—she even gave me her card."

Russ reaches into his shirt pocket and pulls out a business card, white with gold fleur-de-lis wrapped around cursive script so ornately curved I can barely read it.

Susan Tracy
Novelist
A P.O. box in the 'burbs
An AOL e-mail address
A website: www.romantrix.com

I don't even have to look at Daniel this time.

A card?

We've all got cards.

"Me—Writer."

So what?

"If I sent her a story, do you think she'd critique it?" Russ asks.

"Sure. Send her one of your zombie sex stories," I suggest. "Those are romantic."

"Yeah," Daniel says. "She should know all about zombies. That's her audience, right?"

Daniel and I chuckle, sounding a little like Beavis and Butthead, and I feel a touch of shame as Russ slips the card back into his pocket and mumbles, "My stories are about *vampires*."

I give him a slap on the back, swatting at my own guilt.

"Oh, come on, man. You don't need advice from someone like her."

"What the hell does she know, anyway? What the hell did any of those clowns know?" Daniel adds, helping me get things back on track: us versus them. "I mean, I only heard one guy all day who had any clue at all."

Russ smiles, recovering instantly, suddenly all tail-wagging puppy-dog enthusiasm again.

"Jack Beaghan?"

Daniel nods. "He was cool."

"Yeah," Russ says. "I thought so, too."

"Wait," I say. "The Irishman?"

Daniel looks at me, his gaze wary. He knows he's taken a gamble here. He's expressed approval of something, faith in someone. He's saying he liked the guy, and I'm saying, "The Irishman?"

Jack Beaghan. The Irishman. Writer of midlist Dublin domestic dramas, obscure award-bait slices of Irish life, Jim Sheridan films that will never be shot. Not crap—as far as I know. I don't read writers like Jack Beaghan. And I usually don't listen to them.

The star of the day had been Patrick Powers, writer of *Imminent Threat, Deadly Force, Morbid Obsession*, Whatever Whatever, Adjective Noun, Crappity Crap. But good crap, well-crafted crap, successful crap. All the other speakers and busy-work exercises had just been one long warm-up act for Powers' bestselling Elvis.

So when the Irishman took his turn at the front of the overly refrigerated Hilton Hotel banquet hall in which the suckers du jour had been corralled, I passed the time thinking up a question for Patrick Powers. Not the typical timewaster. Not "Where do you get your ideas?" or "How do you build suspense?" or "Who's your agent?" I was going to set myself apart. I was going to be the guy who stands up and asks the question that displays such discernment, such wit, such dazzling *potential* that it wouldn't just squeeze oohs and ahhs out of the wannabes, it would win an appreciative chuckle from Patrick Powers, a wave of the hand when the Q&A was over.

*Come here. Talk to me. Yeah…*you.

I wrestled with the question for nearly an hour, slowly bending and twisting it toward perfection, only glancing up whenever the Irishman won a big laugh from his audience. There were more than a few glances. Beaghan was a crowd pleaser, I could tell that much, though I had no idea what was so pleasing. I was always a split second behind the joke, saying "What? What?" to Daniel and Russ, who were laughing too hard to hear me.

I paid attention to the man just long enough to catch one sample of his "wisdom."

"Storytelling doesn't come from here," Beaghan said, tapping a bony finger against the side of his head. "It comes from here." And he gave his lean stomach three quick pats.

"And your advice," I wanted to say, "comes straight from here." And I would stand up, drop my pants and swat my ass.

But I didn't. I just went back to crafting the perfect question for Patrick Powers, building it slowly, word by painstaking word, on the back of a handout about how to create "Prose Like the Pros."

So cut to three hours later and there we are, three writers in a faux-Irish pub, and Daniel says he liked Jack Beaghan, gives him his official endorsement, and I say, "The Irishman?" And a voice behind us says, "Be careful now, lads. Speak of the devil, you know!"

We're sitting one-two-three at the bar and we all spin around on our swivel-top high-chairs like kids on the Tilt-a-Whirl, and there he is: a wiry, weathered, white-haired little man, a pint in his hand, a grin on his face and a twinkle in his eyes.

And I'm not just falling into cliché when I write that. The Irishman's eyes are actually twinkling. I never even knew what that meant—eyes "twinkling"—until I see Jack Beaghan's eyes up close. They're shimmering with a dancing light that doesn't come from anywhere in the room.

"You were here for the fleecing then?" Beaghan says, and the way we laugh fans his wee twinkle into a flashing-crackling blaze. "Well, come have a pint with me, boyos, and I'll make sure you get your money's worth."

Does he really say "have a pint with me, boyos"? Maybe he says "have a drink with me, boys" or "have a seat with me, gents" or "ketchup mustard applesauce." I don't know. Beaghan's got an accent and a smile and that damn twinkle, and it casts a spell on me, enchants us all. The three of us slip off our stools and follow him to a booth, grinning and dazed, like sailors who've heard the Sirens' song.

Just seconds before, I'd been about to diss Jack Beaghan, write him off as yet another hack kept aloft by nothing more than his own hot air. But meeting him now—all *atwinkle*, for Christ's sake—changes things. He's magic, this guy. He's wearing a dark plaid shirt and worn jeans, but what I see is a green suit and a bowler hat with a shamrock in the band. I'm at the end of the rainbow, only Beaghan's not offering me a pot of gold or a bowl of Lucky Charms. He's offering much, much more.

The Irishman raises his beer and says "sluncha" or "slawn chair" or something like that, obviously a Gaelic toast, and we bellow "sluncha!" and clink glasses and take long, deep, manly, Irish pub drinks. Daniel and I catch each others' eyes over the rims of our beer glasses, exchanging a look that says, "Can you believe this, man? Can you *believe* it?"

I was wrong before. Daniel, Russ, me—we weren't three writers in a bar. We were three "writers" in a "pub." But with the Irishman there with us, I feel the quotation marks evaporating, lifting a weight I'd been only dimly aware of until it was gone.

Now we're four writers in a pub, and to prove it what are we talking about?

"Writing," Beaghan says. "The 'storyteller's craft.' That's what you came to learn about, did you? Well, let me tell you one thing straight off, lads. What you heard today? Blarney, every word of it—and that includes what *I* said!"

Does he actually use the word "blarney"? Does he really talk like something out of *Darby O'Gill and the Little People*? Now I'm not sure. Maybe he says "bollocks." Maybe it's "bullshit." What matters is I hear "blarney," and we all laugh.

"I'm Jack Beaghan, by the way," the Irishman says, stretching his long, gnarled hand toward Russ.

"Oh, we know! I'm Russ. I write speculative fiction."

Beaghan gives him a neutral "You don't say?" nod as they shake, then turns to Daniel.

"My name's Daniel. I write...."

He catches himself before he can say "*literary* fiction."

"Fiction," Daniel says instead.

"Just fiction?" Beaghan asks innocently as they clasp hands. "You don't do any speculating?"

Daniel smirks, jerks his head at Russ. "Not about the same things he does."

"And you are?" Beaghan asks as he swivels around to face me. I'm to his right, on the same side of the booth, sharing his view out at the others, the world.

I try to make my grip forceful but not desperate, my gaze steady but not creepy.

"Robert Potts. Mystery writer."

"Oh," Beaghan says, cocking an eyebrow, seeming to reappraise me without quite judging me. "So you're interested in crime and punishment, then?"

"Well...crime, anyway."

Beaghan's soft chuckle sends a tingle across my shoulders.

I made him laugh!

"Then you'll find plenty to write about in this world of ours, Robert. Crimes we've got around us all the time. But punishment— at least if you're talking about *justice*—that's fookin' scarce."

His gaze drifts downward, gets lost in his beer. But before any awkwardness can settle over the table, Beaghan whips his head up and points his long jaw at Russ like the barrel of a pistol.

"So tell me, Russ—what do you think writing's all about?"

Russ stutters, blinks, grins awkwardly. He's the kid who didn't do his homework.

"Maybe...maybe escapism?"

"Oh, it's an escape, is it?" Beaghan says. "For who, then? Your readers? Or *you*?"

Before Russ can stammer out another answer, the Irishman's swinging his twinkle toward Daniel.

"Maybe you can tell us. What's writing all about?"

Daniel throws a nod at Russ, obviously hoping to one-up him, earn the Irishman's approval.

"It's the opposite of what he said. It's a writer's job to unearth the dark truths of life and report them without flinching."

"'Unearth the dark truths of life'? Sweet Jesus, lads—we've got a poet in our midst!"

Russ and I laugh, and Daniel flushes pink. Beaghan reaches across the table and gives him a no-hard-feelings slap on the arm.

"Ahhh, I've written a bit of the purple stuff myself. It's nothing you won't get over eventually. I did."

Daniel smiles, then joins in the laughter, obviously deciding to wear the bruise as a badge of honor. We're in a scene from an old chop-socky movie. Before you can have killer kung-fu, the master has to kick your ass.

And now it's my turn.

"What about you, then?" Beaghan says to me. "What do you think writing is?"

I'm ready for him.

"Telling lies for fun and profit."

My answer's superficial, glib—stolen from the title of a how-to book. But glib seems to suit the Irishman, and I think maybe I've won the contest.

Beaghan nods and puts down his glass. (He's taking long, gulping swallows each time we speak, I notice now.)

"Well, it is fun, yes it is." Suddenly his nod turns into a shake. "But there's damn little profit in it for most of us, believe me. Why do you think I was up there whoring myself this afternoon? As for lies...no. You can't just tell lies. A story's got to feel utterly and completely true." And he tilts his chin down, drops his voice and honors me with a conspiratorial wink. "Even if it's shite."

Beaghan finishes his beer as we chuckle, throwing his head back to swallow the last slug-trail of foam.

"No, you can't write wrongs, ho ho," he says when he's through.

"And pardon me if that sounds like *real* blarney, but I happen to believe it. Before you can tell a good lie, you've got to know the Truth."

He capitalizes the word with a hard rap on the table. His beer glass rattles, and he looks down at it, seemingly surprised to find it there before him so heartbreakingly empty.

"Well, now," Beaghan says, pursing his moist, rubbery lips. "If you kind sirs were to stand me to a drink, I'd tell you what writing means to *me*. What storytelling means, anyway. And what's more, I'd tell you in a story. A *true* story."

I expect Russ or even Daniel to hop up and fetch the man his beer—expect it even as I'm coming to my feet saying, "What do you want?"

"Guinness. Thanks."

When I come back a few minutes later, a pint glass in each hand, I find three writers laughing uproariously. I've missed the joke again—just like at the seminar—but I don't feel left out. Beaghan takes his beer and gives me a "Sluncha," and we clink glasses, just the two of us. He takes a drink, and I take a drink, and I don't put down my glass until he does. When I do, a third of my Guinness is gone.

"How old do you think I am?" Beaghan says to Russ.

Russ stutters, shrugs, on the spot again.

"I...I don't know. Maybe sixty?"

"Sixty, he says?" Beaghan shakes his fist at Russ with mock outrage. "You heartless bastard! So I look like a withered old man, do I? Well, I'll have you know, boyo, that ol' Jack Beaghan here isn't a day over forty-five!"

He smiles as he lays out this obvious lie, his grin putting even more lines and creases in his already wrinkled face. But Russ and Daniel don't seem to know how to react. Russ's doughy features flutter between amusement and embarrassment, the urge to laugh and the urge to apologize. Daniel just nods, either playing it safe or genuinely clueless.

Even before he's really begun his story, Beaghan's spreading on the "shite" with a trowel. He's going to show us what storytelling's all about, alright—show us by whipping up a big pot of bull right on the spot.

"Wow! Forty five?" I say, the only one of us who knows how to play along. "Geez, Jack—what the hell happened to you?"

Beaghan sneaks a peek at me, throws me a sly smile.

I'm his accomplice in this now. His second banana.

His student.

"Bangladesh, that's what fookin' happened," the Irishman says. Suddenly he's straight-faced, somber. "Twenty years ago, my mate Dan and me, we set off to have an adventure. Around the world in eighty-plus-ten days, that was the plan. But, boyos...we didn't make it home for *two years.*"

Russ and Daniel are both wide-eyed now, like kids around a campfire hearing "The Man with the Golden Arm" for the first time. I'm amazed at how easily Beaghan draws them in. He doesn't need my help here, he's got these suckers hooked, but I throw out a little bit of business just to show which side of the table I'm on.

"You couldn't stop someone and ask for directions?"

"We weren't lost," Beaghan says, bringing just the right hint of irritation to the curt shake of his head. The guy's an Irish Olivier. "It was a matter of crime and punishment, Robert. Not that there was much crime to it. Not at first. But it was a hell of a lot of punishment. Drunk and disorderly in Dublin—why, that's a given for a couple of young lads. Hell, it's a fookin' rite of passage. But in Bangladesh, have a few too many of these—" He lifts his Guinness and gives it a swirl, the dark liquid sloshing to the lip but not quite spilling over. "—and they look at you like you're Charlie bloody Manson. I mean, it's not just illegal to be drunk and disorderly. It's illegal to be a wee bit tipsy. It's illegal to wet your damn whistle. And Dan and me, we got wet. Ohhhhh, boys—we got soaked!"

Beaghan's really rolling now, he's not even pausing to drink, so I just settle in and watch him work his magic. Across the table from me, Russ and Daniel stare at the Irishman, slack-jawed, hypnotized, and I have to fight to keep a smirk off my face.

"Now Bangladeshi justice—if you want to call it that—is a swift business, conducted in volume without much worry about niggling details like a man's rights. Before you know it, Dan and I are thrown into the deepest, darkest pit of slime, misery and degradation you could imagine. In fact, I'd bet you *couldn't* even imagine it, it was so awful. You've seen *Midnight Express*? The movie? Well, a Bangladeshi prison makes that look like fookin' *Bambi*."

I lose it there for a few seconds, break into a chuckle I had to drown in my beer, but it doesn't throw Beaghan off. He plows on, focusing all his attention on Russ and Daniel now, not letting anything break the spell.

"So you want to know why I look a little rough? Well, it's rough surviving a beating each and every day. It's rough fighting off the men who want to steal from you and rape you and wipe their feet on your soul. It's rough having your head jammed into a bucket of your own filth until you think you're going to drown. And it's rough watching your friend go through it all with you—watch him die inch by inch, day by day. And that's just what happened to me and Dan, boyos. We were both dying in that hellhole, and we knew it."

Finally Beaghan stops here for a long pull on his beer. He's picked just the right spot for a pause—a cliffhanger. Daniel glances at me, a look of awe on his face.

Can you believe this shit? he's saying.

But I can't return the look. Instead I fight more giggles, and our psychic link is shattered. Daniel's expression changes, darkens. He still doesn't see the joke, can't smell the blarney. If he did, he'd be giggling, too.

"Two things saved us," Beaghan starts up again. "First, half the miserable sods in there with us spoke English. And second, I knew how to tell a good story. Now you've got to know your audience, and I knew these sons of bitches pretty damn well. So I could give them just what they wanted to hear: stories about brutal, heartless, evil bastards doing brutal, heartless, evil things. And my stories all starred the same two bastards."

I can't resist.

"George Bush and Dick Cheney?" I say.

Beaghan manages a soft, good-natured laugh, but Daniel and Russ glare at me, and I quickly realize how close I've come to blowing my mentor's cover. I hide behind my glass for a moment, washing the grin off my face with beer, noticing only when I put the glass down that it's already almost empty.

"No," Beaghan says. "The two bastards were Dan and myself. I told the story about the time we went to work for a bookie and ended up kneecapping the man's own father over a twenty-pound bet. And the one about us kidnapping a barrister's wife and leaving the body on his doorstep in Christmas wrap after we got the ransom. And the one about us shoving an entire Pekingese up a man's arse. Hell, I even told them about the time we shot a man in Reno just to watch him die. All of it a big, steaming pile of shite."

Beaghan smiles, so we have permission to laugh. I laugh a little harder than Russ and Daniel because I've got more to laugh about. I can see what they can't—that Beaghan's toying with them, practically admitting that he's making the whole thing up on the spot. And the more he hints at the Truth, the more the suckers eat up the Shite. It's a lesson in storytelling I'll never forget.

"But you know what, boyos? People started to believe those stories. I told them so many times, *I* started to believe. Only once did a man in that prison call me a liar. Of course, he was right, yet still it made me so furious, filled me with such rage that anyone would dare doubt my word, doubt that I was the cold-blooded killer I made myself out to be, I brought one of those stories to life right then and there."

The pub we're in serves food—fish and chips, bangers and mash, all that brick-in-your-stomach British crap. So there are place settings in our booth, little napkin-wrapped bundles of silverware. Beaghan casually unravels the one in front of him and slides out something long and gleaming.

"You can kill a man with a fork, you know." And he turns to me and moves his hand up fast, and I feel the cold metal tines tickle the flesh beneath my chin, sending a jolt through me that stiffens my spine. "You just have to get him right here, where a man's soft, and drive straight up. Do that hard enough—" The fork digs a little into my saggy flesh. "—and you'll have yourself a brain-kabob."

And then the fork's back on the table in front of Beaghan, and the Irishman's grinning at me. And when the surprise and fear melt away, I actually feel *honored*. Whether I'm the magician's assistant or his prop, it doesn't matter. He's made me part of the act.

"We were in the cafeteria when I did that," Beaghan says, turning back to our audience. "There were men all around me, but not a one ratted me out. Because they knew then for sure that those stories about me were true. And what's more, *I* knew they were true. And after that, no one so much as said 'Boo' to me or Dan. That's the power of storytelling, my friends."

The Irishman eases back, rests against the wood behind him. The tension around the table releases, deflates like a balloon, and it's clear where we're headed next. The epilogue.

"Well, we made it back to Dublin eventually. Dan and me, we're still mates. But we're different men now. Because stories have the power to change you, lads—both in the hearing and in the telling. There are times I think back on those stories I told and they seem as real to me as actual memories. And Dan, he lives completely in that world now. He went and became a real criminal—this a man who was in *art school* when we started our trip, for fook's sake! He's been in prison again—in Ireland, in England—three, four more times. And every so often I'll meet a hard-looking man, a man with that scared-angry way about him, and I'll know where he's been before he even asks me what he wants to ask.

"'Tell me, Jack,' he'll say. 'That story about you and Dan Kelly and a Pekingese...is that true?'

"And I'll feel that old fire kindle up in me again, feel that other Jack Beaghan, the one I created through my stories, trying to burn his way back into the world. And I'll look the dumb bastard doing the asking dead in the eye, and do you know what I'll say to him?"

Beaghan leans forward, his hands gripping the edge of the table not far from his knife and fork.

"'Every…fookin'…word.'"

His gaze bores into the man across from him—poor, pop-eyed Russ—like a drill into butter.

"So here's the lesson," Beaghan says softly. "Storytelling doesn't come from your head or your heart or even your gut. If it's to be any damn good at all, it has to come from right here."

His right hand disappears beneath the table—and Russ jumps out of his chair squealing, his hands cupping his crotch.

"You've gotta grab 'em by the *balls*, boyos," Beaghan says, and I just can't keep it in any longer.

I'm roaring with laughter, beating the table, turning heads throughout the pub. There's maybe a five-second pause before Daniel joins in with a few uncertain laughs of his own, and then Russ is giggling along with us as he slides slowly, cautiously back into his seat.

Beaghan smiles smugly, a Picasso of bullshit who's just put the final brushstroke on his latest masterpiece.

"Damn, you're good!" I say. "You had these suckers going from word one." And I reach over and slap the Irishman on the back.

And what I'll end up asking myself not a minute later is this: When did his smile waiver? When did his twinkle start to flicker? Was it when I touched him? Or when I spoke?

"I think you'd best buy me another drink, Richard," Beaghan says.

"No problem, man," I reply cheerfully. "You earned it!"

I'm out of my chair and almost to the bar before it hits me.

Did he call me "Richard"?

It stops me dead, and I stand there for a moment, rewinding and replaying the sound bite in my head.

"I think you'd best buy me another drink, Robert"?

No.

"…best buy me another drink, Richard"?

Yes.

"…another drink, Richard."

"…*Richard*."

I manage to start moving again, but I'm not through thinking.

Is he calling me a...dick?

Do the Irish even use that phrase? Wouldn't he call me "Wally" or something?

And then the look on Beaghan's face takes shape in my memory, the way his grin soured into something bitter just before he spoke. I make it to the bar, put in my order—two Guinnesses—before letting myself glance back at our booth.

The Irishman's talking, but he's not looking at Russ or Daniel. He's looking at *me*. And that expression is still on his face. He's staring at me like I'm a turd in his soup.

I turn away, dread suddenly pressing down on me, trying to squash me like a bug.

Am I that drunk? Am I that dumb?

Was Beaghan's story *true*?

I feel nauseous with doubt and shame. Again. I'd been in the "pub" with my "writer" friends (the quotes are back in full force) to drown out the memory of my moment in the spotlight—my question for Patrick Powers, bestselling author, potential guru, asshole. His presentation had been as rote and meaningless as his novels. Practice makes perfect. Believe in yourself. Blah blarney blah. All of it delivered in a monotone by a man who appeared to be in the grip of a boredom so powerful it was practically narcoleptic.

He wrapped up early, leaving twenty-five minutes for questions, and my hand was the first in the air. I was the third person called, after a redheaded PYT who asked where he got his ideas and an aging Botoxified beauty trying to land an agent for her unpublished series of dog-grooming mysteries. When it was my turn, I stood and cleared my throat—and felt my mind clear, too.

"In *Primal Fear*...no...[Damn!]...*Mortal Fear* you...the protagonist, the character of...[What was that name again? Screw it.]...the writer you depict is a...a writer of thrillers and you... he says something like fear doesn't come from the in-...[Shit!]...I mean, the outside. Fear is always with us. Inside. Inside is where it comes from and certain...things, events let it out. And I'm wondering if...if you were to deconstruct your...["Deconstruct"? Shit, I'm lost.]...if you have a philosophy that...."

I finally gave up, reaching down for the paper on the table in front of me, thinking I'd just read the damn question. I'm a writer, not a performer. But before I got the paper in my fingers, could even finish my question, Powers was giving me an answer.

"Yeah, O.K., I think I see where you're going with this," he said, squinting at me as if I were something he couldn't quite pull into focus. A distant cloud, a fuzzy picture, a mirage. Then he looked away, addressing his answer to everyone *but* me. "Actually, that quote comes up all the time. Don't take it too seriously, folks. It's B.S."

A hundred soft chuckles rose and fell in unison, sounding like a gentle wave rolling up a beach before retreating back into the sea. Powers called on someone else—a dowdy grandma who launched into a harangue about "nasty words" in modern books—and I sank back into my seat. Not long afterward, when the seminar was over, I left my "perfect question" behind in a thousand pieces, confetti sprinkled around my chair.

I needed a drink, some alcohol to send me home with the buzz Patrick Powers and the rest of the day's charlatans hadn't provided. And then along came Jack Beaghan, and I got that buzz. Until it curled up inside me and died.

Had I just laughed and wisecracked my through the most horrific memory of a man's life? Had Beaghan been teaching me— or merely tolerating me? And what about that fork at my throat? Was that part of an act? Or a genuine act of rage?

What kind of man was Jack Beaghan? What kind of man was *I*?

My beers come, I pay, I head back to our booth. I see the Irishman hunched over the table, his lips moving fast. Russ and Daniel nod, then all three of them turn to look at me as I walk up. Their faces are blank, unreadable, even Beaghan's now.

I hand the Irishman his Guinness.

"Thank you, Richard," he says as I sit down.

No one corrects him. Not Russ, not Daniel. Certainly not me.

If he thinks I'm a Dick, I'm a Dick. I'm not going to contradict him. I'm just going to finish my beer and get the hell out of there.

Beaghan raises his glass toward me.

"Sluncha."

I clink his pint glass with mine.

"Sluncha," I mumbled, unable to fake cheerful, ignorant bliss.

Beaghan eyes me as he gulps at his beer, his twinkle growing brighter than ever. Hotter. When he puts his glass down, he keeps his hand resting on the table, and his pinky stretches out, comes down on the fork, idly slides the metal back and forth over the smooth lacquered wood.

"Do you remember what I said about lies, Richard?"

I don't, actually. Not then. I feel cornered, and it's hard for me to remember anything. So the Irishman reminds me.

"You can't tell a proper lie unless you can recognize the truth. I really believe that."

He pushes down harder on the fork, two fingers on it now. I can see the red of blood around his nails, the flesh over the joints going white under the pressure.

"So I have to wonder about you, Richard. Because unless I'm seriously mistaken...."

The Irishman's words slow, finally stop, and he lets a beat pass in silence, telling me that what's come before this is just a prologue, a warm-up. When he speaks again, it's with a different voice. It's not the voice of shamrocks and "the little people" and the Blarney Stone anymore. There's no blarney about it. It's the voice of a prisoner, a desperate man. A killer.

"You looked the truth in the face just now—and you spat in it," the voice says. "You didn't believe a word I said. In fact, you think I'm a bloody fookin' liar, don't you? *Don't you?*"

And his fist curled around the fork. I swear it did. Just like before. Just like in the story. I saw it. I can see it now.

So how the fork ended up in *my* hand, I'm not sure. But I can tell you this: Beaghan wasn't lying when he said you can kill a man with a fork. All you have to do is swing, hard, one-two-three-four times into the neck. And hit an artery while you're at it.

Beaghan tilts back off his chair, sprawls across the floor. He presses his hands up under his chin as if he's trying to strangle himself, blood spurting through his fingers. It only takes a few minutes for him to bleed to death, but I don't get to see the twinkle in his eyes go glossy, freeze. I've already been dragged away, beer-fueled action heroes jumping me, prying the fork from my hand, pinning my arms behind my back.

"Let me go!" I hear myself screaming. "It was self defense!"

And Russ looks at me from across the room where he's kneeling over the Irishman, uselessly pressing napkins against the man's gaping, gurgling wounds, and he says, "Jesus, Robert! He was joking! He was just *joking*!"

Just joking. Just "taking the piss." Just having a little fun with me. That's what Daniel says, too. The detectives told me.

"Your friends say the guy was kidding."

"Your friends say you were drunk."

"Your friends say you were agitated."

Was I drunk? Yes. Was I "agitated"? I suppose so. Was the Irishman kidding?

The cops are checking on Beaghan's story—his Bangladeshi prison saga. But I can tell it doesn't matter to them whether it's true or not. And you know what? It doesn't matter to me. Not what Beaghan's records say, anyway. That might be the truth, but it's not The Truth. Not the one Beaghan created in that bar with nothing but words.

I know what I saw. And I know there's only one way to make everyone else see it, too.

So I said to the detectives, "Turn off the video camera. Bring me a pen and a pad of paper. Or better yet, put me in front of a keyboard, if you can. I need to *write* this."

And here it is. I guess some people will say it's my confession, but that's not right. It's not a "confession" or a "statement" or whatever else the cops and lawyers might call it. It's a story. And sitting here now, I'm thinking it's the best one I've ever written. Because you know what?

I believe it.

ABOUT THE AUTHOR

Steve Hockensmith is the author of the *New York Times* bestseller *Pride and Prejudice and Zombies: Dawn of the Dreadfuls*. He is also the author of several non-*New York Times* bestsellers, including the Nero Award finalist *The Crack in the Lens*, the Edgar, Shamus, Dilys and Anthony Award finalist *Holmes on the Range*, the Audie Award finalist *Dreadfully Ever After* and the not-nominated-for-anything-but still-quite-entertaining *Dear Mr. Holmes* and *Naughty: Nine Tales of Christmas Crime*. You can learn more about him, his books and his ego at www.stevehockensmith.com.

CPSIA information can be obtained at www.ICGtesting.com
Printed in the USA
LVOW01s1553250614

391686LV00015B/678/P